STONE PRINCESS

USA TODAY BESTSELLING AUTHOR
DEVNEY PERRY

STONE PRINCESS

Copyright © 2019 by Devney Perry LLC

All rights reserved.

ISBN: 978-1-950692-11-8

Editing & Proofreading:

Elizabeth Nover, Razor Sharp Editing

Marion Archer, Making Manuscripts

Julie Deaton, Deaton Author Services

Karen Lawson, The Proof is in the Reading

Judy Zweifel, Judy's Proofreading

Cover: Hang Le

OTHER TITLES

The Edens Series

Indigo Ridge

Juniper Hill

Garnet Flats

Jasper Vale

Crimson River

Sable Peak

Christmas in Quincy - Prequel

The Edens: A Legacy Short Story

Treasure State Wildcats Series

Coach

Blitz

Clifton Forge Series

Steel King

Riven Knight

Stone Princess

Noble Prince

Fallen Jester

Tin Queen

Calamity Montana Series

The Bribe

The Bluff

The Brazen

The Bully

The Brawl

The Brood

Jamison Valley Series

The Coppersmith Farmhouse

The Clover Chapel

The Lucky Heart

The Outpost

The Bitterroot Inn

The Candle Palace

Maysen Jar Series

The Birthday List

Letters to Molly

The Dandelion Diary

CONTENTS

CHAPTER ONE

PRESLEY

That's today?

That's today.

That's *today.*

There were only so many ways to interpret two words. Only so many ways to alter their meaning with various inflections.

that's today

No matter how many times I'd spoken Jeremiah's text aloud, none of the options held appeal. The bastard hadn't even bothered with a question mark or period to alleviate some confusion.

The ugly words jumped off my phone's screen, and I snarled as I shut it down. There was no point reading them over and over and over again. I'd been doing it constantly since Saturday.

Those two words were the last in our thread. He'd sent them the morning of our wedding—the wedding he'd forgotten. Jeremiah hadn't texted a panicked apology. He hadn't called me endless times to fill my voicemail with excuses. He hadn't driven the three hours from Ashton to Clifton Forge to get on his knees and beg for my forgiveness.

His text might as well have read *the end.*

Well, fuck him. Fuck his text. Fuck all the years I'd wasted on a man who claimed to love me but didn't have a damn clue how to show it. I wouldn't even get the satisfaction of breaking up with him face-to-face. Or maybe standing me up on our wedding day had been his chicken-shit way of breaking up with me.

After calling off the wedding Saturday, I'd spent yesterday in tears, nursing a broken heart and a raging hangover. Presley Marks was not a woman who cried easily. I'd given up on tears at a young age because they only earned me another slap. But yesterday, I'd let them fall freely.

I'd cried for being so damn stupid. And pathetic. And alone. And humiliated.

How many times had my friends warned me about Jeremiah? How many times had I defended him? How many times had I looked at my naked ring finger, deluding myself that I didn't need an engagement ring when a wedding band was the real prize?

The sting in my nose threatened more pitiful tears, but I sniffed it away, blinking rapidly before a stray tear could ruin my mascara. Then I shoved my phone into my purse and pushed open the door of my Jeep. The white paint gleamed, reflecting the early morning sunshine.

I'd had it cleaned and detailed last week. I'd wanted it to sparkle when Jeremiah and I drove away from the wedding reception. I'd wanted the interior spotless when we drove it to Ashton.

Today was supposed to be moving day.

The majority of my belongings were in boxes, and I'd reserved a U-Haul trailer. I'd signed a lease on an apartment in Ashton because Jeremiah had been temporarily bunking at his motorcycle club's clubhouse—for three years.

Stupid, Presley. So damn stupid. I'd been so busy planning how to merge our lives into one that I hadn't noticed my fiancé was perfectly content living apart.

Maybe I should have stayed home and dealt with the fallout today. I had a landlord to contact and numerous deposits to lose. Instead, I'd followed my normal Monday morning routine and driven to work, detouring to swing by the grocery store and shove my thousand-dollar wedding dress into the clothes donation bin.

The Clifton Forge Garage had been my constant for the past ten years, and today, I needed the familiar. I unlocked the office door and slipped inside, flipping on the lights before settling in behind my desk and taking a moment to revel in the silence.

I'd come in an hour earlier than normal and the quiet wouldn't last. Soon, there'd be tools clanking in the shop, customers chatting in the waiting area and phones ringing in the office. But for now, it was peaceful.

I drew in a deep breath, searching for Draven's scent. He'd died over three years ago, but there were times when I could still smell him. Maybe it was only my imagination conjuring a hint of Old Spice and a breath of mint swirling in the air.

When I'd woken up this morning, I'd known the wedding fallout was mine alone to handle, so that was exactly what I'd do. One step at a time, day by day, I'd survive.

At least the hardest part was over. I'd already marched

3

down the aisle to tell the wedding guests that my fiancé had forgotten about our big day. The rest would be easy, right? It was simply logistics. Bartenders and caterers would be paid. *By me.* Gifts that hadn't been collected would be returned. *By me.* My life would go on and one day, it wouldn't hurt as much to know that my fiancé hadn't wanted to marry me.

But could I really blame Jeremiah? This was my own fault. I'd been deaf to the truth and blind to the signs. I should have ended this engagement years ago. Maybe I was just as much a coward as Jeremiah.

Burying those thoughts, I rattled the mouse beside my keyboard, waking up my computer. Then I dove into my email inbox and tried to get ahead for the day.

Once the garage crew knew I was here and not wallowing at home, they'd swarm the office. They'd hover over me all day, checking to make sure I wasn't on the verge of a breakdown. I wouldn't get shit done because I'd be busy maintaining a brave face and listening to them curse Jeremiah up one side and down the other. I'd tell them I was fine —which they'd know was a lie.

I hadn't been fine in a long, long time.

There were only three unread emails to go when footsteps echoed outside. The metal staircase that extended to the apartment above the office vibrated as Isaiah, one of our mechanics and my friend, came downstairs.

I took a deep breath and spun my chair to face the door as it opened. "Morning."

"Hey, Pres." Isaiah stepped inside, wearing a pair of faded jeans and a black T-shirt. His short brown hair was damp. He crossed the room and sat in a chair across from my desk, leaning his elbows on his knees.

"It's good to see you in that chair," I said.

He grinned. "It's good to be sitting here again."

Isaiah and his wife, Genevieve, had been living in Missoula for the past three years while she'd gone to law school. Now that they were back, Isaiah would be working at the garage again, and Genevieve would be working alongside her mentor at a small law firm in town.

"How's Genevieve?"

"Good." He cast his glance to the ceiling. "She'll be down soon. She's excited for her first day back at work."

"How was it staying in the apartment again?"

"Like old times. Don't tell Genevieve, but I'm hoping the contractor is behind a couple weeks so we can crash upstairs a little while longer."

Years ago, that apartment had been their home, and it hadn't been rented out in the years that they'd been gone. Like their jobs, it had been waiting for them to return. Except this time, they wouldn't be calling it home. The two of them had bought a new house in a quiet neighborhood and would be moving in soon.

Still, no matter how much time passed, I'd always consider the apartment Isaiah's.

"I'm excited to see your new place."

"You can have the first tour." His grin widened.

I studied his face. It was strange to see Isaiah smile, but a welcome strange. He'd changed a lot from the tortured soul who'd started working here years ago.

Genevieve deserved all the credit. She'd rescued my friend and brought life back to his eyes. She'd worked a miracle in that little studio apartment.

"What?" He ran a hand over his mouth. "Do I have something on my face?"

"No. It's just good to see you happy."

He sighed, the grin fading. "How are you?"

"Fine." That was the first one of the day. I'd likely repeat it twenty times before I left at five. "I don't want to talk about it."

"Okay."

Isaiah would be the only one who didn't push today. I could hug him for it.

The two of us had formed a fast friendship from the beginning, the only two outsiders working at a garage staffed by former members of the Tin King Motorcycle Club. Before Isaiah, I'd ignored the hushed conversations alone. I'd dutifully gone to the post office or bank whenever my presence hadn't been wanted in the office. I'd overlooked the parties and booze and women.

But then the club had disbanded and life at the garage had changed. They'd hired Isaiah, and when the others whispered about secrets, Isaiah and I had each other.

We'd drink coffee together every morning. We'd talk about nothing. I wouldn't ask him about his past or why he'd spent three years in prison. He wouldn't ask me how I'd come to Clifton Forge and why I refused to speak of my childhood. Yet we were friends. I trusted him.

And it was good to have him home.

"How are things at the garage?" he asked.

"Busy. We had to hire two mechanics to cover what you did on your own."

His forehead furrowed. "I'm not taking anyone's job by coming back, am I?"

"No. Dash and I talked and we're keeping them both on to do the routine stuff so you can apprentice on the custom work."

"I'm happy to do the oil changes and tune-ups."

I waved him off. "It's already decided."

Isaiah stood and walked into the waiting room. The clank and pop of a K-Cup slotting into the coffee machine drifted my way.

The space as a whole had two enclosed offices along with the reception area where I sat. One of the offices belonged to Dash, the owner of the garage and my boss. The other had been Draven's—Dash's father.

Draven had managed the garage his entire life, passing it down to Dash. He'd been more than my boss, he'd been my family. I'd gladly give up every one of my material possessions to have him back for a hug this morning or to have had him with me on Saturday, walking me down the aisle.

After Draven had died, Dash had offered me Draven's office. It had a door so I wouldn't have to sit out front with waiting customers, but I hadn't been able to sit behind Draven's desk.

No one, especially me, would ever take his place.

So we'd converted that office into a waiting room. We'd brought in couches and set up a coffee station.

Isaiah came out with two steaming mugs in his hands.

"Thanks." I smiled as he set down my cup. I spun the swirl stick, mixing the packet of sugar he'd poured in and the dollop of French vanilla creamer floating on top. "And thanks for Saturday."

He lifted a shoulder, sipping his black coffee. "No problem."

On Saturday, after I'd announced the wedding canceled, I'd tried to run away. Isaiah had caught me before I'd been able to get into the Jeep and disappear into a black hole. He'd dragged me to the apartment upstairs before anyone could see. Emmett and Leo, two more mechanics and my friends, hadn't been far behind. Leo had snagged a bottle of tequila from the bar. The three of them had fed me shot after shot until I'd passed out on the couch.

"I suppose I have a mess to clean up out back," I muttered.

"I think Dash and Bryce took care of most of it."

"Oh." I shook my head. "Damn. They should have just left it for me."

How many hours had I spent planning this wedding? How many favors had I called in from my friends? *What a waste.*

My friends shouldn't have had to clean up my mess too.

There was a field behind the garage and I'd always thought it had the potential to rival any city park, so I'd asked Dash if I could clean it up and host the wedding there. Draven hadn't been there to walk me down the aisle, but what better place to include his memory than the garage that had been his business for so many years?

Dash had agreed, insisting that I let everyone help with cleanup. We'd spent three backbreaking weekends working in that field, clearing away the shop's overflow. Spare rusted parts were moved to the other end of the property. Old cars were pushed out of sight. The overgrown grass was cut, revealing a lush green carpet beneath.

On Thursday and Friday, we'd set up the white tent, rolled in tables and placed chairs. Too busy doing the decorations, I hadn't planned a rehearsal dinner. Skipping that dinner had been my biggest mistake—besides picking the groom. Maybe if we'd had the dinner, I would have known Jeremiah wasn't going to show.

"They didn't mind, Pres," Isaiah said.

"This is my fault. I should deal with it."

"This is Jeremiah's fault."

"No," I whispered. "It's mine."

A door slammed above us. Isaiah and I cast our gazes to the window as Genevieve's heels clicked down the staircase and she joined us in the office.

"Morning." Her dark hair was up in a fancy twist and she was dressed for work, sophisticated and perfect for Isaiah.

He stood to pull out the chair beside his, holding her hand as she eased into the seat. "You look beautiful."

Had my man ever held out a chair for me? Had he ever stood when I'd come into the room? Was complimenting your fiancée so goddamn difficult?

"How are you feeling?" Genevieve asked, her brown eyes full of concern.

"Yesterday was bad. I haven't been that drunk in a long time, so I was fairly useless all day." I'd spent hours hovering over the toilet, retching from the tequila. The hangover hadn't mixed well with my emotional state. "Sorry I didn't text you back."

"It's okay." Her gaze softened.

Genevieve had inherited Draven's eyes. I envied that she could look in the mirror and see a living piece of him. All I had was a photo in my desk drawer to pull out when I was feeling alone.

"Ready for your first day of work?" I asked, changing the subject.

"I think so. It will be nice to work with Jim again. I've missed him." She smiled, smoothing out the hem of her black pencil skirt. She'd paired it with a pale blue blouse and stiletto heels. Genevieve Reynolds walked into a room and stole the show. She was stunning, inside and out.

I was pretty, maybe not show-stopping gorgeous, but I was comfortable in my own skin. That confidence had taken me years to build. As a child, I'd perfected the art of blending in and following instruction. Attention had only meant bruises to cover up and explain.

Not until moving to Clifton Forge had I truly let go and embraced who I was.

The hair that I hadn't been allowed to cut as a kid was now short and bleached white. No one would ever again use my ponytail as a way to hold me hostage while they shouted in my face. At first, the pixie cut had been more a boy's style than a woman's. Lately, I'd taken to shaving the sides while keeping the top longer and draped over one eyebrow.

My hair made a statement. My clothes did too. I had a petite frame that didn't look good in pencil skirts or blouses because I didn't have the curves to fill them out. Besides, that wasn't me. I preferred thick-soled boots to heels. My go-to outfit was a pair of baggy overalls with a skin-tight tee underneath. I'd wear cargo pants held to my frame with a cinched belt to give the illusion of hips. If there was *boyfriend* in the description, chances were, I'd bought it. I'd shunned girly the day I'd left Chicago at eighteen.

The most feminine I'd been since leaving home had been on Saturday, dressed for my wedding.

Maybe Jeremiah had woken up on Saturday morning and realized he'd made a mistake. That he was still in love with the girl with long, blond hair who'd worn pastels and floral skirts. That he wanted the girl I'd left behind.

"Did, um . . ." Genevieve scrunched up her nose. "Did he call you?"

"No."

The rumble of an engine saved me from another question, though I doubted the grace period would last long.

Leo and Emmett rode in on their Harleys, both parking against the chain-link fence on the far side of the parking lot. They dismounted as Dash pulled in on his own bike. It was rare for all three of them to be in this early and to arrive together, especially Leo, who didn't like to work before ten. Dash must have called them in for a meeting, probably about me. *Fan-fucking-tastic.*

The office door opened and the three men strode inside. The clock on the wall read seven thirty, and the other mechanics wouldn't be in until eight.

"Pres, how you doin'?" Dash sat in one of the chairs beneath the windows.

"Fine."

"You sure?"

I nodded. "I'm sorry—"

"Don't." He held up a hand. "No apologies."

"I haven't been out back yet, but I'll go out there soon and get everything left put away."

"We got it yesterday. There's a few boxes of stuff for you to take, but everything else is done."

My shoulders fell, heavy with the guilt that my friends had cleaned up my failed attempt at marriage. "I would have—"

"We know you would have done it," Emmett said, leaning against a wall. His dark hair was trapped in a knot at the nape of his neck. "But we got you."

"Thank you. And I'm sorry."

"Don't be sorry." Leo took up the space beside Emmett. "You feelin' better?"

"Yeah." Physically, at least.

Leo had come over to my house yesterday. He'd been the

only one who'd visited, not just texted. He'd brought me Gatorade, saltine crackers and pickles. He hadn't stayed long, just enough to deliver his *hangover kit* before leaving me to wallow. He'd probably left my house and come here to help tear down the wedding tent.

"We gotta talk about something." Dash shared a look with Emmett and Leo. "Two things, actually. First up, Jeremiah."

"I don't want to talk about him." My pleading eyes found his. "Please."

"We can't ignore this, Pres." His gaze softened. "Doesn't sit right with me that he's done this to you. But . . . he's a Warrior, and we don't need them back in Clifton Forge. As much as I'd like to beat the shit out of his punk ass, we don't need that kind of trouble."

Jeremiah had moved to Ashton three years ago to join a motorcycle club. He lived there and worked there, while I'd split my life between the two towns because he'd *needed this kind of family.* His family in Chicago hadn't spoken to him in years. He'd been an accidental pregnancy and his parents had always treated him as such. So I'd supported him. I'd stood back as he'd become part of a brotherhood.

Even when it was the wrong brotherhood.

The Arrowhead Warriors had been rivals of Dash, Emmett and Leo's former club. I'd split not only my time, but my loyalty too. I'd spent three years straddling a barbed-wire fence between the family I had here at the garage and the man who'd asked me to be his wife.

Jeremiah deserved to have his ass kicked. Repeatedly. But I would never advocate for it. I was firmly on the right side of the fence now and wouldn't put this family of mine in danger.

"Come on, Dash." Leo stood taller. "That's bullshit. He—"

"Please, Leo." I met his gaze. "Just let it be over. If you go after him, it'll just cause drama for me."

He frowned, running a hand over his shaggy blond hair before muttering, "Fine."

Genevieve let out an audible sigh. "I'm glad that's agreed. We've had enough trouble."

"That's the truth," Dash murmured, nodding at his sister. The siblings had different mothers, but they'd both gotten their chocolate-colored hair from Draven.

"What's the second thing?" Genevieve asked Dash.

"Got a call from Luke Rosen this morning."

The room went silent. Why was the chief of police calling Dash?

"What did he want?" Emmett's eyebrows furrowed. "I just talked to him yesterday."

"It's a courtesy thing about Dad." Dash looked to Genevieve. "He was going to call you, but I said I'd tell you myself."

"Okay." She stiffened. "Why do I feel like you're going to give me bad news?"

"Because I am." Dash rubbed his jaw. "There's a production company from LA that's making a movie about your mom's murder."

"What?" She shot out of her chair, Isaiah quick to follow. "Can they do that?"

"It's public knowledge," Dash said. "They'll put the Hollywood spin on it so who knows what'll come out, but yeah, they can do that."

"How did Luke get the tip?" Emmett asked.

"The director wants it to be authentic, so they applied

for a permit to shoot here. The mayor approved it on Friday. He called Luke early this morning."

"They're filming a movie in Clifton Forge." My mind couldn't quite wrap itself around that statement. "When?"

"Within the next month or so. Luke doesn't know exactly when. The city wants the money, so they gave the production company a twelve-month window."

"What does this mean for us?" Genevieve asked.

"I don't know," Dash answered. "But my guess is we'll see them around."

"Who? Like actors and shit?" Leo asked.

Dash nodded. "Luke said the mayor hinted that a director and maybe some of the cast might be out to meet the people they're playing. We might get some visitors at the garage."

My stomach plummeted. The last thing I needed was for the rich and famous of Hollywood to be at my workplace. I didn't need to be the sad, pathetic side character they tossed into a movie script for *authenticity*.

"Do we know who to watch out for?" Genevieve asked Dash.

"Luke said the director's name is Cameron Haggen."

"The Oscar winner?" Emmett whistled. "Damn. Who else?"

Dash rubbed his jaw, hesitating. "The only other name Luke knew of was Shaw Valance."

Shaw Valance.

"Holy fuck," Emmett muttered as my jaw hit the floor.

Then this would not be a small movie. Even a woman who didn't have much time for television or movies knew that Shaw Valance was Hollywood's elite, leading male star. He was America's hero. I'd seen an article in the salon's latest issue of *People* that had estimated his salary for his latest blockbuster at fifteen million dollars. His handsome face was in each issue thanks to the paparazzi who stalked his every move.

Shaw Valance was the last thing we needed in this town and this garage.

Isaiah took Genevieve's hand, squeezing it tight. "It'll be okay."

"I don't want this." Her face had paled.

"I know, doll." He pulled her into his chest, wrapping her up tight. "We'll lie low. We'll stay away from it all."

My friend had just come home to settle into a life with her husband, but now she'd be forced to relive old memories of her parents' deaths.

"Let's hope they stay away, do their own thing and are gone before we notice," Dash said, trying to ease Genevieve's worries. "I doubt they'll bother us individually. If anything, they might give some attention to the garage. Presley and I can field questions."

Leo scoffed. "Or we tell them to fuck off."

"Best thing we can all do is say 'no comment,'" Dash said. "Give 'em the cold shoulder."

Cold? No problem.

I'd made a decision yesterday while I'd been lying on the cool tile of my bathroom floor. I was done letting men hurt me. Jeremiah was the last, and I had no more shits to give.

From here on out, I was the woman with ice in her veins. The woman with a heart of stone.

If Shaw Valance or his award-winning director came anywhere near the garage, I was following Leo's suggestion.

They could fuck off.

CHAPTER TWO

SHAW

"This is *not* what I expected," Shelly muttered.

I glanced over from the driver's seat, gripping the steering wheel tighter. She'd been bitching about everything all damn day. "What's the problem?"

"It's so . . . flat. It's nothing like the pictures."

"What pictures?" If she'd googled *Clifton Forge, Montana* like I had a month ago, she'd know that the view through the windshield was identical to the photos from the search results.

"Are those the mountains?" She leaned forward, squinting through her purple-framed glasses. "They're far away."

I bit my tongue.

The mountains weren't far away, maybe fifty miles at most. They cut across the horizon, standing proud and drawing a jagged line between heaven and earth. Beneath them rolled an open plain of green fields interrupted only by straight sections of barbed-wire fence. The breeze tickled the tops of the tall grasses growing along the road. Overhead, the azure sky was clear except for wisps of white clouds.

Some people, like me, might call this paradise.

I shot Cameron a look through the rearview mirror. He was wearing his signature round sunglasses, but I caught his eye roll.

"Is that it?" Shelly pointed ahead at a cluster of buildings in the distance.

I double-checked the map on my phone, my heart rate speeding up with every racing mile. "Yeah. That's it."

Clifton Forge.

I could see it with my own eyes. No more Google searches.

This movie had been announced a month ago, and I'd been itching to visit since. Hectic schedules and working to clear my plate for the foreseeable future had delayed my arrival, but finally, we were here.

I hit the gas, speeding down the highway. Blood pumped through my veins faster than it did during my morning run. Excitement and anticipation buzzed through every nerve ending. Goddamn, I was ready to get this project underway.

I hadn't been truly anxious to play a role for five years. The films I'd been working on lately had all been variations of the same. I'd played the good guy, because that's what the world saw when they looked at my face. In every movie, I won the girl at the end. I saved the day. American Hero was my brand, and I'd been reveling in it from the start. So had my assistant, manager and agent.

Well, fuck the brand.

I was tired of playing the game, sticking to safe roles and delivering common lines. Not even doing my own stunts had helped break up the monotony. It was time for something different. It was time to see if I actually had talent, or if the only reason I was making millions was because I hit the gym religiously each morning and my face looked good on magazine covers.

"It's small," Shelly said as the edge of town neared. "That's good. Maybe we can add some mountains into the background with CGI."

I huffed. "I thought we were going for authentic."

That was the reason we'd hired Cameron, wasn't it? Because of his reputation for keeping things real and raw and honest. As a general rule, Hollywood lacked honesty. Cameron's vision for this film was the reason I'd gone full tilt, why I'd thrown so much of my own money in to make it happen.

I didn't want to shoot in front of a green screen. I didn't want to be sequestered in studio sets. I wanted to walk down an actual street lit by the actual sun.

"No CGI." Cameron's tone left no room for debate.

"Right," Shelly agreed. "Forget the CGI. I just expected . . . something else. But this will work. It's, uh, rugged."

I could use a little rugged. The phony polish of Hollywood was wearing thin.

But here in Clifton Forge, life was real. The town didn't thrive on tourism or cater to rich guests like some other areas of the state—something else I'd learned from Google. This town was fueled by agriculture and people who carved their living out of the land.

I respected that. I admired it. There were times when I longed for the hard days working on the force, when life had been a hell of a lot simpler.

Businesses sprang up along the road as we neared the

town's limits, welcome signs on doors and sandwich boards on sidewalks. It was the beginning of a parade, the early onlookers waving you down the road, inviting you into the fray. Windows were decorated with red, white and blue for the Independence Day festivities taking place in a few days. The GPS took me off the highway and straight down Central Avenue, a street packed with local shops and restaurants. The wide Missouri River flowed along one side of the street. A man stood at the helm of a fishing boat, casting his line into the rippled water.

I missed fishing. Maybe before shooting wrapped, I'd find some time to work in a day along the river.

"Motel first, Cam? Or do you want to drive around town?"

"Let's get our bags dropped off and check in."

I nodded and followed the directions to the Evergreen Motel, located two miles on the opposite end of town. Navigating two miles in downtown Los Angeles could take hours. Here, the miles went by too fast. My eyes struggled to stay on the road as I scanned storefronts and side streets.

Every cell in my body hummed. I itched to stop driving, get out and just walk. The schedule for this short trip was Cameron's to dictate, but next time, I'd come alone. I'd spend time wandering and learn everything I could about this town and its people.

For once, I was going to enjoy being on location.

Most of the films I'd done had been made in LA. Any trips out of California were always short and grueling. I'd arrive at an airport after dark. I'd go immediately to the location, shoot for hours and hours on end—sometimes up to twenty per day—and the moment shooting wrapped, I was wheels up and headed home. There'd always been something next, either another project or a premiere or a press stop.

My agent and manager had pushed for me to do the same here. *Get in and get out of Montana, Shaw.* But I'd put my foot down.

During shooting, I was not flying back and forth to California. I'd stay in Montana to make sure everything went smoothly. Shelly had the official role of producer, but I was staying active. And once this film was done, I was taking time off. Six months. Maybe a year.

It was time to take a break.

From work. From the media. From the city.

Ahead, the single-story motel came into view. The building was shaded by pine trees on three sides, and its name on the dated sign fit perfectly.

The Evergreen Motel.

Our soon-to-be headquarters.

The scene of our crime.

I parked beside the office, hopping out to stretch my legs. Cameron, Shelly and I had flown in on my jet this morning, then rented the Escalade and gotten on the road. The nearest airport of any size was in Bozeman, two hours away. Next time, I might fly direct to Clifton Forge, but for this first trip, I hadn't minded seeing more of the Montana countryside.

"This is great." Shelly smiled, bouncing from foot to foot. "I hope they let me stay in her room."

"Jesus, Shelly." I cringed.

She shrugged and took off for the motel's office.

The *her* Shelly referred to was Amina Daylee. Four years ago, Amina had been murdered right here at the Evergreen Motel. She'd been stabbed to death seven times by the former chief of police, Marcus Wagner.

The villain.

The man I'd be playing in *Dark Paradise*.

Cameron and I shared a look—we were equally annoyed with Shelly—then followed her into the office. It was no more than a kiosk in the center of the motel. I stayed back as Shelly took the lead, greeting the clerk, who identified himself as the owner. Shelly rattled off our names for him to find our reservations. I cringed again as she asked to be put in the room where Amina had been murdered.

So much for a low-key visit to blend in and learn the layout of the place.

The motel owner's expression turned hard as he retrieved three keys, each hooked to a green oval disk stamped with our room numbers.

"Thanks," I told him when Shelly forgot.

He nodded. "Just, uh . . . let me know if you need anything."

"Appreciate it." I waved, key in hand, and held the door for Shelly as she marched outside.

Now I understood why Cameron had insisted on coming here alone during his other visits. Blending in with Shelly was nearly impossible, and it had nothing to do with her magenta hair.

We huddled around the rear of the SUV, scanning the U-shaped motel for our rooms. Cameron and I had adjacent rooms. Shelly's room was on the opposite end. *Thank God.* My temples were beginning to throb.

Shelly and I had worked together for years. At times, her personality grated on me, but she was hardworking and reliable. She'd get the job done and done well, so I could deal with a slight headache.

Cameron and I hadn't known each other long, having only crossed paths occasionally before he'd agreed to come on as director. As I'd gotten to know him, I'd learned his reputation lived up to reality. He was a legend. He worked with dedication, precision and utmost sincerity. If this project was my baby, it was his grandchild.

Most actors weren't involved with the preproduction stage of a film's making, but I wasn't just the bankable star. I was a moneyman.

My production company was making this movie, and I'd made a significant personal investment. Funding a movie took millions of dollars, so we'd pulled in other investors. But if I could have, I would have funded this entire venture myself. That was how strongly I believed in this script.

The screenplay had come to me via my gardener, John. His next-door neighbor Ann was a young screenwriter who'd regaled him with stories of a Montana murder. Ann had spent weeks in Clifton Forge researching the crime she'd read about in an online article the year prior. Then she'd returned to LA and written her screenplay.

Lucky for me, she hadn't worked up the courage to send it out. After he'd begged for a month, Ann had relented and given John a copy of her screenplay to pass on to me.

John had brought it to me on a Monday morning. By Tuesday, I'd purchased it from Ann. By Wednesday, I'd optioned the rights to Valance Pictures. By Thursday, I'd funded the initial development costs and given Shelly the green light to hunt down more investors and kick off preproduction.

I was wasting no time.

I'd started Valance Pictures five years ago, and for the most part, I was too busy to get involved with the day-to-day activities. I had a reliable team who ran the business and producers, like Shelly, I trusted to oversee each film. The CEO churned out a report I read each quarter, and thus far, I'd had no dreams of grandeur. While Shelly and my CEO wanted to build the company into the next Warner Bros. or Universal Pictures, I'd been content to simply see the bottom line in black.

We'd released two movies so far, both with moderate success. Others were still in the pipeline, but nothing we'd picked stood out.

Dark Paradise was unique.

It had the potential to be something great for Valance Pictures, or it had the potential to ruin everything I'd worked for over the past eight years as an actor. Which meant I'd stay here, in Montana, and hope like hell the outcome was the former.

"Let's get settled and regroup in thirty." Cameron dragged his backpack out of the SUV.

"Sounds good." I hefted out Shelly's suitcase. Had it gotten heavier since the airport? We were only here for one night.

As she wheeled it behind her, practically running to her room, I slung my weekend bag over a shoulder and walked beside Cameron toward our own rooms. "Sorry about Shelly."

He lifted a shoulder. "She's a producer. I'm used to it. And she's better than some."

"Let me know if she crosses a line."

"We'll be fine. She's keyed up, but things will settle once we start shooting."

I waved to Cameron as he disappeared into his room and I ducked into mine. The room was as expected, clean but old. This motel had likely been built in the seventies, though the owners had kept it up. The siding had been painted a sage green within the last decade. Outside each room they'd hung flower baskets overflowing with a riot of spring petunias.

Setting my bag aside, I flopped onto the bed. My six-foot-two frame would have to sleep diagonally to fit on the mattress, and even then, my toes would dangle off the end.

My phone buzzed in my jeans pocket. Without looking, I knew it was either my mom, one of my sisters, my agent Ginny, my assistant Juno, or my manager Laurelin. The women in my life didn't believe in letting me rest.

The call went unanswered as I raised my arms and laced my fingers behind my head, staring at the ceiling. This hadn't been her room, but it was odd being at this motel, knowing this was where a person's life had been stolen.

Had Amina Daylee studied the popcorn on the ceiling as she'd died? Or had she closed her eyes as Marcus had driven a hunting knife into her body seven times? What had it taken for him to kill her? Rage. Pain. Maybe a crazy mix of both.

I'd been pondering Marcus's character for months and mentally rehearsing scenes. I hadn't been a shoo-in for the part, even though my company was making the movie. Cameron had made me audition. After he and the casting director had offered me the role, we'd spent hours talking through my performance and his expectations. As far as jobs went, I'd never been more prepared.

Or terrified.

This movie might flop, sinking my reputation and image.

But my gut screamed there was something here, that this was a winner, and I always listened to my gut.

Always.

Still, I hadn't been this scared my first day at the police academy or my first day on the force. The nerves would settle eventually, but for now, they were nearly crippling.

We needed to start shooting. We needed to get the opening scene of the movie behind us so I could stop dwelling on it.

That scene wasn't slated for shooting until later in the schedule, and it would be the hardest to perfect. It was the shot we needed to make our first impression and we'd shoot it right here, at this very motel.

It was the scene where Marcus kills Amina.

Cameron wanted the focus to be on Amina and how the life drained from her eyes. The killer, me, was to be an afterthought. My face wouldn't even be in the shot.

The audience would suspect that Marcus was investigating the murder for the majority of the film. If I did my job, they'd only suspect he'd been her killer toward the end.

Because in reality, Marcus Wagner had nearly gotten away with Amina's murder. He'd lived and worked in Clifton Forge for a year before being caught. The entire time, he'd been trying to frame an innocent man.

Draven Slater.

Draven had been the past president of a former motorcycle club and Amina's lover. Only hours before her death, they'd been together in the room where Shelly was now. According to speculation by the *Clifton Forge Tribune*, Marcus had killed Amina in a crime of passion. He'd been in love with Amina, and her night with Draven had been the ultimate betrayal.

It had cost Amina her life.

Draven had faced trial for her murder. He'd nearly been sentenced too, but the day before the jury had been scheduled to deliver a verdict, Draven had hung himself inside his home. He'd escaped life in prison for a crime he hadn't committed by claiming his own life.

With Draven gone, Marcus had been home free.

Almost.

Marcus had made a mistake. He hadn't counted on one thing—or one woman. Genevieve Daylee, Amina and Draven's daughter.

Genevieve had discovered Marcus's obsession with her mother and tricked him into a confession that had landed him in prison. He was currently serving a life sentence without the possibility of parole.

Along with the screenplay of the film, Valance Pictures had purchased the life rights to Marcus Wagner's story. That had taken us longer than a few days to procure. The movie was using facts based on a number of different sources, but from a liability standpoint, we'd sent Marcus a request anyway, hoping to get his consent.

He'd shocked the hell out of us when he'd agreed to the one-million-dollar payout. No counteroffers. No arguments. Just a signed agreement funneled through his lawyer and a hefty sum deposited into his former bank account, now controlled by his ex-wife.

We'd also bought her life rights too—the former Mrs. Wagner had negotiated an even bigger payday and was now living alone in Hawaii while her ex-husband rotted in a cell.

I'd tried to visit Marcus in prison, but he'd refused my invitation. I'd try again. And again. And again. One day, I'd sit across from him and look him in the eyes. I had to see for myself the man who'd once been a decorated officer. The man who'd hidden his crime for a year. A man who could turn his back on the oaths he'd taken to serve and protect.

Because maybe if I could understand why Marcus had turned, I'd be able to forgive my father for his crimes.

The minutes ticked by as I stared at the ceiling. When I heard Cameron's door open, I pushed off the bed and snagged the keys beside the TV. I met him outside on the sidewalk. "Where to?"

"I'd like to show Shelly the shooting locations, let her get a feel for what we're dealing with. Then debrief with her for a few hours."

"Sounds good." I nodded as Shelly came out of her room and joined us by the SUV.

"It's a little creepy," she admitted.

No shit. A woman had bled to death in that room. I doubted the motel's owners advertised that in their brochures.

We climbed into the Escalade and I drove through town, following Cameron's directions to each of the locations he'd marked for shooting. Cameron had been to Clifton Forge three times already, scouting locations himself. From the moment we'd hired him for this project, he'd immersed himself in the details. He remembered street and business names. He knew which bar served the best cheeseburger and where to get a stiff drink.

The more we traveled around Clifton Forge, guided by Cameron's directions, the more my nerves calmed. The stiffness in my shoulders eased. There was a sense of peace in this town. A sense of normal.

People meandered down the sidewalks. No one walked in a frantic march. We stopped at a sandwich place for a late lunch and nothing about the meal was hectic. Our waitress didn't rush us in and out to make room for another tipping customer. Even the stoplights, what few there were, seemed to change at a relaxed pace.

Cameron had chosen a ranch house about three miles out of town to use as Marcus's home. The owners had agreed to let us do some exterior and interior shooting for a hefty price. It was where we'd film the scene of Marcus's confession and arrest. The city had given us an all-access pass to public areas—after we'd opened the checkbook. And then there was the Evergreen Motel. The owners were allowing us to film on-site. That slice of authenticity had cost a quarter of a million dollars, plus we'd rented out the entire place for a solid two months for some of the crew.

Some interior scenes, like those in the police station, would be at the LA studio. We'd fabricate Marcus's workplace and a few other locations. But otherwise, most of the action would happen in Clifton Forge. Shelly had spent months on the phone ironing out agreements with the locals.

The only place she hadn't even bothered approaching was the Clifton Forge Garage.

Shelly might be a bulldog, but she knew when not to bark.

Once owned by Draven Slater, the garage was now operated by his son, Dash. According to Google, Genevieve had just graduated with honors from law school. I'd found her name listed on the staff directory for a firm in Clifton Forge.

We had decided not to approach either for life rights. We were using facts to craft their part of the movie, their fictionalized characters. And the rest was all make-believe. It was a risk we were willing to take since the focus was so heavily on Marcus.

I knew that filming this movie, let alone filming it in Clifton Forge, would be difficult for the victim's family. My plan was to approach them personally. I hoped they'd see this project as a way to set the story straight for Draven and show the world his innocence.

I'd explain that the script was mostly focused on the murder and the downfall of a cop. This story would travel with Marcus down his road to corruption and violence.

When the words *Based on a True Story* faded in, they'd be as close to history as possible, thanks to Ann's research. She'd pulled articles and court reports. She'd written letters, corresponded with both Marcus and his ex-wife. She'd spent time in Clifton Forge. I doubted the citizens here had even noticed the quiet woman sitting in the corner of a bar or restaurant, eating alone and soaking it in.

Ann had even braved a trip to the garage for an oil change. She hadn't included it in the script, but she'd told me one day how sitting in the waiting room of the garage had been like standing in the corner of a dining room, eavesdropping on another family's Thanksgiving dinner.

Approaching the garage—this family—would take finesse.

"Are we going to the garage?" Shelly had a thick notebook on her lap and had checked the small boxes she'd drawn beside the shooting locations.

"Not today."

Shelly didn't have the delicacy to walk into the garage and not ruffle feathers. Besides, it was likely a no-win situation. I wouldn't send her into the lion's den. As her boss's boss, I'd be the one to make the first introduction.

"Anywhere else?" She twisted in her seat to look at Cameron.

"No." He was scrolling through pictures he'd taken of the various locations. "I really like how everything looks right now. It's green but not too green. It's—what was that word you used earlier?—rugged. I want rugged. How fast can we get rolling?"

Shelly flipped to a different page of her notebook. "With a skeleton crew? Two weeks. If you need the full staff, a month minimum. We're nearly done with preproduction but I don't have any of the crew scheduled to arrive here until August one. We could do some without, but it will be clunky."

"We've managed clunky so far," I said.

She nodded. "This is true."

We hadn't hired a location manager for this film because Cameron had insisted on scouting locations himself. And Shelly had jumped in to negotiate contracts for the different places.

The casting was done. We'd used our in-house casting director for the smaller roles while Cameron had hand-picked the leads to submit auditions. This film didn't have a huge cast, which had made hiring efficient. Cameron had also insisted on a well-known production designer he'd worked with numerous times in the past.

Shelly had the rest handled. Costume design. Sound. Hair. Makeup. Catering. Housing. She'd spent months putting all the dominos in a row so they'd fall in exactly the right order.

God help us if she ever lost that notebook.

"I'd like to go with the skeleton crew." Cameron tapped his chin. "At least get some of the scenery shots done before the summer burns hot. Can you be here, Shaw?"

"No problem." This movie was priority.

"If we're going to do this, I need a few hours to make some calls," Shelly said, already jotting notes in the margin of a page.

"I'll take you back to the motel." I eased off the gas and flipped a U-turn to go the other direction.

"I want to get in touch with my assistant too," Cameron said.

"Let's break," I said. "We can regroup for dinner."

"What are you going to do?" Shelly asked.

"Explore."

And make an introduction.

After dropping them at the motel, I punched a new location into my GPS and aimed my wheels along the resulting blue path. The calm I'd found earlier evaporated as the garage came into view.

The towering shop stood stately on the street, like the mountains in the distance. The tin roof gleamed under the July sun. There were four bay doors, each open and occupied with a car. I parked in a free space beside the door marked *OFFICE*.

The sound of an air compressor whirling filled the air. Metal scraped metal. Socket wrenches cranked as they tightened bolts. The barely there smell of grease and gasoline tinted the air.

I opened the office door, my eyes aimed at the shop, searching for faces. When I spotted one, I faced forward with a smile.

My smile had won me the hearts of countless women across the world. Normally, it was met with a blush and dropped jaw.

Today, I was met with blue. Two of the bluest eyes I'd

ever seen. Eyes that paled the Montana sky and dulled the Caribbean shores.

I staggered.

It was my turn to flush and force my mouth closed as I studied the woman behind the desk, making sure she was real.

Her hair was the color of the purest sand. It was short, swooping over one perfectly arched eyebrow. Her lips were as hard as her expression, but I suspected that when she wasn't scowling, they'd form a natural, sexy pout.

I had no idea who she was, but she clearly knew me.

Her eyes weren't just blue. They were an angry blue.

She knew me and she knew exactly why I was here.

By some miracle, we'd managed to keep the tabloids out of preproduction. If anyone in Clifton Forge had noticed Cameron on his visits over the past few months, they hadn't cared.

But as production neared, everyone in Clifton Forge would notice the activity, the influx of visitors. Some in town, like the mayor, were counting on the commerce. About a month ago, after Shelly had signed the final agreement with the town council, the mayor had announced the movie alongside our Hollywood press release. I'd been keeping watch on Clifton Forge's local newspaper ever since, and they'd published an article shortly thereafter. My name had only been mentioned once.

I'd hoped that people would have adjusted to the idea of a film cast and crew, accepted it even, after a month. That did not seem to be the case at the Clifton Forge Garage.

I spotted the latest *Entertainment Weekly* tossed on a table beside an empty chair. My face was on the cover, decorated with a devil's pitchfork and horns.

So much for finesse and a smile.

"Hi." I flashed her the grin photographers salivated over.

Her stare narrowed. "Can I help you?"

I crossed the empty room, my hand extended. "Shaw Valance. I'm guessing you know who I am and why I'm here."

Her eyes darted to my hand and she crossed her arms over her chest.

"I, uh . . ." I dropped my hand. "I was hoping to introduce myself to Mr. Slater."

"Dash isn't available today." Her voice was flat. "Would you like to make an appointment?"

"Tomorrow morning?"

She shook her head. "He's busy."

Why did I get the feeling that Dash would be busy no matter what time I suggested? I blew out a deep breath. "I'm not here to cause trouble. I only want to introduce myself. Talk a little about the project."

"Right." Her tone dripped sarcasm. She didn't give a shit what we were doing here or why.

I held her stare, unable to move my feet. I was getting nowhere with this woman, so why wasn't I already back in the car?

The angry waves pulsing from her captivating face set me on my heels, but the soles of my boots were glued to the floor. She was a little thing, probably just over one hundred pounds, but damn, she was a force.

The last person who'd intimidated me this much had been my father before he'd fallen from grace.

Wavering under that livid blue gaze, I glanced around the room. My eyes landed on a framed photo tacked to the wall. I leaned closer, taking in the man I knew had been

33

Draven Slater—yet another Google score. His sons, Nick and Dash, stood by his side and beside them were three motorcycles.

The door behind me opened and my feet came unstuck. I turned as one of the men from the photograph stepped inside.

Dash cleaned grease from his hands on a red rag. He eyed me from head to toe as I did the same, noting we were about the same height and build.

"Dash Slater." I held out my hand. "Nice to meet you. I'm Shaw Valance."

His handshake was firm, his expression guarded. "What can I do for you, Shaw?"

"I'm looking to build a bike." The idea came from the ether and spewed from my mouth.

"A bike?"

"That's right." I nodded, pretending that I hadn't just hatched this brainchild. "I heard you're one of the best."

"Sorry. We don't have openings in the schedule." Dash crossed his arms over his chest and looked past my shoulder. "Isn't that right, Presley?"

"Yep. We're booked out for two years."

Damn. That actually sounded like the truth.

Their wait list was my way out the door. I'd stopped to introduce myself. I'd offered them business. Neither one of them seemed to want to know anything about my film. So why was I still standing here? Why did I suddenly feel guilty about filming a movie in their town?

This was good commerce. We'd bring money to this town during production and, afterward, notoriety. Didn't everyone want that elusive claim to fame?

No. Not everyone enjoyed the limelight. Not even me.

I should leave, but once again, I didn't even glance at the door. Now that the idea was out there, I *did* want a bike. I wanted to get to know these people who'd only been characters on a page until this point.

"I should have figured you'd be busy and called sooner. It was a last-minute idea. Sorry. We'll figure something out for the movie. I'm sure Harley-Davidson will send over something stock for the guy playing your dad to ride. It won't be as cool as that bike in the picture, but I bet people won't notice."

"Stock?" Dash's jaw clenched.

He knew I'd just baited him, and he knew he was going to take it. Because Draven Slater, the man in the picture standing in front of a fifty-thousand-dollar bike, would never have ridden a stock bike.

Dash would build the bike so his father's image was as accurate as possible.

Shelly might not understand the concept of authenticity, but Dash Slater sure as hell did.

"It'll cost you," Dash said.

"Dash—"

He held up his hand, silencing Presley's protest.

"How much?" I asked.

"Seventy-five grand. Three months. I have design control."

In three months, we'd be long gone from Clifton Forge. "Six weeks. Design whatever you want, and I'll pay ninety for the rush."

"Done. Presley will draw up the contract." Without another word, Dash exited the office and returned to the shop.

When I turned around, I was met with an icy glare.

"Please have a seat." Presley pointed to the chair across from her desk.

I obeyed. As I sat across from her, the scent of citrus and sweet vanilla wafted over the desk. The smell was inviting, unlike the woman whose eyes were aimed at her computer screen.

"Name?" she asked.

"Shaw Valance."

"Your legal name."

"Shaw. Valance."

Her fingers hesitated over the keyboard before punching in my name. She took down my address and phone number, clicking her mouse about one hundred times and never once looking at my face. Then she twisted in her chair to pick up the contract pages fresh from the printer.

She set them down in front of me along with a pen. "Sign the last page."

I scribbled my name.

Presley slid the sheets from under my hand before the ink had a chance to dry. She signed her own name below mine.

My lips fought a grin the whole time.

Who was this woman? When was the last time a single female—I'd checked, there was no ring—hadn't thrown herself in my direction? Presley was ice and fire with cool blue eyes that blazed with fury. Except every word, every movement, was full of indifference.

She pretended not to care, but her eyes betrayed her.

"I'd like a copy of that." I nodded to the contract.

"And I'd like a deposit."

I shifted to yank my wallet from my back pocket. I pulled

out my credit card and tossed it on her desk. "Run it for the full amount."

Her eyes flared but only slightly. Not a lot of people could charge nearly one hundred thousand dollars on a credit card, and yeah, it was a gross display of wealth. But her attitude, this apathy, was making me fucking crazy.

Presley dragged the credit card through the machine beside her computer, giving it back as the receipt printed. She ripped it off with a clean tear, pushing it across the desk for another signature.

I signed it and stood, walking for the door. I paused at the handle, glancing over my shoulder. I expected to see her eyes snapping up from my ass—that was normally what happened when I walked out of a room. But there was nothing. No look. No glare. Presley's attention was firmly fixed on her screen.

Huh. That dented the ego.

"Goodbye, Presley."

She blinked. The mouse she'd been moving froze for two seconds, then she was back to work. Not a damn word . . . because I'd already been dismissed.

When I returned to the motel, I didn't stop by to tell Cameron or Shelly that I was back. I went to my room and stared at the ceiling, not thinking about the movie or the murder.

My mind was fixed on Presley.

She was different than the women who'd caught my fancy these past few years. They'd all been beautiful, but Presley stood apart. She had strong cheekbones and a pretty chin. I'd been right about the lips. When she wasn't pursing them tight, they had this perfect, soft swell. She'd caught the bottom one between her teeth as she'd signed the contract and I'd almost reached to set it free. Presley had slight curves because she was a slight woman, which happened to be just my type. And goddamn those eyes.

She was . . . real.

I craved real.

"Damn," I muttered. I shouldn't have given Dash design control over that bike.

Because now I'd have to think up another excuse to visit the Clifton Forge Garage.

CHAPTER THREE

PRESLEY

"What about Leo?" Genevieve asked.

My face soured. "Ew."

"Emmett?"

I gagged. "Double ew. I just ate. Do you mind?"

Genevieve laughed. "Sorry. I had to ask. They're both single and not hard on the eyes."

"Yeah, they're easy to look at, but the idea of kissing them . . ." I shuddered. "No. They're like annoying older brothers and always have been."

When I'd started working at the garage, there'd been no shortage of handsome men to gawk at and drool over. There'd been a couple Tin Kings who'd caught my eye, but not Dash, Emmett or Leo. Yes, they were handsome, equally so in their own way. But I'd always seen them as friends—the closest thing I had to older brothers—and nothing more.

Besides, back then, I'd been too busy figuring out how to survive adult life to dare bring a man into the mix.

When I'd started at the garage, I'd been a naïve eighteen-year-old girl working her first job and living on her own in a new town. I'd grown up fast because there hadn't been another option. Despite the smile I'd worn to work every day, I think Draven had suspected I was frazzled and at my wits' end.

He'd sheltered me from the men in the club those first few months, afraid I'd either break or quit. He'd hired me to take over the office duties because he'd decided to retire. Except retirement hadn't really been Draven's style, so he'd cut his hours some but showed up at the garage each day.

To this day, I wasn't sure how he'd warned the club members away, but whenever one of the guys would see me in the office, he'd nod politely, then scurry in the opposite direction.

Draven had been my guardian while Dash had become my champion. Dash had slugged down cup after cup of my shitty coffee, never once complaining. When I'd finally gotten the hang of it, he'd just shrugged and said he'd known I'd figure it out eventually.

Emmett had worked at the garage then too. He'd come into the office on his lunch breaks and ask me what I was having. After two weeks in a row of watching me cook ramen noodles with a coffee mug in the microwave, he'd *accidentally* started cooking double the night before. One morning I'd shown up at the garage to find two Tupperware containers sitting side by side in the fridge, both marked with sticky notes. One had my name, the other Emmett's.

His hair had been shorter then, and he'd been going through a rough time. Morning after morning I would take him coffee and wince at the dark circles beneath his eyes. On particularly bad days, he'd reek of alcohol and smoke. But no matter how thick the grief, no matter how dark the cloud that threatened to swallow him whole, Emmett had never failed to bring me lunch.

Until the day I'd figured out how *not* to burn Hamburger Helper and brought in plastic containers of my own.

Draven, Dash and Emmett. My protectors. Not that I'd needed them. The one and only time a member of the club had dared hit on me, I'd handled it fine on my own.

It had been Leo.

He'd been drunk by five o'clock, which at the time had been Leo's norm. He hadn't started working at the garage yet, and to this day, I didn't know what he'd done for money. I suspected it had something to do with the club—I'd never know.

Leo had been loitering outside the office, hovering beside my car with an amber beer bottle dangling from his fingertips.

Presley, right?

I'd nodded.

You feel like—burp—*goin' for a ride?*

I'd burst out laughing, doubling over and nearly peeing myself. When I'd recovered, I'd told him to stop by the office the next morning, promising to give him lessons on how to ask a sober woman out on a date.

Much to my surprise, Leo had stopped by the next day, though not in the morning. Leo didn't do mornings. He'd come by around noon with sandwiches for us both and another for Emmett. Obnoxious as he was, there was a sweet streak to that man. Someday, I hoped a woman would whip Leo into shape. She'd have a fight on her hands, but it would be worth it.

A smile tugged at my mouth as I thought of the day we'd get to meet her.

"What?" Genevieve asked.

"Nothing." I shook my head. "I was just thinking about the old days."

"You've worked here for, what, ten years?"

I nodded. "Ten years in August. A lot has changed since then."

"I bet. You were here when the club was still going, weren't you? What was it like?"

"Wild. Even from the outside, you could feel the energy and excitement. It scared me a little, though I'd never admit it to Dash or Emmett or Leo. Draven kept me pretty far removed from it all, but I sit here. I can see." I gestured to the window. "I'd catch glimpses of the guys as they rode into the parking lot. They'd breeze by on their way to the clubhouse, wearing their cuts. There were so many of them. Eventually, I stopped trying to figure out who was who. The only ones I really knew were the guys working in the shop or some of the older ones who'd come in to bullshit."

"Were all the mechanics a part of the club?"

"Yeah. I was the first non-club member to work here. Draven told me that once. Isaiah was the second."

"Huh. I didn't know that."

I nodded. "Draven ran everything in the office. He didn't do much work in the shop by that point. That was Dash and Emmett's domain, especially after Emmett's dad, Stone, was killed."

"Oh." She blinked. "I didn't . . . I don't know much about Emmett's family. I've only ever heard him talk about his mom."

"She's lovely, and he adores her."

"Tell me again why you'd never be interested in dating Emmett?"

42

I giggled. "Never gonna happen."

"Worth a try." She took a bite of her sandwich, then lowered her voice. "Emmett's dad was killed? Was it because of the club?"

"I think so. No one ever told me the details. I only know that he died shortly before I moved here and Emmett was devastated."

The drinking had been obvious. I'd worried there'd been drugs. On more than one occasion, he'd come to work with cuts and bruises on his hands and face that I'd known had come from fighting.

"He worked it out eventually," I said. "Leo told me once that Emmett smiled a lot more back then. He was kind of like Dash—he loved working alongside his dad."

"I had no idea." Genevieve's eyes turned sad.

"A lot has changed."

Genevieve had only spent a year around the garage before she'd gone to law school. When she'd lived here, the Tin Kings had been just a memory.

But I'd seen it all. I'd seen them in their glory. I'd watched on as they'd lost members and hadn't replaced them. I'd been here the day the bikes had stopped roaring into the parking lot.

There were still days when I missed the noise.

I yawned, quickly covering it up and slugging down another gulp of Dr Pepper.

"Tired?" Genevieve asked.

"Leo," I muttered. "The jerk called me at one thirty in the morning last night to pick his drunk ass up from The Betsy."

"And you went?"

I lifted a shoulder. "He's Leo."

"But it's a no on dating him." She smirked.

I giggled. "A firm no. The man's a child."

Genevieve had come into the garage for lunch today. She'd picked up sandwiches for the entire crew to celebrate the end of the week. Since they'd moved back, she'd been working full-time for Jim Thorne, the best lawyer in town. Jim had closed the firm down early, so Genevieve had surprised us with food.

Except the guys were too busy watching Leo freehand airbrush a hood panel in the paint booth to be disturbed. There was no way I was waiting for those slow asses to show so I could eat my food, so Genevieve and I had started—and finished—without them.

She'd asked me if I was ready to start dating. I'd surprised us both with my *yes*.

I hadn't dated. Ever. Not once had a man taken me out on a first date to dinner and a movie. Jeremiah and I hadn't dated, we'd just been . . . together.

I was almost twenty-eight years old and wanted to be desired. For once in my life, I wanted to be *pursued*.

The only problem was no man in Clifton Forge had piqued my interest. Granted, I'd been with Jeremiah, but Clifton Forge wasn't known for its singles scene. I knew most of the single guys around, had met them when they'd come to the garage with their vehicles, and they were single for a reason.

The newest single man in town—at least, I assumed he was single—was a movie star, and there was no way I'd ever be sitting across from Shaw Valance in a restaurant.

Gorgeous as he was, I'd let millions of other women lust after him. It was fitting that he'd played a Greek god not long ago. He had the body for it. With his dark blond hair styled to perfection and those straight white teeth, Shaw had probably melted all the female togas on set.

I was not interested in melting.

And the last thing I needed was Hollywood glamour.

I needed real. Honest. I needed a man with a kind smile, a steady job and humble roots.

Jeremiah had been that guy, minus the job and the humility. If only the idea of kissing Leo or Emmett didn't sour my stomach.

"So . . ." Genevieve glanced over her shoulder toward the shop, making sure we were alone. There was still no sign of Emmett, Leo or Isaiah. Our other two mechanics, Sawyer and Tyler, usually ate their lunch out back at the picnic table, and Dash didn't work on Fridays. "Has Jeremiah reached out?"

"Not. A. Word." I poked the last bite of my turkey sandwich, discarded on its paper wrapper.

"Asshole."

"You said it."

I pretended it didn't hurt that in the six weeks since the wedding, Jeremiah hadn't reached out once. I pretended that things were better this way. They weren't, but I was good at pretending.

I'd been pretending life was *peachy* since birth.

"Did you get the landlord thing squared away?" Genevieve asked.

"For the most part." I sighed. "I'm trying not to think about how much money I lost."

On rent. On the wedding.

Jeremiah hadn't offered up a penny because the bride paid for the wedding, right? Or the bride's parents? As far as I was concerned, I didn't have parents, so I'd carved a chunk out of my savings to pay for the entire disaster myself.

The landlord in Ashton hadn't been pleased when I'd called to cancel my lease. He'd kept my deposit and the first month's rent I'd prepaid.

Thankfully, I had my job. I could kiss Dash for refusing to accept my resignation until the wedding was over.

It wouldn't take me long to rebuild my savings cushion, especially now that I wasn't funding Jeremiah's poker habit. Or his drinking habit. Or his rent and utilities. I wouldn't be spending hundreds of dollars in gas each month driving back and forth to Ashton each weekend to visit my fiancé.

Since Jeremiah had joined the Warriors and moved to Ashton, he'd only been back a handful of times. Each time he'd left, I'd noticed all the cash in my wallet had left with him.

I truly hadn't minded floating him some money. After everything Jeremiah had done for me, I could afford to indulge my fiancé.

I'd loved him. Once.

Or maybe I'd loved the boy he'd been.

He was in the past now. Any affection had shriveled up and suffered an angry death during the past six weeks.

Sleepless, miserable, humiliating nights had a way of turning love into resentment.

Maybe the reason Dash hadn't attempted to hire a replacement manager for the garage was because he'd hoped things would turn out this way. I couldn't blame him. He'd seen Jeremiah's true colors when I hadn't.

Still, wedding disaster aside, I was lucky. I was happier now than I had been as a kid. I had my modest home with a landlord who'd been overjoyed when I'd asked her if I could stay.

My life looked exactly the same as it had before June, sans Jeremiah.

I had my independence, and that was more precious to me than all the dollars in my savings account.

The boxes I'd packed had been unpacked. I hadn't had to pawn an engagement ring because Jeremiah hadn't bought me one; he'd wanted to save that money for our life together. *Lies.*

Jeremiah was nothing like the men here at the garage. Dash had put a ring on Bryce's finger weeks after they'd met. He'd married her almost as quickly. When Emmett and Leo met the women destined to ride on the backs of their motorcycles, they'd do the same.

When had I become a pushover? Here I was, thinking I'd become this strong, independent woman over the past ten years. But maybe I'd become what I feared most—my mother.

Was I a doormat for everyone? Or had Jeremiah been my weak point? I'd ponder those questions later tonight, when I was home alone and again shrouded in self-doubt and shame.

"How's your house?" I asked Genevieve, more than ready to shove Jeremiah out of my mind.

"It's coming along." She smiled. "Isaiah keeps telling me not to be in such a hurry to get it decorated, but I can't seem to stop ordering stuff online. I'm just ready to have a home. These last three years with school, everything has felt so temporary. The year before that too. I want stability."

"I get that."

"Can I tell you a secret?"

47

I leaned forward. "Always."

"I'm pregnant."

"What?" My hands flew to my mouth, then up in the air. "Oh my God. That's amazing. Congratulations."

She beamed. "It's early but we're so excited."

I stood and rounded the desk, bending down to pull her into a hug. "You're going to be the best mom."

Genevieve had the heart of a mother—a good mother. Unlike my own, she'd never let her children suffer.

"Thanks. I needed to hear that. I wish my mom was here so I could ask her questions."

I hugged her tighter.

"We haven't told many people yet," she said as I returned to my chair.

I zipped my lips shut.

The door between the office and the shop opened and the guys burst inside. Isaiah immediately went to kiss his wife. Emmett and Leo dove into the fridge.

"I forgot to tell you something last night," Leo said, his mouth full as he sat beside Emmett underneath the window.

"Last night?" Isaiah looked between the two of us.

I waved it off. "I collected his drunk ass from The Betsy."

Leo swallowed his bite. "I saw this chick who, swear to God, looked just like you."

My body tensed. There was one *chick* who looked like me but . . . *no. Impossible.* "You were drunk, Leo. Very, very drunk."

"True." He chomped another bite of his ham and swiss.

"No one looks like Pres." Emmett chuckled. "She's the only fairy sprite in Clifton Forge."

I rolled my eyes. "One Halloween. One. And I'll never live it down."

"Live what down?" Genevieve asked.

"Let me tell it." Emmett held up a hand before I could talk. "So Pres had been working here for a couple of years. She wasn't twenty-one yet and Draven would have smothered us with our own pillows if we'd invited her to the party at the clubhouse. We decided to have a party here after work. We all clocked out and Pres disappears into the bathroom. She comes out dressed as a fairy. Wand and everything."

"Okay," Genevieve drawled. "Why is that funny?"

"Ask her where she bought the costume."

"The kids' section," Leo blurted. "None of us would have teased her about it except she left the tags on."

Emmett and Leo burst into hysterics.

"I'm a small person!" I shouted over their laughter, fighting my own smile. I'd never understood why that story amused them so much, but they always laughed, and I liked their laughs. "I hope you choke on your food." I feigned a scowl. "These dickheads called me Pixie for months."

"Anyway," Leo said. "This girl looked just like you except she had long hair."

The tension returned, mounting. Could it have been . . . *no.* There was no way Scarlett was anywhere near Clifton Forge. If she were here, I'd know about it. "You're not to be trusted when you're wearing beer goggles."

He chuckled. "True."

"What's on the board for the rest of the day?" Emmett asked.

I rattled off the list of scheduled appointments. Being a Friday, both he and Isaiah wanted to leave early, so they offered to take some of the oil changes and help out Sawyer and Tyler.

Genevieve hugged me goodbye and declared she was going home to take a nap. Isaiah escorted her to her car and kissed her goodbye before returning to work.

The noise in the shop picked up as I resumed working on payroll. When the door opened, I looked up, expecting to see the customer scheduled for a tire rotation. Instead, I was met with a pair of golden-brown eyes that had *not* been haunting me for two weeks.

"Ugh," I groaned as my heart skipped. "You again?"

"I've missed you too." The corner of Shaw's mouth turned up.

Other women probably called that mouth delectable. Not me. *Never me.*

"What do you want?" I carefully kept my tone flat.

If Shaw Valance knew that he made my pulse race, there'd be no tolerating him. His ego barely fit through the door as it was. He'd think it was attraction that made my voice shaky. That I liked having him here, when this physical reaction was nothing more than irritation.

I was on edge because Shaw was well practiced at delivering a line, and nothing he said could be trusted.

"I was hoping to see how my bike is coming along."

"Dash isn't here today. You'll have to come back next week."

Isaiah was actually working on Shaw's bike, but he didn't need to know the details.

I focused on my screen. The muscles in my legs were bunched tight to keep my foot from bouncing on the floor, and I held my breath, eyes forward, waiting for him to leave.

The chair across from mine dragged on the carpet as he took a seat.

A low growl rumbled in my chest.

Shaw chuckled and—*sweet Jesus*—his voice was so smooth, like a satin ribbon running through my fingers. It was deep but not too deep. Low but not quiet.

Irritating. The man was wholly irritating.

I hadn't resorted to googling Shaw yet, but I had spent my sleepless nights over the past two weeks watching all his movies. His voice had lulled me to sleep. A secret I'd take to the grave.

"Like I said, Dash isn't here." As in, *go away*.

The last thing I needed was a superstar invading more of my life. I'd let him do that enough with just the one visit.

What the fuck kind of name was Shaw Valance anyway? I would have bet my life it was a stage name and not his legal name. I guess it could still be fake; maybe he'd legally changed his name. But something about the way he'd said it felt familiar, like he'd been saying it his whole life.

His gaze burned a hot trail down my body as he took me in. It was times like this that made me wish I still had my long hair to drape over my tiny breasts.

I'd worn a pair of boyfriend jeans today. They were baggy and cinched tight around my waist with a camo cloth belt. But it was hot outside so I'd paired it with a thin black tank top. The red straps of my bra showed from collarbone to shoulder blade.

Shaw's gaze was locked on those red bands. "I'd like to watch."

What? Watch? *Me?*

"The bike," he added. "I'd like to observe, maybe learn a few things as they build it."

"Oh." My cheeks flamed, something else hard to hide with short hair.

I was an idiot. Why would a famous actor want to watch

me? He wouldn't. Besides, I didn't want him here either. I was busy and the way he wore his jeans, loose but not too loose, was an unnecessary distraction.

He was too . . . polished. Too refined. Too perfect. I wasn't going for perfect. I was going for good enough.

Because good enough wouldn't shatter my soul.

"Why?" I asked. Didn't he have better things to do than lurk at a small-town garage?

He shrugged. "I've always been interested in cars and motorcycles. While I'm here, I'd like to see how it's done."

"No." No way in hell. I could not have this man around me for weeks on end. "Don't you have a movie to make?"

"I'll have free time between shooting."

"It's a liability. You can't be in the garage. Employees only."

"Hire me as an employee. I'll work for free."

"No."

He quirked an eyebrow. "How much?"

"This isn't a negotiation or something you can buy with your platinum credit card."

I'd never touched a credit card like Shaw's before. It was heavier than the ones we mere mortals were granted for our wallets. Hell, he could buy the house next door to mine with one swipe.

"How much?" he asked again. "Just to observe. I promise to stay out of the way."

"Were your parents the type who never said no to you as a child?"

"I understand the meaning of *no*."

"Do you though?" I raised an eyebrow.

Neither of us was going to give. He'd probably go over

my head and ask Dash. Most men didn't like being told no by a woman, let alone a woman the size of a teenager.

"This is the safe zone, right? A place for the public?" He lifted a finger and twirled it in a circle. "I can observe through the window in that door."

"Excuse me?"

"That window." He shifted and pointed to the door. "I'll just watch from here. Probably better that way anyway. You can keep me company. Hours between shoots are boring."

"Then read a book. Go hiking. Work on your tan."

"Nah." He grinned. The son of a bitch knew he was getting to me. Was this how Dash had felt when Shaw had backed him into a corner with that stock Harley bullshit?

If he were bluffing, I would have stood my ground. But I had no doubt that Shaw would show up here each and every morning to stand beside the door and irritate me for hours.

"You'll have to sign an insurance waiver."

Sorry, Isaiah. I was passing this nuisance off to him. Hopefully Dash would boot his ass out of the shop.

"Happy to." His grin turned into an arrogant smile as he stood and walked to the door. "Goodbye, Presley."

I ignored him. I ignored the way my name sounded in his voice.

I ignored that chuckle, that glorious fucking chuckle, as it echoed in the office long after he'd closed the door.

CHAPTER FOUR

PRESLEY

"You were supposed to kick him out," I grumbled.

Dash scoffed. "You're the one who had him sign the insurance waiver."

"Which I thought you'd tear in half."

"Well . . . I've been thinking about it." Dash rubbed his jaw. "What better place to keep tabs on him than here? I don't have to go anywhere. The asshole comes to me."

My lip curled. "This is not how I'd imagined this going."

"Hey, at least he's not in the office, bothering you."

"Yeah," I muttered as Shaw crouched beside Isaiah.

Dash and I were standing at the other end of the shop, watching as Isaiah pointed out various parts on the bike's engine and frame. Shaw nodded along, licking it up like he was actually committing it to memory, but the guy was an actor.

He was a professional faker.

It had been nearly a week since Shaw had come by the office wanting to *watch*. Monday had passed without a visit. I'd been on edge Tuesday and Wednesday, waiting for him to show. But this morning, I'd been relaxed as I'd unlocked the door, thinking we were home free. I'd foolishly gotten my hopes up that he'd been busy with the movie and had forgotten about the garage.

Not thirty minutes after I'd flipped on the neon OPEN sign, Shaw's black Cadillac had rolled into the space beside my Jeep, and when he'd entered the office, he hadn't balked at the insurance waiver.

The word around town was that Shaw was staying at the Evergreen Motel along with other members of the cast and crew. The KOA campground was filled with shiny white and silver trailers. The other two motels were rumored to have a zero-vacancy rate starting in two weeks when more of the crew and cast arrived.

Everyone was talking about the movie. The cashier at the grocery store. The girl at the coffee hut. My next-door neighbor and Mrs. Franklin across the street. The town was buzzing.

Last night, I'd gone to the salon for a quick trim and my hair stylist had talked about Shaw the entire time.

Have you seen him? He's so hawt. I saw him jogging down Central yesterday morning and about died.

Shaw. Shaw. Shaw.

I was so sick of that damn name, except when he'd swaggered into the office and flashed me his killer grin, my traitorous heart had skipped.

Dash had been in his office reviewing the parts order, so I'd let him deal with Shaw. Meanwhile, I'd snubbed our guest like it was my superpower.

"We need to find out what the movie is about," Dash said quietly. "I know you don't like the guy. I don't either. But let's play along. See if he'll tell us what it's about. I don't really give a fuck what they're doing, but Genevieve does."

My sweet friend was having a hard time with this movie. Genevieve was scared about how they'd portray her mother and father. She didn't care at all that she'd be a character in the film too. She simply fretted over the memory of those she held most dear.

"You're right." I sighed. "I'll be civil."

"Thanks." He squeezed my shoulder.

"I'm going back to work." I left Dash in the shop, who continued watching Shaw, as I retreated to my desk.

So much for keeping Shaw at a firm distance, but Dash had a fair point. For Genevieve, I'd put my own feelings aside.

None of us knew exactly what the movie was about or what type of story they planned to tell. The script was a mystery and not even the mayor or Luke Rosen had a clue to the movie's plot—Dash had called Luke on Monday.

We knew it was about Amina's murder. Obviously, Marcus Wagner would be a focal point since he was her killer. But what about Draven? What about the garage? Would there be mention of the Tin Kings or the Arrowhead Warriors?

The old rivalry between clubs had flared up a few years ago during Draven's trial, but it had ended peacefully, and the Warriors had stayed out of Clifton Forge ever since. As far as I knew, the only person who'd had contact with them since was me, and that was because Jeremiah had dragged me into their world.

If I'd wanted to see him, I'd had to drive to Ashton and stay in his room at the Warrior clubhouse.

It wasn't until I'd walked through one of the wild

Warrior parties that I'd understood why Draven had kept me far away from the Tin Kings when I'd been young.

The booze had flowed like a river, past shores of drugs and islands of scantily clad women. My first Warrior party was the first time I'd seen someone snort a line of cocaine.

About a year ago, I'd gone to visit Jeremiah like I had nearly every weekend. The two of us had been alone in his room, on his bed, watching a movie while a party raged beyond.

I'd tried the party scene, for Jeremiah, but after my tenth visit, I'd told him I was done. So he'd given them up too, choosing to stay with me in his room on Friday and Saturday nights instead of drinking with his brothers.

We'd been in the middle of the latest *Jurassic Park* movie when the door had burst open and a naked woman had stumbled inside. She'd gotten the rooms mixed up. In the middle of her slurred apology, she'd bent over and puked on the end of the bed and over my feet.

Had I been replaced with a skank who was drinking her daddy issues away? Jeremiah of all people knew I had daddy issues of my own. Maybe it had been a turn-off that I'd battled my demons, for the most part, alone. When Jeremiah had found me in Clifton Forge, I hadn't needed him to rescue me.

Was he *rescuing* someone now?

The idea of him with another woman made me grimace. The week after the non-wedding, I'd gone to the clinic to be tested. I'd barely been able to make eye contact with the doctor. The results had come back clean, but I still wondered if Jeremiah had been faithful while we'd been together.

Had he loved me? Or had I just been easy sex on a Friday and Saturday night? It wasn't like sex at the Warrior clubhouse didn't come easily to any man wearing a cut. Jeremiah was easy on the eyes and hadn't needed me to get off.

So why had he stayed with me only to leave me so brutally on our wedding day?

Damn it, I wanted an answer. I wanted the chance to yell and scream in his face, but I refused to reach out.

I would not seek him out. I would not waver.

I would not be my mother and accept whatever excuse he'd throw out.

The door between the shop and office opened and Shaw walked in. My mood, already sour, nose-dived, yet my heart rate spiked. This man had my insides twisted, pulling in opposite directions. I frowned as he took his normal chair across from my desk, but my breath hitched as he grinned.

"That was cool," he said. "Worth your waiver to learn how they build the bikes. Do you spend much time in the shop?"

"No."

"Have you worked in other garages?"

Wasn't he here to watch his bike? This wasn't get-to-know-Presley day. "No."

"Did you grow up in Clifton Forge?"

My mouth flattened into a thin line. Seriously, the show was over. Why was he still here? "No."

"Is this you making sure I've been told *no* enough times this week?"

I shot him a glare. If Shaw turned out to be funny, I was screwed.

"Isaiah seems like a nice guy. I appreciate that he took the time to humor me today."

"He is a nice guy," I said. "You do realize he's connected

to this movie you're making, right? His wife's mother was murdered."

"Yes." He nodded. "I know about the connection."

"How much else do you know?"

"Enough to do the story justice."

I crossed my arms over my chest. "Says a guy who wasn't here and doesn't know the actual story."

Shaw picked up a pen from the edge of my desk and spun it around his fingers. "You don't like that we're making this movie."

"Of course not. You're glorifying a crime that stole my friend's mother."

"Trust me. We're not glorifying anything. Certainly not Marcus Wagner."

I arched an eyebrow. "You're playing him, aren't you?"

"I am."

That was a different role for Shaw. Every movie I'd watched, he'd been the hero who saved the day. Marcus's role didn't fit his roster. He'd be better suited to playing Chief Rosen.

"What about the rest of the characters? Who's playing them?" I pointed to the picture of Draven, Dash and Nick on the wall. "These are real people. Draven was a good man. Is that how you'll show him? Or is this going to be a movie about a bad cop going after a bad guy? Is this more interesting than any other murder in the past decade because the person framed had ties to a motorcycle club?"

Shaw spun the pen again, then caught it and placed it back on the desk. "This story is interesting because of all the elements involved. People want to watch interesting movies. Don't you?"

"This isn't fiction. This is my family. Did you ever once

ask yourself who was on the other side of the murder? Or have you been too busy worrying about Marcus? That man deserves to rot in prison. What happens after this movie? Does he start getting fan mail from other sickos in the world?"

Shaw frowned. "There's no way he comes out of this movie looking like anything other than a villain."

"So you say." I shrugged. "Until then, I get to watch my friend worry about how her mother is going to be portrayed in a movie. How her father will be portrayed. I get to watch her husband come to work with circles under his eyes because she had a bad night and couldn't sleep. You're here, years after we've started putting the past behind us, and now we have to relive it over again."

There was a flicker of remorse in his gaze as he shook his head. "That's not our intention."

"But it's reality," I fired back. My mouth was running away with itself. "How far are you going to go? Will you show Amina's murder? What about Draven? Is the world going to know he was a good man?"

Shaw didn't answer.

"That's a no," I muttered.

The world would see a glimpse into Draven's life and be told he was a criminal. This movie would focus on his death, and everyone would think he was a coward for taking his own life when I thought—no, I *knew* he'd done it to save the rest of us from watching him wither away in prison.

"Presley, we're not doing this to hurt people."

"I actually believe you think that. But you will."

Shaw was quiet for a few long moments. Over his shoulder, Dash approached the door but I gave him a slight headshake that turned him in the opposite direction.

"How does it go?" I asked. "The movie."

"We aren't telling anyone. The cast and crew have all signed NDAs."

"Tell me anyway."

He narrowed his gaze. "Why? So you can sell it to the press? Spoil it before it releases?"

"No." I barked a dry laugh. I had no desire to bring any more attention to myself than necessary. "Because no matter what I say, you're going to make that movie. You can at least tell us what to expect so we don't have to walk into the movie theater and find out ourselves."

He studied my face, then nodded. "Fair enough, but not today. What I can tell you now is that we're trying to keep it as authentic as possible."

"Authentic." I rolled my eyes. "*Authentic.* What does that even mean?"

"It means we're here, aren't we?"

"You're here shoving authentic horseshit in our authentic faces and expecting us to like how it smells because you're tossing authentic money around like it grows on authentic trees."

"I'm not the bad guy."

"No. You're just playing one on TV."

Shaw flinched at my insult, the slash deep. Pain crossed his handsome face and his eyes pleaded with me to understand.

If I stared at him too long, maybe I would, so I turned my attention to my computer screen, dismissing him.

Guilt snaked its way through my veins, his stare hot on my profile. I'd been harsh, too harsh, and Dash would scold me later for not playing along.

My runaway tongue was Shaw's fault. His presence

unsettled me, and he made me say the first thing that came to mind instead of thinking it through.

Shaw finally stood, not saying a word as he walked to the door.

I braced, waiting for my *Goodbye, Presley*, but it didn't come.

He was gone and I'd likely ruined our chance at finding out about this movie. I hadn't been able to resist the opportunity to rain on his Clifton Forge parade.

Stupid, Pres. Damn it.

In my defense, Shaw was living in la-la land, and he had to know how hard it would be for Genevieve to see him on the street. He had to know how much Isaiah had probably hated entertaining him today.

I waited until his SUV crunched over the gravel on its way out of the parking lot before ungluing my eyes from the screen. Then I dropped my head into my hands and blew out the breath I'd been holding. The wounded look on Shaw's face was burned into my brain.

"Shit."

Why did I feel so guilty? Everything I'd said had been the truth, though I could have delivered it with more grace. Why did I care if Shaw's feelings had been hurt?

Because I'd built this image of him in my head based on his movies. He was the good guy. Good guys didn't deserve the kind of attitude I'd served him cold.

But what if he wasn't so good? Would this softness I had for Shaw go away if I learned he was a massive prick and not the dream guy from his movies?

I sat up straight and clicked my mouse. So far, I'd avoided the tempting combination of Google and Shaw. He already steamrolled through most of my thoughts, so I hadn't wanted to add oil to that engine. And looking him up felt . . . sneaky. Underhanded.

Though that was probably how Shaw had learned about us. I was sure he'd spent time reading through Bryce's newspaper articles and looking at our social media profiles.

He was exploiting the sliver of information he'd found, and it wasn't fair.

Yet here I was with my hypocritical fingers typing his name into the search bar.

The first thing to pop up was a row of pictures. In each, Shaw was at a movie premiere. His shined shoes gleamed atop the red carpet and the man wore a black tuxedo well.

The few times Shaw had come to the garage, he'd been in a button-down shirt with the sleeves rolled up his tanned forearms, his jeans draped down his long legs. I had purposefully not let myself look at his ass because my imagination was running rampant on its own.

Shaw had been casual. Natural. And even without a hair and makeup team, he was billboard worthy. He really was just that good-looking.

Natural didn't play into these photos. Every line of his suit jacket had been tailored to his strong body. His slacks tapered with precision down his muscular thighs. In most he had one hand in a pocket. In some, he was waving to a fan.

He was utterly gorgeous, and everything was for show, including his smile. It was a practiced version of the easy grin he'd been flashing me.

The cameras ate it up.

Beneath the photos, the first link was to Wikipedia. The next was a movie database. I clicked through it, making sure I'd hit all of the movies on Netflix that he'd filmed.

I had—twice.

On his Wikipedia page, the most recent movie listed was titled *Dark Paradise*. Was that this movie? Our movie?

According to the status, it was in preproduction, whatever that meant. Given the influx of Californians to Clifton Forge, I was guessing the page hadn't been updated recently. There was nothing *pre* about what was happening in town.

I went back to the photos, expanding the results, and did a double take. Woman after woman. Model after model. If Shaw had a type, it was simply beautiful.

There was only one woman repeated in multiple photos. She was tall, much taller than my five two, though most women were. In one photo, she was holding Shaw's arm as he escorted her down the sidewalk on a sunny day. Both were laughing. In another, the couple was dressed to the nines without smiles, standing on the steps of what looked like a museum.

Christ. Here I was lusting over a man who had supermodels as companions. For all I knew, this repeat woman was his girlfriend. The idea made me squirm. Why was I more jealous of the blonde in a photo than I was whatever Warrior club slut was hooking up with Jeremiah?

"And we're done with the photos," I muttered, going back to Wikipedia.

Shaw had been born and raised in Southern California. His mom was a retired drama teacher. His father had been a decorated police officer and Shaw had followed in his footsteps.

I snapped my fingers, remembering a story I'd heard ages ago on the news. I scrambled to type in a new search. *Shaw Valance school bus.*

How long had it been, seven or eight years? The details of the story came rushing back as I scanned the words of the first article I found. It was about a cop who'd gotten national media attention for saving a school bus full of children from an armed psycho who'd taken it hostage.

The hazy images from the past mixed with the details of the present. That cop was Shaw. Why hadn't I put that together sooner? Maybe because I'd been too busy back then, at barely twenty years old, to think about much other than my own problems.

He'd been so popular, so heroic, after the school bus incident that his face had been splashed over every news outlet. Someone from Hollywood must have snatched him up after that and made him a star. Clearly his mom had taught him a thing or two about acting.

I kept reading and researching, and according to what I could piece together, Shaw had quit the police force a year or so after the school bus incident. In the last picture of him in uniform, he was wearing a pair of dark sunglasses over those brown eyes and holding a large, automatic rifle.

He looked like a cop, stoic and serious.

So why had he quit? He'd been such a hero. Was it because of the media attention? Was it for the money? Most actors didn't make squat, though I was learning that Shaw didn't exactly fit the mold.

I spent the rest of my morning hunched over my screen, ignoring the work I was being paid to do. I'd make it up to Dash by staying late.

By lunch, I was in a fog.

I'd opened Google, hoping it would make me hate Shaw Valance, except he came across so freaking nice and genuinely kind.

How was it the paparazzi hadn't caught him on one off day? Hadn't one of them ever managed to piss him off?

Shaw's smile never seemed to falter. Hell, in most of the photos, he was waving to whomever had the camera aimed his way.

So why was he playing the criminal in *Dark Paradise*? Why not play Draven?

I trusted Shaw as the good guy, to play Draven as a good guy. But as Marcus? It seemed like too much of a jump. Would Shaw, just by being Shaw, make Marcus some kind of hero?

The door to the shop opened and Dash walked inside, chugging a bottle of water. "So? Did you find out anything?"

"No." I shook my head, then looked out to the parking lot. "But I will."

If Shaw Valance returned, I'd lay off. I'd find out why he'd chosen to play Marcus in this movie, and I'd make sure he knew down to the bottom of his soul that Marcus Wagner had been a vile and evil human being.

Because while I hated the idea of this movie, while I hated that it was happening right here in my own town, Shaw was the only person wrapped up in this movie visiting the garage. He was the only one who might listen.

And trusting him with the truth might be the only way to set the record straight.

CHAPTER FIVE

SHAW

"Ann, I should have asked this question months ago." I paused, hating what I was about to ask. Ann would no doubt see this as me doubting her screenplay. Maybe I was. But mostly, I was doubting my own conviction. "You said this was based on a true story. I know you did a lot of research and spent time in Clifton Forge, but how true are we talking?"

"It's true, Shaw."

Yeah, she was irritated. "I'm sorry to ask. I just . . . I had to know."

The line was quiet for a few moments, then she blew out a breath. "I get it. You're there and people are questioning what the movie is about."

"Exactly."

"It's true. It's as true as I could make it. Marcus answered my questions and so did his wife. Ex-wife, I guess. Unless they lied, which I don't think they did, because it matches up with other sources. It's true."

Thank fuck. "Then we're good. That's all I needed to know."

When I'd received the screenplay, I'd instantly gotten caught up in the story. When I'd called Ann to ask her about buying it, she'd told me it was based on a true story—the words were on the front page—but I hadn't stopped long enough to ask exactly how true.

I'd found a unique script. I'd seen an opportunity to play a different role. And I'd gone from zero to sixty in less than a week, and my foot had been on the gas ever since. Sure, I'd spent time reading articles online about the murder and Marcus. I'd spent hours on Google. But I'd skimmed articles and glazed over facts.

Then came Presley.

She'd challenged me and I hadn't liked not knowing if I was standing on solid rock or quicksand.

"I took some liberties to fill in the gaps," Ann said. "I had to. But I cross-referenced everything with the newspapers. I bought the transcript to Draven's trial. And I only used a piece of hearsay if I'd heard it more than once. Maybe they were rumors, maybe some of the gossip was wrong, but that's all I had to go on."

"Okay." Hearsay wasn't great, but it was all we had. And if the rumors were common enough, I was confident we could sell this story to the vast majority of people in Clifton Forge.

But could I sell it to Presley?

She probably had a different opinion than most people in town. She had a different perspective.

The real truth, the one we'd never be able to replicate, was likely somewhere in the middle.

"Thanks, Ann."

"Yeah," she muttered. "I really did try."

"You succeeded," I assured her. "Put this phone call out of your head. We're good."

She hung up the phone and I tossed mine beside me on the bed, closing my eyes and rubbing my forehead. A headache was brewing behind my temples, probably from all the time I'd been hunched over my laptop.

Over the past four days—since Presley's questions had stirred this slurry of self-doubt—I'd gone over the script with a fine-tooth comb. I'd scoured the news archives at the *Clifton Forge Tribune*, grateful they were all kept online. I'd matched scenes and dialogue as best I could to the news.

I'd dried up two highlighters marking lines as either fact or fiction. Yellow or blue. In the end, the pages blended into green.

Ann had done a fantastic job writing a tale based on the truth. But this was a movie and the line between entertainment and reality was often what kept viewers glued to the screen. That line, if we got it wrong, was where Presley would nail my balls to the floor.

Why the hell did Presley's opinion matter so damn much? How had this woman, this stranger, managed to turn me inside out about my own movie?

Because she made it real.

She'd turned a movie into life. This project had taken on a whole new meaning. It wasn't about satisfying investors or turning a profit. Now, I had an urge to do this story, the real story, justice.

Financial gains and academy accolades didn't mean success anymore. For me to consider this a win, I wanted Presley's approval.

I was going to have to break confidentiality to quiet her

69

voice. I'd already considered asking her to sign an NDA, but I suspected she'd tell me to shove it up my ass, so I'd take a leap of faith and trust her with the truth.

There'd been vulnerability in her voice when she'd asked me to tell her about the movie. Her curiosity didn't seem devious, and I'd been replaying our conversations on an endless loop.

When had life gotten so complicated? When had I started measuring every single conversation?

I missed the simple days, the early days, when I was a new cop. Back then, I'd been so focused on following orders and enforcing laws, life had been easy. The world was black and white for a kid barely twenty-one years old. I'd gotten my associate's degree. I'd gone to the academy. I'd joined the force. Wrong was wrong, and right was right.

Then it had blurred to gray.

Kind of like this movie. The vision had been so clear before I'd set foot in Montana, but it was blurring now too.

Who was Draven Slater? Presley spoke about him with such reverence and love, but he was a criminal. In the movie, we were showing him as a criminal. He'd been arrested for murder and according to my research and Ann's storyline, it hadn't been the first time Draven had been in handcuffs.

The newspaper hadn't mentioned too much about Draven's motorcycle club, which made the entire thing suspicious. But since the reporter and owner of the newspaper had the last name Slater, that hadn't been a shock. Bryce Slater was Dash's wife, Draven's daughter-in-law. She'd written clean, informative news for the *Tribune*. She'd covered Draven's trial fairly. Marcus's too. There was just a big hole when it came to the Tin Kings. Any references were vague and dismissive.

The key dynamic in the film, besides Marcus's own internal conflict, was the battle between Marcus and Draven. The plot centered around their old rivalry. Draven's past crimes had been embellished slightly from his rap sheet, and Marcus's inability to keep him in a jail cell would be the catalyst for his breaking point.

There was no way to know, but I had a hunch we were closer to the truth than even we'd realized.

I was hungry for details, not because it would change the movie, but for myself. The former cop in me wanted answers. I wanted to know more about these people, and I wanted to know more about Presley.

I stood from the motel's bed and grabbed my phone. I'd been staying at the Evergreen since I'd returned to Montana and my time here was about over. The room was clean, but the shower was too short for a guy my size and the queen-sized bed wasn't big enough. I needed room to sprawl. Come tomorrow, I'd have a space of my own and a decent bed.

The morning sun warmed my face as I stepped outside, sunglasses and keys in hand. I wasn't shooting today. Cameron and the crew were doing setup for a night scene, so I had a while before my call time.

My plan was to talk to Presley and hopefully work the doubts out of my head, but before I went to the garage, I was heading to the police station.

I'd meant to swing by last week, but shooting had been busy. This morning I was making time to see the place where Marcus had worked. I wanted to introduce myself to the chief, the guy who'd arrested Marcus, and get a read on him.

The motel's parking lot was nearly empty as I left, everyone else having left before six this morning. We were rotating out cast members to keep location time at a minimum.

Last week, we'd shot a few outdoor scenes so Cameron could get his rugged look. One had been of Marcus as a young cop, patrolling town and helping an elderly woman change a tire at the end of his shift. Another had been of Marcus taking his wife out to dinner. They were scenes to lay a foundation, to show Marcus had been a good man.

Despite Presley's hatred toward him, I needed to believe he'd been a moral man once. That one horrific act didn't erase the good he'd done. The good I'd assumed he'd done.

Tonight, we were shooting a scene at Marcus's home. He —me—would be on his couch in his living room, sitting alone and drinking a glass of tequila. His wife, played by a nice actress I hadn't met before, would come in and kiss his forehead good night. She'd exit the shot with the tails of her nightgown floating over the carpet. And when she was gone, Marcus would cringe. He'd wait, sipping his drink, until he was sure she was asleep. Then he'd call Amina.

He'd smile and relax, because he was on the phone with the love of his life.

Tomorrow night's shoot would be one of ten depicting the night Marcus had been arrested for Amina's murder. Then the actress playing his wife would fly out and a new set of characters would fly in.

The only constant through the movie was me. I was in every scene.

It would be grueling, and sleep would be scarce. What I should be doing during my free time was resting and running lines, but until I had some answers, I wouldn't be able to concentrate.

I didn't need my GPS to navigate the streets of Clifton

Forge any longer and the police station was easy enough to find along the river. I parked beside a cruiser, hopped out and jogged up the steps to the front door. The cement radiated heat, even this early, and I was glad I wouldn't have to stand under the scorching sun in full makeup.

The lobby of the station was as expected, plain and beige. I walked up to the officer stationed behind a glass window. "Morning. I was wondering if the chief was in."

"I'll check." He pointed to the row of chairs along the wall.

I took a seat, balancing my elbows on my knees as I waited. The officer hadn't asked me for my name. I guess he hadn't needed it.

Five minutes later, a door opened with a loud click and a tall man about my height and size walked out wearing a navy uniform shirt, jeans and cowboy boots. "Shaw Valance?"

"Chief?" I stood and met him in the middle of the room.

He shook my hand. "Luke Rosen."

"Nice to meet you. Sorry to just drop by."

"No problem." He waved for me to follow him. "Come on back."

The smell of coffee, leather and aftershave filled my nose as we entered the station's bullpen. Cluttered desks. Empty chairs. It was familiar and comforting, and while a part of me longed for the past, another part of me was glad I didn't have to walk into this every day.

There were only two officers in the bullpen, one man and one woman. Both were wearing shirts like Luke's, but they had on the coordinating pants with guns and badges hanging from their belts. They stopped talking when I passed their desks, so I lifted a hand and waved. They nodded.

"Coffee?" Luke asked as he crossed the threshold to his office.

"No thanks." I stepped in so he could close the door behind me.

"So, Shaw"—he took his chair behind his desk—"what can I do for you?"

"I just wanted to introduce myself," I said as I sat down. "And I wanted to see the station."

"Is it what you expected?"

"You've got a nice setup," I answered. "Was this his office? Marcus's?"

"It was."

The beige walls were dotted with certificates and pictures. There was a window behind Luke's chair that gave him a view to the river, rolling and glittering under the sun. The leaves of the trees outside danced in the gentle breeze.

Had Marcus sat in that chair each morning after the murder, knowing he hadn't deserved the badge on his hip? Or had he compartmentalized Amina so completely that he'd justified his actions?

I was planning on playing him a little bit of both. He'd kept working. After the murder, he'd done his job as chief and he'd done it well. But he had to have known that he was a hypocrite. There had to have been some moments of self-loathing. He must have had some reservations, putting on his shirt each morning.

"You worked for Marcus, right?"

Luke nodded. "Since my first year on the force. I grew up here. Went to the academy and came home."

"What was he like?"

"Why do you want to know?" Luke leaned forward.

"Because I want to make sure I do this movie right." It was part of the reason.

"He was a good cop. Until he wasn't. He was a good man. Until he wasn't."

"Were there signs?"

Luke narrowed his gaze. "Are you asking me if I knew my boss was a murderer but didn't do anything about it?"

"No." I held up my hands. "No blame here. I'm just curious."

"Why?"

"Because I was a cop. Graduated community college and went right into the academy. I served on the force for five years before I quit. I've known good cops and bad. I guess I'm just . . . I'm trying to understand. I don't want to glorify Marcus." I was stealing Presley's words.

"Good. He doesn't deserve glory. He killed a woman and used his position to pin it on an innocent man. I think that explains it all."

"I guess it does."

I looked around the room again, taking in the personal touches. There was a picture of Luke fishing on the river. Another of him in uniform, standing between an older couple I assumed were his parents. And then one of him standing on a ridge, overlooking a mountain valley.

This guy had the life that would have been mine if not for the school bus incident.

"You feel like getting a beer?" I blurted. *Where the hell had that come from, Valance?*

"A beer?"

"Yeah," I said as the idea sunk in. "I miss the force. I miss the stories. And I bet you have some good ones."

"To go in your movie?"

I shook my head. "Just to talk. Promise. The truth is, I miss being a cop. I miss the camaraderie. And it's hard for me to keep in touch with the guys I used to work with in California."

The guys from my former SWAT team didn't want to risk being caught on camera. I didn't blame them. Most of them preferred quiet lives when not on the clock. Most didn't have social media accounts, because exposing themselves meant putting their families at risk.

Even though I hadn't been on the team anymore, they'd done their best to include me in summer barbeques, but after about a year, I'd stopped going. I hadn't fit into that life anymore. With travel, my schedule was unpredictable, and we'd drifted apart.

But I missed it. I missed them.

"What do you say?" I asked. "I'll buy you a beer and you can let me live vicariously through you for an hour."

Luke gave me a sideways glance.

"I'm serious." I chuckled, raising my right hand. "Honest. I just feel like talking about cop stuff with a cop and knowing we aren't going to get caught on camera."

He studied me for a long moment, then nodded. "All right."

"Thanks." I stood and fished my wallet out of my pocket. I took out a business card for Valance Pictures, flipped it over and scribbled my private number on the back with one of his pens. "How about we meet Friday at The Betsy? I haven't been there yet."

"Six?" Luke took the card.

"Sounds great." I shook his hand again, then let myself out of his office.

Luke followed me out, escorting me to the lobby. He

waved, I waved, and then I was outside, driving to the one place I couldn't seem to stay away from.

The Clifton Forge Garage.

The parking lot was full of cars, more than I'd expected for a Monday morning. There were cars in each of the bays and three parked in a waiting line. My normal spot was taken by a black Yukon beside what I'd determined was Presley's white Jeep.

She was on the phone when I walked inside the office and caught me from the corner of her eye. "We have an o-opening—" She faltered, blinking twice before focusing on the phone conversation. "We have an opening at three o'clock. Okay, great. See you then."

"Hi," I said as she hung up.

"Hi." It wasn't a warm welcome, but it wasn't her icy glare. *Improvement.*

"Pres—" A woman came out of an office and stopped mid-step when she spotted me. Her dark hair fell down her shoulders as she eyed me up and down with pretty brown eyes. Then her mouth turned up, not in a smile, but a cunning grin. "Shaw Valance."

"Bryce Slater." I'd seen her picture and read her bio on the *Tribune's* website while I'd been researching.

"Here to check on your bike?" Her shrewd gaze reminded me of other reporters in LA, the ones who made me think through my words carefully. Bryce knew I wasn't really here about the bike.

"Sure."

"Dash is—"

A small body collided with her legs, cutting her off. Then another little boy appeared on her other side. Both kids were dressed in bright swim trunks and coordinating rash guards. They had flip-flops on their feet.

"Mommy, can we have a sucker?" the older boy asked. The *s* came out as *th*, the word *thucker*. He looked to be about three, the same age as one of my nieces.

"Not before swimming lessons," Bryce said.

"Pwease," he begged.

"Sorry." She ruffled his hair and bent to pick up the smaller boy, who had wrapped himself around her calf like a monkey. "These are my boys. Xander." She glanced to the older boy, then bounced the other on her hip. "And this is Zeke."

"Hey, guys." I crouched to greet Xander, then held out my fist for a knuckle bump. He hesitated, then wacked his fist against mine. "Nice. How old are you, Xander?"

He held up three fingers.

"Three? I have a niece named Brittany and she's three too. But you're taller than she is." He gave me a shy smile as I stood and winked at Zeke. "And how old are you?"

He buried his face in Bryce's neck but kept one eye on me.

"He's two," Bryce answered.

"I have another niece who's two. And then a whole line of them. Four, five, six, seven, eight and nine."

"Eight nieces?"

"That's right. Each one a year apart, give or take a few months. No nephews. The girls all belong to my three sisters."

Bryce grinned. "That's a lot of girls."

"Family reunions in about ten years are going to be interesting." I chuckled. "I've got to admit, I feel like I know you.

I've spent the better part of the past weekend reading a lot of your articles from the newspaper."

She hummed. "And?"

"Let's just say, I'm glad you run the *Clifton Forge Tribune* and don't work at a magazine in California. I have enough trouble with the reporters and paparazzi there. Someone like you would eat me alive."

She laughed. "Hollywood isn't my thing, but thanks."

"You're welcome."

"It was nice to meet you, Shaw. We've got to get going."

"We're going thwimming," Xander declared as Zeke squirmed to get down.

"Let's say goodbye to Daddy." Bryce took Zeke's hand as Xander bolted through the door.

There was one customer in the waiting room but none out front, leaving Presley and me alone. When I turned, her assessing stare was waiting.

I assumed my usual chair. "I heard what you said last week."

"Good." She met my gaze, giving me her full attention. There was something different about her today. Her guard was still up, but the fortress wall wasn't ten feet thick or twenty feet high.

"I'm trying to do the right thing, and I think we are. But you're right, I wasn't here during that time so I'm asking for dinner."

She blinked. "Dinner?"

"I want to take you out."

"Out? Like . . . on a *date*?" Her last word was tortured.

What was so bad about dinner with me? I ate with a fork. I chewed with my mouth closed. And I'd been told my company was rather charming.

Maybe I wasn't making progress after all. No woman in history had rebuked me like Presley, not even the girls in high school, when I'd gone through my awkward phase at fourteen.

"I didn't say date," I corrected. "I said dinner."

"And I say no."

"Why not? It'll give us a chance to get to know one another. You can tell me about what happened. I can tell you about the movie."

"We don't need to go out for dinner to discuss either of those topics."

"Come on. Why not?"

Her gaze narrowed. "You don't even know my last name."

"What's your last name?"

"Marks." That wall was coming down, inch by inch.

"Okay." I grinned. "Presley Marks, would you go to dinner with me?"

"This sounds more and more like a date. And my answer is still no."

"But you still haven't given me a good reason."

She shrugged. "I think you're ugly."

My laughter filled the room. *Christ.* When had a woman called me ugly? Even that hadn't happened at fourteen. "Liar."

The corner of her mouth twitched. "I can't be seen around town with you."

"What? I'm a good guy. I'm even having a beer with your chief of police on Friday at The Betsy."

"You? At The Betsy? You might scuff those fancy boots. Or is this you trying to be authentic?"

I leaned forward, holding her stare. "I'm not afraid of getting dirty."

The word sent a zing between us. My mind jumped to her black T-shirt and how quickly I could peel it off to find out if that red bra was underneath.

Presley's cheeks turned pink and her eyes darted to my mouth before she turned away and cleared her throat.

"So what do you say? Dinner? I'll tell you all about the movie. You can tell me where I'm fucking it up."

"No." She shook her head. "No dinner. But we can discuss it here."

"When?" I grumbled, trying not to take this as a complete loss.

"Friday. The office is quiet on Friday afternoons."

I nodded. "Then Friday afternoon it is."

CHAPTER SIX

PRESLEY

Two people were whispering in the ice cream aisle. Maybe it had nothing to do with me, but I abandoned my quest for chocolate chip cookie dough and turned the other way.

This was not my day.

Today had been long, and I didn't have the courage to suffer through gossip with my chin held high.

The garage had been packed. I'd come in, expecting a nice steady stream of Tuesday oil changes, and it had become chaos. Tyler had called in sick. Leo had decided this particular Tuesday wasn't one he'd felt like working. He and Dash had gotten into a fight over the phone. And we'd had more walk-ins in one morning than we'd had combined for the past two weeks.

But as Draven had taught me, we didn't turn walk-ins away.

So the guys had hustled. I had hustled, grateful that Shaw hadn't stopped in for one of his random visits, and by the time I'd left at six o'clock, I'd just wanted some ice cream.

But there was no way I was waiting for those people to stop talking about me. Okay, maybe they weren't talking about me, but maybe they were. I wasn't risking it.

My paranoia that the town was talking about me, pitying me, was as strong as it had been the day after the wedding. Maybe in a year or two, I wouldn't be that *girl* who'd been dumped at the altar. Maybe they'd see me as the *woman* who stood on her own two feet.

Sometimes small towns sucked.

The gossip mill in Clifton Forge wasn't particularly interesting, but I'd always kept my ear to the wind. I'd stayed on the fringe. I knew who was cheating on whom. I knew who had hooked up with whom at The Betsy. My source was almost always my stylist at the salon. I might be on the outer edge of the circle, but the women who worked at the salon were in the thick of it. Since I got my hair done every two weeks—it grew fast and the short style required maintenance—I usually knew what was happening. Plus, I'd overhear things at the garage while waiting customers talked about folks around town.

Since the wedding, I'd vowed no more.

Call it ignorance, but now that I knew how it felt when people were talking about me behind my back, I'd never spread a lick of gossip again. If I could avoid hearing it, I would. Even if that meant I had to grow my hair out and drive the two hours to Bozeman for a new stylist.

I pushed my cart to the checkout line and loaded my things onto the conveyor belt. My eyes stayed fixed on the items in the cart, not wanting to make eye contact with the cashier until the last possible second.

When I did, she gave me a sad smile—all the smiles aimed my way were sad—and I turned to the candy display to hide an eye roll. As the last items beeped through, I plastered on a smile and went through the motions of checking out.

My groceries were loaded and I was pulling out of the parking lot when the phone rang. I almost answered Jeremiah's call like I had a thousand times before. *Hey, babe.*

He wasn't mine anymore. And I wasn't his. So why was he calling me?

It rang, twice, three times, as my heart raced. Should I answer? What did he want? Why was he calling me now?

It rang a fourth time, then the noise stopped. I blinked, placing my hands on the wheel as I focused on the road.

I didn't need to talk to him. I didn't need to hear his voice, and nothing good would come of this. Maybe he'd called me accidentally, an old habit.

"I'm not calling him back," I muttered.

I didn't need to. The phone rang again and his name came up on the display.

"Grr. What do you want?" I spat.

He had to know we were over. I wasn't taking him back after this. Never. But what if something was wrong? Was he sick? Or hurt? Maybe he'd gotten into some trouble with the club.

I gritted my teeth as the phone kept ringing. The leather wrapping the steering wheel squeaked as I strangled it beneath my palms. Every ring seemed louder than the last, jolting me in my seat.

Then, silence descended—blissful silence—and I could breathe again. I blew out the air in my lungs and relaxed my spine.

My heart had climbed down out of my throat by the time

I turned off Central to take the residential streets home. I was five blocks away when my phone rang again.

Jeremiah.

"Ugh." Was he going to keep calling all night? Should I get it over with? Tell him goodbye, get that closure for *myself*, then hang up and move on with my life? My thumb made the decision for me, pressing the button to answer. "What?"

"Hey, Pres."

I gritted my teeth.

His voice sounded soft and kind. Apologetic. I hated Sorry Jeremiah. He was pathetic in all the ways that made me forgive him. But not this time. The line had been drawn and if I crossed it, I'd only be that much closer to becoming my mother again. I'd die before that happened.

With my foot on the brake, I slowed down and steered the Jeep to the curb, putting it in park. "What do you want?"

"I just wanted to hear your voice."

To hear my voice? Wrong answer. How about to fucking apologize? "I'm busy."

My voice was flat. Was that the voice he'd wanted to hear?

"Oh." The silence dragged on, itchy and uncomfortable. But he'd called me. If there was something he wanted, he could speak up. "You're mad."

My mouth fell open. Seriously? This was the guy I'd chosen to marry? I was so dumb. "Mad doesn't begin to cover it."

The silence returned.

Why hadn't I listened to the guys? Why? Draven, Dash, Emmett and Leo had all badmouthed Jeremiah. For years, they'd muttered words like *loser*, *dumb fuck* and *piece of shit* under their breaths whenever I brought him up. Each time, it would start a fight. I'd defend Jeremiah while they'd rake him over the coals. Fight after fight.

I'd gotten so sick of their commentary that I'd eventually flown off the handle. I'd scolded them for not being supportive and told them to mind their own business. At that time, none of them had been in relationships and none of them had been in a position to tell me how to conduct my love life.

My stubborn streak had reared its ugly head.

They'd only been trying to help.

Draven had gone so far as to try and warn Jeremiah off. It had been right before he was supposed to receive his verdict in Amina's murder trial. We'd all known he was going to be pronounced guilty, and he'd spent weeks putting his affairs in order, which included actually retiring from the garage and deeming me the office manager.

That was when there'd been a lot of animosity between the former Tin Kings and the Arrowhead Warriors. I'd stayed on the cusp, careful not to get involved, but I'd heeded warnings and kept a close watch out for Warriors in town. Draven and Dash had suspected they were lurking and might try to hurt one of us.

Yeah, they'd been lurking.

In my house.

Jeremiah had brought over some friends he'd met at the poker table. He'd play cards two or three times a week. Some days, he'd win. Sometimes, he'd lose. But it made him happy so I'd kept my mouth shut.

I'd been so scared of losing him that I'd walked on eggshells about his lack of a job and lack of money and lack of . . . love.

Jeremiah's friends had actually been Warriors. I hadn't known, obviously. Unless they were wearing their cuts, making a statement with those leather vests, they'd just been Jeremiah's friends.

When I'd learned who they were and that they'd been trying to glean information from me about Draven and Dash, I'd been floored. I'd told Jeremiah they weren't welcome in our home, hoping he'd cut ties. *Nope.* Instead, he'd decided to join their club.

To be part of a brotherhood.

You know my family, Presley. This is a good thing for me.

Draven had gone to Jeremiah and encouraged him to prospect for the Warriors. He'd been sure that if Jeremiah moved to Ashton, that would be the end of our engagement.

But then Draven had killed himself.

He'd left me.

And I'd clung to the one man who, for better or worse, had never abandoned me.

Until the day he had.

"Pres, you there?"

"Yeah."

"Are you gonna talk?"

"No."

He sighed. "I'm sorry."

The wound he'd slashed in me in June ripped wide open. "You humiliated me."

"I forgot."

"Our wedding?" My voice cracked and my temper spiked. "After everything, all we'd been through, you forgot? Fuck you." Now that felt good. Too good.

"I didn't want to get married."

"Uh, I gathered that," I seethed. "But why not tell me

sooner? You sat by and watched me plan the wedding. I bought a dress. And you never said a word."

"I was confused. I didn't—"

"Oh, shut the fuck up. I don't care about your reasons. It was wrong and you know it." No matter what his excuse, it would never erase what he'd done.

"Pres." He paused. "Look, I need something."

I scoffed. So that was what this phone call was about. Jeremiah always needed something and I was sick and tired of being the one to give it to him. "No."

"Hear me out."

"No."

It was like talking to Shaw. Except saying *no* to Shaw felt like foreplay, a battle of wills to see if I could hold up my stone heart against his persuasive smile. Saying no to Jeremiah just felt overdue.

"Was there anything else? I'm busy." My eyes were aimed down the road as I waited. I was giving him five seconds, then I was hanging up.

Five. Four. Three.

"I need Scarlett's phone number. I lost it and I just . . . I need it."

My stomach dropped. The elation I'd had, the pride in my backbone, was gone. "Why?"

"Because I do. Can you give it to me?"

"No."

"Presley." The pitiful tone to his voice disappeared, replaced by a thread of frustration. "I need Scarlett's number."

"Why?" I repeated.

"Do you really want to know?"

I closed my eyes, my heart breaking all over again like it had at the altar when I'd told people to take their gifts home. "No. I guess not."

"Then give it to me."

"Did you know I invited her to the wedding? Is that why you didn't show? Because you were worried she'd be there? She wasn't, by the way."

Jeremiah and I are getting married on June 1st in Clifton Forge, Montana.

There'd been no reply.

I'd invited my sister because she was my sister. I'd texted the number that had been hers in high school—ironically, on the phone Jeremiah had bought her. He should have remembered it. But maybe it wasn't her number anymore, I wasn't sure. She'd never texted me back, not after the wedding text or any of the others I'd sent her over the years.

I hadn't spoken to my sister in ten years. My parents the same. The day I'd left Chicago, I'd promised myself that this new life, my life, would be of my own making. I'd been eighteen years old and the only way I'd been strong enough to start fresh had been by cutting them out.

I'd refused to live in fear.

Not a day had gone by that I'd missed my parents. Not once had I regretted leaving without so much as a goodbye.

But Scarlett, she was different.

I thought of her often. I hoped, with all my heart, she'd freed herself and found happiness. I hoped she'd found someone to love her, like I'd once believed Jeremiah loved me.

Or maybe Jeremiah had been in love with Scarlett all those years.

Maybe I had been the stand-in. Maybe, when it had come time to make a real commitment, he hadn't been able to say my name instead of hers.

"Do you love her?" I whispered. "Still?"

He didn't answer, which was Jeremiah's way of saying yes.

"Why did you even propose in the first place?" I wanted to scream. *Why?* "We were good as friends. Why?"

"It doesn't matter."

"It does to me. Please," I begged. "Do this one thing for me. Tell me so I can put it behind me. You owe me that and you know it."

"I don't know. Things were crazy back then. You left. Scarlett and I broke up. I went on with my life. Then I wanted to see how you were doing."

Jeremiah had left Chicago five years after I'd made my escape. He'd shown up in Clifton Forge one day and I'd been shocked. He'd told me he'd needed some space from his parents—their cold shoulders and dismissive waves. Though given that he hadn't worked, clearly they hadn't dismissed his wallet.

None of the reasons had mattered because it had been so good to see him and have that connection to the past. Jeremiah had been a constant source of light in my life as a teenager. He'd been in love with Scarlett, but he'd been my friend. My only true friend.

Then the boy who'd been my friend and my savior had become the man I'd loved.

"Why did you leave Chicago?" No matter how many times I'd asked, Jeremiah had never given me a straight answer. He'd been *bored.* He'd been *ready for a change.* "Was it because of Scarlett? You said you two had been done a long time. Is that true?"

"She cut me out of her life, Presley. Just like you did. Except I knew if I came to see you, you wouldn't slam the door in my face."

"Then why do you want to talk to her now?"

"Just give me her number and we can be done with this."

This. Us.

We'd been done since June first.

And we'd probably been doomed from the start.

"Goodbye, Jeremiah." I ended the call on the steering wheel's control, then dove for my purse. My hands trembled as I dug out my phone and maneuvered through my contacts, pulling up his name. My finger hovered over the screen for a split second before I tapped *Block*.

This had never been about me. It had always been Scarlett.

Jeremiah and Scarlett.

How many times had I said their names paired together? How many times had I told myself that if she really loved him, she would have left ten years ago too?

A tear slipped from my eye. A pathetic, broken tear.

He loved her, after all this time.

He couldn't marry me when he loved my twin sister.

Not a soul in Clifton Forge knew that Jeremiah had been Scarlett's. Not a *living* soul, that is.

When I'd shown up in Clifton Forge, I'd been eighteen with no credit cards and a pay-by-the-minute cell phone number. I'd had a car that I'd bought with the money I'd hidden away in my room since I was sixteen. It had cost two thousand dollars and I hadn't known if it would survive the trip from Chicago to Montana.

It had. I'd driven to this small town where a garage owner had taken a risk by hiring a barely legal adult after a phone interview where I'd promised to make coffee and learn.

Draven Slater had saved my life.

He'd given me the means to break free from my parents.

I never spoke about them, my parents or my sister. Draven had been the only person to know that Jeremiah had made it possible for me to leave Chicago.

That car? Jeremiah had found it. He'd bought it with my cash so my parents wouldn't know. That phone? Jeremiah had given it to me. He'd given the same kind to Scarlett.

He'd tried so hard to get her out, but she'd refused.

I'd left her behind.

Were these tears, this humiliation, my punishment? Was this the universe's way of reminding me that I should never have left her in the first place? Or was this my punishment for taking what was hers? Except Scarlett had given him up. Maybe she'd clued into the real Jeremiah long before I had.

I dried my cheeks and swallowed the lump in my throat, then I put the Jeep in drive and eased onto the road.

No matter how things had unraveled at the end, I missed my sister.

There were days when I was so alone, like now, and wished I could tell her about my day. I wished I could have one of her hugs.

The guys at the garage were always teasing me for being a hugger, but I had nothing on Scarlett. Her hugs had been magical. They'd saved me on the horrific days. They'd kept my world from turning black.

I turned right onto my quiet cul-de-sac, expecting to see

a neighborhood kid riding their bike or the little girl across the street playing in her splash pool like she did every evening, her mother watching on from the front steps.

Instead, a huge yellow moving truck was parked in front of the house next door, blocking the view to my driveway.

It had sold? When? Had the owners finally given up and decided to rent it instead?

The neighbor's house had been for sale for months. I'd contemplated buying it myself, before Jeremiah had moved to Ashton. I didn't want to be a lifelong renter and I loved my tiny street.

Damn. I'd missed my chance. The yellow home, bright and cheery, now belonged to someone else. My spirits plummeted as I pulled into the driveway. Normally, I'd go over and introduce myself, but I wasn't in the mood. I didn't need to fake a smile right now. I was going to go inside, unload my groceries and order a pizza.

Screw cooking.

I went to the back of the Jeep and looped the handles of the paper bags over my palms. Footsteps echoed next door as I collected my groceries, a guy climbing into the driver's seat of the moving van.

"Miss." He tipped an invisible hat.

I was always *miss*. No matter that I was probably five or six years older than that kid, I was a *miss*. People saw me as a child.

I ignored him and finished loading up my bags. My hands were full, and I had to close the Jeep with an elbow as the truck pulled away, its diesel engine rumbling through the whole block. It took three steps for me to notice my new neighbor.

He stood at the top of his stairs. Four stairs, to be exact, identical to the four that led to the small porch of my own front door. Our homes were identical from the outside, except for the color. Mine was a pale blue so light it was practically white. His was the color of a fluffy baby chick.

Shaw lifted a hand. "Hey, neighbor."

CHAPTER SEVEN

SHAW

My realtor would have earned a higher commission if she had mentioned that the woman who lived next door was Presley Marks.

"Isn't this a surprise?"

"Is it?" Presley asked, frowning as I descended my steps and crossed the lawn, meeting her in her driveway. She raised a dark blond eyebrow. "Because it sort of feels like stalking."

I chuckled. "I swear I had no idea you lived next door."

But what a bonus.

I wouldn't have to make excuses to stop by the garage to see her. She could tear that insurance waiver to shreds. Presley had to know I didn't give a damn about that bike they were building for me.

"You bought this house?"

"Yeah." I reached for the grocery bags she had in her hands. "Here, let me help."

She twisted away. "I've got them."

"Come on." I stepped forward and she took a step back.

Wait, did she really think I was stalking her? "I'm just trying to help. I mean, I'll probably start writing down your daily schedule so I can make sure our paths cross at least once a day. But that's normal, right? For stalkers?"

"Are you being funny?"

My smile flattened. "I guess not."

Presley took a wide step around me, hefting the grocery bags higher as she walked toward her porch.

I caught up to her with a long stride and slipped my hand through the handles of her paper bags, stealing them from her grip.

"Hey." She shot me a glare.

"Let me help before you dislocate a shoulder." Stubborn woman. "If you want to return the neighborly favor, I've got about fifty boxes to unpack."

She climbed two of her steps, shifting bags to her now free hand to balance the weight, then she turned and met me at eye level. "I'm not going on a date with you, or to dinner, or whatever you called it."

"Did I ask again?"

She rolled her eyes.

"Can I help you take these groceries inside? Or would you like to stand out here all evening? Because I really do need to unpack." I needed to unearth the sheets for my bed and towels for my bathroom.

She grumbled something under her breath and took the rest of the stairs, digging her keys out of a pocket of the baggiest pair of khaki cargo pants I'd ever seen in my life. They probably would have fit me, except the hems had been cut off to accommodate her shorter legs.

The bottoms were cuffed, rolled halfway up her calves. These hideous pants allowed no hint of the curve of her hips or the shape of her ass. Except they were oddly not so hideous and kind of sexy because they were cinched tight by a red belt low on her waist, highlighting her trim physique.

One tug of that belt and the pants would pool at her feet. That's why they were sexy. They tempted, they *begged* to be set free.

Presley's gray tank top was thin and tight and, unfortunately, covered her bra straps. Was it the red one to match her belt? My imagination took off like a sprinter from the starting blocks. Let it be the red one biting into the smooth skin of her shoulders.

"How was your day?" I asked as she unlocked the front door, needing a distraction before I touched the bare skin of her arm.

She snarled.

"That good?"

"I'm ready for it to be over." She pushed inside her house and flipped on a light, brightening the entryway as she walked down the short hallway and turned to the kitchen.

"Have you ever been next door?" I asked, following her to the kitchen and setting the bags on the counter.

"No. Why?"

"Everything is opposite. My kitchen is on the other end of the house, which means our bedroom windows are facing each other."

She gave me a sideways glance. "Am I going to hear you grunting some woman's name in the middle of the night? Because if so, I'll need to buy new ear plugs."

I slapped a hand over my heart, feigning insult. "You think I'm a grunter? How could you? After all we've been through, you'd degrade me to a grunter. I'm wounded."

That earned me a lip curl as she began unloading groceries.

I had no desire to bring any woman to my home unless her name rhymed with Wesley and her last name sounded a lot like larks. Every minute I spent with her intrigued me more. Presley rarely did what I expected, and for a guy who was fairly good at anticipating other people's reactions, it was refreshing.

I dove into the bags I'd brought inside, taking out a loaf of bread and bag of baby carrots. Then another bag of carrots. And another bag of carrots. "Do you have rabbits?"

"No." Her cheeks flushed as she swiped a bag from my hand. "I just like carrots."

"How long will it take you to go through all of these?"

She shrugged and opened the refrigerator door. "I don't know. A week?"

"A week?" My eyes bulged. "That's more carrots than I eat in a year."

"Carrots are good for you. They're good for your vision."

"And they make your skin orange. You'd get along with one of my nieces. She used to love carrots as a baby. That was all she'd eat—carrots from those little glass jars. Until one day I came over to visit and her skin was orange. My sister had to limit carrots from then on out."

"I eat these many carrots regularly. Do I look orange?" She waved a hand up and down her body.

"No. You don't." Not orange, but she did look fucking delicious. My mouth watered at her imagined taste. I bet she was sweet, and that pert mouth would taste better than honey.

My gaze zeroed in on her lips, so soft and the perfect

98

shade of pale pink. I'd be able to cover them with my mouth, suck them until they were their own shade of red.

Presley's breath hitched and she twisted away, hurrying to unload another bag like she'd heard my thoughts.

I turned my back to her, hiding as I made a quick adjustment to my dick. Between the attitude she dished out and that firm body, being around her was taking more and more restraint.

Did she feel this tormented tension too? Did she have any idea how much I wanted to shove the groceries onto the floor, heft her up on a counter and take that sweet mouth?

I sucked in a sharp breath through my nose, taming my arousal before it got out of hand. If I didn't stop imagining Presley naked, I'd have to hobble my hard-on home. As it was, I'd be in for a cold shower.

I really needed to find the towels.

Behind me, Presley rustled through bags, opening and closing cupboards as she put her items away. "So what are you doing here?"

"Helping unload groceries."

"No, here. As in the house next door. I thought you were staying at the Evergreen."

"I was." I handed her the loaf of bread. "Motels are fine for short location shoots, but I'm going to be here too long to stay cramped in a single room. Someone else can have that spot. I needed more space anyway, and I didn't want to take a trailer. Besides, real estate is a good investment and that house was cheap."

"Cheap?" She stiffened. "Owning that house would take me twenty years to pay off. It's not cheap."

Shit. Someday, I'd get through a conversation with this woman where I didn't manage to piss her off.

"I'm sorry." I held up a hand. "I'll admit my perspective on money is skewed."

I had to watch myself around my family too. On more than one occasion, I'd shoved my foot into my mouth when it came to wealth. My parents and my sisters were proud of my success but didn't want handouts.

I'd offered to buy my mom a new car. She'd informed me she could buy her own vehicle, thank you very much. I'd gone overboard with Christmas presents a few years ago, buying my sisters each a diamond bracelet. They'd been gracious, but Matine had pulled me aside later and said the gifts were too much. Apparently, diamonds made things weird. So last year I'd bought them each a fancy new coffee maker. The year before that, house slippers and a massage.

The only extravagant gift I'd been able to arrange in recent years had been getting my sisters and brothers-in-law to let me pay for my nieces' college educations.

Now that I was getting to know Presley, I saw that same kind of pride. My wealth held no appeal. Hell, it was probably working against me.

That credit card stunt the first day I'd met her had definitely been a bad move.

Presley wouldn't look at me as she folded the paper bags into a neat stack.

"Truly, I didn't mean any offense," I said. "I'm going to be in Clifton Forge for a while and wanted a place of my own. It's a very nice house, as is yours."

Her shoulders eased and she met my gaze. "How long are you here?"

"We're on an aggressive shooting schedule, but we're trying to be authentic—your favorite word—so we're filming most scenes on location. Right now, we're projecting eight weeks total. Two down. Six to go if we stay on track."

"Then what?" she asked. "Wait. You're not going to stay here, are you?"

"No." I chuckled at the panic in her voice. "I'll be out of your hair as soon as we wrap here. We'll go back to California and shoot some scenes on set. The movie will go into postproduction. We'll have edits and retakes and sound. By the time we actually start marketing the movie, you'll have forgotten all about me."

She nodded along as I spoke, though I could tell she had no idea what any of the movie terms meant. Not many did unless they were part of the Hollywood world.

I'd done the same thing when Isaiah had walked me through the custom bike design. He'd named parts I'd never heard of, and besides the seat, handlebars, gas tank and wheels, I'd been at a loss to understand how the pieces fit together.

My blank stare had probably looked a lot like Presley's at the moment.

When I'd first started acting, I'd been a mess—going the wrong way, standing on the wrong mark, looking at the camera. My first movie had been a crash course, and luckily, I'd had a good tutor in Laurelin, my manager. She'd given up acting to become a manager and had taken me under her wing. So had the producer, director and the cast and crew members. Not a single person on that set had given me shit when I'd screwed up early on. After that project, I'd walked into the next with more confidence and it had shown on screen.

"Have you lived here long?" I asked, changing the subject.

If we kept on this path, I feared we'd begin talking about the movie, but I was saving that for Friday. I wasn't going to deviate from the plan. Once we were done discussing *Dark Paradise*, I'd have to come up with yet another excuse to spend time with Presley. This bought me a few days.

"Almost ten years," she answered.

"Ten?" Presley wasn't old enough to have lived here that long. "Did you grow up in this house or something?"

"I moved in when I was eighteen. I rented the guest bedroom from the lady who owns this place. She was looking for a roommate to take care of the place while she was gone because she worked for the railroad and traveled a lot. So I took care of her cat and made sure the house was clean. When she moved a few years later, she was going to sell but I asked her if I could rent it instead."

"So you're twenty-eight?" She did not look twenty-eight.

"Twenty-seven. My birthday is in August. You?"

"Thirty-four."

Presley stepped across the kitchen, passing me by. I followed, stopping by her side as she looked down the entryway to the front door. "Thanks for your help."

"No problem. Are you sure I can't convince you to help unpack boxes?"

"I've had enough unpacking for a while," she muttered.

"Huh?" Hadn't she lived here for ten years?

"Nothing." She waved me off, then looked once more to the door.

But she wasn't getting rid of me that easily. I strolled past her into the living room, ignoring the grumble that came from her mouth.

"No picture?" I picked up an empty frame from a table beside the couch.

"No." She yanked it from my hand, laying it facedown.

I walked to the TV, crouching down to examine the row of movies stacked neatly on the stand's shelves. "I wouldn't have pegged you for a horror fan."

"I'm not," she muttered. "Those aren't mine."

"Oh, do you have a roommate?"

"Not anymore."

That distant tone I'd gotten the first day at the garage was back. I stood, the chill in her voice setting the hairs on my arms on end. What was I missing? What picture had been in that frame? Who had left the *Saw* movies behind?

She tapped her foot, reminding me it was time to leave.

I ignored that too and kept searching for clues.

When I'd been a cop, I'd walk into a room and catalog everything within the first minute. I'd gotten out of that habit since changing careers, and it took me longer than it would have back then to pick up on the details in Presley's home.

The empty frame. The *People* magazine turned upside down on the coffee table. The cushion on the left side of the leather couch that looked slightly more worn than any other seat.

There was an entire row of photographs hanging on one wall and I moved in to get a closer look. The largest in the center was of Presley and Draven. He had his arm around her and his cheek bent low, pressing into her hair. She was hugging his waist and smiling wide.

"You two were close."

"Very." There was longing in her voice. Heartache. She joined me in front of the photo, staring at it hard, like she was wishing she could hop inside and go back to that moment.

That same nostalgia hit me whenever I saw a photo of myself in uniform, standing beside my dad wearing the same.

There were days when I wished we could leap into the past, to relive the moments when he was my hero and the notion of giving up the police force for some action movies would have made us both laugh hysterically.

The longer she stared at Draven, the more it began to sink in. Presley's defense of his character. Her constant reminders that he'd been a good man.

Draven had been a father figure for her. She longed to be his daughter.

She tore her gaze away from the photo. "You'd better go."

"Okay." There'd be no breaking down that wall of hers tonight. "Are we still on for Friday?"

She nodded and led me to the door, her spine stiff and shoulders pinned as she opened it wide.

I followed but didn't leave. Instead, I leaned against the frame and let the warm air seep past us both. "I don't know which box my dishes are in."

"Probably the one marked dishes."

I grinned. Everything in the boxes was brand new. I doubted there'd be many items labeled. "I'm ordering pizza. Want to share?"

"I'm eating in tonight."

"That's right. You've got all your carrots."

"I have bad eyes," she snapped. It sure was fun to irritate her. "When I was a kid, the eye doctor warned me I'd probably need glasses. I didn't want glasses because what already tiny first grader wants to stand out more than she already does? So I ate a ton of carrots. I still had to get glasses, but . . ."

"The carrots stuck."

She nodded.

"Do you wear glasses?"

She nodded again.

I bet glasses would only make her blue eyes bigger. They'd be sexy on the thin bridge of her nose. They'd accentuate the daintiness of her chin. I'd have to come over one night, surprise her with something neighborly—carrot cake maybe—just to see if I could catch her in glasses.

"What else do you like to eat?"

"Go away, Shaw."

I chuckled but didn't move. "Tell me."

"Why?"

"Because I want to know about you."

"You're leaving in six weeks. Doesn't this feel like wasted effort?"

"Not at all." These questions felt like some of the best I'd asked in a long, long time.

"I like pasta. And bread. And chips. And cereal. And all the things that come in a box because even though they're supposed to be bad for you, I love them anyway."

"A box? Like a pizza box? Because I'm ordering pizza for dinner tonight. Want some?"

"You're impossible. Go. Home." She planted one of her delicate hands on my arm and gave me a not so delicate shove.

I didn't budge.

She growled.

"Fine." I pushed off the door and winked as I walked down the steps.

I didn't rush my steps but I kept my eyes forward, waiting for the sound of her closing door. When I hit the driveway, I still hadn't heard it, so I glanced back.

And *fuck yeah*, Presley's eyes darted up from my ass.

She could pretend she didn't like me all she wanted, but

we both knew there was something here. Something worth exploring for six weeks.

How convenient, since Presley was my new neighbor.

I whistled as I crossed my yard and waved to the woman across the street watching her daughter play in a splash pool.

Goddamn, I loved my new yellow house.

CHAPTER EIGHT

PRESLEY

F ridays were my least favorite day of the week.
Dash didn't work on Fridays unless he'd gotten behind. He'd put in long days early in the week so he could spend Fridays with Bryce and their boys. Emmett and Leo loved to duck out early and get their weekend party started. When he'd lived here before, Isaiah used to stick around in case a last-minute walk-in showed, but now that we had the other mechanics, he was gone early too.

And without Draven, that left me alone in the office, watching the clock tick toward five.

The slowest hours of the week came on Friday afternoons.

But not today. I couldn't wait for *this* Friday. I'd driven to work with jitters this morning that had yet to fade.

I had no idea what time Shaw would come to the office, but when he showed, I'd be ready. I'd worked ahead the last few days, preparing so that once he arrived, I'd be off the clock and all ears.

My afternoon cup of tea was steaming. My foot bounced on the floor. I'd be a mess if Shaw made me wait until five.

He didn't.

At ten after three, his gleaming SUV pulled into the lot.

"Hey." He walked into the office and whipped the sunglasses off his face.

"Hey," I breathed, the air from my lungs stolen by the square cut of his jaw and his glittering eyes. The man was handsome to distraction.

I hadn't seen much of Shaw since the evening he'd helped me unload groceries at my house. His vehicle had been missing more often than not whenever I came home from work. I'd done my best not to watch.

I'd followed my normal routine and lived like that house was empty. I didn't check the windows when I heard a car drive by. I didn't turn down the television at night so I could hear the slam of his door. A movie star might live next door, but I refused to treat him differently than I would any other neighbor.

I respected his privacy that much.

Except ...

Then the nights came. I'd retire to my bedroom and slip into my pajamas. I'd settle underneath my covers and fluff my pillow. But instead of closing the blinds like I had for years, I'd leave them open. I'd crack the window.

Only when the light from his bedroom window shone across the expanse between our homes, twinkling in my own room, would I be able to relax and sleep. I'd had a hard time falling asleep whenever he was gone at night because there were too many questions rattling through my mind.

Was he working? What had he done for dinner? Was he with a woman?

The nighttime hours were the only ones when I couldn't seem to control my obsession with Shaw Valance.

"Would you like some coffee or water?" I asked.

He gave me a sideways glance, like he didn't trust my offer's sincerity. To be fair, it was the first time I'd greeted him without a glare. "Water, but I'll get it."

"It's in there." I pointed to the waiting room and filled my lungs as he disappeared to fill a cup.

The foot I'd been holding flat on the floor began bouncing. My limbs felt loose and uncontrollable. The electricity between us, the anticipation of this discussion, was unnerving.

Shaw unsettled me with his bright gaze and I lost track of my wits. The more time we spent around one another, the harder it was to keep up the icy façade.

It was a miracle I'd managed to kick him out of my house on Tuesday. He'd been funny. He'd been entertaining and kind. How was I supposed to deal with a charming movie star standing in my kitchen? When I'd bent to put my carrots in the fridge, I'd lingered inside the door, hoping the chill would cool me down.

The man walked into a room and the temperature spiked. It was no wonder he was melting me into a puddle.

Shaw emerged, a paper cup of water in hand. The way he walked was so . . . graceful. Manly. His hips swayed with confidence, like every step had been preordained. He knew exactly where to place his foot to make his leg look as long as possible. He knew how to highlight the perfect curve of his ass and draw attention to his zipper.

When he sat, the muscles on his shoulders and arms tightened, showing off the definition between the sleeves of his shirt.

I was so used to seeing men in T-shirts, bulging arms covered in tattoos on display. Shaw's button-ups and rolled sleeves hid the bulk of his biceps, hinting at what I knew to be sexy muscle beneath.

He set his water on the desk and the smooth cotton stretched, revealing the definition of his bicep. It disappeared when he leaned back, placing his hands on the armrests, making his shoulders look impossibly broad.

"So where do we start?" he asked.

Right. We were talking about the movie. I tore my eyes away from his shirt and shrugged. "It's your movie."

"Then the beginning."

I shifted in my chair, rolling it over an inch or two until he was directly in front of me and his words would hit me straight on. "Okay."

"It starts with the murder. The scene is all about Amina, and it's not a pretty one."

Then no matter what she said, I would not let Genevieve see this movie. I knew Isaiah would be on board with me too. "Does it show Marcus?"

Shaw shook his head. "You don't know he killed her until near the end. It's just Amina, her eyes aimed at the ceiling and a trickle of blood coming from her mouth."

Maybe I wouldn't be seeing this movie either. I'd been debating back and forth, but I was leaning toward no. "Who is playing Amina?"

"Dacia French."

"Oh." They weren't holding out on the cast, were they? If Shaw was one of Hollywood's most notable and in-demand actors, Dacia French was his female counterpart. She was equally as beautiful and as captivating on screen as Shaw.

I'd recognized Dacia in one of the pictures with Shaw on the internet. They'd been a couple once, hadn't they? Were they still? Was she in town? I hadn't heard, but true to my vow, I'd been steering clear of all things gossip.

It didn't matter. She'd be gone, like Shaw, before winter.

"What happens next?"

"The next morning, Marcus arrives on the scene at the motel," Shaw said without hesitation. He was trusting me with this. I knew it was confidential and he was violating a rule, but he kept talking anyway. "He examines the body and starts the investigation. He finds out that Draven was there the night before. He walks around the property and finds the knife in a field. He crouches down and pulls an evidence bag from his pocket. He picks up the knife and sees Draven's name engraved on the side."

"I bought him that knife. For Christmas." I turned my gaze to the window. "I wish I had bought him socks instead."

"Listen, if this is too hard—"

"No." I shook my head. "Keep going."

"Marcus rejoins the cops in the room. They tell him the victim's name is Amina Daylee. He tells them he knew her once, long ago. Then it flashes back to the time they met, as kids. That's how the whole movie goes. It follows his investigation at the time but jumps back in time."

"How did they meet? In the movie?" I knew how they'd met in real life. Marcus had been Amina's neighbor. When she'd moved to town, he'd lived next door, though a few years younger.

"As neighbors." He raised an eyebrow. "How am I doing so far?"

"So far you're *authentic*."

He chuckled. "That was such a good word before I met you."

"Keep going."

"The next scene is him arresting Draven."

"Where?" I'd been here the day Marcus and two officers had come and arrested Draven. We'd all been here.

"At a garage."

"Which garage?"

"A fake one in LA. None of us wanted to try and shoot scenes here."

So they weren't completely heartless or insensitive about this film. "Thank you for that."

I would have had to be the one to tell them no, because I answered the phones and would have taken that call.

"The next scene is in an interrogation room. We're doing that in LA too. Then it's another flashback of Marcus and Amina walking home from school one day. They're friends. And when it cuts back to him in his office, he's sad that she's gone."

Marcus probably had been sad. Maybe he'd been angry. Maybe he'd been heartbroken. But as far as I was concerned, he didn't get to feel anything for Amina but shame. "See? Now you're making me mad. The viewer is going to sympathize with him."

"Probably," Shaw admitted. "If I'm doing my job right. The next scene is him on the phone with Genevieve. She calls to find out about the investigation. He promises to get justice for her mom. She cries. It's hard for him to hear."

My molars ground together. "No one should feel bad for Marcus Wagner. I hate this."

I understood what they were doing. The audience would be shocked. They'd drive home from the theater with popcorn kernels stuck in their teeth and wonder if they'd missed a hint or a sign at the beginning of the film.

Fucking Hollywood.

"I know, just . . . stick with me." Shaw's pleading eyes made me clamp my mouth shut. "The next scene is one from the past. Marcus comes to the garage to ask Draven questions about a guy who was beaten at a bar. Marcus thinks it was Draven or someone from his club. Of course, Draven knows who did it but he's smug. He doesn't say anything incriminating and Marcus has no choice but to let it go."

They'd show Draven as the bad guy and Marcus as the cop who couldn't seem to take down a criminal.

The most infuriating part was that Shaw wasn't wrong. Draven hadn't always been an upstanding citizen. Even after the club had disbanded, there'd been some questionable activities. But I'd kept my mouth shut about a lot of things that I'd seen happen or comments I'd overheard in my years working here.

"Is it wrong?" Shaw asked.

"Keep going." It was the only answer he'd get.

"The next scene is in the present again. Marcus is talking to the prosecutor about the case. He's . . . excited. Hesitant."

"Because he's had evidence against Draven before but hadn't been able to make it stick."

"Exactly." Shaw nodded. "Then it flashes back again. There's three more times when he goes up against Draven and comes out the loser."

Draven would be the smug, untouchable criminal. And in a way, that's exactly who he had been. People had gravitated toward Draven because of his confidence. His power. He'd been a natural leader with a sharp mind and a no-bullshit attitude.

You loved him fiercely.

Or you hated him with equal passion.

Dash was like that to a degree, though Bryce and the boys had mellowed him over the years.

We'd all mellowed after the Kings had closed their clubhouse doors.

"There's a scene with a young cop Marcus is mentoring," Shaw said. "Another where he butts heads with Luke."

"Luke's in this?"

"Yeah. He's the hero."

"No." I shook my head. "Genevieve is the hero."

"True." He sipped his water. "Luke and Marcus don't agree on a burglary case. This kid breaks into a store, and Marcus wants to let the kid off with a warning because he plays golf with the kid's dad. Luke argues that since the kid is twenty-one and was drunk off his ass at the time, he doesn't deserve a break. It's the first time you question Marcus as a cop."

"Good." Maybe that story was true. Maybe it wasn't. But it was time to start infusing some doubt about Marcus himself.

"The scenes after that jumps into the present timeline. Draven was arrested but is out on bond. Genevieve has moved to town. She came because she wants to investigate her mother's murder, but then she learns that she's Draven's daughter. Though her story is shown from Marcus's perspective. He's out to dinner with his wife and overhears a rumor. He's upset. He liked Genevieve and he feels like she's on the other team."

"Because she was." Genevieve's determination to find her mother's killer was the reason Marcus was in prison.

Though Shaw had it wrong as to why she'd moved to

114

Clifton Forge, but since that truth was known by only a handful of people, that was no surprise.

Genevieve hadn't moved here to watch the investigation. She'd come here to see her mother's grave and had been kidnapped along with Bryce. It had taken them a year to learn that Marcus had been their kidnapper. Still, it had never been made public knowledge. That was one of the few Tin King secrets I'd been privy to.

The day of the kidnapping, I'd come to work and the entire place had been abandoned. I'd tried to call Dash and Draven with no luck, and I'd known instantly that something bad had happened. So I'd done what I'd always done: I'd taken care of the business. I'd claimed a family emergency and rescheduled appointments. Then I'd waited, hoping everyone would be all right.

God, what a year that had been.

The year of death. It had started with Amina's murder, then the kidnapping and then Draven's suicide.

We'd all been scared and on edge. There had been a murderer at large. The Warriors had been threatening retaliation for the death of one of their members—they'd suspected their man had been killed by a former Tin King.

Everyone had been stressed. Bryce had been pregnant with Xander, and Dash hadn't let her out of his sight. Bryce used to come in and work here every day because Dash wouldn't leave her at the newspaper.

It had been such a miserable year, yet we'd all become closer for surviving it together.

"We get more flashbacks," Shaw spoke, his smooth voice pulling me into the present. "Marcus runs into Amina in Bozeman. He asks her out and they start dating."

"Do you show that she knows he's married?"

Shaw shook his head. "He never tells her. In one scene, he's taking off his wedding ring before he meets her."

Thank God.

None of us knew if Amina had known Marcus was married when they started dating. According to Genevieve, her mom hadn't talked much about the man she'd called Lee —a nickname from when Marcus and Amina had been kids. Maybe Amina had known that Marcus was married. Maybe he'd promised her that he was leaving his wife. Or maybe he'd hidden it, along with so many other things.

For Genevieve's sake, to protect the memory of her mother, I pretended Marcus had lied.

"Marcus hides Amina and the affair from his wife. He sneaks in phone calls and weekends to visit her. He starts drinking more. He isn't as focused at work. My makeup in the movie gets more and more haggard."

"He's becoming the villain."

"That's right." Shaw nodded. "I told you we'd get there."

I gave him a small smile. "As long as the audience hates him as much as I do when they walk out, we're good."

"I'll do my best."

"How does it end?" We needed to skip forward. At some point, I was sure there'd be a scene for Draven's death. It was yet another reason seeing this film probably wasn't good for my mental state. If I couldn't listen to Shaw give me the CliffsNotes version, I doubted I'd be able to watch the fictional retelling.

Shaw humored me. "Genevieve finds a picture in Amina's things of Marcus. Again, it's from his perspective, but she takes it to his house one night. She asks him about it. And it all clicks. It crumbles around him as she puts it together that he killed her mom."

How hard had it been for Genevieve to go to his house? There hadn't been a picture, but she had been the one to piece it together—Shaw had that right. Genevieve had been the one person able to give Draven and Amina justice.

She'd done that for them. For herself. For us all.

"Are you using their real names?"

"Marcus's," Shaw said gently. "Most of the others have been changed. I just thought it would be easier to refer to them as the names you know."

"Thank you. For the names. For talking this through."

"You're welcome."

The explanation, though helpful, didn't make this project easier to accept. Shaw was trying to help me find peace with the movie but . . . it wasn't there.

I didn't want this movie to happen. It would, regardless of Shaw's time spent answering my questions.

And that was a fact, a disappointment, I'd learn to live with.

Still, I appreciated his time. Shaw didn't have to answer my questions. He didn't have to spend his Friday afternoon in an uncomfortable chair.

Why me? Was it because I sat in the front? Because I'd been the first to ask? Would he have told Dash if Dash had been the one to press for answers?

Or was it because something simmered in the air when Shaw and I were in these seats? There was attraction here, more than I wanted to admit. But there was something else too. I didn't hold back words with Shaw, afraid of how they could be turned against me or used to punish me.

My words flew, ripping, raw and honest.

At the first hint of my attitude, he could have left the

garage and never come back. That's what I'd wanted, right? But he'd returned.

He'd listened.

To me.

I was fucked. If he kept listening, if he kept being his charming self, I was fucked.

Shaw straightened in his chair. "You told me you were worried about the truth. How close are we?"

"Close enough," I said, watching as the tension in his shoulders eased. "You have the main parts right. The rest . . ." I looked up at Draven's picture. "The rest died years ago."

"I'm sorry you lost him."

I gave him a sad smile. "So am I."

The room went quiet except for the noise from the shop. Sawyer and Tyler were likely finishing up for the day, anxious to clock out.

"I'd better go." Shaw picked up his empty cup. "Trash can?"

"I'll take care of it." I stood and rounded my desk as he set the cup aside. Then for the first time, I followed Shaw to the door. He opened it and stepped outside, the sun glinting in his eyes, making the gold striations jump. "Did this earn me dinner?"

I laughed. "No."

"Worth a try." He stepped away but stopped and looked back. "You still don't approve of this movie."

"No. I doubt I ever will."

Did he need my approval? Not really, but it seemed important to him. I'd been focused on the description and visualizing it in my head as he'd talked. But there'd been something about his voice. Reverence. Like with every scene, he was begging me to like it as much as he did.

"Why is this movie so important to you?" I asked.

"Reasons."

"Are they the same reasons you're no longer a cop?"

He studied my face, then slid on his sunglasses. "That's a different movie. Goodbye, Presley."

"Goodbye, Shaw." I stood in the doorway as he strode to his Escalade, waving as he left.

That's a different movie.

That was a Shaw Valance movie I wanted to see.

CHAPTER NINE

SHAW

"You did *what?*" Presley's shriek permeated the walls. I'd been on my couch, pondering—dreading—the scene we were shooting tonight, when her voice echoed around the cul-de-sac. I shot up and rushed to the door, nervous about what I'd find outside.

It had been five days since I'd told her about the movie and we hadn't spoken since. I'd seen her in passing, but I'd had a punishing week of shooting and hadn't been home much. Had something bad happened in the past few days?

Presley wasn't one to get loud. She'd get stony and speak with a sharp bite, but no matter how much I frustrated her, she stayed ice cold. What I saw from my porch was a woman on fire.

"How could you do this? Why would you do this?" she seethed, her arms flailing wide before she poked a man with shaggy-blond hair in the chest. "He was gone. I was moving on."

"Had to be done, Pres. He doesn't get away with this."

Away with what? What the hell was going on, and why was it happening at seven o'clock in the morning?

"That's . . ." She growled and reached into the air like she was choking an invisible neck. Then her hands balled into fists. "You're stirring up trouble we don't need."

I slowed my pace as I approached them in Presley's driveway.

The second she spotted me, her hands dropped and she shot me her notorious *go away* look.

"Hey. You okay?"

Her shoulders were rigid. "Fine."

I looked at the guy standing across from her. I'd seen him at the garage the day I'd shadowed Isaiah. His name was Leo, if I'd overheard correctly.

He crossed his arms over his chest. "Did you need something?"

"Did you get in a fight?" I pointed to his split lip.

His tongue darted out and licked the cut, but otherwise he didn't move. His knuckles were red and angry, at least the ones I could see. If he'd gotten into a fight, the other guy had to look worse.

The tension stretched long and awkward. Neither of them was going to tell me what was happening, but no way in hell was I leaving Presley alone with a guy who made her this angry.

The seconds ticked by, the silence painful, until finally Presley broke, turning in a huff to storm inside her house. She stomped up the steps, slamming the door with a boom that rang around the block.

"Shit." Leo dropped his arms, shaking his head.

"Is there something I should know?"

"Fuck off."

I held up my hands. "I'm just looking out for her."

Leo scoffed. "No, *I'm* looking out for her."

"Is that what this is about?" I nodded to his split lip. "Who was he?"

"Her ex. And he deserved what he got for hurting her."

My mind jumped straight to the extreme conclusion. "He hurt her?"

Because whatever pain Leo had inflicted, I'd double it on the son of a bitch. Rage ignited in my veins, off to on, like the flick of a light switch.

"He left her at the fucking altar," Leo said. "What do you think?"

What? I replayed his answer once. Then twice. Presley had been left at the altar? When? I'd assumed "hurt" meant cheating or abuse. But leaving her at the altar would never have occurred to me.

What kind of dumbass left a woman like Presley Marks?

"You took care of it?" I asked.

"Yeah, I took care of it. She's ours." As in, not mine.

Leo spat on the ground and the white blob landed dangerously close to my bare feet. Without another word, he walked to the motorcycle parked behind Presley's Jeep, started it up and thundered away.

I stayed in place until he was gone, then turned and walked to Presley's door. I knocked.

"Go away."

"It's Shaw."

The door whipped open. "I know. I heard Leo leave. I'm not deaf."

"Are you all right?"

"Dandy." The stone princess had returned.

Maybe this attitude was supposed to scare me away, but it was having the opposite effect. I fought the urge to pull her into my arms and hold her for a solid five minutes.

"He told you," she whispered. "Goddamn it, Leo."

"I don't think he meant—"

"Do *not* defend him. I don't need him sharing my problems and I don't need your pity."

"Pity?"

"Please." She rolled her eyes. "That look you just gave me? That was pity. I know because I've been staring at looks like that for two months, and I don't fucking want it from you."

Presley stepped back to slam the door in my face, but my hand shot out, slapping against it to stop it from closing. "I don't pity you. But I can be sorry that you got hurt."

"Aren't they the same thing?"

"No." I stepped closer.

Presley tipped up her chin, her feet planted on the floor. Her jaw was clenched hard.

If I cupped her cheek, would some of that strain go away? My hand lifted only to drop beside my thigh. "I feel a lot of things for you, Presley, but pity is not one of them."

She blinked, her eyes going wide behind her black-framed glasses. As I'd suspected, it made them bigger. The blue was brighter. Bolder.

And they seemed truly shocked.

She had to know I had a thing for her. She had to know the reason I kept coming to the garage was for her. So why the surprise? I wasn't hiding my interest, but maybe I needed to make it crystal clear just how much she intrigued me. Just how desperate I was to caress her skin and taste her lips.

My hand lifted, this time without hesitation. The apples

of her cheeks bloomed as I skimmed the bottom of her chin with the pad of my thumb. I leaned in, our eyes locked, as a loud rumble filled the air.

Presley blinked, stepping away from my still-raised hand and looked past me to the street.

Leo came racing back, like his wheels were on fire. He parked behind her Jeep and was up her steps in a flash, stepping into Presley's doorframe like I wasn't standing there. He forced me aside and wrapped his arms around her. "Sorry."

She relaxed into his embrace, winding her hands around his waist. "You suck."

"Yeah." He dropped his cheek to her hair.

A bubble enclosed them as they stood there, holding on to one another like I wasn't on this porch.

I didn't *want* to be on this porch.

Without a word, I turned and walked home, shutting myself inside as my heart clawed its way into my throat. What the hell? Were they a couple?

Presley hadn't said anything about being with Leo. She'd turned me down for dinner but I'd kept asking. If she had told me she had a man in her life, I would have stopped. Why hadn't she told me?

Because we're not friends, dumbass. I was a fleeting breeze in Clifton Forge, and once this movie was done, I'd be gone. She knew that. Hell, I knew that, but I was still jealous, and I hated that Leo had stolen the hug I'd wanted to give her.

I waited, standing beside the door, listening for the sound of Leo's bike to leave. It was silent. Did he still have his arms around her? My pride wouldn't let me go to the window and check.

The knot in my gut tightened, jealousy spreading in a wave until I was green, head to toe. There wasn't time for this. I had work to do, a scene to shoot. Dacia was at the motel and we hadn't spoken since she'd arrived last night in Montana. But did I leave? No, I stood there like a goddamn masochistic, waiting for the sound of a Harley.

It never came.

Leo was inside. Presley had welcomed him into her home, probably without him having to hold her carrots hostage.

I scrubbed a hand over my face and unglued my feet. I walked toward the bedroom, my heart dropping with every step. Would I hear her mattress springs squeaking? My eyes snapped right to the window when I crossed the threshold.

Her room was dark. The blinds were drawn.

They were never drawn.

Whenever I came home late at night, her blinds were open and the window was cracked. I did the same to mine so all that separated us was air, and I'd fall asleep with a smile on my face.

Fuck. Time to go.

I plucked a pair of socks from the dresser and sat on the edge of the bed to pull them on. Then I slipped my feet into the tennis shoes I'd worn running before dawn. They were still damp with sweat but they were close by. I tied them up and got out.

Leo's bike earned a glare as I backed my Escalade out of the driveway.

This jealousy was pissing me off. I wasn't a jealous guy by nature. When I was with a woman, I expected exclusivity, but if we were casual and she showed up at a party on

125

someone else's arm, I didn't have this gut-twisting urge to beat the guy to a pulp for putting his hands on my woman.

Presley wasn't my woman. Why was that idea not sinking in? She wasn't mine. She was an acquaintance and my temporary neighbor. If I didn't get her out of my head, I was going to screw up this movie, and that's why I was here. The movie.

I couldn't afford to be twisted up in Presley today of all days.

My part in the scene we were shooting tonight was simple enough.

I had to kill a woman.

Dread chased away part of the jealousy as I crossed town to the motel. The drive to the Evergreen took minutes and it was abuzz when I arrived. Even though we had hours and hours before the cameras would roll, everyone was up and moving, anxious for this shoot.

Now that Dacia had arrived, the crew would be keyed up about her too. She had an uncanny ability to put the people around her on a razor-sharp edge.

Dacia French was a thorn in my side, but she had the name and face to draw a crowd to this movie. We needed both. She was making a killing for playing a small role, but her name would be on the billboard. Her face would be on the poster.

And I only had to survive her for two weeks.

Once she was done shooting her scenes, I had no plans to see her again until the movie's press junket.

The motel's lot was full so I parked along the street. The keys in one hand rattled as I walked toward the action. I checked my watch. My hands had been fretting since I'd left home. Was Leo still at Presley's house? Didn't she need to get ready for work?

She left about seven thirty each morning, or at least she had on the mornings I'd been paying attention—which was nearly every morning.

If everything went perfectly with filming today, it would be past midnight by the time I made it home, and so help me, if his bike was still there, I was moving. Again.

I'd trade Cameron my house for his motel room. He could have my king-size bed, leather couch and spacious shower. If Cam didn't want it, then I'd swap with Shelly. Because there was no way I was staying in my yellow house for another month if there was even the remotest chance I'd overhear Presley getting it on with another man.

"Hi, Shaw." One of the crew members waved as I approached a group gathered outside the room where we'd be shooting today.

"Morning," I said to all five bodies huddled together and reading off the same iPad. With no sign of Cameron, I continued past them toward his room.

His face, covered in his new gray beard, was not the one that answered.

"There you are." Dacia cocked a hip as she held the door. "I tried to find you when I came in last night, but the crew said you weren't staying at the motel."

"I've got my own place." I pushed past her to enter the room. She didn't move, forcing me to brush against her as I stepped inside. The smell of her perfume made me gag. "Hey, Cam."

He was sitting in the chair beside the window, watching something play on his laptop. "Morning. You're here early."

"I figured you'd want to run through this one a few times."

"You're right." He shut the laptop and stood. "I do."

Then, like every other day working with Cameron, he consumed our attention. I didn't have time to think about Presley and whether she was wearing her glasses to work today. I didn't have the chance to worry that Leo had pulled them off her nose to kiss her after I'd left. I didn't have a free minute to ponder why a woman I'd just met had me so completely unnerved.

We were too busy trying to get Dacia to look genuinely terrified that she'd been stabbed by her lover and was about to fucking die.

"I'm sorry, Cameron." She sniffled after the thousandth run-through.

I pinched the bridge of my nose, the headache that had been brewing since lunch finally breaking through.

The woman could cry on command, but Cam didn't want fake tears. He wanted one—one real tear to leak out of the corner of her eye and fall to the floor.

As much as Dacia frustrated me, I got why she was upset. Cameron was asking for perfection and she wasn't delivering. Maybe no one could deliver. His expectations were . . . extreme.

But we needed his extreme. This was the opening scene. This was the scene where we had to hook the audience. Where we had to make them fall in love with Amina so they'd care about her death and have a vested interest in watching more.

Beginnings.

They were always the hardest scenes for me to shoot.

"Maybe we should take a break," I suggested.

"Good idea." Cameron nodded. He was as frustrated with this as I was.

"Come on, Dacia." I waved for her to get off the bed and follow me.

"Where are we going?" She walked by my side as I crossed the parking lot.

"Let's go get some dinner."

"But the caterer is that way." Dacia pointed to the tent set up beside the motel's office.

The owner of the motel and his wife were making their way through the buffet line. Shelly had invited them to eat with us for the meals we hosted here. A couple cameramen were sitting at a collapsible table in folding chairs.

"I think maybe we both need some space from the motel." I dug my keys from my jeans pocket and clicked the fob to unlock the Cadillac's doors. The inside was stifling from sitting outside all day in the summer sun.

Dacia hopped into the passenger seat, hissing as the bare skin of her legs touched the black leather seat.

I hit the ignition and cranked up the air conditioning. "How about a burger?"

"That's fine." She waved a hand, not caring what we'd eat. Probably because she wouldn't eat.

Dacia and I had gone out three times, each to a nice LA restaurant. She'd ordered a meal. She'd held her fork and knife. She'd chewed. But when the waitstaff had come to clear the table, my plate had been empty and hers barely touched.

Like she had on those dates, she'd watch me eat tonight, and when we returned to the motel, she'd eat the meal specially planned by her nutritionist.

My diet was normally regulated and my exercise

regimen set in stone, like hers. The lax hold I'd had on food in Clifton Forge was mostly because this part didn't require my abs to sell tickets. I was playing an aging police officer, fit in his later years but not unrealistically so. Any extra weight on my face actually made it easier for the makeup team to turn me into a sixty-something-year-old man.

Dacia didn't have that luxury. She'd be mostly naked in the murder scene.

She had an incredible body. She was long and lean, fit with curves in the right places to fill out a gown. Dacia had a certain image to uphold and this industry was unsympathetic, especially toward women.

That was the reason I'd taken her home after that third date. The reason why I knew exactly what Dacia French looked like without a stitch of clothing.

I'd been stupid enough to think an actress who was dealing with the same media onslaught I did might actually want a meaningful connection. A refuge from the attention. A person who knew how exhausting it was to constantly smile and gauge every move. To eat just right. To work out, day in and day out. A person who would be there in the unwind to talk about her day.

But Dacia had been too wrapped up in her own life to bother asking about someone else's. Dacia, to put it mildly, was a rattlesnake.

She'd taken a picture of me the day after the two of us had hooked up. I'd been in bed, asleep on my back with an arm tucked beside my head. A white blanket had covered my groin and a leg, but the rest was all bare skin and wrinkled sheets.

Lazy morning.

That had been Dacia's caption. Her face had been on

one side of the picture. Mine on the other. The photo had gone viral and I'd woken up to fifteen messages from Laurelin asking me why I hadn't bothered telling her I was in a relationship with Dacia. Managers needed to know that kind of thing.

I'd called Dacia a cab and kicked her out of my house. She hadn't cared. She'd gotten what she'd been after—speculation in the tabloids and an influx of social media followers.

Dacia had been the last actress on my arm. From then on out, I took one of my sisters to movie premieres. It was usually Matine, because she liked dressing up more than Astrid or Becca. If I wanted to take a woman to dinner, I invited my mother. There hadn't been a woman in my bed in months.

If it had been my call, Dacia wouldn't have been picked for this film, but Cameron thought she had the talent for the part. Was he regretting that decision after today's rehearsals?

"I'm trying, Shaw." Her eyes were aimed out her window as I drove through town. "I don't know what he wants."

She was trying, and as much as I hated to admit it, she had the talent. Besides, it was too late to find someone else anyway.

"You'll get it," I said. "We'll take a break. Get out of there for a while and then regroup."

"Yeah," she muttered, conversation closed.

The drive to town was silent because neither of us cared to find out what the other had been doing since we'd seen each other two years ago. I'd caught a glimpse of her at the Academy Awards last year, but we'd been going in opposite directions, each swarmed by people, so I hadn't been forced to make small talk.

I pulled into Stockyard's and parked, grinning as Dacia's

lip curled. Clearly she hadn't explored Clifton Forge much, because Stockyard's was the quintessential Montana bar and it matched the rest of the town.

It was rustic without any fanfare or polish. The parking lot smelled like grease and smoke. To her, I'm sure the place looked . . . dirty. Beneath her.

But while I was on a diet reprieve, I wanted one of the Stockyard's damn good burgers. It was worth the added hour in the guest room I'd turned into my temporary gym. It would be worth it watching Dacia squirm as she took a rickety stool, then doused herself in hand sanitizer when we left.

Cameron had introduced us to the place when we'd come back to start shooting and I'd been five times since. I'd even bought Luke Rosen a burger here after we'd met for beers at The Betsy this past Friday.

"Here?" Dacia asked, gulping as we walked toward the door.

"It's not that bad. Just relax and enjoy a break."

She scowled as I held the door for her, making sure not to touch it as she slipped inside. "I'm relaxed."

"Sure," I deadpanned.

The inside of the restaurant was dark and it took my eyes a moment to adjust. When they did, I scanned the tables, searching for an empty high-top.

Instead, they landed on white-blond hair and my heart skipped.

Presley was sitting at the bar. She caught me in the reflection of the mirror behind the liquor bottles and her spine straightened.

She was alone.

A slow grin spread across my face. It stretched, wider

and wider, when she didn't look away and a smile of her own tugged at her lips.

Lost in that blue gaze, I didn't notice Dacia staring between the two of us until her hand slid into mine and she stood on her toes to nibble on my ear.

Dacia really was a bitch.

CHAPTER TEN

PRESLEY

W hy did I ever listen to Leo?
            I dropped my gaze from the mirror and stared at the napkin on the bar. Was it too late to cancel my order? My stomach growled but a cheeseburger didn't sound appetizing anymore. I didn't want to be here by myself anyway, but especially if Shaw was here with Dacia—*holy shit, she's pretty*—French.

Why did it hurt to see them together? Of course he'd be with a movie star. He *was* a movie star. I kept forgetting.

Lately, he'd just become . . . Shaw. My wickedly sexy, flirtatious neighbor.

Dacia was stunning. Her long, blond hair was shiny and thick. It was actually similar to the hair I'd once had. She was tall though, and she had breasts bigger than B cups. Standing beside Shaw, with her lips at his ear, they were the perfect pair.

I raised my hand to snag the bartender's attention from where she was talking to another customer. "Can I get my order to go?"

She smiled. "Sure, hon."

I should have just gone home after work, but Leo's words from this morning had been playing in my head all day.

Don't hide away from the world, Pres. Don't let Jeremiah win.

I didn't think I was hiding, but Leo had made some good points. I used to be out, visible in town more often. I loved grabbing a coffee at the coffee shop on Saturday mornings and meandering along Central, especially in the summer. But since the wedding, I hadn't set foot downtown unless it had been to stop by the bank and make the garage's deposits.

I'd been humiliated and hiding my bruised heart at home, like my mother had done with her black-and-blues.

I refused to become my mother.

So here I was, not hiding, still humiliated, but the agony had faded.

Leo had told me to stop worrying about gossip and other people's opinions. He was right. Who cared if people whispered behind my back? Eventually, it would stop if I showed the world I was happy on my own. But if I became a hermit, the pity would continue. I'd be that broken woman who avoided life.

So after work tonight, I'd gone to get a burger rather than escape into chores at home.

I had to wash my bedding tonight. Leo's drool was probably on my pillow along with the stale scent of blood and wind. After he'd apologized and hugged me, he'd nearly passed out from exhaustion. Staying up all night, riding to Ashton and beating the shit out of my ex-fiancé before riding home could really wear a guy out. I'd pushed him toward my bed and told him to take a nap while I went to work.

While I did the wash, I'd eat my burger. Alone.

Stockyard's wasn't as busy as the diner. This was a bar with bar food, but their burgers were delicious and the owners made sure families were welcome. The room was dimly lit and quiet music played over the speakers. The only thing I didn't like was the poker table at the back.

This had been Jeremiah's preferred poker stop. He used to bring me a burger and fries on the nights when he'd get home before midnight. We'd eat them together on the couch while he'd tell me about his game.

The appeal of the game eluded me, no matter how many times he explained the rules and strategy. But I'd been innately supportive, like my mother.

Supporting a man with horrific habits was her ultimate weakness.

If—*when* I began dating, I was breaking that cycle.

And I would not hide.

Starting tomorrow.

Shaw had stepped away from Dacia, shooting her a glare and jabbing his finger toward a table. When his back was to her, she sneered at me through the mirror.

I kept my head down, blocking out the sound of their hushed voices. Dacia laughed, too loud, and it carried across the room. My eyes caught them again.

She wore her multi-million-dollar smile as she placed her hand on Shaw's arm.

He removed it.

So maybe they weren't together, but regardless, it was a good reminder.

He might *feel a lot of things toward me* but getting involved with Shaw Valance would only lead to disaster.

The bartender came out of the kitchen with a paper sack in her hand. "Here you go."

"Thanks." I smiled and left a twenty on the bar. "Keep the change."

I slung my purse over my shoulder, took my food and walked straight for the door.

"Presley." Shaw's voice was like honey, smooth and thick and sweet.

"Hey." I looked up, and *damn it,* one glimpse of those eyes made me shiver. "What's up?"

"Are you okay?"

I nodded. "Hungry."

"About this morning. I, uh . . ."

"Forget about it." I waved it off as he struggled for what to say.

His jaw ticked. "You and Leo seem close."

"So do you and Dacia."

"There's nothing there."

I lifted a shoulder. "Not my business. See you around, Shaw."

"Presley—"

I was out the door as my name floated off his lips. My Jeep was waiting around the corner. I got in and wasted no time going home.

Leo was right. I needed to rejoin society.

But not until Shaw Valance was gone. Not until there wasn't a risk of seeing those golden eyes and letting myself daydream that a rich and handsome star had his sights set on me.

———

"GOT A SEC?" Dash asked from the doorway between the shop and office.

"Yeah." I stood, following him into the shop, smiling at the customer waiting and reading on her phone.

Emmett, Isaiah and Leo were standing beside a tool bench. I scanned the room, searching for our other two mechanics. "Where are Sawyer and Tyler?"

"Out back." Dash tossed his thumb to the wall. "We need to regroup on the Warriors."

Leo groaned. "We talked about this yesterday."

Yes, we had. At length.

When Dash had come to the garage and I'd told him about Leo, he'd gone ballistic. I hadn't seen him that mad in years. When Leo had finally crawled out of my bed and joined us at the garage, Dash had hauled him into the office and proceeded to lecture him for an hour about the Warriors.

"Yeah, we talked about it yesterday," Dash snapped, the anger lingering. "But we talked about it in June too. I used to not have to repeat myself, but since you didn't listen the first time, I want to make sure it's clear. Stay the fuck away from the Warriors."

"I know." Leo threw his hands in the air. "I fucked up, okay? I'm sorry."

"Have you heard anything?" Emmett asked.

Dash shook his head. "Not yet, but one of their members got his ass kicked by one of us. You know them as well as I do. They'll retaliate."

"Goddamn it." Isaiah dropped his gaze to the floor. "We don't need this."

"It's not going to blow back on you," Leo said. "That fucker knows exactly why I did it. If the Warriors come after anyone, it'll be me."

"We don't stand alone." Emmett clapped a hand on his shoulder. "Never have."

"I shouldn't have done it," Leo muttered. "I was drunk and stupid. I mean it. I'm sorry. I'll get ahold of Tucker and explain."

Tucker Talbot was the president of the Arrowhead Warriors. He was ruthless and cunning. The man scared the hell out of me. He was not like Draven. There was no soft side to Tucker.

"No. I'll be the one to call Tucker." Dash's entire body went rigid. His fists were so tight he could have crushed bolts to glitter.

There was no love lost between the Tin Kings and the Warriors, but I hadn't seen Dash like this before. His fury vibrated around us.

Was I missing something?

"Sorry, Dash." Leo looked truly miserable. His knuckles weren't as red as they had been yesterday morning at my house, but the crack in his lip almost seemed worse.

I gulped. What did Jeremiah look like?

"I get it." Dash huffed. "I wanted to do the same."

My frame slumped. This was not what I wanted when I'd planned my simple, classy wedding.

"This isn't your fault." Isaiah threw his arm around my shoulders, pulling me into his side.

"I just want to forget the whole thing ever happened."

"It's forgotten," Dash declared. "As of today, it's done. I'll do what I can to smooth things over with the Warriors, and we'll put it behind us."

He made it sound so easy.

Maybe it was.

I didn't think about Jeremiah much these days, and I had Shaw to thank for that. He occupied the thoughts that had once been reserved for my fiancé. He and his movie had taken the place of wedding planning.

"Let's get back to work," Dash said as Sawyer and Tyler rounded the corner of the shop, returning to work after a cigarette break.

I was glad those two had each other. They'd bonded quickly when they'd started working here, much like Isaiah and I had after his first day. Sawyer and Tyler probably wondered why the five of us were always talking without them. What did they say about us as they smoked out back?

I made a mental note to tell Dash we needed to include them more in our regular activities. I didn't want either of them to feel like an outsider—I knew all too well what that was like.

"Hey, guys." I waved at them before heading to the office.

They nodded and Sawyer returned the gesture.

Leo followed me to the office with Dash bringing up the rear. The minute we entered, Dash's shoulders fell with the weight of a thousand bricks and he trudged to his office, closing the door. He was probably calling Tucker.

Leo met my gaze and his was full of so much regret, so much sorrow. It was rare to see past his cocky, playboy exterior to the fears underneath.

"It'll be okay." I walked right into his space, wrapping my arms around his waist.

"I'm sorry, Pres," he said, returning my hug. "It was eating at me and I lost my head."

"You're going to get yourself killed," I whispered so the customer waiting couldn't hear. "Don't make me bury you too."

"Never." He held me closer.

Dash had labeled me a hugger years ago. It was true. I hugged. But what people didn't seem to understand was that I didn't only hug for them. I hugged for me. When my emotions got the best of me, when life got to be too much, I always went for the hug.

My sister had taught me that.

Leo dwarfed me. My head only came to the center of his chest, but I held him as tight as my arms would allow. Maybe if I held tight enough, this would go away. Like Dash had promised, today would be the end. Leo wouldn't be in danger of some violent retribution delivered at the hands of the Arrowhead Warriors.

All because he'd been drinking at The Betsy and had gotten a wild hair up his ass to punish Jeremiah.

Leo had told us that Jeremiah hadn't been hard to find. He'd been at a bar, playing poker—shocker. Jeremiah wasn't going to change. Leo had ordered a drink and hung out until Jeremiah had spent his chips, after two in the morning. Then Leo had *beat the hell out of him.* I'd been spared the gory details.

Then he'd driven home, stopped at a gas station to wash up and come to my place.

"What's up with that Shaw guy?" Leo asked, letting me go.

I shrugged. "He's my temporary neighbor."

"He likes you."

"Maybe." I suspected Shaw liked a lot of women and they liked him in return. "It doesn't matter."

Leo's face soured and he glanced toward the shop. "He's getting the bare minimum paint job on the bike Isaiah's building."

"Ha!" I laughed. "No, he is not. That bike is making us a

141

lot of money, and it's going to be in a movie. You'll do the best damn paint job of your life on that motorcycle so that when the fictional Draven rides it down the street, it'll be one the real Draven would have been proud to ride."

He grumbled and shook his head, but he'd do his best work. Leo loved Draven as much as I did, if not more. It was the reason Leo's drinking had increased ever since Draven's funeral. His nights at The Betsy used to be limited to two or three a week, but he went nearly every night these days. And Draven died three years ago.

Dash had tried talking to Leo about it. So had Emmett. But lectures about drinking and women fell on deaf ears. Besides, who was Emmett to talk? He didn't flaunt it as much, but he partied too. Leo's crutch was alcohol. Emmett's was women. I heard the rumors about who he hooked up with on any given weekend.

"Are you going to be okay?" I asked Leo.

"Are you?"

"Yes." I'd said it automatically, but deep down, there was truth behind that word.

Leo winked and returned to work. I smiled at our customer and returned to my desk, taking a moment to face my screen and close my eyes.

What a damn mess.

Behind Dash's closed door, I heard the low rumble of his voice but couldn't make out the words.

I glanced up at the picture of Draven and his sons, wishing more than ever he was here. He'd fix things. Draven would straighten out Leo and take some of the weight off Dash. He'd tell Emmett to stop messing around so that when a woman with staying power showed up, he'd be ready.

But Draven was gone.

We'd buried him beside his wife in the cemetery. The service had been small, no more than twenty people invited to huddle around the casket.

Bryce and Dash. Genevieve and Isaiah. Emmett and his mom. Leo had stood by me. Nick and his wife, Emmeline, had been there with their two crying kids, who had adored their grandfather. Some of the former Tin Kings who still lived in town had attended.

Dash had attempted some words, but when he'd stumbled over them, Nick had taken over.

After he was done, we'd left. I'd gone home alone—Jeremiah had been in Ashton, vying for his position as a prospect for the Warriors—and cried all day.

No matter how many times I tried to imagine Draven's death, it left me unsettled. Suicide? That hadn't been his style. Draven had been the kind to go out in a blaze of glory, not hanging from a noose in his own home.

Was it possible that he hadn't killed himself?

My thoughts were interrupted when Tyler came in with the customer's car keys. I hurried to take her payment and smiled as she waved goodbye. Then the office was quiet again.

I hated the quiet.

I stared at Dash's closed door, waiting for it to open. I didn't have to wait long. He stepped out and looked . . . beaten. Dash Slater never backed down.

"Are you okay? How did it go?"

"I don't know," he muttered, coming to the chair across from my desk.

It was days like this when I wish Bryce still wrote her stories at the garage instead of at the newspaper. She'd know what to say to Dash. He'd confided in her about the club, things I'd never know.

"I think we'll be okay," he said. "I just don't want to get a call one night from Paul at The Betsy, telling me that Leo is drowning in a pool of his own blood."

My stomach turned. "Me neither."

"Sorry, Pres."

"If this is anyone's fault, it's Jeremiah's."

Dash chuckled. "I'm good with blaming him."

"Me too." I bit my lower lip, hesitating to ask the question that had been on my mind before he'd come out, but I had to know. "Can I ask you something?"

"Course." He relaxed into the chair.

"I've been thinking a lot about your dad lately. With the wedding and the movie, he's been on my mind. I need to know something. Was it really suicide?"

Dash's eyes flooded with grief, and a pained expression crossed his face. "Pres, I—"

"Please? Tell me the truth. Trust me with it."

He blew out a long breath, then shook his head. "No. It wasn't."

A stab of pain hit me in the chest, like I was experiencing Draven's death all over again. Tears flooded my eyes and my lungs struggled to hold in air. Wasn't I supposed to feel better, knowing the truth? Instead, I felt like I'd grieved the wrong way. Was that possible? To grieve incorrectly?

There'd been blame inside my grief. Resentment that Draven had left us behind. When really, there should have been anger and fury and revenge.

"Who?" I asked.

"I can't tell you that."

"The Warriors?"

Dash stayed quiet, giving nothing away, which gave everything away.

"You should have told me. Did you think I'd betray you?"

"No, but you were marrying one of them, Presley. You were going there every weekend. It would have made things worse for you. I didn't want that."

"Except it's worse now. I've spent three years asking the wrong why." I took a deep breath, giving my emotions a minute to level. Then I raised my gaze and, this time, asked the right question. "Why? Why did they kill him?"

"He made an arrangement with Tucker to save Genevieve and me."

"Oh." My hand covered my aching heart.

Draven had protected his children. It made perfect sense because that was who he'd been. He'd sacrificed his life to save his kids from Tucker and the Warriors.

And because of me, because of Jeremiah, I'd brought Tucker back into Dash's life. No wonder he'd looked so angry in the shop. That phone call was probably the last one he'd ever wanted to make.

"I'll text Jeremiah and tell him it was my fault for Leo," I said. "Maybe that will help."

Dash shook his head. "Just leave it. I doubt it will do any good."

"But will it hurt?"

"It might. Leave it. Leave him. With any luck, we'll never have to see the guy again."

"Okay." I wanted to help defuse the situation, but if there was a chance I'd make it worse, then I'd take Dash's advice.

He stood from the chair and walked toward the shop. Dash would go lose himself in a car for a while, then he'd go home to his family and be all right. He paused at the door, his hand on the knob when he glanced over his shoulder. "Happy Birthday."

"Shh." I put a finger to my lips.

I hated my birthday, something Dash and the guys knew. Emmett had winked at me this morning but hadn't muttered those words. Leo had whistled "Happy Birthday" under his breath. Isaiah had brought me a latte from the coffee hut.

"Are you sure you don't want to celebrate?" he asked. "I'll buy you a beer."

"I'm sure. But thanks."

Dash left me to get back to work, and I treated the afternoon like any normal day. I paid bills. I got started on the month-end financial report. I bid farewell to the guys and locked up at five.

It wasn't until the drive home that loneliness crept under my skin.

It happened every year on my birthday, and I was surprised it hadn't hit me sooner.

I missed Scarlett. Today especially, I missed my sister.

Our birthday was something we'd always made special for one another. It was the one day my mother would put us first. She'd make us a cake. She'd spend hours cleaning so the house was spotless. She'd let Dad give us our presents and take credit for buying them even though we knew she'd done all the work.

She'd bend over backward making sure there was nothing that might set him off.

It worked. I couldn't remember a birthday when Dad had raised his hand to any of us. There were never any bruises or welts to hide the next morning.

My birthday used to be a good day.

Celebrating without Scarlett held no appeal.

I parked in the driveway and took out my phone, sending Scarlett the same text I sent her every year.

Happy Birthday.

There'd be no reply, but I'd sent it into the universe and hoped, wherever she was, that it found her well.

I scooped up my purse and opened my door just as Shaw's shiny, black SUV pulled into the driveway next door.

"Hey." He waved after getting out.

I waved back. "Hey."

He had a backpack slung over one shoulder, his sunglasses in his hair. "How was your day?"

"Fine." I shrugged, unable to move away from my Jeep and disappear inside. "You?"

"Good." He waited for me to say more and when I didn't, he took the first stair toward his porch.

"Shaw?"

"Yeah?" His foot backed down to the sidewalk, like he'd been waiting for an excuse to come closer.

I gave him one. "It's my birthday."

He crossed the lawn, a small smile toying at his mouth. "Happy Birthday."

"I'm ordering pizza."

"Pizza's good." Shaw grinned. "But I've been craving carrots."

I laughed and nodded for him to follow me inside. "I happen to have some carrots."

CHAPTER ELEVEN

SHAW

"Thanks." I took the beer bottle from Presley.

"You're welcome." She sat in the chaise lounge by my side, the hinges squeaking as she kicked her feet up.

"This is a nice yard." I tipped the top of my bottle toward her lawn, then took a swig.

The grass was green and lush, a carpet as nice as some fairways I'd played at golf resorts. It was almost out of place here in this little neighborhood. Or would have been if her other neighbor's yard weren't exactly the same. There was no fence back here, and the grass flowed in a green wave across property lines. Except the green of my lawn wasn't nearly as brilliant.

"My neighbor on the other side owns a small landscaping company," she said. "We trade. I do his bookkeeping and he takes care of my yard."

"Ah." Tomorrow I'd call Juno and have her hire the guy.

We drank our beers, listening to the subtle noises around the block. A kid laughed. A lawn mower rumbled. Birds chirped. Our two chairs were the only thing Presley had on the square deck that jutted out from the sliding glass door off her dining room.

The evening was warm, and though she'd positioned the chairs in a patch of shade, I was grateful for my white linen shirt and pair of cargo shorts.

Presley was wearing a pair of shorts that, for once, didn't need a belt to keep them on her frame. They were black and fit tight to the curves of her hips, exposing those mouthwatering, trim legs and golden skin. When I'd spotted her beside her Jeep earlier, my eyes had zeroed in on her legs, stirring my dick to life.

Her shirt was baggy over the shorts, more like a man's T-shirt than the normally tight tops she wore. If it hadn't had a vintage pink and orange flower on the front, I would have worried the shirt was her ex's. She'd tied it in a knot at her side, showing the smallest triangle of skin above the waistband of those shorts.

I was drooling into my beer, feeling like a lucky son of a bitch that I'd come home at just the right moment to catch her. I still wasn't sure how I'd scored a pizza invitation, but I was taking it.

"It's your birthday."

Presley nodded. "Yep."

"No big plans or a party with your friends?"

"I don't celebrate my birthday." Her tone was crisp and cool, that subject closed.

She'd told me it was her birthday but she didn't want to talk about it. Interesting. I'd play along.

At this point, I wasn't going to push anything that might make her kick me off her deck. After she'd run out of Stockyard's last night, I'd figured she was done with me for good.

Dacia's stunt had been typical, something I should have

expected. She'd seen the desire I had for Presley and, since she'd been having a rough day, decided to torment someone else.

As I'd eaten my burger and she'd twirled a french fry in a dollop of ketchup, never actually eating the damn thing, I'd told her that if she ever put her mouth on me again, I'd blacklist her from my social circles and do everything in my power to get her fired from *Dark Paradise*.

That had shut her up.

Dacia might be a snake, but she wasn't dumb. She knew I had a broad network of connections in this industry and I was not fucking around.

"Sorry about last night," I said.

Presley shrugged. "For what?"

"For Dacia."

"It's fine." She took a drink.

I shifted so I could look at her square on. "There's nothing between Dacia and me. She saw the way I looked at you and decided to play a game."

"Okay." Presley kept her eyes forward, but the corner of her mouth lifted.

One of these days, I'd do something to make her smile and laugh. She'd be gorgeous, smiling with no walls in place. "So what was the deal with Leo?"

She sighed, bringing her knees up to her chest. "It's a long story."

"I've got nothing to do tonight."

Presley stayed quiet, something I was learning didn't necessarily mean she was shutting me out. She was simply careful with her words and cautious with her trust. I respected that. I didn't trust many with the details of my past either.

"I was engaged," she said, letting the words hang in the summer air. "Jeremiah decided to break it off with me on our wedding day by forgetting to show up at the ceremony."

I winced. Leo had told me as much yesterday, but it hurt to hear the pain and humiliation in her own voice. And it still made no sense. Who would leave Presley? What kind of an asshole would break up with someone on their wedding day? What kind of prick didn't turn up for her? "And Leo settled the score with his fists."

She nodded. "It's a little more complicated than that, but yeah."

"Is there, um . . . something with you and Leo?"

"No. Definitely not." She barked a laugh. "He's the annoying older brother I never had."

The air rushed from my lungs. *Thank fuck.* That hug had been bothering me since yesterday morning. It had seemed intimate, but now that I replayed it again, maybe I'd read too much into it. Maybe it had been a tight hug between friends. Maybe it looked like that when I hugged my sisters too.

"Can I admit that I was jealous yesterday?"

The color rose in her cheeks. "Can I admit I was jealous too?"

My gaze dropped to her pink lips. My tongue wagged behind my teeth, desperately wanting to be set free, but I swallowed hard and tore my eyes away.

This woman was testing the limits of my restraint.

This woman might push me over the edge.

"How was your beer with Chief Rosen?" Presley asked.

"Fun." I grinned. "He's a good guy, and I appreciate him humoring me. He told me some interesting stories about Clifton Forge and being a cop here. It was kind of like old times. Turns out, some idiots are just as stupid in Montana as they are in California."

"Do you ever miss being a cop?"

"Some days," I admitted. "It was a stressful job, but rewarding. I miss feeling like I do a little bit of good every day."

I tried to make up for my lack of civil service through donations. Every year I gave money to different inner-city charities, especially those that helped kids.

"What was the best day you had as a cop?" Presley asked.

"The best day? Easy. The day of the school bus."

"Really?" She sat up straighter and shifted so her knees were aimed my way. "I would have thought it was the hardest."

"It was also the worst day. I'll never forget all those crying faces. Seeing that guy with the gun. Those kids . . ." That day, I'd learned what true fear looked like. It had nearly sent me to my knees.

Her eyebrows came together. "Then how was it the best?"

"They lived."

Understanding dawned on her face and she reached over, placing her hand on my forearm for the briefest touch.

Those kids might have been traumatized, but they were alive. Seventeen lights shining in the world.

"I hear from them sometimes. Or their parents. I have a secret Instagram account under a fake name, and I follow most of them." Once I'd made my first million, I'd also set aside money to fund their educations. If there was a way I could help them succeed in life, I'd do what I could.

"What happened that day? Can you talk about it? It's fine if you don't want to. I can't imagine it's easy to relive."

"It's okay." I hadn't spoken of that day in years, but I had this overwhelming urge to confide in Presley, maybe because I trusted her with my secrets.

I trusted so few people, and it didn't come naturally.

Presley was . . . different. Special. I looked at her and saw a safe harbor. A vault. She guarded the people at the garage so fiercely that I wanted a sliver of that loyalty too. And she was asking because she wanted to hear it from me, from my perspective.

Most people assumed they knew the whole story from the news. They made assumptions about how it had gone down. So rarely did anyone ask for my point of view.

The last time I'd spoken of it had been with one of my sisters. Becca had wanted to know the details about six months after I'd resigned from the force. Just like Matine and Astrid, she thought it was why I'd quit.

Only Mom, Dad and I knew the truth.

The day I'd quit was also the last day I'd spoken to my father. Something else my sisters were sure had to do with the bus.

"It was just a normal day," I said. "Started my shift early, right as the sun was coming up. I was on patrol that day and had a new partner, Margaret. It was her second year and she'd just transferred to my precinct. I was the senior officer but we were both young. Want to hear something stupid?"

"Sure."

"Promise not to judge me too harshly?"

"Oh my God," Presley groaned. "Did you sleep with your partner?"

"No." I laughed. "I most definitely did not sleep with

Margaret. She was—is—beautiful, but we were definitely not attracted to each other."

"Okay, so what am I going to judge you for?"

"I was glad to be paired with a female officer because I thought I'd get to show her the ropes. That I was already superior because I was a guy."

"Yeah." Presley frowned. "I'm judging you."

"As you should." I lifted a hand. "In my defense, I was a closed-minded idiot. But I was an idiot who learned. Margaret taught me a lot that morning, and after the school bus, I started to see things differently. I saw my sisters differently. My mom too. I opened my ears and listened to their opinions, not assuming mine were already right."

Because Margaret was strong and sure. Because Margaret was brave and balanced. Because Margaret had saved those kids. And because I admired her.

"Still judging me?" I asked.

"A little." Presley smirked. Some of those qualities I saw in Margaret were staring back at me with vivid blue eyes.

"Fair enough." I chuckled. "I hired mostly women after quitting the force. My assistant, my agent and my manager are women. Before you ask, I didn't hire them because they were women. I hired them because they were the best, and I think as a younger man, I wouldn't have given their résumés a chance. I'm not proud of it but . . . I'm man enough to admit my flaws."

"Okay, you're forgiven." She took a drink of her beer. "So what happened that day on the bus?"

"Margaret and I were driving around. It was sunny and hot already, even in the morning. That's how I knew something was wrong on that bus. Every window was up. Those buses don't have air conditioning, so the kids always have their windows down. Kids see a cop car, normally they wave out the windows, especially if they're younger. You drive by and see all these little fingers sticking out."

"Makes sense. Did you pull it over?"

"No, it was parked in the lot of a grocery store. Another thing that seemed strange. Full buses don't park until they're at school. I was driving and eased off the gas for a long look. This guy was standing beside the driver. The driver had his hands on the wheel, eyes forward. And the guy standing was dressed completely in black, with a coat and hat. On a hot day in that bus without the windows down, he'd be sweating bullets. The whole thing was off, so I slowed when on any other day I probably would have kept driving."

My gut had been screaming.

"We took another lap around the block and I pulled into the grocery store's lot from the other end, coming at the bus from a different angle. That's when I saw it."

"The gun?"

I nodded. "An assault rifle. We learned later he had a handgun too."

"What did he want, the guy?"

"To this day, I don't know. The driver said the guy had come out of nowhere on his last pickup. One of the kids had climbed up the steps, smiled and walked down the aisle. The driver watched the kid in the mirror as he took his seat. Then when the driver went to shut the door, the guy was just . . . there. He'd been waiting. Came onto the bus, yelled at the kids to shut up and close their windows. Then he ordered the driver to drive through town. Had him stop in the parking lot. The whole time, he was mumbling this crazy shit about saving the kids from themselves. Saving them from society."

"He was crazy."

"He was something. There was no connection to that bus driver or any of the kids other than he lived in the neighborhood where that route went. If there was more to it, we'll never know."

"He's dead?"

I nodded. "He shot Margaret. I shot him."

Presley gasped. "Did she—"

"She's alive. He hit her in the shoulder."

"Thank God." Her frame relaxed. "How did it happen?"

"Fast. I called for backup and parked in the middle of a bunch of cars, hoping he wouldn't see the cruiser. We got out with weapons drawn. Margaret went to the back of the bus as I went to the front. He didn't see either of us. We were planning on waiting until SWAT arrived, but then everything went to shit. One of the kids opened the emergency hatch. And then . . . it was over. Maybe thirty seconds and it was done."

I'd seen the entire thing from my position. The kid spotted Margaret from his seat at the rear and ducked low. I had already been moving at that point, dodging cars to get closer. When the hatch door opened, I was running full tilt toward the front window.

"The back opened and the guy went crazy. He started screaming loud enough that I could hear it outside. He lifted his gun, aimed it at a kid. I screamed something, hoping I'd get his attention. I figured if he saw me, he'd shoot me instead of a kid."

My feet had felt like cement blocks. The driver noticed me first, then a couple kids in the front. They bent low, leaning past the seat in front of them, their faces twisted in fear.

To this day, I saw them at times. Small faces covered in blood.

"I fired at the same second he did. I shot him right through the glass. Three bullets. That was it. *Boom. Boom. Boom.* One hit him in the back of the head, the other two his spine. Blood and brain matter everywhere."

Presley flinched.

"Shit. Sorry. I didn't mean to be so graphic."

She waved it off. "I'm not scared of some blood. I just . . . that's insane."

"The driver opened the door for me. I got in and expected to hear kids crying and screaming, but it was silent. They'd all huddled down in their seats, and it wasn't until I walked down the aisle they began to look up. Seventeen terrified faces all looking at me. I-I didn't know what to do with them."

"But Margaret did," Presley guessed.

"She saw me frozen and immediately took over. She wiped the kids' faces clean with her shirtsleeves. She helped me unload every one of those kids from the back and was calm the whole time. Touched each kid, hugged the ones who needed it. I didn't even realize she'd been shot until the bus was empty. She didn't say a word."

It wasn't until another police car arrived that the kids started crying. Then it was deafening wails as they clung to Margaret and me.

"Wow."

I nodded. "Like I said, it was the best day because they all lived. And the worst day too."

"I read an article about it, after you got to town."

I raised a teasing eyebrow. "You googled me?"

"Yes," she admitted. "Sorry. I was hoping it would make me dislike you."

"Did it?"

"You're drinking my beer and I gave you the good chair."

I chuckled. "Touché."

"There was no mention of Margaret. If you hadn't told me about her, I would have thought you saved those kids yourself."

"The official press release included both of our names, but the mainstream media latched on to me. Mostly because some asshole from the grocery store took a bunch of pictures with me and the kids and sold them to the tabloids. Margaret had already been loaded into the ambulance."

"That's unfair."

"I thought so too, but she was actually glad for it. She didn't want any part of the publicity. Our commanding officer asked if we'd make a statement, and she told him no, so I did it all. She doesn't get much credit for that day."

"Sounds like she didn't want it."

"True. I might have killed the guy, but she was the hero."

"You both are."

"I'm no hero. I just play one on TV." I stole Presley's words, hoping to lighten the mood, but her expression remained serious. "I did what every other cop in my position would have done. What most do every single day."

Then I'd quit.

I was no hero. I was a selfish, greedy coward.

"Did you have a hard time taking a life?" she asked.

"No." There was no hesitation in that answer. "Never."

"So why did you quit?"

Why? That was a whole other story, one I wasn't ready to tell. But I'd explain *when*. "I went into SWAT training after that and joined a team, but the media were still following me around. The paparazzi could make a buck from my pictures so they took it. An agent tracked me down and asked if I'd ever thought of making a movie. One thing led to another and I had this contract in front of me for half a million dollars."

"You were a sensation."

"He wanted to exploit the situation and I let him." Thanks to some lucky breaks and the fact that I had talent, I'd ridden that wave to the top. "I wish I could say I had a noble reason for quitting, but I don't."

"You did it for the money." Presley's tone wasn't judgmental, more matter-of-fact.

"I'm still doing it for the money. This money, it's . . . it's life-changing money. It's legacy money. My kids won't have to live on ramen noodles or peanut butter sandwiches when police department budgets get cut. My parents don't have to worry about retirement. My sisters and their husbands won't go into debt paying for my nieces to go to college."

"I think working for your family is a fairly noble cause, Shaw."

"I've always felt like a sellout."

My old squad had teased me about it after that first movie. They didn't know the whole reason for me leaving, neither did Presley, but the money had been a major factor. Their teasing had felt more like accusations than jokes.

I bet that new car rides smoother than my Honda.

It only took me twenty minutes to get here from the station. How was traffic from Malibu?

Surprised you can even stomach the cheap beer.

"You're not a sellout." Presley's hand was on my arm again, sparking desire and soothing worry with a single touch. Then her hand was gone, and I wanted it back. "I'm going to go order pizza. Want another beer?"

"Sure. Thanks."

She stood and walked away, her perfect ass encased in those shorts. I savored the natural sway of her hips, drinking in the chance to stare before she disappeared inside.

The warm air filled my lungs and a lightness settled in my chest, the weight of the past drifting away. I hadn't talked much about that time, maybe because there hadn't been a person around I'd trusted to listen.

Presley had my trust. I wasn't sure why, but my gut said she deserved it. She'd guard it fiercely.

I stood from the "good" chair and followed Presley inside.

She'd just hung up the phone when I found her in the kitchen. "I forgot to ask what kind of pizza you like."

"I'm not picky." I stood against the counter beside her, our shoulders nearly touching. "And it's your birthday."

Leaning closer, I let my elbow brush the skin of her forearm.

Presley darted for the fridge before the touch lingered, pulling out two more beer bottles. She handed one to me and took up a rigid stance three feet away. "We should be able to hear the doorbell from outside."

Except I didn't want to go outside. I put my beer on the counter and stepped into her space. If she really wanted to go, she could sidestep me and leave the kitchen, but she didn't try to make another escape.

Her gaze stayed locked on mine as I shuffled her backward until her tailbone was pressed against the counter. "What are you doing?"

"Something I've wanted to do for weeks." I lifted a hand

and ran my knuckles down the curve of her cheek. I bent low, my mouth hovering above hers. If I left Clifton Forge without one taste of Presley Marks, I'd regret it for decades.

"What would you say if I asked to kiss you?"

Her eyes darted to my lips.

"What would you say?" I repeated.

Presley's lashes lifted, those blue eyes sparkling. Then, on an exhale, she whispered, "Yes."

I crushed my lips to hers, not giving her a chance to rescind. Then I pinned her to me, wrapping her petite frame in my arms and holding her close.

She sank into me, her soft lips gentle under mine, hesitant at first. Cautious. Then it was like she said fuck it, because she dropped any pretense and kissed me within an inch of my life.

The hold I had on her was nothing compared to the way she gripped me with her free hand, hauling me down by my shirt. Her cold bottle of beer between us pressed into my abs. She licked the seam of my lips, demanding entrance, and when it slid against mine, I swallowed her moan. Or was it mine? With the licking and the tangling and the heat—*holy shit, the heat*—the world around us disappeared. There was only me and her and this inferno. There was only her fresh, citrus scent tinted with the sweetness of vanilla.

My blood thundered in my ears. My head was dizzy. This kiss was likely going to make my brain combust but I dove in deeper, shuffling my legs closer and pressing my arousal into her hip.

It was her gasp I swallowed that time.

Then she was gone, just when it was starting to shift from a kiss to foreplay. She ripped her lips away, planted her palm against my heart and shoved me onto my heels.

"Sorry." I swiped a hand over my wet lips. "I got carried away."

"No, it's—" She shook her head and dried her own mouth before burying her face in her hands.

Son of a bitch. Was she going to cry? Maybe she was thinking about her ex. Was it too soon since the failed wedding?

One day, maybe I'd remember that Presley rarely did what I expected. Her hands fell away and she burst out laughing. The smile I'd hoped for on the deck, that carefree, unguarded laughter, made my knees weak.

There she was. The wall was gone and it was just her. Breathtaking. Real. A beautiful, magnetic woman, and I couldn't look away.

Presley pulled herself together, her musical laugh ended too soon, but the smile stayed. "That was . . . wow."

My heart dropped from my throat. *Wow.* Wow was good. "Wow, yourself, woman. I'll need a cold shower later."

She giggled. "Someday, years from now, I'm going to remember that time the gorgeous movie star kissed *the hell* out of me in my kitchen on my birthday."

And any time I thought of Montana, I'd remember the woman with eyes bluer than the big sky. Or maybe I'd just think of her, no trigger needed.

Maybe when it was time to go, there'd be no leaving her behind.

CHAPTER TWELVE

PRESLEY

I approached the corner to my street, my foot hovering over the brake as I held my breath and scanned Shaw's drive.

Phew. Empty.

It had been a week since my birthday, a week since Shaw had kissed me in my kitchen, and I'd been avoiding him like I avoided public places during flu season.

Last night, his SUV had been in the driveway when I'd come home from work. I'd parked and run inside like a bear was chasing me.

Four nights ago, he'd knocked on my door. I'd crept through my entryway like a ninja, barely breathing, and watched him through the peephole.

Suffice it to say, I wasn't dealing with his kiss very well.

In the moment, it had been everything I'd wanted. That kiss had been hot and consuming and so incredibly passionate. I'd laughed and smiled because that kiss had blown my mind.

It was the best kiss of my life.

Cue panic attack.

After Shaw had kissed me, he'd gone about the night like it had never happened. The pizza arrived. Shaw carried the conversation, talking about the movie shooting they'd done that day. He told me about his three younger sisters and their collective brood of girls, his nieces. He showed me pictures and I recognized Matine from my Google search—the woman I'd thought was his girlfriend. We ate on the deck with our beers and when we were done, he went home. Not once did he touch me again. He didn't kiss my cheek when I escorted him to the door. Shaw just waved and jogged down the steps.

Meanwhile, every moment that passed, I became more and more freaked out.

I loved that kiss. I wanted a kiss like that every day until I was in dentures. But Shaw was leaving. He wasn't boyfriend material. He was a goddamn movie star.

What exactly had I been thinking? I was supposed to be protecting my wounded heart, not tossing it to a man destined to smash it to smithereens with his *very* capable hands. What the hell was he even doing with me?

Shaw Valance.

He was *the* Shaw Valance.

And I was . . . me.

I was a random woman from Montana with enough baggage to sink a cargo ship. Except Shaw didn't make me feel random. He looked at me with those stunning eyes and I felt in the spotlight. I was in the room and I had his attention. Entirely.

He'd confided in me too, about the movie and the school bus. He couldn't know how I treasured that trust. Shaw had told me there were *feelings*, and damn if I didn't want them.

It had been so long since I'd felt that anticipation and excitement around another person. The anxiety that came with standing close, wondering if he'd touch me.

Had Jeremiah and I ever had that electricity? Or had I conjured a spark that hadn't really been there? Jeremiah had been a constant. He'd been easy and familiar.

Shaw had pushed me so far out of my comfort zone I didn't know how to act. Hence, my avoidance—something I couldn't afford.

The days were ticking by too fast. Shaw would be gone before long and I was wasting time being a chicken, hiding in my own home.

But here I was, doing it again tonight.

I went inside, shutting the door behind me, and flipped on the lights. I went into the kitchen and my gaze landed on the spot where he'd kissed me senseless.

My fingers drifted to my lips. It had been a week and I could still feel him there. He'd tasted so incredibly masculine. His spicy cologne, sandalwood and musk, had disappeared days ago, but I searched for it in the air all the same.

Sweet lord, that man could kiss. His costars were lucky, lucky women.

I shivered and opened the fridge, searching for my open bag of baby carrots. I took a handful and began crunching. Then I wandered into the living room and plopped down on the couch, taking my phone from my pocket.

There was nothing interesting on Instagram. I scrolled aimlessly through pictures and then pulled up the search bar. I entered Shaw's name, like I had every day this week, and looked at his latest post.

He was fishing.

When had he gone fishing? The post said yesterday. He

was holding a fish with a wide smile stretched across his face. Sunglasses shaded his eyes and his baseball cap was turned backward. #Montana.

More like #sexy.

And this man, with over a million likes on that photo, had kissed me. *Me.*

I swiped through his pictures for the thousandth time, chewing my carrots. None of Shaw's posts from the time he'd been here indicated anything about the movie. If anything, it looked like he was on a vacation. There were only five photos, three of his face, one of the mountains at sunset, and one he'd taken at the garage of the unfinished bike. It was from the day he'd shadowed Isaiah.

The bike was nearly done now. Dash had told me this afternoon I could call Shaw and arrange for him to pick it up next week. I'd avoided making that call too. Shaw was giving me time, he was being respectful—which I appreciated—but my time was running short. It was like an egg timer, winding down to zero. With every tick, you knew it was coming, but you'd still jump when it buzzed.

Shaw was getting close to zero, of that I was certain. Hunger. Excitement. Desire.

There was the threat of *more* in that kiss.

He wanted it.

So did I.

It was only a matter of time.

There was no way Shaw would finish this movie without seeing me again.

After Shaw had summarized *Dark Paradise* for me, I'd passed it along to the guys at the garage. We'd agreed that while the movie wouldn't paint anyone in a great light, it also wouldn't do much damage. Isaiah would ensure Genevieve stayed far away, not that she had a desire to go. It had taken her a while, but when she'd learned that her mother's portrayal would be mostly positive, tragic but positive, she'd accepted it.

Her strength astounded me.

She had no interest in seeing the movie, but curiosity was a funny thing. It made you do dumb things.

Like kiss a movie star in your kitchen, just to see if his lips were as delicious as they'd looked.

They were.

The doorbell rang and I leapt from the couch, my phone falling to the seat.

It was Shaw. I was sure of it.

The egg timer was dinging, and avoidance was no longer an option.

I walked to the door and hovered behind the lock.

"Presley." His voice carried through the door. "I know you're in there. I can hear you breathing."

I froze. *Damn it.*

"Not to sound like an arrogant asshole, but most women open the door if I'm on the other side."

"Smug bastard," I muttered. He was goading me, and I took the bait. I swung the door open and scowled. "Your ego is beyond comprehension. You should see a doctor about it."

He grinned. "But I got you to open the door."

"Whatever." I rolled my eyes and stood aside, gesturing for him to enter.

His deep chuckle filled the space between us as he strode toward the kitchen.

"Oh, no." I stopped him and pointed to the couch. "You're not allowed in my kitchen anymore."

"And you think a living room with this plush, soft couch

is better?" He sat down and threw an arm over the back like he owned *my* sofa.

This was the problem with movie stars. They commanded attention and we mere spectators were helpless to resist.

I stayed standing, making sure I wasn't in a place where he could back me into a counter or a wall or a bed. Near the coffee table, I had an escape route on both sides.

Shaw glanced at my phone, which had landed face up where I'd tossed it. Face up with *his* face on the screen. *Oh, hell.*

He smirked. "Anything good on Instagram today?"

I stomped to the couch and swiped up my phone, then retreated to my safe spot. "How was fishing?"

"Awesome," he answered. "You've been avoiding me."

"Yep." There was no use denying it.

"Care to tell me why?"

"Because you kissed me."

He sighed, the bravado dropping. "Was it a mistake? Because it didn't feel like a mistake, but if it was, I apologize."

"No." Maybe it wasn't smart, but definitely no mistake. "Don't apologize."

"I like talking to you. I don't want to lose that. I mean, I like kissing you too, but if I had to choose, I'd pick talking."

"Really?" I cocked my head and studied his expression. It was so sincere.

"Every day of the week."

I fought a smile. "I like talking too."

Discussion with Shaw was different than with most people, especially the guys at the garage. I was a good listener, I was always available in the office, so I was the one Emmett or Leo came to if they needed to unload. Dash too until he'd met Bryce. But no matter what, I always felt like the guys held back, just a little, because they were in protection mode.

Shaw didn't shelter me from his truths.

So I wouldn't hide away in mine.

"I'm confused," I admitted.

"Because of your ex?"

I scoffed. "No. He's a memory. Because you're you. You have millions of people who follow you. People across the world stalk your Instagram, desperate to feel some sort of connection with you. It's hard for me to wrap my head around the fame."

"It's not real."

"Isn't it? Because it seems like you're *really* famous."

"The fame is real, but that guy, the image, isn't. This is." He waved a hand up and down his torso. "I spend more time working out than I want. I hate running, but I go at least four times a week. My signature on autographs is nothing like the one I put on your contract at the garage. I have two smiles: camera and off camera."

"What's your camera smile?"

He flashed it at me. It was the one I'd found on Google. The one I'd seen on social media.

"What's your off-camera smile?"

He stood from the couch and crossed the living room, and my feet stuck to the carpet as he crowded my space.

I had these incredible escape routes, but did I use them? No, I stood there and let Shaw drop his confusing, magnificent lips on mine.

The kiss was short and soft. Not the best of my life—the kitchen kiss was—but this was the sweetest.

Then Shaw let me go, leaned back, and there it was. The most blinding, beautifully handsome smile in history.

"Oh, fuck," I groaned and dropped my forehead to his chest. I only stood tall enough to reach his sternum. "You are killing me here."

He chuckled. "You make me smile."

"Shut up." I pinched his side, making his laugh louder as I stood and soaked in that smile. "Maybe I'm confused because this seems too good to be true."

"It's not too good. If it was too good, you'd live in California and I wouldn't have to say goodbye in a month."

Reality came crashing down around us, sobering us both.

Shaw wasn't a *neighbor* neighbor. He was fleeting. Soon, we'd say goodbye, and the only connection I'd have to him would be on social media and in the movie theater. I'd share him with the world, limited to the camera smiles.

But I didn't have to share him tonight.

"Would you like to stay for dinner?" I asked.

"We could go out."

I scrunched up my nose. "What's with you and wanting to take me out to eat?"

"My parents always had this thing." He shrugged. "They'd go out to eat once a month, and only once a month. With one income and four kids, they couldn't afford restaurants often, so it was a big deal. Mom would spend the day at home, cleaning and doing laundry for all of us kids. Then she'd get dressed up so when Dad came home, she was ready to go. He'd change out of his uniform and put on slacks and a starched shirt. Then they'd go on a date. I don't date much, but I'd like very much to date you, at least once before I go."

Hadn't I told Genevieve weeks ago that I wanted to

date? Hadn't I wanted Shaw to be the man sitting across from me?

But I couldn't do it. That was a step with Shaw I wasn't ready to take. He'd put me in his spotlight, which was fine when we were alone. But in public? Not yet. And definitely not before I told the guys at the garage.

The entire town would know if I went out to dinner with Shaw and word traveled fast in Clifton Forge. Everyone would speculate that we were dating or that Shaw was my rebound or that I was his easy fling. It would probably be a combination of that and more.

I wanted to enjoy my time with Shaw on my own terms.

"No."

His frame slumped. "Huh. I thought that story would work. I mean, I just made it up but . . ."

"What?" I smacked his arm. "Seriously?"

He laughed. "I'm just kidding. The story is true."

"I don't know if I can believe you."

"Want to call my mom and ask?" He shoved his hand in his pocket.

"Put your phone away." I scowled. I was definitely not calling his mother. "Would you like to eat here instead?"

"Sure." He ran his thumb across my cheek, sending a rush of tingles to my toes. He didn't make me explain my refusal, and he didn't ask for a date again. Maybe he thought he'd have a better chance at another kiss if we were alone.

He would.

The two of us ended up on the deck after I'd whipped together some simple turkey sandwiches with potato chips. A no-fuss meal made special because I wasn't alone.

"How's shooting going?" I asked as we ate.

"Good." He nodded. "We're on schedule, which is

important. There've been some long days, but we're getting through. I just hope . . ."

"Hope what?"

He sighed. "I hope I'm doing a good job."

It was strange to see insecurity on his face. "You are."

"Maybe."

"You are. You're a good actor and I know this because I've watched every one of your movies at least twice. You're doing a good job."

The light in his eyes danced. "Twice?"

"Is this going to inflate your ego?"

"Most definitely."

"Well, that backfired," I muttered.

Shaw tipped his head back and laughed at the cloudless blue sky.

I hid my smile by chewing a chip.

His laughter was like music, and the more I heard it, the more I could make out different notes. Like his smile, it was different when it was real. It was huskier and came from deeper in his throat. It was raw and unrefined. It ignited a pulse between my legs that would stay long after our meal.

"Any word from your ex?" he asked.

"Nope." I'd blocked Jeremiah's number, so if he'd tried to call, I wouldn't know, and he hadn't tried to reach me at the garage.

The Warriors hadn't contacted Dash since his phone call to Tucker, and we all hoped he'd managed to smooth things over. But I wasn't blind to the risks. Leo had screwed up, and I suspected he spent his nights at The Betsy looking over his shoulder.

"You said something that day, the one where Leo was here after he kicked your fiancé's ass. You said, 'You're stirring up trouble we don't need.' What did you mean? I'm missing something here, aren't I?"

Yes, he was. "If I tell you something, can you promise me it won't go into your movie?"

Shaw frowned and shot me a glare. "I'm kind of pissed you'd even ask."

I cringed, replaying my words. "Sorry. That's not— I trust you."

"Do you?"

"Yes." I held his gaze. "I trust you."

But the Tin Kings and the Warriors had been our secret for so long, it felt strange to let the words loose.

"Jeremiah, my ex, joined a motorcycle club. The Arrowhead Warriors. Back when Draven and Dash were still running the Tin Kings, they were rivals."

"I've heard of them. In the paper, Bryce speculated that one of their members was the one to steal Draven's hunting knife and kill Amina."

It had actually been Marcus, disguised as a Warrior because he'd known about the rivalry. But he'd been smart. Everyone had immediately suspected the Warriors given their history.

"Jeremiah, in his infinite stupidity, decided he wanted to join their club. He moved to Ashton years ago, even though we stayed together. That was my infinite stupidity."

"You're not stupid," Shaw scolded.

"No, I am. When it came to Jeremiah, there's a lot of stupid there." I waved off another one of his frowns. "Anyway, Jeremiah is a Warrior. Leo was a King."

"Enemies."

"Exactly." I nodded. "Jeremiah deserved what he got, but when you mess with one member of the club, you mess with them all. We don't need trouble with the Warriors. I don't want to see my friends get hurt."

"Hmm." Shaw nodded. "Your ex sounds like a fucking asshole."

I grinned. "You're not wrong."

"You can tell me to mind my own business, but why'd you stay with him?"

I'd been asking myself that question for weeks. "I don't know. Honestly, I don't know. We have a long history, and I think that clouded my feelings toward him. But it's done now and that's all that matters."

"You're sure?" Shaw sat up, swinging his long legs between our chairs. He leaned his elbows on his knees so he was close. "I thought maybe the reason you were avoiding me was because you need some time to get over the ex."

"No." I shook my head. "It's done."

The heartbreak, the humiliation, was fading too. Turns out all I'd needed was some time to see Jeremiah's betrayal on our wedding day as a gift. He'd given me my freedom.

I wasn't going to say thank you, but I wasn't angry anymore.

"Does that mean I can keep kissing you?"

I sat up and mirrored his pose, one knee threaded between his. "You're here for a month?"

"If shooting goes as planned."

"Then how about I make you a deal? I'll trade you that dinner out you so desperately want for a kiss every day for a month."

"No-brainer." He held out his hand. "Shake on it."

My hand slipped in his.

Then he smiled, the real one, and took today's kiss.

CHAPTER THIRTEEN

SHAW

P resley was hiding our friendship—relationship—from the world.

She hadn't offered up much explanation as to why, but I understood. She'd been the talk of the town once this summer after the wedding, and she didn't need to tie herself to me publicly and go through it all again.

I'd leave Clifton Forge in a few weeks and she'd be here to deal with the gossip. If Presley needed me to be her dirty little secret, I'd play that game. The alternative was not having her at all, which wasn't an option.

The nights I wasn't shooting, I went over to her house. I'd let her feed me dinner, then kiss her senseless. Before things escalated past heavy petting, I'd excuse myself and go home for a cold shower.

It was easy behind her closed door. There was no pretending.

But walking into the garage today and not pulling her into my arms was going to take some major restraint. Maybe, if no one was watching, I'd be able to steal a taste of her lips.

As I approached the garage, my hopes were dashed. My usual parking space was taken. Every space was taken. I had to park on the street, and when I walked inside, I was met with chaos. Not a seat was empty. Was everyone in Clifton Forge getting their oil changed today?

Presley's fingers flew over the keyboard as she sandwiched the phone between her shoulder and her ear. "Great. See you at three."

She spotted me standing by the door and for a brief moment smiled. Then she either remembered I was her dirty little secret or she remembered she had a million other things to do—I preferred the latter—and she shot out of her chair, scrambling for a piece of paper on the printer and a set of keys hanging on a pegboard. She breezed past me, flying through the door to the shop as the customers waiting drank coffee, chatted and buried their noses in phones.

Since all the chairs were full and I'd signed that insurance waiver, I headed into the shop.

I found Isaiah standing beside a tool bench, chugging from a canteen of water. "Hey."

"Hey," he said, wiping his mouth dry. "Here to pick up the bike?"

"Yep." I smiled, clapping my hands together. "Can't wait to see it."

"Come on." He grinned and jerked his chin for me to follow him through the shop.

Two mechanics I hadn't met were each busy with a car. Emmett slammed the hood on a third and nodded his hello. Presley was nowhere to be seen.

How had she disappeared? I glanced around, searching, and finally spotted her rushing inside from the parking lot.

She threw a pair of keys to Emmett and went right back for the office, not sparing me a glance.

That stung.

When she was in the room, she had my attention, but that didn't seem to be the case with her. She had a surprisingly easy time ignoring me. It was probably good for my ego, but . . . *damn, woman.*

"Haven't seen you around much," Isaiah said, leading me toward the far corner.

"Yeah, I've been busy." I'd only shadowed him the one day. "I, uh . . . thanks for letting me watch you work on the bike that day. I realized after that"—because Presley had made me realize—"it might be tough to have me lurking over your shoulder. I didn't want to get in the way or cause any hard feelings."

Isaiah slowed, eyeing me carefully. "Appreciated."

"So this is it?" I waved my hand at the machine covered with a tarp.

"Yep." He jerked off the cover, revealing a gleaming black motorcycle underneath. My fingers skimmed the gas tank. The machine was truly a work of art. I bent down to get a closer look. The tank was painted a gleaming black, but hidden in the shiny surface were matte-black flames. "Wow."

"Let's take it outside." Isaiah lifted the kickstand with his toe and put both hands on the handlebars, steering it through the open bay door and into the sunlight.

If it had been glorious inside, outside it was magnificent. The bike was meant for the road. It was meant to be in a movie. "I-I'm . . . speechless. Thank you."

"Better take it for a ride." Isaiah nodded to the seat.

"Hell, yeah." I took the bike from him, straddling the seat. I hadn't been on a motorcycle in years, but once upon a time, I'd ridden regularly to and from the police station. I started the engine, the rumble sending a wave of excitement through my veins.

I slid my sunglasses over my eyes, grinned at Isaiah and rode to the street. I glanced at the office as I passed and found Presley standing on the sidewalk outside, her hand shading her eyes, but there was a smile on her face.

So maybe she wasn't ignoring me completely.

I smiled back.

Then I raced away, opening up the machine as I sped down the streets. It was the best ninety grand I'd spent in years.

We'd be using it for two movie scenes, but then it was coming home with me. This was *my* bike.

The road beneath the wheels was smooth and the motorcycle rode like a dream. I wanted nothing more than to take it out for hours, but I had to be on location to shoot today. So after thirty minutes, I headed to the garage, my hair wind-blown and my smile firmly fixed in place.

And tonight, no matter what she thought about being seen with me, I was taking Presley for a ride. I wanted to feel her toned thighs pressed against my hips. I wanted to feel her chest against my back and the whisper of her breath on my neck.

"So?" Isaiah asked as I parked it in the lot. Emmett came out to join us.

"That's one hell of a bike." I held my hand out to shake his. "Thanks. You did an incredible job."

"Tell your friends in Hollywood." Emmett chuckled. "We'd do projects like this one every day of the year."

"Done." I'd gladly send them business. "Mind if I leave it

here? I drove over but I can have someone come with me later today to pick it up."

"We can get it to your house," Isaiah offered. "No problem."

"Are you sure?" Because that would mean I wouldn't need to bring Shelly or another crew member to the garage. There was a clear boundary between the film crew and the garage, and I'd like to keep it that way.

"We'll drop it off at lunch." Emmett nodded. "We'll leave the keys with Presley."

"Sounds good." They both turned to leave, but I stopped them. "Can I ask you a question?"

Isaiah turned and nodded.

Emmett did the same, crossing his tattooed arms over his chest. "What's up?"

"Presley's ex. Is he going to be a problem?"

The two of them shared a look.

"What's it to you?" Emmett's eyes narrowed.

"I was a cop. I want to know if she's in danger."

"No," Emmett answered at the same time Isaiah said, "Maybe."

My spine stiffened. "Maybe?"

"Her ex is an epic fuckup." Isaiah ignored Emmett's glare. "Will he hurt her? Probably not. But she needs to stay away from him. He's tied up with a nasty crowd. If you see him around, you need to tell us."

"I'm not scared of the ex." Or his motorcycle club.

"There are things you don't know," Emmett said. "No matter what Presley told you, there are things you both don't know, so if you see him around, don't be the hero. Make the call."

179

Something about his tone, the sincerity and the protectiveness in his voice, made me nod. "All right."

Until my time in Clifton Forge was up, I'd do my best to keep a watch on Presley. While I was here, she was mine.

With one last wave, I walked across the parking lot toward the street. Through the office's window, I saw Presley on the phone. I was tempted to go in there while she was distracted and kiss her cheek, but she'd fillet me for that one.

So I'd wait, shove the urge deep, until I could claim that kiss tonight on my new bike.

———

"THIS IS QUITE THE VIEW," she breathed over my shoulder, her eyes aimed into the distance.

"Montana has some stellar sunsets."

She hummed her agreement, pressing her cheek into my shoulder.

The ride along the highway with Presley at my back had been better than I could have imagined. Having her pressed against me, her small body holding tight to mine, was both bliss and agony.

Even after we'd found a secluded place to pull over and watch the sun set, she hadn't climbed off. She was still there, her arms around my waist and her cheek against my shoulder.

My hand was on her leg and my thumb circled her knee. Every lap, I found it harder and harder to breathe. Every stroke of my finger against her jeans made me wish I could rip the loose denim from her legs and find out what she looked like wearing nothing at all.

I'd need two cold showers by the time we made it home.

My day had been spent on set, rehearsing tomorrow's shoot and doing a retake of a small scene Cam hadn't been happy with. We had some days set aside for retakes, but no one wanted to use them. They caused stress and levels were already on the rise now that we were in the final half of our shooting schedule. Thankfully, Cam was happy with the retake and I'd managed to sneak out before being pulled into the tent for the cast and crew dinner.

Shelly was already on my case for skipping out each night. She wanted me there to help support morale.

Sorry, Shelly. Presley ranked higher than morale.

My bike had been in the driveway when I'd arrived at my house. Presley's Jeep had been parked in its normal space. I'd dumped my backpack at home, then rushed to her door, taking her hand and dragging her outside the moment she'd answered my knock.

I'd put her on the bike and shot out of the driveway, her yelp of delight ringing in my ears. My plan had been to stick to the roads in town, ride for thirty minutes, but she'd pointed at the sign to the highway and away we'd gone.

Fifty miles away from town, we'd crested the top of a hill with a wide, gravel pullout. I'd parked us here, the kickstand down, and we'd watched the sun make its way toward the horizon.

Her hair was blown away from her face, like mine. Next time, I'd put her in a helmet, but for today, neither of us seemed to care about safety. Tonight was about adventure and the wind and the open road.

On nights like this, I wasn't sure why anyone would want to live in the city. The plains spread below us and the mountains rose in the distance. Above us, a few stars glinted in the vast, sapphire sky. We had at least an hour of light left, but as the evening turned to twilight, the magic of Montana found its way into my heart.

Or maybe it was Presley.

"I was dying to kiss you today," I whispered into her ear. "I almost did."

Her eyes dropped. "Shaw, we—"

"I know. I'm temporary. You don't need the gossip. I get it, but that doesn't make me want to kiss you any less."

"If people knew, if the guys knew, it would only make it more complicated."

I suspected the guys at the garage already knew, but I wasn't going to burst her bubble. "I'll keep this quiet, but when we're alone, you're all mine."

She grinned and let me go to swing her leg off the bike. I expected her to walk to the edge of the bluff and take in the sunset from her feet. Instead, she turned her back to the view and straddled my lap, looping her arms around my neck. "We're alone now."

My mouth fused to hers, and I kissed her like I'd wanted to kiss her all day. Our tongues collided in a messy, wet duel that we both won. As the sun continued to fade, my need for Presley surged to a fire even a dozen showers wouldn't cool.

"We gotta slow down." I broke away from her mouth, panting. "Otherwise I won't be able to stop."

Her hands came to my face. "What if I don't want you to stop?"

My jaw dropped. My cock, already hard, wept. *Please let me have heard her right.* "What are you saying?"

"We only have a month." She looked up at me with those blue eyes, matched by the sky above our heads. "You'll leave and we'll both let go. But for now, when we're alone . . ."

"Let's make the most of it."

"Yeah." She smiled and dipped her lips to the underside of my jaw, peppering it with kisses.

I growled, my cock begging to be let out of my zipper. I hauled her to me, holding tight, and I lifted us both off the machine.

I would have liked nothing more than to fuck her on the bike, but it was brand new and this was going to be hard and fast. I didn't trust my balance that much. There was a picnic table in the distance, shielded partially from the road by two cottonwood trees.

Her legs wrapped around me as I walked us to the table, her mouth sucking and licking at the skin on my neck.

I set her on the edge of the table and her hands went right for my jeans. I tugged on the strap of her belt, loosening its hold so her jeans draped over her hips, exposing creamy skin and the black lace of her panties.

"Condom's in my pocket."

She raised an eyebrow, digging into my pocket. "Expecting this?"

"Hoping for this." I chuckled, dropping my lips to hers. "So damn hopeful."

She smiled against my lips as she retrieved the condom.

I put a hand in the center of her sternum, checking over my shoulder for any oncoming traffic. The road was empty—we hadn't seen a car since we'd parked—and the trees shielded us along with the fading light.

I flicked open the button on her jeans, dragging down the zipper, though I could have slid them free. Presley arched her hips, helping to shimmy them toward her knees. She toed off her shoes and those jeans pooled on the gravel by my boots. My fingers caressed her skin, dragging trails along the flesh of her legs.

I started at the outside, then worked my way in, first to her knee, then up an inch. Down an inch, up two. Until my fingers were barely centimeters from the gusset of her panties.

I dragged my thumb up her covered slit.

"Shaw," she moaned, squirming under my touch. "Quit playing around."

"I like to play."

Presley lifted up on one elbow, her chest heaving. "Play later. When we're behind a closed door. Right now, I need you inside."

I loved the desperation in her voice. It shredded my control and I leaned over her, dragging my nose along the lace panties, inhaling her scent. I placed kisses up her belly, over the top of the white Clifton Forge Garage tee that molded to her flat stomach and firm breasts. I found her lips with mine and kissed her as I undid the zipper of my jeans and set myself free.

Taking the condom from her hand, I rolled it over my shaft and slipped my tongue out of her mouth. I leaned back, and with one yank, I shredded those lace panties.

Presley laughed to the sky. "I always wanted to know what that felt like. A man ripping off my panties."

"Yeah?" I leaned in to whisper against her lips. "What other fantasies do you have?"

"Keep going and maybe you'll find out."

I chuckled, savoring every shiver and hitch in her breath as I let the stubble on my jaw scrape against her chin and the cool breeze wash over the wet I left on her lips.

I reached between us, gripping my cock to drag it through her entrance. She moaned, the sound loud and long because there wasn't a damn soul out here to object. Presley could scream at the top of her lungs and only the birds would hear.

I'd love to hear her shout my name.

I inched forward, stretching her. It took every ounce of control not to thrust in deep and feel the pulse of her slick, wet heat, but I worked us together with patience.

She shifted each time I went deeper, her breath gasping as she adjusted to my size. "You're big."

And she was tiny. I'd known this was going to be a snug fit, and I gritted my teeth to keep from exploding. I wanted to make this good for her, for both of us.

My fingers splayed between us, holding her wet folds apart as I rocked us together, until finally, I was seated as deep as she'd take me. Presley's eyes were squeezed shut.

"Good?"

She bit her lip. "Move."

Fuck, yeah. I took her knees, holding up her legs as I withdrew. She hissed a breath when I drove forward, grinding the root of my cock against her clit. Her hands gripped the table.

"You feel fucking incredible, baby."

"So do you." One hand reached for mine.

I took it, lacing our fingers together, and thrust in again. My jeans fell farther down.

God, I wanted her naked. I wanted that T-shirt gone and Presley spread out beneath me so I could watch her rosy nipples. But we were scratching an itch. We were letting loose and fucking under the sky.

Tomorrow, or maybe tonight, we'd take the time to explore.

My pace picked up and I slammed into her time and time again until she writhed on the table. White spots broke in my vision as I took her hard, loving the clench of her around me.

"Shaw." She gave me a warning gasp.

I planted deep, hard, and dropped her leg. I found the bundle of nerves between us and stroked, three times before she shattered, her back arching off the table and her mewls fading into the coming night.

When her cries subsided, I began stroking again, this time in short, hard thrusts. It didn't take long for the build, the pressure to consume me, and I let go with Presley's hand still in mine and her scent floating on the night air.

I collapsed on top of her when we were both spent. "Damn."

The fingers of her free hand dove into my hair. "Damn."

I didn't want to let her go, but I did. I stood, sliding out and picking up her jeans, brushing off the dirt. As she stepped into them, I yanked up my own jeans and took care of the condom, tossing it in a trash bin a few feet from the table as Presley cinched her belt.

We didn't speak as we made our way to the bike. I climbed on first, steadying the bike as she straddled me from behind.

Then she sighed, wrapping herself to my frame and holding on tight.

"See?" I kissed her temple. "I don't grunt."

The sound of her laughter rose above the roar of the engine as we rode home.

CHAPTER FOURTEEN

SHAW

I shook Luke Rosen's hand. "Good to see you."
"Thanks for the beer. You change your mind about ditching work and going fishing again, give me a call."
"Wish I could."

Luke was taking a vacation, his first since becoming chief of police, and spending two weeks on the river. He'd camp out at night and sleep under the stars. No cell phones. No showers. No schedules.

The trip sounded like bliss, but there was no way I could leave. We were in the thick of shooting and every available second I wanted to spend with Presley.

Maybe I'd come back one day. Luke and I had bonded over police talk and beers at The Betsy, a seedy bar that reminded me of a spot me and some of the SWAT guys in LA used to hang out in. He'd also taken me fishing one afternoon, giving me a taste of something to look forward to.

"Rain check?" I asked.

He nodded. "I'll hold you to it."

"If you're ever in LA, let me know."

"I'll do that." He slid on his sunglasses, then turned for his truck, waving as he rounded the hood. "Take care, Shaw."

"You too." I waved back, then walked to the Escalade on the other end of the gravel parking lot.

My phone had five texts when I took it out of my pocket. All were from Shelly. She was in full-fledged triage mode, trying to figure out how to rework the filming schedule to account for our recent delays.

We'd been doing so well, staying on track. Dacia had left long ago, which had been a blessing for the on-set vibe. The cast and crew were getting along. Cameron had been happy. Shelly had been constant smiles.

Then everything had gone to shit this week.

It had started with a cold traveling around the crew. Cameron had caught it first, constantly coughing and sneezing. He'd passed it along to the cameramen next. From there the virus had raged.

People were miserable. Every scene took twice as long to shoot because Cameron was so unhappy. Nothing was good enough. The script morphed to accommodate the changes, and I held my tongue, trying not to make it worse.

These types of things happened on all movies, things evolved as you shot, but this was becoming extreme. I'd rehearse one set of lines in the morning and the afternoon's delivery would be entirely new.

The only thing I had going for me was that I wasn't sick, because I was staying the hell away from the infected motel. I ate my meals separately and went home at night. Well, not home. I went to Presley's house, my destination as I pulled away from The Betsy.

Shelly had finally convinced Cameron that we should

delay today's scenes and let everyone take a day to recuperate. He'd reluctantly agreed.

I'd spent some time today catching up on emails and phone calls. I'd spent half an hour on the phone with my mom, then checked in with each of my sisters. They'd updated me on all aspects of their lives and had made sure to tell me about Dad.

I didn't talk to Dad. I wasn't going to talk to Dad.

But my mom and sisters refused to let that rift grow. They fed me information about him, and I was sure they did the same in reverse.

After family calls, I'd talked at length with my agent and manager, reminding them no matter how hard they pushed for this or that audition, once *Dark Paradise* was over, I was taking a break.

They still pushed.

By early afternoon, I'd been done with the phone and texted Luke to see if he wanted to meet up for a beer. He'd been off work already, packing for his trip and getting his boat ready, so we'd spent a couple hours bullshitting at The Betsy while I watched the clock, waiting for five to roll around, when Presley would be on her way home.

The past week with her had been one of the best. Time was passing too quickly and there hadn't been enough hours in the day to spend with her. The ones we did have, we'd made the most of. The second I was in her house and the door was locked, her clothes were off.

We'd spent a week mauling one another. Inhibitions went out the door as we went after one another with abandon, clawing and biting until we were both breathless and passed out in her bed.

Earlier this week, I'd managed to make it in and out of a

189

gas station without being recognized to replenish my stash of condoms. Thank God for baseball hats and sunglasses. I had one in my pocket, waiting for the moment Presley opened the door, took a fistful of my shirt and dragged me inside.

I grinned as I drove across town.

Presley Marks was an explosion.

She'd destroyed the plans I'd had for Montana. My focus hadn't been on the movie like it should have been. Besides one afternoon fishing with Luke, I hadn't done any exploring of the area. My attention had been on my petite neighbor, as it would be for the next two and a half weeks, before I was scheduled to leave Clifton Forge.

None of us wanted the movie to run past schedule. That cost money and frustrated crew members who were itching to get home to their families. But if it did, I wasn't going to be broken up about it. I'd take the extra time with Presley.

Could I delay my commitments for October? I should have asked Laurelin when we'd spoken earlier. There were some scenes we had to shoot on location, but after they were done, could I come back to Montana? I was supposed to attend a children's charity fundraiser at Halloween and had some press engagements to promote an upcoming movie—one I'd shot eighteen months ago. If I asked Laurelin, she'd grumble and tell me to get my ass back to California.

My phone rang and I chuckled at the name on the screen. "Speak of the devil. I was just thinking about you."

"Shit," she muttered. "You already heard."

My grin dropped. "Heard what?"

"Oh, uh . . . you haven't heard. So, there's a picture floating around."

"What kind of picture?" My stomach dropped. There were a lot of pictures of me out there. Ones taken by the paparazzi. Ones taken by fans. I did my best to always wear a smile when I was in public because with today's technology, no place was safe.

"It's of you and a woman. Shaw, you're supposed to tell me when you start seeing someone, remember? Do you not recall what happened with Dacia?"

"I'm not seeing anyone," I lied. There was no way she could know about Presley. "What's the picture?"

"*TMZ* just bought it and posted it on their website."

"Details, Laurelin. What's the picture?" My mind instantly jumped to the worst. To another Dacia incident. Who was the last woman I'd been with? A travel agent in New York. We'd met at a hotel bar and hooked up that night. But that had been, what, nine months ago?

Not that the tabloids cared about the time stamp.

"It's nothing bad. It's you and a woman on a motorcycle, but *TMZ* is speculating you're dating someone."

The air rushed out of my lungs. *Fuck. Fuck. Fuck.* Presley was going to lose her shit. "More. What else?"

"I don't know what else. She has short blond hair. You're at a stoplight or something. You're looking back at her and smiling. She's got her arms wrapped around you."

"Damn it." How many stoplights had we hit on the way out of town when I'd taken Presley for a ride? One. Two, maybe? Just my luck a tourist or local with a cell phone had snapped that photo at the right moment.

If the paparazzi started digging into Presley, she'd be a target. That was the last thing she needed just weeks before we were all out of her life. "Bury it, Laurelin. Buy it from them. I don't care how much it costs, but get it down."

"I already did, and you got lucky, it was cheap. I told

them that she was your assistant on set, and that you were just testing out a motorcycle you were using for a film."

"Good." There was enough truth to that statement that if they started asking about the movie, they'd find out we had a whole crew in Montana, if they didn't know already. "What else?"

"Nothing else. You know how these things go. Some photos go viral. Others die. Don't be seen with her again and you should be fine."

Repeats of the same woman were when the paparazzi began to drool.

"Send me the picture," I ordered.

"It's in your inbox. Who is she, Shaw?"

"A woman I met here."

"No shit." I could practically hear her eyes roll. "Is this something I'm going to need to explain later? Or will I need to get an NDA sent over?"

"No and no." I sure as hell wasn't having Presley sign an NDA. My secrets were safe with her and I didn't need a piece of paper to prove it. Besides, after I left Montana, there'd be nothing to explain.

"Are you sure? Because—"

"I'm sure."

"Fine," she muttered. "I'll let you know if something else comes up."

"Okay. And, Laurelin? Thanks."

"Just doing my job," she said and ended the call.

Fortunately for me, she did it well.

Laurelin had assumed the role of my manager and didn't stifle her opinions. For the most part, I listened and took her advice. She was peeved with my decision to step away for a while. Laurelin feared I'd lose my position at the top.

But it was time for a damn break, and the top was a lonely place to be.

It was hard to trust that people didn't befriend you because of your fame. Most had ulterior motives, wanting to use me in hopes of springboarding their own success—which was why being around Presley was so refreshing.

Hell, she didn't even want to be seen with me.

I pulled into my driveway, Presley's Jeep already in hers. Opening my email, I took a look at the photo and grumbled. But it wasn't horrible. We could deal with this.

The zoom was too far and the shot partially out of focus. Presley was in profile, and her face wasn't the primary target. Mine was.

We'd gotten lucky.

Shit. That picnic table stunt had been a stupid-as-fuck move. If a photo of that had been taken and leaked, Presley would have cut my balls off. I would have handed her the knife for being so careless.

I got out and jogged over to her house, checking over my shoulder to make sure no one was around. Besides me, the street was quiet. The next block over, some kids were playing outside.

At my knock, Presley swung the door open, greeting me with a sly smile. "Hey."

"Hey." I stepped inside, closing the door behind me. Then I cut right to it. "I've got something to tell you, and you're not going to like it."

Her smile dropped. "What?"

"Someone took a picture of us on the bike last week. Probably someone trying to make a few bucks and sell it to the tabloids."

"What?" Her eyes went wide. "What does that mean?

Do they know who I am? That we're"—she fluttered her hand between us—"together?"

"My manager told them you were my assistant on location and that we were testing a bike for a movie. That's all."

"That's all?" She wrung her hands in front of her chest and walked to the living room. "I don't—I'm not sure what to do."

"There's nothing to do." I followed her into the room. I put my hands on her shoulders, turning her to me. "Sorry. I know it sucks, but the best thing to do is ignore it."

"Ignore it?" She looked at me like I'd grown another head.

"Yeah. Ignore it. The photo will go away. As long as we aren't photographed together again, it will disappear. They don't know your name, so it's not like they can track you down." *Yet.*

Presley's eyes darted to the windows that overlooked the front yard. She raced toward them, dragging the blinds down.

I chuckled, but when she shot a glare over her shoulder, I pulled my lips together.

"I don't want to be in pictures." She stomped to the kitchen and opened the fridge, emerging with a fistful of carrots. She snapped one between her teeth, chewing with fury.

"It's no big deal," I promised. "It will go away as soon as I go away. But if you're worried, we can end this now."

I held my breath, waiting and watching her think it over. The last thing I wanted was for this to end. I wasn't ready to give her up, that time would come soon enough. But I wouldn't put her in a bad position. I wouldn't force her to risk exposure to the vipers of Hollywood.

Presley's chewing slowed, then it stopped and she swallowed. "No."

Sweet relief washed over my body. I smiled and stepped closer, framing her face in my hands. "I love it when you tell me no."

She lifted another carrot to her mouth, but I caught her wrist before it could travel past her lips.

And I put my own mouth there instead.

————

"WHAT DID YOU DO TODAY?" Presley asked. She was draped over my side.

"Worked this morning. Had a beer with Luke. Waited for you."

"Another beer with Luke. Do I need to be jealous of this bromance? We are exclusive, you know. I didn't mention that, but I expect you to be completely mine while you're here."

I grinned, tracing a circle on her bare shoulder. "I mean, I like you. But Luke? He's something special."

"He is dreamy." She licked her lips. "He's friends with Emmett. Sometimes I see him around town. He fills out that uniform shirt so well and the jeans he wears are—"

I pinched her ribs.

"Ahh!" she cried, laughing and swatting my hand away. "Kidding. I don't even know the guy."

"That's right you're kidding." I laced my fingers with hers. "They'll be no talk of dreamy cops unless it's about the dreamy ex-cop currently naked in your bed."

She propped her chin up on my chest. "Will you tell me

about why you stopped being a cop? You said it was a different movie."

"It's a mess." I blew out a long breath, brushing a lock of hair that had fallen over her eye away. I loved her hair, that it was unique and stylish and different, but I didn't like that at times, it covered her eyes. I wanted to soak in the blue for as long as I had it.

"You don't have to tell me." She pressed a kiss to the sprinkling of hair on a pec. Then another.

If she kept it up, we wouldn't be talking about anything.

We'd stumbled from the kitchen to her bedroom earlier, leaving a trail of baby carrots in our wake. Then we'd spent a few hours in her bed, safe behind her walls and covered windows where I could do whatever she'd let me do to her lithe body without the risk of anyone noticing.

Fuck, she was flexible. Presley could do this thing with her legs where one was wrapped over my shoulder and the other hooked around my knee. We'd been experimenting with positions and though I was twice her size, she had this way of wrapping herself around me.

Presley was the best lover I'd had in my life, bar none.

"I'll tell you," I said, shifting us both to our sides. My stamina was at its peak, but she'd worn me out and I needed a minute to replenish my reserves. Then she could kiss me wherever she wanted.

She propped up on an elbow, her beautiful eyes locked onto mine. Presley listened so intently. She gave me her entire focus, something that seemed rare these days when there was always a screen to steal someone's attention.

"I grew up in California," I told her. For this story, it was important to start at the beginning. "My dad was a cop, and I always wanted to be a cop. It was simple. Every Halloween, I dressed up as a cop. Every time a teacher asked me to draw a picture of a hero, it was a cop."

Actually, it had been my dad. I'd wanted to be my dad.

It stung, thinking of those days and the blind adoration I'd had for my father. I had so many good memories to recall, but when I saw them now, they were covered in a gray film. They'd been clouded by his actions.

"I'm going to tell you something you're not going to like," I said.

"You keep saying that to me today." Her body tensed beside mine. "What?"

I gave her a sad smile, silently pleading for her to understand. "I know you hate him, and I get why. But a part of me needs to believe that once, Marcus Wagner was a good man. That he wasn't always a bad cop."

Presley was motionless, not moving even to blink. She kept her gaze on me as my confession stole into the room.

I wouldn't blame her if she got mad. From her pillow, I would have been angry too.

But slowly the tension eased from her body and understanding seeped into her expression. "Your dad. Something happened."

"Yeah." I nodded, so damn grateful she'd listened and heard the vulnerability in my words. "I haven't talked about it, at all really. Just with my mom. She's the only other person in my family who knows, not even my sisters."

"You don't have to tell me."

"I want to." I touched her jaw, needing the softness of her skin before I continued. Her face, that skin, it grounded me. "Dad was a cop his entire life. A good cop. He worked hard and was honest. Then I don't know what happened. Money got tight. All three of my sisters were in college or just graduating. Dad . . . I don't know what he was thinking."

To this day, I didn't understand. How had a man with such character, such integrity, made such a catastrophic, moral mistake because of money? If he had talked to us, we would have pitched in. My sisters would have taken out loans. I would have thrown my salary into the mix. But Dad had shouldered the burden alone.

The one and only time I'd tried talking to him about it had ended in disaster. I'd been too angry to listen, and I hadn't spoken to him since. The disappointment was too crushing, because he'd been my hero.

"Dad was collecting evidence at a drug bust. I've been to a few of them before and it's insane. Usually, there are drugs everywhere. Sometimes, there's money too. Mostly it's left out in the open, but I've found money stashed in toilets and kitty litter bins and dryers. Dad found a roll in a little kid's shoe. Instead of cataloging it for evidence, he put it in his pocket."

Presley gasped. "And he got caught?"

"His captain was going through Dad's report a week later and there were some inconsistencies. Mistakes Dad never made, so he called Dad in to ask about it. Dad said it didn't take more than one questioning look before he confessed to the whole thing. He returned the money, every dollar."

"W-wow," Presley stuttered.

"Yeah, wow. He did the right thing, owning it and not spending that money. But he shouldn't have taken it in the first place. He crossed the line."

"Did he get fired?"

"Pretty much. Technically, he retired early. His captain made him turn in his badge, but he got to keep his pension."

"Did he tell you about it? How did you find out?"

"He told me." I nodded. "He invited me over the day he admitted it to his captain and laid it all out for me and Mom. It was six months after the school bus."

"And that's why you quit."

"Yeah." I turned on my back to stare at the ceiling. "I was the new guy on a SWAT team and still in training. I left Mom and Dad's house and drove home. I was supposed to work a night shift, but I called in sick. I don't know why but I couldn't go to work."

Maybe I feared that I'd become my father. Up until that point in my life, I'd followed in his footsteps.

"There was an agent who'd been calling me since the bus. It wasn't the same agent I have now. I fired him because he was a ruthless bastard and hired Ginny instead. But I had this guy's number. He kept calling me once a month to see if I was interested. He said he could get me in with a well-known casting director. He had a hookup. I'd been dodging him but had never outright told him no. That night, I went home and called him. I just . . . I couldn't be a cop anymore. I was too heartbroken. I didn't want that to happen to me."

"It wouldn't have."

"How do you know?" I turned on my cheek to look at her. "Cops don't make a lot of money. You have kids. You get strapped. I see my buddies struggling with it all the time. They have nothing extra to go around if their wives don't work. And I had this once-in-a-lifetime chance, so I took it."

I'd turned into Dad after all.

I'd given up my righteous career for money.

"I'm ashamed of it."

"Why? People change jobs all the time, Shaw. They do

what they need to do. You're not a sellout. You just changed."

She made it sound so simple. So innocent. Would I have had this internal battle if I'd become a banker or a mailman or a football coach?

"Maybe you're right."

"Of course, I'm right." She grinned. "Why didn't your parents tell your sisters?"

"Because I asked them not to. Dad wasn't just my hero; he was theirs too."

"And you didn't want to take that from them."

I nodded. "By some miracle, no one found out. A lot of people have dug into my past, but it's stayed quiet."

Hopefully by now, there was nothing to find. If it surfaced, it would destroy my father.

It would destroy my family.

"I'm sorry." Presley put her hand on my heart.

I covered it with mine. "Me too."

She lifted up and pressed her bare chest into my side. Her hands dove into the strands of hair above my temple and her lips hovered an inch from mine. "Thank you for telling me."

"Thanks for listening." There was a lightness in my chest, one that hadn't been there in a long time. I flipped us both, pressing my growing arousal into Presley's leg. "Now that's enough talk."

She smiled. "Agreed."

CHAPTER FIFTEEN

PRESLEY

"I'm going to miss this," Shaw said, his eyes glued to the yard. "I forgot how nice it is to do nothing and relax."

His profile was toward me, highlighting the straight line of his nose and his square jaw. I'd forgotten how it felt to *like* someone. How it felt to crave someone.

I would miss this too.

We'd started this as a fling but it had morphed into an eye-opening experience. Shaw had reminded me how it felt to be touched. How it felt to be kissed. He'd reminded me how it felt to race home so excited to see another person that you stood beside the door, bouncing on both feet, practically coming out of your skin until finally they arrived and it was the best part of your day.

Saying goodbye this week would be brutal, but I was grateful he'd come into my life. Shaw had shown me what I'd missed with Jeremiah, what our relationship had lacked— passion, trust, friendship. He'd shown me what to expect down the road when I was ready to date again.

It would take time.

Shaw had stolen a part of my heart and I was planning on holding on to the piece I'd stolen from his, just for a while.

Since he'd told me about his father, our conversations hadn't been heavy. We'd spent most of our time hidden away in my house, mostly in my bedroom. He'd been so busy that our hours together had been limited. Tonight was the first time he'd come over before midnight.

So we were on the deck, drinking a beer and doing nothing. We were simply together.

Relaxing.

That was not an easy concept for me to grasp or practice.

I'd spent my childhood walking on eggshells. Even after I'd moved to Clifton Forge, it had taken me a long time to calm my constant nerves. They hadn't truly settled until I'd lived alone. With my roommate—now landlord—I'd been on my best behavior, making sure I'd tidied up at every turn.

After she'd moved out, I'd kept it up because that was how I'd lived my life. Then one day, I'd left a pan in the sink to soak. Normally, I would have scrubbed it clean, no matter how long it took. Instead, I'd left it and gone to work.

I'd nearly had a panic attack that morning and had come home at lunch to clean it up, but it was the first time I'd let go a little.

That was harder to do with another person. What if they saw my flaws? What if I messed up and was punished or hated? Maybe the reason Jeremiah and I hadn't worked was because I'd been too focused on perfection.

Or maybe he was just an asshole.

Asshole. Definitely.

Shaw had broken through my defenses and left me untethered. To the past. To my insecurities. To expectations.

He was leaving in five days, so why hold back?

I hadn't, and I was better for it.

"Thank you," I said.

He looked over. "For what?"

"For being perfect." I'd been so rude and cold to him at the beginning, but he hadn't given up on me. He was still here. He'd trusted me with his skeletons, and I was learning to trust myself. If I wasn't perfect in every way, he wouldn't leave.

"I'm not perfect, Presley. I'm just a man, flawed like any other. The perfection is an illusion."

No, that wasn't right. He was perfect because he saw his flaws. Because they made him human. He embraced them. Owned them.

He'd shown me it was okay not to fear my own shortcomings and their consequences.

"Then thank you for being kind."

Shaw's forehead furrowed. "How else would I be?"

"Unkind."

Until I'd moved to Clifton Forge, I'd known mostly unkind men. To this day, the jerks were easy to find.

"We don't talk about you," he said.

"No." I turned my eyes to the yard.

"Why?"

I lifted a shoulder. "I don't like my story."

It was not a movie I'd want to see.

Shaw reached over with his free hand and rested it on my elbow.

There was no question behind the gesture. He wouldn't pressure me into talking about my past. He told me without words that if I wanted to talk, he'd listen.

With the few days I had left with Shaw, I wasn't going to waste them with ancient history. I had a family, one he'd already met at the garage. I'd found them the day I'd started working there, and Draven had been the father I'd needed.

While Shaw had taught me it was worth trusting a man in a relationship, Draven had taught me how to trust a person, period. He'd shown me that unconditional love was no myth.

Draven had loved his children, and I liked to think he'd always lumped me in with them as an unofficial daughter. Draven had loved his wife. I'd never met Chrissy Slater, but Draven's love for her was undying. It was so strong, I loved her, a stranger, because *he'd* loved her.

I missed him.

I missed my sister.

I'd miss Shaw.

I was tired of missing people.

A sting hit my nose and I rubbed away the threat of tears. I'd been doing so well, seeing Shaw for all the good things he'd brought to my life. But he was leaving. He'd disappear and the only place I'd see him was on screen.

"You okay?" he asked.

"Who was the worst costar you ever had to kiss?" I blurted, wanting to change the subject.

Shaw squeezed my arm, then brought it back to the armrest of his chair. "Dacia."

"Really?" My jaw dropped. "I would have thought it was the time you had to kiss Aquaman on *Saturday Night Live*."

"That clip will haunt me forever." He chuckled. Both huge, handsome movie stars had cringed afterward and laughed hysterically, trying to regain composure to deliver their lines. "But no, it was Dacia."

"When?" I couldn't remember them being in a movie together. "What movie?"

"This one. I didn't want to kiss her because I wanted to kiss you."

"Oh." I blushed.

This man could deliver a compliment. I mean, Dacia was *Dacia French*. I was just . . . me. But Shaw Valance wanted *me*.

"Does it bother you?" he asked. "Me kissing other women?"

"Yes," I admitted.

He grinned. "Good."

The doorbell rang and I hopped out of my chair.

"Expecting someone?" Shaw asked, standing too.

"No." When we got inside, I set my beer down on the end table beside my couch and walked toward the door.

Shaw stayed back, hovering close to the wall so he wouldn't be seen, but he was close.

I stood on my toes to check the peephole and my stomach dropped. A face I hadn't seen since I'd ripped his picture out of my frame waited on the other side. *No.*

What was he doing here?

I unlocked the door and opened it, staring at my ex-fiancé's face.

"Hey." He lifted a hand.

I crossed my arms over my chest. "What do you want, Jeremiah?"

"Can I come in?"

Was he high? He didn't live here anymore. "No."

Shaw's heat hit my back and Jeremiah's eyes went wide, tipping up an inch. Shaw had inches on him, and Jeremiah wasn't short at six feet tall.

Jeremiah studied Shaw, recognizing him instantly. There was a gleam in his eyes, something I'd seen around town whenever anyone spoke of the stars visiting Clifton Forge. It was that greedy lust when you wanted to be associated with someone powerful and popular and rich.

I focused forward, not turning to Shaw. He'd let me take the lead, though I felt his anger radiate from his chest to my shoulders.

Jeremiah's lip had a dried gash in the corner. It had matching friends on the bridge of his nose and through an eyebrow. Were those from Leo? How badly had Leo beaten him up if they hadn't healed yet? That had been over a month ago. Or had Jeremiah gotten into another fight since?

The pity I normally would have had for him was long gone. His bruised and battered face wasn't my problem anymore. So far, we'd heard nothing from the Warriors about retaliating against Leo, and I was holding out hope it would vanish, but I didn't like seeing Jeremiah back in town.

"Can we talk for a second?" Jeremiah's gaze darted between me and Shaw. "In private?"

"No," Shaw and I answered in unison.

"Come on, Pres." He dragged a hand through his hair. The brown locks were longer now than they had been when we'd been together.

Jeremiah was wearing a black leather Warrior cut over a rumpled white T-shirt. His jeans were dirty at the knees, and it looked like he hadn't slept. His motorcycle was parked on the street.

I hadn't seen him since two weekends before the wedding. I'd gone to Ashton to sign the lease on the apartment, and we'd gone to dinner together that night. I'd decided not to sleep over because I'd had packing to do.

He'd been so handsome in the restaurant. It wasn't a fancy place, but the light from the window we'd been sitting beside had made his hazel eyes dance and his smile glow. I remembered thinking, my God, I'm marrying him.

The man on my porch was nothing like that handsome man who'd, for once, bought my dinner.

Maybe he'd never been that handsome in the first place. Had Jeremiah's lips always been that thin? His shoulders weren't as broad as I'd remembered. He was lanky and not in a good way. There was no grace or fluidity to his movements.

Had he changed that quickly? Or were my rose-colored glasses finally off? Maybe I was finally seeing what everyone had told me all along. Jeremiah was not worthy.

Granted, I'd been sleeping with Shaw Valance, so my standards had changed drastically as of late.

Take that, Jeremiah.

"Pres, come on. Five minutes."

"You had your chance to talk to me. You had years to talk to me. But you didn't. You avoided everything."

"So did you," he fired back.

"You're right, I did. But I didn't do it to hurt you. I *never* would have hurt you like you hurt me."

"I apologized."

"And I don't care. You need to leave."

"I'm not leaving until you talk to me." He pounded a fist on the doorframe, then caught himself. "Please."

Shaw stiffened, inching closer. The rage roaring at my back was ready to rip Jeremiah's head off, and I had a feeling he'd do far more damage than Leo could have dreamed.

I placed my palm on his bulging thigh, hoping to calm him with a touch as I spoke to my ex. "Goodbye, Jeremiah."

"I just need to borrow some money and—"

"Do not finish that sentence," I seethed. "You get nothing from me. Nothing. Don't come here again."

"Presley—"

I stepped back, forcing Shaw with me, and slammed the door in Jeremiah's face.

My chest heaved as I dragged in some air, blinking at the door. The sound of its slam echoed in my ears.

Shaw placed his hand on my shoulder. "Okay?"

"Yeah," I breathed, calming myself down.

When was the last time I'd stood up to Jeremiah? I should have broken off our engagement when he refused to buy me an engagement ring. I should have told him no the first time he asked for money. I should have told him goodbye when he joined the Warriors.

I didn't have trouble saying no to other people in my life. I barked at Leo or Emmett or Dash whenever they pissed me off. Telling Shaw no was one of my favorite things because he'd turned it into foreplay. But Jeremiah was so tied to my past, I'd never had the guts.

Until today.

I turned and looked up at Shaw. "That felt . . . awesome."

A giggle escaped and I pulled my lips in to silence it. Jeremiah was still outside. I hadn't heard his boots on the porch steps.

"I should have done that years ago," I said, then spun for the door and whipped it open. As expected, Jeremiah was still there. "You were never good enough for me. I didn't see it. But you were never good enough for me, or for Scarlett."

His jaw dropped but I slammed the door again.

I waited, holding my breath, until his footsteps drummed on the porch and he was gone. Then I laughed, this time not holding it back.

"So that was the ex."

I nodded, my cheeks pinching with a smile. "That was him."

"Emmett and Isaiah warned me he might come around. Asked me to tell them if he did."

"He's harmless." I waved it off. "And Emmett and Isaiah are overprotective."

"Presley," he warned.

"I'll tell them about it if that will make you feel better." Or not. I didn't want the guys getting riled up about Jeremiah's visit to beg for money. Now that it was clear he wouldn't get a penny from me, he'd disappear.

"Do you want me to—"

I launched myself at Shaw before he could finish.

He caught me, hoisting me up as I wrapped my legs around his waist. His hands gripped tight to my ass as I wrapped my arms around his neck.

"No more talking," I whispered, then devoured his mouth.

Our tongues slid against one another in frantic sweeps. My hands dove into his hair, one hand in the short fringe at his neck and the other in the longer strands on top. My legs clamped around his hips as he walked us backward and away from the door.

I used my grip on his hair to steer him, left down the hallway, then right into my bedroom. We bumped and crashed against the wall and doorframe, eventually bursting into the room.

Shaw hoisted me higher, using one hand to hold me while the other dove into the neck of my tank top, yanking it down over a breast. The cool air hit my naked skin as he did the same thing to the cup of my bra. His fingers pinched my nipple and I broke away from his mouth, moaning to the ceiling as he rolled it between his fingers.

There was a delicious bite as he plucked. My core throbbed and desire pooled.

"Down," I panted, but he shook his head.

Then he lifted me even higher, the muscles in his arms bunching and flexing tight as he brought my nipple to his mouth and wrapped it in his hot lips.

"Shaw," I whispered, my neck going limp as my head lulled to the side.

The man's mouth was magic. He could bring me to the edge from a kiss alone. My center was against the firm ridges of his abdomen and I arched my hips, squeezing my legs to get some friction.

He groaned, the vibration of his deep voice running down my spine before he broke away, dropping me so we were eye level. Then he gave me a devilish grin. "I can't go to work bald tomorrow."

I loosened the grip on his hair. "Then put me down and let's get serious."

He chuckled and then I was flying, sailing backward as he tossed me onto the mattress.

I bounced, laughing as he came on top of me. I'd changed from a pair of jeans to a pair of tiny cotton shorts when I'd gotten home from work. It was hot outside and I'd planned on hanging out on the deck even before Shaw had come over to join me.

When I'd opened the door for him, he'd taken one look at these shorts and gulped. The same heated look was in his eyes now, and his fingers dove for the waistband.

I arched my hips and *whoosh*, my shorts and lace panties landed with a dull thud on the floor.

Shaw dropped to his knees.

My heart skipped.

I propped myself up on my elbows, my breast still exposed.

He reached up and cupped it with one hand as his tongue swirled on the skin of my knee. He moved from one leg to the other, leaving wet trails with each lick.

Up and lick. Over and lick. Sideways and lick. Down and lick. By the time he finally met the apex of my thighs, I was close to coming apart.

My hand went for his hair to drag him up, but he swatted it away and continued his ministrations, torturing me with that talented tongue.

"Shaw, please," I begged when he licked the edge of my folds. I didn't need him to kiss me there. I needed him to kiss me on the spot where he knew I'd unravel.

But did he listen? No. He kept licking until I was a quivering mess and the pulse in my core drummed harder than my heartbeat.

"Shaw." I gritted my teeth, ready to reach down and take care of it myself, but then, oh *sweet Jesus*, he found my center.

One fast lick through my slit and my body came off the bed. This orgasm promised to ruin me, and I vowed he'd get one just as powerful.

I squeezed my eyes shut, arching above the mattress. My arms reached above my head, fisting my pillows as my hips twisted, unable to keep still as Shaw worked his tongue up and down my slick folds.

"More," I begged. "More."

He flicked my clit, then sucked it into his mouth as I cried out. He alternated, toying with me before giving me punishing kisses until I couldn't hold on anymore. The burn was so hot and fast, I broke on a wave.

White spots broke in my vision and I pulsed, over and over while his tongue darted in and out, lapping me up with every twist and clench.

When I was wrung out and boneless, Shaw kissed the inside of my thigh and stood. I cracked an eye open and grinned, lifting a hand to motion him up with a finger.

Shaw had taught me about multiple orgasms. He'd turned me into a greedy, hungry woman.

His clothes disappeared. He sheathed himself in a condom and stroked his long, thick cock as he knelt on the bed. I inched back to make room and opened my legs as far as I could.

His breath hitched. "Fuck, you're flexible."

I was unguarded.

I was open and wanton.

For him.

Shaw's hands took my knees, pulling me close as he lined up to my center. "And beautiful. You are so goddamn beautiful."

"Sweet talker," I whispered into his ear, nibbling on the lobe and dragging in his spicy scent.

Then with one smooth, devastating stroke, he filled me.

"Oh, fuck," I hissed, stretching and adjusting to his size. It always took me by surprise, the feeling of us connected.

He gave me a second, then moved, slowly inching out and in. His pace was unhurried and deliberate. He was taking his time, working me back up. He knew it took me a little longer after that first orgasm, so he'd work for it. He never left me wanting more.

"You feel so good," he groaned, his hips working faster and faster.

I nodded, unable to find the words as the build came on me again. My skin was too hot. My muscles too tight. The second my orgasm broke, I let out a string of incoherent noises. I was in a fog of lust and sensation, lost to anyone in the world but Shaw.

"Presley." My name came off his lips in a low murmur, then he planted deep, shuddering through his own release.

We collapsed beside one another as we came down, the only sound in the room our heavy breathing. I righted the cup of my bra and tank top, then sighed. "Wow."

Shaw chuckled. "What an interesting development."

"What?" I looked over at him.

"Did you hear yourself?"

"No." My mind raced. Oh, hell. What had I said? I hadn't blurted out something stupid, like *I love you*. Because that would be crazy. I wasn't in love with him. I mean, I liked him. More than liked him. But love? We'd only been together for a few weeks. He was my fling. My rebound. My neighbor.

I wouldn't have said I love you, right?

Shaw's chuckle filled the room. "Presley Marks, you are a grunter."

"What?" I sat up, my mouth hanging open, partly in relief that I hadn't said something stupid and partly in mortification. "I'm—no way."

"Baby, you grunted." He sat up and nuzzled his lips into my neck, tickling my skin with his stubble. Then he mimicked the sound I'd made.

"Oh my God." I covered my face with my hands. Being

left at the altar was humiliating. This? Definitely a close second. "We're never having sex again."

He laughed as I shoved off the bed, searching for my panties. I cast a glance over my shoulder, seeing him on his side, naked and perfect.

Somewhere along the way, he'd become more than Shaw Valance. The fame had worn off. Now he was just the beautiful man in my bed who made me feel special.

"Never?" He quirked an eyebrow.

I'd embarrassed myself and it was like he wanted me more than ever. I fought a grin. "At least let me nurse my pride until after dinner."

He chuckled and licked his lips. "I already ate."

I bent down and swiped a pillow that had fallen off the bed and threw it at his face. The sound of our combined laughter rang through the house.

I was really going to miss him.

CHAPTER SIXTEEN

SHAW

I hung my head as the water beat over my shoulders. The shower had turned cold, but the longer I stood here, the more I could avoid the day.

This movie shoot, which was supposed to have been long and grueling, was over too fast. The house was packed with my personal things, clothes mostly, and in an hour, I'd pick up Shelly and Cameron from the Evergreen so we could drive to the airport in Bozeman and get on my jet for California.

Today, I'd say goodbye to Presley.

I was fucking sick over it.

We'd gotten up early today out of habit. We didn't share our mornings together, never had. I'd leave and go for a run while she did yoga in her living room—that was why she was so flexible.

The nights were ours. The mornings had always been colder.

But this morning had been frigid.

Presley hadn't even looked at me when I'd walked out the door. She hadn't uttered a word.

We were both miserable.

I dragged a hand over my face, pushing the water off my nose, then I shut off the stream and got out. The pit of dread in my gut was heavy and dark.

Would I find her in tears when I went over to say goodbye? I wasn't sure I'd be able to handle that.

I dried off, wrapped a towel around my waist and shaved. I put all my toiletries in a leather case, then took it into the bedroom and tossed it into my suitcase. I had two others full and waiting by the front door.

This house was going on the market furnished. The furniture was brand new, having been bought specifically for me and this shoot. Juno was already coordinating with the real estate agent who'd sold me this yellow house.

I dressed quickly in a pair of jeans, tennis shoes and shirt. I rolled up the sleeves to my forearms, leaving the tails untucked, then I walked out the door. Every footstep was heavier than the last as I walked to Presley's and let myself inside.

I found her in the kitchen.

"Hey." I leaned against the counter, the same one I'd backed her against for our first kiss.

"Hi." At least she was speaking to me now. She lifted her to-go mug of coffee. "Want some?"

"Nah. Shelly will make us stop on the way out of town."

"Breakfast?" She took a bite of buttered toast.

"No, thanks." I shook my head and sighed. "I hate this. If I didn't have to get back to shoot the rest of the movie on set, I'd stay for a couple more weeks."

Though maybe that would only make this harder. Every

night spent in Presley's bed made me dread returning to my own.

"Think of how nice it will be to be in your own home," Presley said, chomping another bite of toast.

She smiled as she chewed, easy and light.

What the fuck?

Was she ready for me to go? Was I the only one hating this day?

I studied her face, looking for any signs of sorrow or pain, but came up empty. Her eyes weren't red rimmed from crying in the shower. Her skin was smooth, not splotchy. And her blue eyes sparkled like they did every day.

She seemed . . . happy.

What. The. Fuck?

"What are you going to do today?" I asked, hoping she'd answer with something to make me feel better. *Stare at your pictures on Google. Call you a million times. Cry in the bathroom at work.*

"Today should be busy at the garage. Dash's brother, Nick, is coming to town. He's bringing a car for the guys to work on, and usually his visits are a fun time. We'll probably all go out to dinner or something."

So she'd go out to dinner with these people, but not me?

My jaw ticked. "Sounds like fun."

"It is." She nodded, popping the last bite of toast in her mouth while she put her plate in the dishwasher.

"So, uh . . ." We hadn't talked about keeping in touch after I left. I'd planned on asking her if she was okay if I texted or called her now and then. Was that why she was acting so normal? Because she knew we'd have more conversations?

"I need to grab my shoes." She patted me on the stomach

217

as she walked past and out of the kitchen with that smile on her face. That goddamn pleasant smile.

Wait. Why was she getting shoes already? I glanced at the clock. We had thirty minutes before she normally left for work. I had plans for that thirty minutes.

I was going to kiss the hell out of her so that her taste would linger on my lips for the trip home today. I wanted her to feel me for the rest of the day too. To touch her lips and think of me.

My feet pounded on the floor as I marched after her. She was on the edge of her bed in her room, lacing up her black boots. I frowned at her from the doorway, my hands on my hips.

"What?" Her lashes lifted as she kept tying.

"You remember what today is, right?"

"Wednesday." She finished with her boot and stood.

"I'm leaving today."

"I know." Her eyes flicked to the carpet for a moment, her shoulders fell.

There. There she was.

I took a step forward, but when she looked up, whatever glimpse of sadness I thought I'd seen was gone.

"Are you okay?" she asked.

Me? I blinked. "Are you?"

"Yeah." She shrugged. "I'm okay."

Well, I wasn't. Not at all.

She flashed me that smile again as she slipped past me through the door.

I was left standing like a damn fool.

Maybe she didn't like it, but Presley wasn't torn up over me leaving. I was a fool over a woman who maybe didn't care about me as much as I cared about her.

Every one of our moments together played through my head. The nights in bed when we'd laughed and talked about nothing. The day last week when I'd shown up at her door, still in makeup from the shoot. I'd been in such a hurry to see her I hadn't washed it off after Cam had called cut.

Presley had dragged a finger through the flesh-colored cream, cringed, then giggled. She'd grabbed my hand and pulled me to the bathroom, where she'd wiped my face clean with a warm washcloth.

There were countless moments like that one. More than I ever would have thought could fit into a month.

We'd had fun, every single night. Hell, it had even been fun when her asshole of an ex had shown up at her door.

I'd been so proud of her, slamming him out. And she'd been so proud too. Proud in a way that I'd wondered if that was the first time she'd ever stood up for herself. Maybe it had been.

But how was I supposed to know? I'd talked. She'd listened.

Had I read this whole relationship wrong? Here I'd been, pouring my heart out to this woman, and she'd kept me at bay. I'd thought this was something . . . I didn't have a word for it. Special? Different? But was she really in this for the hookup?

Was I just the movie star rebound she was using to get over the ex?

Fuck.

"I'm a fucking schmuck," I muttered, needing to get the hell out of this house and away from the vanilla scent that hung in the bedroom from her lotion.

Presley was in the kitchen, drinking her coffee and digging her sunglasses out of her purse. She might be okay waving goodbye with a smile, but that was not how I wanted this to end.

I marched into her space and took the coffee tumbler from her hand.

"Shaw—"

My lips crushed hers and she melted into me. A sigh washed over us both. This was my Presley.

Her hands came between us, fisting in my shirt so tight, there'd be creases when she let go. Her tongue slid into mine, stroking and savoring. My hands slid up and down her body, memorizing every curve and line.

I wasn't sure how long we kissed, but she was the one to break off. She shivered, then released her hands.

I dropped my forehead to hers. "Thank you."

"For a kiss?"

"For all the kisses."

She took a step away, refusing eye contact. She took a long breath and grabbed her coffee mug, and when she met my gaze, my Presley was gone. She'd softened for a minute, but now she was back to the stranger inhabiting my favorite body on earth.

Presley squeezed my arm, a gesture that burned *friend zone*. "Best of luck with the movie."

Fuck this shit. "Uh-huh."

I was tempted to kiss her again, to smash through the wall she'd erected since last night, but she was already on her way to the door.

I followed her to the entryway, taking a last look around the house. I wouldn't be here again, not after today's goodbye.

"What time does your plane leave?" she asked from the doorway, sliding on her sunglasses and hiding those beautiful eyes.

"We're hoping to take off at noon."

"You're packed?" She let me out, then closed the door behind us.

"Yeah," I muttered as frustration raced through my veins.

"And the bike?" she asked as we walked down the steps.

I looked across my yard to where my bike was parked in front of the SUV. "There's a crew coming over later today to put it in a crate, then ship it to me."

"Then I guess this is it." She walked to her car door and for a second, I thought she might just get in and drive off, but she opened the door, set her purse and coffee inside, then walked over to me and stood on her tiptoes to brush a kiss across my cheek. "This was great."

Great?

Not exactly the word I would have used to describe my time with her. Maybe it was one of them, but to sum it up with a generic, five-letter word seemed . . . cheap. Before this morning, I would have thought a *four*-letter word was closer to what Presley and I had shared.

She smiled up at me, her gaze hidden behind her sunglasses, and I saw my own reflection in the lenses.

Did she see the utter disappointment on my face? Could she see how badly I wanted this to be different? Was a fucking tear too much to ask for?

Her hand came to my jaw, her fingers soft against my cheek. "Take care of yourself."

"Same to you." I brushed my knuckles down the line of her jaw.

Presley took her hand away and stepped back. "Goodbye, Shaw."

My heart clenched. "Goodbye, Presley."

My goodbyes to her had always been laced with the promise I'd see her again. From the first time I'd gone to the garage and every goodbye since. Goodbye had never meant goodbye, not for her.

But this . . . there was no undertone. No subtle threat I could return.

This was goodbye.

With a wave, she got in her Jeep and sped away, leaving me in her driveway alone. I followed her taillights as they turned around the corner and disappeared.

I wasn't sure how long I stood there, staring down the empty street.

Had she really just kissed me on the cheek and waved goodbye?

Yes, she had.

My feet came unglued as my phone vibrated in my pocket. I pulled it out, Juno's name on the screen. "Hey."

"Morning. I spoke to your pilot this morning and everything is ready to take off at noon." Juno kept speaking, running through my list of things to know and where to return the SUV when I got to Bozeman, but her voice became a dull drone. I blocked it out as I walked to my house.

I paused on the top stair, looking over at Presley's home.

That was it. We were done. That notion wasn't settling in my gut.

Juno hung up on me after she realized I wasn't listening —she'd call again later—and I went inside and finished packing.

When I loaded my bags into the SUV, I refused to glance at Presley's place again. I drove away from that cul-de-sac and didn't cast my eyes to the rearview mirror.

Shelly and Cameron were waiting at the Evergreen as I parked.

"We're all checked out and paid," Shelly said as I hefted her suitcase into the back. "Let's get the hell out of here. If I never see another floral print comforter like the one I've been sleeping under for weeks, I'll die a happy woman."

Cam didn't speak as he loaded his things and climbed into the backseat, silently as eager to leave Clifton Forge as Shelly. Neither asked to stop and get coffee, not even Shelly, so I drove.

It was only after we hit the highway that I cast my glance backward to the town fading in the distance.

That was the most unsatisfying goodbye of my life.

I blinked at the road.

It was probably better this way. The longer I stayed, the harder it would have been to leave. For me, not Presley, apparently. Would she think of me? Would she keep my number in her phone? Or had I already been deleted?

Since that picture had landed on *TMZ*, I'd been so worried about keeping her away from unwanted media attention. I'd hidden away, just like she'd wanted. Now we were done and she'd return to her life, no one the wiser.

"Are you okay?" Shelly asked. "You look pale. You're not getting sick, are you? Because I am not going through another sickness."

"I'm not sick."

She gave me a sideways glance, then hoisted her purse up from the floor and began digging. She came out with a bottle of Vitamin C tablets and popped one in her mouth before handing a tablet to me.

I took it, cringing as the bitter orange flavor burst on my

tongue. This was not what I was supposed to be tasting today.

"We'll have some script changes to the scenes we're doing in the studio," Cameron said from the backseat.

"All right."

I liked Cam, but he'd become so focused on the movie there was little to no personal touches to his sentences anymore. Though that's what we'd hired him to do. Stay focused. Keep the rest of us on track. I probably would have been the same if I hadn't met a certain blonde who'd consumed my every waking thought.

"Will we need to come back for any retakes here?" An hour ago, I would have loved that idea. I would have insisted, begged even, to make a return trip to Clifton Forge.

But now?

I wasn't sure. What the hell was up with Presley? The past few days, we'd been so in sync. Every touch, every kiss, every look. I'd seen regret on her face that time had been running out.

Or maybe I'd imagined it there.

No, goddamn it. She'd felt something. My gut couldn't have been that wrong.

I'd give her the day, but I wasn't ending things like this.

I was calling her tonight and we'd try again.

By the time my plane landed in Los Angeles, I was itching to get away from Shelly and Cameron. I was grateful for their distraction on the trip, talking nonstop about the movie and what was next for shooting.

The set design was done and tomorrow, we'd get started. There would be no delay now that we were in the home stretch. But before I could shift my focus to the movie, I needed to clear up this thing with Presley.

We parted ways at the airport and I raced home, hauling my bags inside but not unpacking them. I walked through my house, turning on lights with my phone in hand.

The glass doors of my bedroom's balcony beckoned and I stepped outside, drawing in a deep breath. I'd missed this view. I'd missed the sound of waves crashing against the sand and salt water clinging to the air.

Except I missed Montana too and it had only been hours. Months there had made a lasting impression. So had my stunning neighbor with a smile that stopped my heart.

My phone rang in my hand. It was Laurelin and I almost declined it, wanting to talk to Presley, but I answered in case it was something important. "Hey."

"You're back?" Laurelin asked.

"Yeah."

"Good. Are you sitting down?"

My spine stiffened. "No."

"Sit down, Shaw."

I recognized that tone. It came with bad news. "What's going on?"

"*OK! Magazine* just published a story that your father was a corrupt cop."

The world tilted beneath my feet, and I gave all my weight to the deck's railing, trying to absorb the words. "What?"

"Tom is already working on a statement to squash it," she said, referring to my publicist. "But I need to know what I'm dealing with. You never said anything, so I just . . . is it true?"

I closed my eyes. The reason that story hadn't gotten out was because I hadn't told a soul.

Not until Presley.

Fuck. Fuck. Fuck.

She'd played me.

How could I have been so stupid? When was I going to learn not to trust the women I was fucking?

Presley didn't want *Dark Paradise* to come out and she'd fucking played me. No wonder she'd been so happy to see me go this morning. Today was probably payday.

All the trust I'd given her. All the times I'd confided in her.

She knew it all.

"Shaw?" Laurelin said into the phone. "Shaw."

"It's true," I whispered. At least, it was close enough to the truth that denying it would only look foolish.

My family was going to be ruined, my sisters heartbroken.

If I had stayed a cop, no one would have given a shit about Shaw Valance's father.

This was as much my fault as his.

"We're not commenting," Laurelin said. "Don't say a word. Tell your family to stay quiet too."

I nodded.

"Do you hear me?"

"Yeah," I choked out.

I had to call Mom. There'd be paparazzi outside their house in the morning if there weren't already. Maybe I should fly them somewhere. They could leave tonight and get away. My sisters and their families too. None of them needed the press infecting their lives when the truth about Dad would be shock enough.

"I need to make a few calls but keep your phone close," Laurelin said. "I'll call back when I know more."

"Can we buy it from them?" I asked.

"I'm going to try." Then the line went dead.

We could buy it, but the damage had been done.

I pushed off the railing and dragged a hand through my hair. The world came into focus as shock became anger.

"Fuck." I pounded my fist on the iron railing. "Fuck!"

The few people walking the beach cast me strange looks. I didn't care. I didn't think. I called Presley's number, my heart racing as it rang.

"Hi," she answered. "I didn't think I'd hear from you again."

"Because you sold me out?" I clipped.

"Huh?"

"You fucking sold me out. I hope you got a decent paycheck."

There was a rustling in the background, like maybe she'd been in bed and was sitting up. "Shaw, I—"

"Fuck you."

I ended the call.

Then I blocked and deleted her number.

Fuck her.

Goodbye, Presley.

CHAPTER SEVENTEEN

PRESLEY

"Hey, Pres." Emmett knocked on the door to the bathroom. "You okay?"

"Yeah." I sniffled, wiping my cheeks dry. "I'll be out in a sec."

I took a wad of tissue and blew my nose, exaggerating the sound because I knew Emmett was hovering outside. When were these tears going to stop? I'd been making excuses for two days, doing my best to convince the guys I was sick. That my splotchy cheeks and red nose were from a cold, not the fact that I'd been crying.

When was I going to learn? When was I going to wise up? This was the second time in months a man had proved me a fool.

I'd been so stupid, thinking I could watch Shaw Valance walk away.

I'd been so stupid, thinking he wouldn't break my damn heart.

Enough. I dried my eyes once more. This was enough. I hadn't cried this many tears when Jeremiah had left me at the altar, and Shaw Valance didn't deserve one more. Shaw Valance was gone, and thankfully, I never had to see the man again in my life.

The news had come out about his father and he'd immediately assumed it was me.

I'd survive him, like I'd survived the others.

Fuck Shaw Valance.

And fuck the movie he rode in on.

CHAPTER EIGHTEEN

PRESLEY

F*ive months later . . .*
        My feet, covered in wool socks, were curled underneath me as I stared out the front window of Genevieve and Isaiah's home.

Snow blanketed their yard, and Isaiah had spent an hour clearing the driveway and sidewalks this morning. I'd watched from this perch as he'd worked, seemingly enjoying the February cold. Then he'd come inside with red cheeks and kissed Genevieve and the baby before taking her grocery list to the store. I'd been in this seat as he'd left and as he'd returned.

Their baby Amelia was warm and safe in my arms.

A couple walked down the sidewalk on the opposite side of the street, both wearing heavy coats, stocking caps and puffy gloves. They looked to be in their fifties. Between them, their hands were linked. Each carried a paper coffee cup covered with a white lid.

It was freezing outside, but they were talking, smiling as their breaths billowed in a trail behind them. Maybe they were newlyweds. Or maybe they'd been together for twenty-five years and were as in love now as they had been at the beginning.

They were the perfect picture for what I wanted.

I wanted someone who'd take a walk with me to the coffee hut ten blocks away no matter the weather because it was ten blocks we could talk and hold hands.

I added it to the mental list I'd been making.

Over the past five months, I'd spent a lot of time reflecting on relationships. I saw how many of my own, romantic and platonic, had been unhealthy. It had started with my family—my biological family. I'd never trusted anyone in my youth besides my sister, but even our relationship had been strained, tainted by constant, simmering fear.

I couldn't remember a time when we'd laughed and played like children, with reckless abandon. I couldn't remember fighting with her with that same recklessness either. And sisters should fight, just a little.

My relationship with my mother had lacked all respect and adoration. I pitied her to this day. I had since the beginning. And my father? I loathed him with every fiber of my being.

Those few romantic relationships of mine had been epically messy. Jeremiah was Jeremiah. I wasn't going to dwell on my mistakes there anymore. And then . . . Shaw.

The man I didn't let myself think about often, because while Jeremiah had hurt me, Shaw had crushed me. I'd let him in. I'd let him see the real me. For the first time in my life, I'd let a man see me completely, and he'd cast me aside. He'd had no faith in me, in our bond.

We'd been tested.

He'd failed.

Thankfully, after those first few days, blocking him out had been easy. It helped to know I wouldn't run into him around town. The television could be shut off when his face appeared. Magazines in the salon could be flipped to another page.

After a couple of months, after I'd set aside my anger and disappointment, I'd been able to examine that relationship too. In a way, I had Shaw to thank for this new outlook. Because he'd wounded me so deeply, I'd vowed to change. I'd vowed to raise my standards.

If a man didn't chin the bar, he was gone. I had my expectations and I would not lower them an inch.

I was learning from the relationships around me, stealing pieces of happy pictures for my own collage.

Bryce and Dash had endless passion. They held each other accountable. They challenged one another. They made the other a better person, never doubting the other's love.

Trust.

Partnership.

Draven had loved Chrissy with his entire being, even in death. He'd made some mistakes, but his heart had always been hers.

Dedication.

Genevieve and Isaiah had so much faith in one another. No trial would tear them apart.

Loyalty.

Friendship. Love. Peace.

Maybe I'd get lucky and put checkmarks beside them all. Maybe I'd have the chance to build a family of my own and have a baby, like the one in my arms.

Shaw's betrayal had inspired this list. I was doing my best to look back on our time together and see it fondly.

Some days I was more successful than others, but I was healing. He was a memory I hoped one day wouldn't taste so bitter.

Genevieve and Isaiah's week-old daughter let out a small sigh in my arms and I shifted us both, swaying Amelia gently.

"You are so precious." I stroked my finger over her button nose.

"Isn't she?" Genevieve said, coming down the hallway from their bedroom. Her wet hair was combed, and she was in a pair of baggy sweats. Her movements were stiff and slightly pained as she sat in the recliner opposite the couch.

"Feel better?"

She nodded. "Thank you. Showering has suddenly become difficult."

"That's expected."

Genevieve and Isaiah had survived their first week as parents but both were exhausted. I'd brought over soup and bread for them today, then volunteered to be on Amelia duty while Genevieve took a long shower.

While her mother was gone, I'd studied the baby's face, trying to decide who she looked like. I hadn't reached a conclusion yet, but her hair was Genevieve's.

"She has Draven's hair. Your hair."

"She does." Genevieve smiled at her daughter. "Can I ask you for a favor?"

"Of course."

The joy in her eyes dimmed. "I've been thinking about him. Dad. You knew him a lot better than I did." I'd had years with Draven whereas Genevieve had only known him for months. "Will you help me?"

"With what?"

"I want Amelia to know who he was. The good parts. Maybe you can help me teach her about him."

Oh, my heart. "I'd be honored."

I looked down at the baby, lowering my voice. "Your grandfather was the best man I've ever known. He saved my life."

"He did?" Genevieve asked. "I didn't know that. How?"

"He gave me a family. He gave me something to fight for. I was a broken girl when I came to live in Clifton Forge, and he didn't pick me up. He expected me to do it myself. So I did."

Draven hadn't believed in victims. After I'd gotten to know him, he'd asked me about my childhood, and I'd summarized the general feel of my childhood home. He'd listened intently. He'd empathized. Then he'd told me something that had set the course for my future.

You're stronger and better than your past. Choose the life you want and work your ass off to make it happen.

There'd been bumps along that road, but I was still working my ass off.

"Draven took me out for my twenty-first birthday," I told Amelia and Genevieve. "He wouldn't let the guys come along. We went to The Betsy and he ordered me a lemon drop. I got to drink two sips and then he took it away. He hauled me down the street to Stockyard's and bought me a burger and a Coke. He was always the protector, your grandpa."

Genevieve laughed. "That sounds like him."

"I never told him that after I went home, Dash, Emmett and Leo showed up at my house and we went back to The Betsy, where they proceeded to get me rip-roaring drunk. I've never puked so hard in my life."

Not even the wedding drunkenness could compare to that birthday.

Isaiah came around the corner from the kitchen. "Huh?"

Genevieve and I both giggled, waving him off. "Nothing."

He walked into the living room and went to Genevieve's chair first, bending to kiss her. Then he came over and knelt beside the couch, gazing at his daughter like the miracle she was. "How we doin', Aunt Presley?"

"Great," I whispered. "Really great."

If "Aunt Presley" was as close to a family as I could get, I'd call myself blessed for eternity. Like Draven had watched over me, I would watch over this baby girl along with Bryce and Dash's boys too.

A pair of boots stomped outside the front door and Isaiah hurried over before the doorbell could ring and wake up Amelia. "Hey."

"Hi." Luke stepped inside, quickly shutting the door behind him to keep the cold air out. He had a bouquet of yellow roses in his hand, identical to the bundle he'd taken to the hospital last week when we'd gone to see Amelia after she'd been born. "I hope these didn't freeze on the walk over."

Genevieve pushed herself up and crossed the room, taking the flowers and pressing them to her nose. "You're so sweet. Thank you."

"My pleasure." He bent to kiss her cheek, then shrugged off his coat before rubbing his hands together, warming them up.

I smiled as he came over and sat beside me on the couch. "Did you wash your hands first?"

Luke grinned. "Yes, ma'am."

"I'm only sharing her for ten minutes. Then she's mine again." I transferred the baby into his arms, my ovaries exploding at the sight of him cooing at Amelia.

Luke Rosen, Clifton Forge chief of police, might just hit every single item on my list.

"How are you?" He leaned over to brush a kiss to my cheek.

"Good." I inched closer, letting the warmth of his arm seep into mine. "How was your night?"

"Quiet, thankfully. It's too cold for people to cause trouble." Luke had filled in last night for a patrol officer who was sick. He'd been out patrolling the streets instead of out to dinner with me.

Turns out, I had a thing for cops.

And Friday nights were reserved for Luke.

Luke and I had met in the grocery store one Friday night, about a month ago. The place had been nearly deserted except for the two of us in the frozen foods section. We'd both been hovering around the frozen lasagnas.

Then he'd formally introduced himself.

I'm Luke Rosen.

I shook his hand and we lamented about how sad it was to cook a large lasagna for one person. One thing led to another, and neither of us left the store with groceries. I went out to dinner with him instead.

We'd had dinner together every Friday since. And some Wednesdays. And a random Monday. And nearly every Saturday. We were taking things slowly, getting to know one another.

Luke had helped me move past Shaw's hurt. He was a genuinely good man and his introduction had come at a time

I'd needed to believe in good men again. And day by day, dinner by dinner, he'd become important.

"What's your plan for the day?" he asked.

Across from us, Genevieve and Isaiah were in the recliner. While we'd been crooning over their daughter, Isaiah had sat down and Genevieve had climbed into his lap. The two of them were almost asleep.

"I was going to hang out here for a while," I said quietly. "Give those two a break."

"Want some company?"

I smiled. "I'd love some."

An hour later, after Luke and I had disappeared into Isaiah and Genevieve's TV room to talk while Amelia napped in his arms, we reluctantly returned her to her mother.

"Thank you," Genevieve said, bouncing Amelia, who was beginning to fuss and nuzzle toward Genevieve's breast. "I didn't realize how tired I was."

"We'll get out of your hair." I hugged her and Isaiah, then Luke and I let ourselves out.

"It's two o'clock," he said, checking his watch as I shivered in the cold. "Want to go to a movie?"

"Sure." As long as it wasn't a Shaw Valance film, a movie sounded great.

"I'd better drive in case I get called in."

"Okay. We can leave my car here."

"You sure?" he asked.

"Yep." I looped my arm with his as he escorted me down the block five homes to his house. Luke was Genevieve and Isaiah's neighbor.

We went to a movie, a comedy that had us both laughing hysterically, then Luke took me to Stockyard's for a burger. I didn't even glance at Jeremiah's former poker table. Or at the high-top where Shaw had eaten with Dacia. I focused on Luke and the meal, talking until all that remained on our plates was a handful of fries.

"That was fun," I told him as he escorted me to his truck.

"Yeah." He winked, then held the door for me.

I tracked him as he walked around the hood, his long legs hurrying so he could get in out of the cold. His dark brown hair was clean cut and short. He had these dark, deep blue eyes with a hint of charcoal around the iris. Luke's smile wasn't flashy, but it was warm and kind.

He held my hand as we drove. "Next week, I want to take you to a steakhouse about an hour from here."

I knew the restaurant he was referring to. It was a popular spot for locals in Clifton Forge when they wanted to get out of town and do something special. "That sounds great."

"Friday." He glanced over and smiled.

When he turned to the road, I studied his profile.

Luke was comfortable. Being with him was easy. There weren't butterflies fluttering every moment he was around, but when he shot me that smile or a wink, I shivered.

Maybe it wasn't blinding passion like my time with Shaw, but there were different levels of passion, right? Besides, passion wasn't number one on my list.

Luke steered us toward his neighborhood, returning me to my Jeep. He'd go start it for me so it could warm up. Then he'd wait until the windows were clear of frost and kiss me before saying good night.

Then he'd go to his home while I went to mine.

We had yet to spend the night together.

The furthest we'd progressed physically were wet kisses in his truck or my Jeep. Luke hadn't even tried to feel me up. Maybe it was time.

"What if you didn't take me to my car? What if you took me home instead and came inside?"

His face whipped to mine and his eyes flashed, sexy and dark. "Yeah?"

And then . . . butterflies. "Yeah."

The corner of his mouth turned up as he slowed, then flipped a U-turn.

"Was that legal?" I asked.

He chuckled and the sound made my pulse race. The anticipation, the slow burn of the past month, hit me like a wave, and suddenly, he couldn't drive fast enough.

I clutched his hand, my foot bouncing on the floor as he raced—safely—through town. "Would it be an abuse of power to turn on your lights so we could get there faster?"

Luke flashed me a white smile as my stomach flipped. "Probably."

He obeyed the traffic laws, not that I was surprised. Luke was a rule follower.

The rebel inside of me, the one I didn't let out much, wished he'd take a risk, but I wasn't listening to her anymore. I'd taken a risk with Shaw only to crash and burn.

So the rebel was muted and I clung to Luke and his rules. He was not a man who'd accuse me of selling his secrets and make me cry for days.

My neighborhood came into view and my heart galloped in my chest.

I was having sex tonight. With Luke.

Luke and me. Me and Luke.

Was I ready for this? I took another look at his handsome profile. *Yes.*

He pulled into my driveway and my seat belt came off, but before we could get out, his phone rang. "Oh, hell. It's dispatch. I have to take it."

My stomach dropped and I forced cheeriness into my voice. "No problem."

Damn it. Every time dispatch called Luke, it meant dinner would be cut short. He pressed his phone to his ear, and given the way his shoulders fell with every passing second, I was guessing there wouldn't be sex after all.

Why wasn't I more disappointed? Maybe I needed a little more time to wrap my head around Luke and me. *Me and Luke.*

"Be there in five." He hung up and growled. "Sorry, Pres. Some old lady drove her car into the gym on Central."

My eyes bugged out. "What?"

"Yep." He popped the *p*.

"That's um . . . she drove into the gym? Wow." I slapped a hand over my mouth to keep from laughing. With Luke, there'd never be a shortage of interesting stories.

"I don't know how late it's gonna be." He sighed. "Tomorrow?"

"Tomorrow." I leaned across the console to kiss him goodnight.

The moment my lips brushed his, he hooked a finger under my chin, pulling me closer. His tongue traced the seam of my lips, asking permission to enter.

When I opened for him and he slid inside, my entire body gave a collective sigh. *Comfortable.*

The kiss wasn't scorching. It wasn't fast-paced or frantic.

There were no curling toes or ripped clothes. But it was delicious, like the man himself.

We broke apart and he dropped his forehead to mine. "There are times when being the chief fucking sucks."

"Sorry."

"Not as sorry as I am," he muttered, making a quick adjustment to his jeans.

"Tomorrow," I promised. He nodded, reaching for the handle on his door but I held up a hand. "Stay warm. Call me later."

"Okay."

I hopped out of his truck, then I waited in the cold as he backed out of the driveway and raced away, this time flipping on the lights.

Tomorrow. *Luke and me. Me and Luke.*

"Luke, huh?" A deep voice echoed in the night and I gasped. "Didn't see that one coming."

I whirled around, searching in the dark for the voice I'd spent five months forgetting. Then he was there, standing on the porch of the house next door. The house that had been empty for months with a for-sale sign in the frozen yard.

Shaw.

He took the stairs deliberately, his natural swagger drumming up an onslaught of memories—reminders of how he moved with grace and determination in my house, in my bedroom. When he was two feet away, he tossed me a bag of baby carrots.

The bag hit my arm and landed on my boots, muffled by the snow.

"Hello, Presley."

CHAPTER NINETEEN

SHAW

I'd forgotten how beautiful she was.

I'd forgotten the way her nose turned slightly at the tip. I'd forgotten how delicate and dainty her ears were and how small she seemed when I was standing this close.

But I hadn't forgotten those eyes. Even in the dark, those enthralling irises jumped out and ensnared me.

"Hello, Presley."

She blinked.

I bent to pick up the bag of carrots and brushed off the snow from the plastic. "Can we go inside? Talk where it's warmer?"

I'd come from sixty degrees in California this morning to zero in Montana. I was wearing a pair of jeans, tennis shoes and a sweater.

When I'd arrived and seen that Presley's Jeep wasn't in her driveway, I'd unpacked my suitcases, then waited. When I'd seen headlights flash in her driveway, I'd stepped outside to meet her.

I hadn't expected to see Luke's rig. I definitely hadn't expected to see Presley lean across the console and kiss him.

The cold had seeped into my bones the minute her lips had touched his.

Fucking Luke? Really?

I'd liked him, but that son of a bitch had crossed the line. Presley was mine. That was my pink mouth and those were my blue eyes.

I was in Montana to fix my colossal fuckup and win back my girl. No more secrets. No more hiding. Presley was mine, and Luke had to go.

"We can go to my place?" I hooked a thumb over my shoulder.

Her eyes darted past me, taking in the light I'd turned on in the living room and the truck I'd parked in the driveway. This vehicle wasn't a rental, not this time. There was nothing temporary about this trip. Presley did a double take, realizing she hadn't noticed either when she'd arrived.

She'd been too consumed with Luke.

Fucker.

There was no way I'd go fishing with him again.

Presley remained silent but crossed her arms over her chest as her teeth rattled.

"You're freezing."

She clamped her teeth together.

"Let's go inside. Please?"

She found her voice, as cold as the winter moon. "No."

"You do love telling me no," I teased.

Not a crack in that exterior. "What do you want, Shaw?"

"I'm sorry. I owe you an apology and an explanation. Can we please just go inside?" I moved to touch her arm, but she shied away. This wasn't going to be easy. I hadn't deluded myself into thinking she'd come running into my arms, but I'd hoped for understanding. If we could just talk, if I could explain, she'd have to understand.

She could rake me over the coals for as long as she wanted, she could hold my mistake over my head for a decade, as long as we were together.

"What are you doing here?" she asked. "It's been . . . months."

"I came to grovel."

Presley arched one of those perfect eyebrows. "You came to Montana in February to grovel?"

"That's right." I nodded.

"A phone call would have sufficed."

"Yeah." I shifted the carrots to my other hand, then back again. "I didn't want to talk over the phone."

I didn't want to talk in the freezing cold either, but she wasn't going to let me inside, not tonight.

"I'm sorry, Presley." If that's all she heard tonight, I'd count it as a win. I had months to tell her the rest. "I know it wasn't you, and I'm sorry for assuming it was. I jumped to the wrong conclusion."

"You thought I'd sold your personal story for money."

"Most people would."

That was the wrong thing to say. Her eyes narrowed. "I'm not most people."

No, she wasn't. "I'm not making excuses, but I would like to explain." I pointed a frozen finger toward my house. "Please?"

"Fine," she grumbled and stormed past me, flying up the stairs and barging through the front door.

I hurried to follow, keeping up until she stopped in the living room.

She looked around, taking in the space and the furniture. The real estate market wasn't exactly booming in Clifton Forge and there hadn't been a single interested party for this house. Five months ago, I'd been pissed, wanting this house off my ledger. A lot had changed since. Now, I was glad to have a place close to Presley as I begged for her forgiveness.

"Would you like something to drink?" I waved a hand to the kitchen.

"No." Her arms were wrapped tight around her torso, closing in on herself.

"Would you like to sit?"

"No." She wouldn't look at me.

"Okay." I stepped past her, drawing in a deep breath of that citrus and vanilla scent I'd missed so much. I took a seat on the couch and leaned forward on my elbows, tossing the carrots I was still carrying to the coffee table. The wood gleamed, having been polished by the cleaning crew who'd come in yesterday to tidy it up.

"What do you want, Shaw?" My name sounded painful on Presley's lips. *Christ.*

"I'm sorry." I met her gaze, pleading for her to hear the sincerity in my words. "I never meant to hurt you."

She rolled her eyes. "If that was true, you wouldn't be here."

"Okay." *Ouch.* "I deserved that."

"You assumed the very worst of me. You deserve far worse."

"You're right." I held up my hand. "Please, let me explain, then you can rip me to pieces."

She glared at me but stayed silent.

Goddamn, I'd missed that glare. I'd missed that scowl and those imperious, angry gestures. I'd missed her. Everything about her. And if dealing with her wrath was the only way to have her at the moment, then I'd take it willingly.

"I hadn't told anyone about my dad, so when I told you, it was the first time. It's been buried for years and then to have it come out after I told you . . . I thought maybe you'd used me. With the way you were so happy that day I left—"

"You thought I was happy?"

There was the fire in my girl. "You seemed glad."

"I was miserable," she snapped. "I was heartbroken. I hated that you were leaving but what was I supposed to do? Beg you to stay?"

"Yes."

She scoffed. "You have a whole life that I'm not a part of. I wasn't going to pretend you'd give it up for me, because we both know you wouldn't have."

"You're right," I admitted. Even if she had asked me to stay, I would have returned to California, but I wouldn't have ended us. I would have found a way to keep us going. "I was upset with how things ended."

It had taken me months to realize that she'd put up the wall because she'd been hurting. I'd been too busy dealing with my own thoughts about leaving that I hadn't seen the truth.

"Dad's story came out right as I got back to California. I thought . . ." I blew out a deep breath. "You know what I thought."

"Yes, you made it very clear."

"I fucked up. I should have asked more questions. I should have let you explain."

Her chin jutted up. "I never would have done that to you."

"I know. I overreacted. I found out about a month after-

246

ward that it was someone from the police department where Dad used to work. The rumor had been spreading. I don't know how it started, but someone got wind of it and leaked it to the press."

The magazine that had published the story first had refused to sell it to me and they'd refused to give up their source. It had taken every one of my resources plus multiple favors to track down the story's origin.

I'd been so sure it was Presley's name I'd find. So damn sure and so damn arrogant.

The story had actually been leaked by one of Dad's old colleagues, a sergeant who'd never liked Lieutenant Shane Valance and had weaseled information from Dad's former captain.

"I'm sorry." I'd repeat it a million times. "I'm so sorry."

She swallowed hard. "So now you know, and now you've apologized. You can go."

"I'm not leaving."

"Then I am." She shot toward the door, practically running the length of the entryway.

"Presley, wait." I leapt from the couch and chased after her. The cold air stung my nostrils as I followed her to her own porch. "Presley."

She kept walking. "Go back to California, Shaw."

"I'm staying."

She skidded to a stop, then whirled around. Those arms came off her torso and flew into the air. "Why? Why are you here?"

"Because I can't stop thinking about you." I stepped closer. "I tried. For months, I tried to get you out of my head, but I can't."

"So what? What did you expect to happen? For me to

247

fall at your feet because the famous movie star Shaw Valance wants to be back in my life as long as it suits his schedule?"

"No, that's—"

"Did you expect me to be waiting around for you?"

Yes. "We have something, and you feel it too."

That obstinate chin lifted. "I'm with Luke."

"That's not an answer."

"It's the only answer you're going to get. Go home, Shaw." She spun on her foot and marched to her house. The door slammed, echoing down the quiet street.

I stared at it, my breath billowing around me until the cold won out and I retreated to my house. The baby carrots on my coffee table mocked me when I sat down.

"Fuck." I ripped the bag open and popped one in my mouth, crunching with fury.

That had not gone like I'd expected. Though to be fair, nothing with Presley had ever been predictable—she hadn't changed.

On the plane ride to Montana, a part of me had wondered if she'd see me and smile. I'd been a daft idiot for hoping that months apart would have cooled her temper.

She had every right to be mad. She had every reason to hate me.

What if she never forgave me? What if I'd come here too late?

I groaned and flopped back on the couch. *Christ.* What if she'd fallen in love with Luke Rosen?

When I'd left Clifton Forge, I'd been half in love with the guy myself. He was a good guy—better than me. In my shoes, Luke wouldn't have screwed up in the first place. But if he had, if he were sitting on this couch in my place, would he walk away? Would he let her go?

It didn't matter. I was me and no matter what Luke would do, I wasn't leaving Presley. Not again.

My phone rang and I dug it out of my pocket, answering my sister's call. "Hey."

"So? Did you see her?" Matine asked.

"Yeah," I muttered. When I'd been grumpy for months, my youngest sister had smacked me upside the head and told me to spill. She was nearly as invested in this apology as I was.

"Uh-oh. That doesn't sound good. How'd it go?"

"Not good. She's dating someone."

"Ooof." She hissed. "Do you think you're too late?"

"Yes. No. I don't know." Was I too late? Had I hurt Presley beyond the point of repair?

"But you're going to fight for her?" Matine asked.

"Of course." The answer was automatic. Presley was the woman of my dreams, and I would not let her go easily.

"Good." There was a smile in Matine's voice. "How cold is it?"

"Cold." I chuckled. "You'd hate it."

She laughed. "I'll plan to visit you in the summers."

"Good idea."

"Keep me posted?"

"Yeah." I nodded.

"Have you talked to Dad?"

"You know the answer to that question, Matine."

"But I'm going to keep asking it, Shaw."

Matine and my other sisters had been pressuring me for years to speak with Dad. Before the story came out about his retirement, they hadn't understood our divide and my hard feelings. The story had answered a lot of questions.

It'd been hard for them to hear the reason Dad had left

the force. Matine had taken it better than anyone else, maybe because she'd confessed to always having felt like she was missing something in our estrangement.

All three of them had been hurt, but my sisters were strong. The story faded into the archives after a few weeks thanks to a cheating scandal and surprise pregnancy with other celebrities. It was old news, and my sisters had already moved past it, loving Dad no differently than they had before. They'd been relentless in pushing me to do the same.

But I wasn't there yet. When I thought of calling Dad, bitterness crept up my throat and made it impossible to speak.

One of Matine's daughters squealed in the background.

"I'd better let you go," I said. "Thanks for calling."

"Good luck with Presley. Sounds like you'll need it."

I hung up and tossed the phone aside, then surveyed the room.

It was a far cry from the enormous house I had on the beach, but it was home. I'd miss the sound of waves lulling me to sleep, but I'd trade them for Presley tucked into my side each night.

I made a mental list of everything I'd have my assistant pack and ship here. Most of my clothes were already on their way, not that my shorts and flip-flops would be useful for another few months. I'd have Juno pick out some sweaters and jackets, plus I'd need another winter coat and some gloves. But then I'd be set. Everything else could stay in California because it wasn't like I'd need my suits or tuxedos here.

As of yesterday, I was on a break.

Dark Paradise had officially been moved into postproduction. It would take months of editing to get to the final cut, but no one expected I'd need to shoot another scene. My time on camera was done for now.

My staff members were freaking out. Ginny and Laurelin were sure that this extended leave—I'd refused to give them a firm return date—would destroy my career. What they didn't understand was that I didn't care.

Fame was lonely. Fortune was empty. This was not how I wanted to live my life, avoiding public places and fearing that every action would be misconstrued.

There were more important things than money and a legacy.

Presley was more important. Her happiness. Her dreams. Her love.

I'd fallen in love with her.

I'd fallen in love with her every time she'd told me no, sitting across from her at the Clifton Forge Garage.

Yeah, I'd fight for her. I'd die trying to earn her trust.

I was going to live in this house and make it my own. I'd show her, every day, how special she was to me.

This time, I'd take care.

I picked up my phone and made my way to my bedroom, flipping off the lights in the house as I walked. It wasn't even eight o'clock yet, but I'd had a long day of packing and travel. I stripped off my clothes, leaving on only my boxer briefs as I slid into bed. The sheets were cool and smelled like soap, but the bed was too empty. I turned off the lamp on the nightstand and stared at the dark ceiling.

Above my head, the window glowed.

A light shone from next door.

I sat up, flipping on the light and grabbing my phone to call a number I hadn't called in months. A number I'd blocked and deleted, then begged Laurelin to hunt down for me when I'd realized how much of a dick I'd been.

It rang and rang.

I knelt on the mattress, my bare shoulder pressing against the window's frame. The call went to voicemail.

Hi, this is Presley . . .

I hung up.

I called her again.

This time, she answered on the second ring. "What do you want?"

"You didn't delete my number."

"An oversight."

"Come to your window."

"No." She huffed. "Good night."

"Pres, come to your window."

"Ugh." Marching footsteps sounded through the phone, then her blinds whipped open. She stood there, so close, with her phone pressed to her ear. "What?"

"I'm sorry. I should have made this phone call months ago."

"Yes, you should have, but it doesn't matter now." Her bravado slipped. "None of it matters now."

"It matters. You matter."

She held my gaze through the glass and the ten or twelve feet that separated our homes. Did she feel it? Even after the time apart, even across this distance, did she feel it?

"Goodbye, Shaw," she whispered.

I lifted a hand and pressed it to the cold glass. "See you tomorrow."

Never again would I tell Presley goodbye.

CHAPTER TWENTY

PRESLEY

It was fucking cold.

I shivered underneath my red parka, burrowing into my hood and quickening my steps. The snow crunched under my boots, the flakes dry and crusted with ice.

Walking across town was not how I'd planned to spend my Sunday morning, but I wanted my Jeep and I wanted to get away from *my neighbor*.

Couldn't Shaw have just called and apologized? What was he doing here? Messing with my life, that's what.

I was in a good place. I'd put Shaw behind me, Jeremiah was a distant memory, and I was dating Luke. The last thing I needed was Shaw living next door.

The asshole had brought me carrots. So help me, if he'd ruined carrots for me, I'd burn his house down. I'd torch it, stand back and smile at the flames. My feet paused. *Should I?*

No. That was crazy. That man made me crazy. I shook off that ridiculous idea because tempting as it was, I was no arsonist.

Avoiding his home, the inside at least, would be simple. Under no circumstances would I set foot in that yellow house again, not until it was empty and fumigated. Walking into his house last night, being wrapped in his scent, was much too dangerous for my heart—my disloyal heart, which had leapt with one long inhale of Shaw.

Damn him.

I marched faster, practically jogging. My breaths clouded above my head like the puffs of a racing steam locomotive. The blocks disappeared quickly as I hurried down the deserted streets, too angry and confused and annoyed to pay much attention to the few cars passing by.

I'd be an icicle by the time I reached Genevieve and Isaiah's house, but I had my fury to keep me warm. Isaiah would have come and picked me up, but this walk was good. I needed the movement to get my head on straight and think through a plan.

First, if Shaw hadn't figured it out last night, I'd spell it out for him. We. Were. Over. No number of apologies would change my mind. We'd been over the moment he'd called me from California. If I repeated the message enough times, eventually he'd go back to his world and leave me to mine.

Second, I was dating Luke. I *liked* Luke. He was a good kisser and a sweet man. He was honest and true. Luke would come over and we'd take our relationship to the next level. *Luke and me. Me and Luke.*

That was happening.

Tonight.

It didn't matter who was living next door. It didn't matter whose bedroom was outside mine.

Maybe *Luke and me* should happen at his house instead.

The crunch of tires on snow at my back startled me and I

jumped to the far edge of the sidewalk. A large, gray truck pulled up beside me, its tires crushing the berm of snow that edged the streets this time of year, made from the snowplows clearing the streets.

Emmett. He must have recognized my coat. Not many wore cherry-red parkas. He rolled down the passenger-side window. "Are you trying to get yourself killed?"

"You scared me."

"Get inside before you freeze, damn it."

"I'm not cold," I lied.

"Hurry up." He rolled his eyes and up went the window. Then the locks clicked open.

I opened the door and hopped inside, buckling my seat belt and sliding off my gloves. My fingers wiggled over the warm air coming from the dashboard vents.

"Where are we going?" he asked.

"I was walking to Genevieve's to get the Jeep."

He scowled as he pulled away from the curb. "That's miles."

"I needed some air."

There was no way I'd tell Emmett about Shaw. No one knew about my fling with the movie star, not even Genevieve or Bryce.

When Shaw and I had started our tryst, I'd been scared about how everyone would react given the movie and his short-term outlook on Montana. As my feelings for Shaw had changed, grown, I'd been scared to slap us with a label, mostly because *location hookup* sounded so . . . cheap.

I'd almost told them when that picture of Shaw and me on his bike had come out, but then it had turned into nothing. Why? Because Presley Marks wasn't news. I was a nobody. If that photo'd had Dacia French in my place, it would have gone viral.

When Shaw had left, I'd been grateful for my foresight not to tell anyone. It meant that I could wallow in heartbreak alone without worried glances or pitiful hugs. Since we were over, there was no point in dragging Emmett into the mess.

Shaw would be gone soon, lost to California for good.

"Want a coffee?" Emmett asked, already slowing for the parking lot of the country and feed supply store. There was a coffee hut in one corner of the lot. Emmett rolled down his window, leaning out, as the barista opened her sliding window.

The blonde's cheeks flushed when she saw Emmett. Her tongue darted out and licked her lower lip. "Oh, hey. Again. Did you, um . . . forget something at my place last night?"

I rolled my eyes and leaned forward. "Could I get a vanilla chai with skim milk, please?"

Her eyes flashed to me and her smile flattened. "Sure. Emmett?"

"Triple mocha."

"Give me a minute." She nodded and slid her window closed.

"The barista?" I shot Emmett a look. "She's probably going to spit in my coffee."

"Nah. She's nice."

"Have you even been home since last night?"

He chuckled. "Not yet."

"Do you remember her name?"

"Yeah. Of course. It's, uh . . . Carrie."

"Carleigh, according to her nametag."

"Damn. Carleigh."

I shook my head. "You're horrible."

"The women love me. What can I say?"

"The women?" I teased. "Do you hear yourself?"

He laughed, digging a twenty from his wallet.

Emmett wasn't wrong. Women did love him. They loved his bad-boy look with his beefy, tattooed arms and the shoulder-length brown hair that he was constantly tying up or brushing out of his face. He wasn't as quick to laugh or flirt like Leo, but Emmett had a smolder that drove *the women* crazy.

Would he ever settle down? Would he find a woman who caught his attention for more than one night? I hoped so. What I wanted most for the people in my life was that they found love, even if it seemed to elude me.

Emmett paid for our coffees and winked goodbye to Carleigh, then he pulled away and aimed the truck toward Isaiah's neighborhood. "So why'd you leave your Jeep at Genevieve's?"

"I went over yesterday to see the baby and spend some time with them. Luke came over too and we went to a movie. He drove me home."

"How's that going, you and Luke?"

I sighed. "Great."

"Doesn't sound great."

"No, it is. He's a really good man, and I like him a lot."

"But . . ."

"There's no but."

"Pres." Emmett shot me a look. "Who are you talking to?"

"You," I muttered. "Why couldn't Leo have been the one to find me? He doesn't ask as many questions."

"Not today. What's wrong? Why are you stomping

across Clifton Forge like you're on a mission to show Jack
Frost he isn't going to get the best of you?"

"It's a long story."

"Does it have anything to do with a certain movie star?
The one you were seen riding on the back of a bike with?"

My mouth dropped. "You knew?"

"Please." He scoffed. "You might be good at hiding your
emotions from some people, but you've never been good at
fooling me."

This was true. Whenever I was sad and forcing happy,
there were two men who saw past the brave face: Draven
and Emmett. Draven would badger me until I talked, ripping
the truth from my lips. But not Emmett. He'd pull me into
one of his bear hugs and not let go until some of the pain had
seeped away.

"We were . . . well, I don't know what we were. Something." Something special.

"Has he been in touch since he left?"

"No. He came back last night."

He looked over, taking a drink of his mocha. "What
happened last night?"

"I'm pretty sure he moved here."

Emmett choked. "No shit?"

"When Shaw was here for the movie, he bought the
house next door to mine. Not because it was the house next
door, it was just a coincidence. During the movie, that was
where he stayed. We started talking and things happened."

Then he'd crushed me, something I wouldn't tell
Emmett because it would mean a U-turn and an awkward—
likely violent—confrontation on my street.

"Shaw left," I said. "Now he's back."

"You still have feelings for him?"

"I don't know," I whispered. "I don't know how I feel. And the truth is, I don't trust my judgment."

"Pres." Emmett reached over and put his hand on my shoulder. "What happened with Jeremiah—"

"Was my fault."

"I was at the wedding, babe. Didn't seem like your fault."

"No, it was my fault. I shouldn't have stayed with him in the first place."

"You loved him."

"Maybe," I muttered. *Maybe not.* I didn't have the energy to delve any deeper this morning. Because of Shaw, I'd barely slept. And we were nearly to Isaiah's. "New subject, please. How is your mom?"

Emmett shot me a look, one that said he wasn't leaving this alone, but answered, "She's good. I'm going over there later."

"Please, for her sake, shower first. You still smell like The Betsy."

"I'll shower." He grinned as he turned down Genevieve and Isaiah's block.

When he parked behind my Jeep, I unbuckled and gave him a smile. "Thanks for picking me up."

"Always. See you tomorrow."

"Bye." I raised my coffee mug in a silent thanks and climbed out of the truck, juggling my drink and my gloves as I dug keys from my coat pocket.

I got in my Jeep, shivering as I hit the ignition and cranked up the heat. My gaze zeroed in on Luke's house as I drove down the sleepy street. His truck wasn't in the driveway where he normally parked—his garage was reserved for his boat—and the lights were off.

Should I tell him about Shaw? Should I pretend it was no big deal that he was in town?

Guilt had clawed its way into my heart last night as I'd lain restlessly in bed. I'd spent the midnight hours thinking of Shaw, not the man I was actually dating. It wasn't like I'd done anything wrong. I'd gone into Shaw's home and listened to him speak. I'd answered a phone call. So why did I feel like I'd betrayed Luke?

The last place I wanted to go was home, where Shaw would be waiting. The stubborn ass wasn't going to leave me alone. So I steered my Jeep to a place in Clifton Forge I had never been.

The police station.

"Hi," I said, greeting the officer stationed inside the front door. He sat behind a glass partition so I leaned in and spoke to the metal speaker between us. "I was wondering if I could see Luke—uh, Chief Rosen."

"I'll check to see if he's available." He collected my driver's license and scanned a copy. Then he pointed to a row of chairs along the wall.

Less than a minute later, Luke came through an interior door. "Presley?"

"Hey." I smiled, hurrying toward him. "Sorry to interrupt. I just wanted to say hi."

"Hi." He grinned and dropped a kiss on my cheek. "Come on in."

Luke took my hand and led me through the station, past rows of desks and empty chairs to a door embossed with *Chief of Police* in gold letters. He held it for me, closing it behind us.

His stately chair sat on the other side of the desk, but

instead of sitting there, Luke held out one of the guest chairs for me, then sat at my side.

Because that's who he was. He was the guy who sat beside the woman he was dating, even in his own office. The guy who brought his neighbor yellow flowers twice after she'd had a baby. The guy who'd been patiently waiting for me to be ready to do more than kiss for a month.

"How did it go last night?" I asked.

"What a cluster." He groaned, running a hand over his square jaw. He had more stubble this morning than normal and he was even more handsome this way, a little rough around the edges.

I put my hand over his, rubbing my thumb across his knuckles. "You look tired."

"It was a long night."

"Anything I can do?"

"No." He gave me a smile. "I'm finishing up some paper-work and then I'm going home to take a nap."

"If you want to reschedule tonight, we can—"

"Never."

I smiled, despite the anxious knot forming in my stomach. I wanted this. I wanted to be with Luke. So why was I dreading tonight? Why was I hoping for any reason to delay a day or two?

Shaw.

Damn him. He didn't get to show up here and ruin everything I had going for me. Luke and I were new, but there might be a future here. A real future, not some Hollywood fantasy.

"Six o'clock?" I asked, doing my best to hide the nerves in my voice. "I'll make dinner."

"Sure."

"How do you feel about frozen lasagna?"

He laughed. "Seems fitting."

"Then I'll get out of here so you can finish." We both stood and I raised onto my toes to brush a kiss to his lips.

He deepened it, slanting his mouth over mine.

A tingle ran down my spine and my heart thumped. It didn't burst into a wild sprint, but the thump was good. The thump meant we had the promise of passion.

Luke broke away and grinned. "I'll escort you out."

"Thanks." I followed him to the door, letting him kiss my cheek once more before I braved the cold and scurried to my Jeep. Then I spent the rest of the morning and early afternoon avoiding my home.

I went to the grocery store, wandering up and down every aisle. I stopped at my favorite sandwich place for lunch. I gassed up my Jeep and went to get some cash from the bank because for a woman who didn't use cash, having some in her wallet suddenly seemed important. I drove by the garage to see if Leo or Dash had randomly decided to work on a Sunday—it was deserted.

Finally, when it couldn't be avoided any longer, I drove home.

Shaw's white truck was in his driveway, and I cursed myself for missing it last night. I'd been too anxious about inviting Luke to spend the night, and I'd trained myself for months not to look at that yellow house.

As I parked, I kept one eye on Shaw's. There was movement at the living room window.

Ugh.

I really wished I had a garage to park inside, but only two of the homes on this street had them. The homes on the cul-de-sac had all been built before garages were a must-have.

Maybe it was time to move.

The apartment above the garage had been empty for years. The last people who'd lived there were Genevieve and Isaiah.

If Shaw wouldn't accept we were over and stayed in Montana for more than two weeks, I was moving. Decision made.

I parked and sent up a muted prayer that I could haul my groceries inside in one trip.

My arms were overloaded with bags when I felt the crackle of his presence behind me. Shaw's spicy scent drifted across the cold air. How had he managed to sneak up on me? The rustle of my bags and thundering, panicked heartbeat must have drowned out the crunch of his footsteps on the snow.

"Let me help." He moved to my side and started taking bags off my wrists.

The heat of his shoulder hit mine and I sidestepped away. "I can do it."

"We've been here before. Let's skip to the end where we both know I'll help carry these inside." He grinned at me, daring me to argue.

Stubborn, arrogant ass. He was not going to leave me alone and I didn't want a standoff in freezing temperatures.

"Fine," I muttered, shoving five bags into his gut.

"Was that so hard?"

I shot him a glare and marched inside. The minute my grocery bags were on the counter, I gave him a tight smile and pointed to the exit. "Thanks for your help."

He chuckled and strode out of the kitchen to the living room, his gait full of grace and sin.

I forced my eyes away from his long legs and thick

thighs, not letting myself remember how it felt to have those hips flush with mine. "Keep going until you hit the door."

He ignored me. "Did you sleep okay?"

"Great," I lied.

"I didn't." He sat down on my couch and cast his eyes down the hallway toward my room. "I kept wishing for a different bed."

My cheeks flushed, not because the mental image of him naked in my bed flashed through my mind. I still had my parka on and it was a warm coat.

"Goodbye, Shaw."

"What are you doing today? You had a busy morning."

"Stalking is illegal," I snapped.

"So I've heard." He leaned back, lifting his arms and lacing his fingers behind his head. "What are you doing for dinner tonight? Want to share a pizza?"

"Luke is coming over. I'm dating him, remember?"

"I remember." His cocky grin soured.

"Then what are you doing here? Go home." And by home, I meant Los Angeles.

"How serious is this thing with Luke?"

It wasn't serious yet, but there was the promise of serious. Luke and I had potential. "We're dating."

"You said that already but it doesn't really answer my question."

"I don't owe you any answers." I stomped past the living room and down the entryway to the door. "Are you going to make me throw you out?" I called.

His laughter filled the hall as he emerged, a sexy grin on his face. Shaw moved into my space, crowding me beside the door. "Answer me. How serious?"

"Does it matter? I'm dating Luke. That won't change just because you're vacationing next door."

"This isn't a vacation, Presley."

I gulped, refusing to let myself believe he'd come to Montana for me. "I think you'd better leave."

He put his palm flat on the door, holding it closed. "How have you been?"

"You're on the wrong side of the door."

Shaw's grin spread into a slow, mouthwatering smile. He leaned closer, his breath whispering across my cheek. "How are things at the garage?"

"Super. Now go." My knees were weak and that smile was melting my resolve. I fixed my gaze on his broad chest and the green sweater that smelled like soap and sandalwood. "Please."

"Why? We're just talking. Unless there's something about me being here that makes you uncomfortable."

Hell, yes, I was uncomfortable. The man put me on edge and made me squirm under that golden gaze. "I have groceries to unload and I need to cook dinner. I don't have time to talk."

"Presley, look at me."

"Shaw." I squeezed my eyes shut and fisted my hands. "Please. Leave."

He was still standing there when I opened my eyes, pure regret etched on his face. "I'm sorry. I never should have doubted you."

I nodded.

If he kept apologizing, I might forgive him, and until I had my feelings sorted, forgiveness was not an option. I yanked the doorknob, forcing him to step away. The cold air rushed past us. "Goodbye, Shaw."

He sighed. "See you tomorrow."

No, he would not. Thankfully, tomorrow was Monday and I was spending it at work. *Unless* . . . My stomach dropped. Shaw would just come to the garage.

Maybe after tonight, after Luke's truck spent the night in my driveway, Shaw would get the hint. Did he think Luke and I had been intimate already? Did that bother him?

Because the idea of him with another woman made me sick. How many women had he been with these past five months? How many women had slept curled into his warm side and woken up to his soft lips on their temple?

That idea stiffened my spine, freezing any desire that had crept through my veins.

Shaw stepped through the door, his shoulders falling as he crossed the porch, but he paused at the top stair when beyond him on the street, a yellow cab parked beside my curb.

"Expecting company?" Shaw asked.

"No." I walked out and stood by his side as the cab's door opened.

I gasped as the woman in the backseat stepped onto the snow.

A face I hadn't seen in ten years looked up.

A face I saw each day in the mirror.

Scarlett.

CHAPTER TWENTY-ONE

SHAW

"Is she still asleep?" I asked, casting my gaze down the hallway toward Presley's guest bedroom.

"Yeah." Presley dropped to the edge of the couch and slumped. "Do you think I should call a doctor? It's been two days."

I took the seat beside her, keeping my voice low. I wanted to put my arm around her shoulders, hold her until some of the worry on her face subsided, but I stayed on my cushion, two feet away from hers. "Has she gotten up at all?"

"I heard her get up in the middle of the night and flush the toilet."

"Then I'm sure she's fine."

Presley leaned back into the couch, looking at the ceiling. "This is . . ."

That was the fourth time since I'd come over that she'd started speaking only to trail off. Her mind was visibly whirling, trying to make sense of her sister's sudden and strange appearance two days ago.

Scarlett had stepped out of that cab, crossed the yard and walked right into Presley's house.

She hadn't hugged her sister or said hello. She'd trudged inside wearing clothes just as baggy as the ones Presley normally wore, except hers hadn't looked cute or sexy or purposefully loose. They'd been wrinkled and dirty, like she'd swiped them from a man's bedroom floor.

Presley had gaped at her sister, lost for words.

Scarlett had spoken instead.

Before we talk, can I crash in your guest bedroom for a minute?

Presley had nodded and pointed down the hallway, then Scarlett had disappeared and left a stunned Presley—and me —behind.

Presley had called in sick to work yesterday and today. I'd come by at ten yesterday morning when I'd spotted her Jeep still in the driveway. She'd let me in without any hesitation—which told me exactly how well she was reacting to her sister's visit.

Today, I'd assumed Scarlett would be awake and that the two of them would have talked. Again, I'd seen the Jeep when normally it would have been at the garage. I'd stayed away until the afternoon, but curiosity had gotten the better of me. I'd expected to find the sisters together. Instead, Presley had opened the door and led me to the living room, where the stress on her face made my gut twist.

"Why is she here?" Presley whispered, her hands wringing in her lap.

"Wake her up and find out."

"No, not yet." She shook her head. "She looked so haggard. I haven't seen her in . . . a long time. She looked bad, right?"

"She didn't look good," I muttered.

The deep circles under Scarlett's eyes had been a purplish blue. Her long, blond hair was stringy and in need of a couple shampoos. Despite the baggy clothes, she was skinny. Too skinny, even for a woman with Presley's petite frame.

"Have you talked to her lately?" I asked.

"I haven't seen or spoken to her in over ten years."

I blinked. "Ten years?"

"Yeah." Presley's gaze fell. "Not since I left home at eighteen."

"Did you have a falling out?"

Presley blew out a long breath. "It's a long story."

"I'm not going anywhere." I shifted on the couch, turning sideways to give her my attention. "You have no reason to trust me after what I did, but you were there for me. You listened when I was ready to talk. If you're ready, I'll be here to listen to you."

She brought her knees to her chest, wrapping them in her arms. Minutes passed as she curled in on herself, her eyes unfocused and sad.

And I waited. I gave her time as she decided whether or not to give me her trust.

"We grew up in a toxic home," she whispered.

I closed my eyes, savoring her honesty for one second, then I looked at her with my full attention.

"Toxic how?" My mind jumped to the worst. Drugs? Violence? Molest—I couldn't mentally finish that word.

"My dad was a cruel man. He beat us."

Violence. My hands fisted on my thighs. "I'm sorry."

She pulled her knees in closer. "I don't remember a time when he didn't raise his hand to us. We didn't get

269

spankings. We got slapped on the cheek if we made a mistake. We would get sent to bed hungry if we cried. But he never yelled. I can't remember a time when he raised his voice. He was just a cruel man who'd come at us with silent rage."

My arms ached to pull her onto my lap, but she was huddled tight, safe in her own world.

"He beat my mom too," she said, her voice quiet and robotic. "She didn't work, so he could hit her wherever he wanted. When Scarlett and I started school, he made sure the bruises were in places easy to conceal. He especially loved to yank us around by our hair or grab us here." She pointed to her bicep. "We always wore sleeves."

"Presley, I-I don't know what to say."

"There's nothing to say." She lifted her eyes to mine. "He controlled every aspect of our lives. We followed his rules completely because the punishments for breaking them were so severe. Even then, even at perfection, he'd find something to get mad about."

"And your mom?"

"She stood there and watched. I actually blame her the most because she didn't protect us. A mother should protect her kids, don't you think?"

"Yes, I do."

"But that was my life. From the outside, we were the perfect little family. We had family picnics on Saturdays. We went to church on Sundays. We had nice clothes and got good grades at school. Our teachers adored us and because we were such good kids, our parents must be doing such a good job to have two perfect girls. No one ever thought that the reason we were so good was because we were scared every single day. We lived in fear."

Presley's gaze shifted and fixed on an invisible spot on the wall. She went quiet, frozen, as she stared.

I put my hand on her foot. This woman was strong. Resilient. She'd chased the terror away. "But not anymore."

"No," she said. "Not anymore."

"Where did you grow up?"

"A suburb of Chicago."

"You left at eighteen."

"Yeah." She nodded. "It wasn't easy. Scarlett and I were living at home, and I don't know if my father expected that we'd try to leave or not, but he was so strict after graduation. More so than before. He didn't let us get jobs that summer. We just stayed home, waiting for fall because he'd agreed that we could go to a local community college."

Her father was a fucking pathetic excuse for a human being. I'd never met the man, even laid eyes on him, but I hated him. *Hated.* My molars ground together but I worked to keep my expression neutral. Presley didn't need me flying off the handle while she was reliving that time.

I'd save my rage for later.

If there was a way to ruin her father without causing backlash to Presley, I'd do it. My first phone call when I left here today would be to Laurelin. She was a kind woman but if you fucked with me, she'd make your life a living hell. Presley was in my life—whether she was ready to accept that or not—and Laurelin would eviscerate her father. If she wasn't able to, I'd step in and get my hands dirty.

"Scarlett was dating Jeremiah."

"Wait, what?" I'd been so lost in thoughts of revenge that I'd barely caught Presley's statement.

"Scarlett was dating Jeremiah," she repeated.

"Jeremiah, as in your ex-fiancé?"

271

"That's the one," she muttered. "He helped me get out and get away."

"How?"

"He found us a car. It was supposed to be for us, Scarlett and me. The three of us, actually. Jeremiah and Scarlett were going to go to California. I had already decided on Montana."

"Why Montana?"

She shrugged. "It sounded so . . . simple and old-fashioned, living in a quiet town with nice people. I didn't need the glitz of Los Angeles or New York City. I just wanted a safe, little town to call my own."

"And what sounds simpler than Clifton Forge, Montana?"

"Exactly." She nodded. "We snuck out one night. I'd been sneaking clothes and stuff from our room for weeks. Scarlett had too. Jeremiah had kept it all at his house because he only lived about half a mile from us."

It sounded like a hostage escape, and maybe in a way it was. "Did your parents suspect anything?"

"Not as far as I knew. I'd already found a job. I'd been searching on the library's computer so no one could trace it. That was one of the few places Dad let us go without supervision that summer. I wasn't sure what I was looking for, but when I saw a classified ad for a receptionist at a garage, it sounded perfect. I wanted to work at a place that wasn't prim or proper."

"You wanted the noise and the grease."

"That, and Draven hired me with only a phone interview. He took a chance on me, and I never asked him why." Presley's face flashed with grief, like it normally did when she thought of Draven. Not for the first time, I wished I had known the man she held so dear.

"I was sure that once we were gone, my parents would forget about us," Presley said. "But Scarlett was nervous. She thought Dad suspected we were leaving. It was a thrill for me. No matter what, I was going. But Scarlett wasn't like that. She didn't test the limits like I did."

"Tested how?"

She smiled a little. "Stupid things. I'd sneak candy home from the vending machine at our middle school and eat it after bedtime. I painted my toenails red in the girls' locker room. Once, my mom took us school clothes shopping and when she wasn't looking, I shoplifted a thong."

My thieving beauty. "Did you get caught?"

"Sometimes. When my dad saw my red toenails, he threw me on the living room floor and kicked me for being a 'slut.' He insisted on a lot of pink for his daughters. I'm pretty sure he broke one of my ribs, cracked it at least, but we didn't go to doctors. Scarlett wrapped them up for me."

"Son of a bitch." I closed my eyes, searching for calm. My heart pounded as I thought about these girls and what they'd endured. Or how her sister had known to wrap ribs to heal. "I don't—I'm sorry."

She gave me a sad smile. "Don't be sorry."

"I can't help it."

"Don't pity me." She glanced down the hallway. "I got out."

Presley got out.

But Scarlett . . .

"Scarlett didn't go with you, did she?"

She shook her head. "I tested the boundaries. Scarlett

stood ten feet away from the lines my father drew and wouldn't dream of getting too close."

My forehead furrowed. If you put Presley and Scarlett side by side and told me to pick the rebel, I would have chosen Scarlett every time. The way she'd held her chin high when she'd stepped out of that cab, the way she'd refused a courteous greeting . . . "That doesn't jive with the woman who marched in here two days ago."

"I know." Presley's cheek dropped to her knees. "I don't know who that was because it wasn't Scarlett."

"You said you haven't seen her in ten years. What happened? How'd you get away and she didn't?"

Presley stared at the wall as she sat in that ball. "We snuck out of the house. I'd done it a couple of times. There was this guy I liked my senior year and he'd meet me at a playground in my neighborhood. We'd make out for a couple of hours, then I'd sneak back home." She shuddered. "I'm glad I didn't get caught for that one. God, I was so stupid."

"You were a kid trying to find some freedom."

"Yeah," she muttered. "Scarlett and Jeremiah were dating but they only saw one another at school. They'd kiss and stuff and sneak around, but it was behind the teachers' backs and far from Dad."

"But she was going to leave."

Presley nodded. "California was Scarlett's idea. Looking back, I think Jeremiah would have followed her anywhere because he just wanted her out of that house. I never told a soul about what really happened at home, but Scarlett had confessed it to Jeremiah and made him promise to keep the secret."

Coward. Jeremiah should have gone to the police. "How'd he get you a car?"

"I saved every penny I made from babysitting neighborhood kids for two years. Christmas money. Birthday money. Scarlett saved too, though not as much, and we hoarded it until there was two thousand dollars. It was enough to buy an old Civic with one hundred ninety thousand miles on it, but the engine ran, and it had four working tires."

My brave woman. She'd forged a new life from two thousand dollars. The swell of pride conflicted with the anger simmering in my chest.

Presley went quiet for a long moment, like her brain was taking her back to that time.

"You okay?"

Her eyes flashed up and a sheen of tears was in her gaze. "I shouldn't have left her. I should have made her come with me."

"Did you try?"

"Of course, but—"

"Then that's all you could have done."

I'd spent time in the academy learning about domestic abuse victims. I'd seen plenty in real life. I remembered the first time I saw a wife rush after her husband in handcuffs, promising him she wouldn't press charges. One of her eyes had been swollen from where he'd hit her. He'd broken her nose. And there she'd been, crying as we'd dragged the motherfucker away.

Breaking the cycle wasn't easy, and Presley and Scarlett had been in it their entire lives.

"We snuck out one night after my parents were in bed. They weren't asleep. I heard some noises like they were . . . like my dad was . . ."

Raping her mother.

My knuckles turned white as my fists squeezed.

"We snuck outside and ran to Jeremiah's house. Scarlett kept saying, 'This is wrong. We're going to get caught. We should go back.' But I kept running. At one point, she stopped and I grabbed her hand and dragged her behind me. I figured that once we got to Jeremiah's, he'd convince her to leave."

"You just wanted to get on the road."

"I was so *sure*. Staying wasn't an option. The second I left that house, I knew I'd never go back."

"But Scarlett wasn't ready," I guessed.

"I think she was, but she was so scared. Jeremiah couldn't calm her down. She was convinced we'd get caught. We got to Jeremiah's and he was there, waiting outside with the car. He'd loaded all of our stuff. Scarlett took one look at that open trunk and the bags inside and started pulling them out. She threw them on the ground, all of them, in this panicked frenzy. She was crying and shaking. She was just so . . ."

"Scared."

"Terrified," she whispered, wiping at the corner of her eye. "That's what he taught us. Fear. He'd broken her—us—long before that night."

Except Presley wasn't broken. She was whole and strong and a goddamn miracle. "How many times have you told this story?"

She met my gaze. "Once."

"To Draven?"

"Yeah." She cast her eyes to the photo on the wall. "To Draven."

He might have been a flawed man, but Draven had loved her like a daughter. What kind of woman would Presley be today if Draven hadn't stepped up for her? What kind of place would she have landed in if Clifton Forge hadn't been an option? I'd seen what happened to a lot of runaway kids in California. Their lives became about drugs, alcohol and sex. Because of Draven, Presley had stopped the cycle.

"What happened next? That night?"

She sniffled, reaching for some composure. "Jeremiah and I tried to calm Scarlett down but she was hysterical. She begged me to go home, but I told her I was leaving with or without her. She started screaming. One of the neighbors turned on a light and it freaked me out. So I grabbed whatever bags I could, shoved them in the car and I left. I left her there."

"You didn't have a choice."

"I could have stayed," she said. "I could have stayed for her."

"Where do you think you'd be if you'd stayed?"

"Dead," she replied immediately. "Maybe not in the physical sense, but he would have killed my soul."

"Then you didn't have a choice. And I, for one, am glad you got the hell out of there."

Presley shrugged. "Maybe."

The weight of her past settled into the room, the air growing thick and heavy. The two of us sat in silence as I replayed her story, over and over. Anger at her father burned under my skin and my mind changed. I wouldn't involve Laurelin in his demise. I wanted that satisfaction for myself, for Presley. I'd always believed there was a special place in hell for those who hurt children, especially their own, and her father belonged in that circle.

My God, she was strong. What had it been like for her to drive to Montana alone? How scared had she been to leave? She'd been lucky to score that job at the garage. I was a man who believed in destiny—and getting that job with Draven had been nothing short of fate.

And she'd lost him.

He was the father she'd never had. The father she'd always needed. And that son of a bitch Marcus Wagner had pushed him to suicide.

I'd made a goddamn movie about it.

Fuck. Fuck me and fuck that movie.

I never should have come here. I never should have bought that screenplay. It would have died and no one would have known that story. But it was too late now. I'd found Presley and leaving her was not an option.

I'd tried to forget her for months, but every night when I'd gone to bed alone, I'd wished she were at my side. I'd thought about her each morning and dreamed of her face, her laugh at night.

Presley didn't have Draven to protect her anymore, to listen to her woes, but she had me. She'd always have me, a man who stood by her side when she slammed the door in an asshole's face. A man who'd carry her to bed when she fell asleep watching a movie.

Luke Rosen was not that man.

Presley would stand on her own, she didn't need me to prop her up, but I would all the same.

"You're the strongest woman I've ever met."

She scoffed. "Your old partner sounded much stronger than me."

"You clawed your way to a good life. That's the definition of strength."

"But was it enough?" she asked. "I set myself free, but I left my twin sister behind."

"You can't always save someone. Sometimes, they need to want to save themselves."

She looked down the hallway again. "I used to text her. All I had was the number she had from high school. For all I know, my parents took that phone away and that number belongs to someone in Skokie, Illinois, now. But I texted her, and I kept her in my heart. I always hoped she'd get out."

"She's here, isn't she? She got out."

"When? Has he been hurting her all these years? Ten years, Shaw. Ten. I know exactly how many bruises a person can get in ten years."

This distance between us wasn't working anymore. I couldn't sit here and watch her try to hold herself together. I slid closer, taking her arms and unwrapping them from her legs. Then I hooked her knees over my lap so I could lean in close. "Don't blame yourself for this. You didn't do anything wrong. You were eighteen and scared too. None of this is on you."

She looked into my eyes, those beautiful crystal-blue pools flooding with tears. "I abandoned her."

"You saved your own life."

"The guilt"—she swallowed hard—"is crushing me."

"Let it go, baby," I whispered. "Stop holding it so close."

She collapsed into my chest and the dam broke.

I wrapped my arm around her shoulders, pulling her into my lap as she fell apart in my arms. Her shoulders convulsed and tears soaked my shirt.

"Let it go," I whispered into her hair. "I've got you."

She buried her face in my neck, then cried and cried until there were no tears left. I expected her to sit ramrod straight and pull away. I was ready for the wall she'd slam up between us.

279

But she stayed.

She held on to me as I held on to her. The barriers, the obstacles, vanished.

Trust. Honesty. Faith.

They cloaked us and sent a surge of hope through my veins.

We were going to make it. I was going to win her back. The crippling pressure in my chest ebbed along with the fear that had settled deep when I'd thought I'd lost her.

The fight wasn't won. Yet. But I'd walk away the victor. I'd win Presley Marks.

She was my anchor.

She was my heart.

"Sorry," she said as she sucked in a deep breath and leaned back. She wiped at her cheeks, sniffling. "I didn't mean to unload on you."

"I'm glad you did. You good?" I cupped her cheek, using my thumb to dry one last tear.

She met my gaze, giving me the weight of her face in my palm. "Yes. For now."

"When yes becomes a no, you come find me. Okay?" I trailed my fingertips along her jaw.

Presley's breath hitched and her eyes flared as I leaned in closer. Our noses nearly touched.

This was closer than we'd been in months. The heat from her skin, the warmth of her touch, her scent—"I fucking missed you, Pres."

She leaned in, her lips almost dropping to mine, then she was gone. She shot off my lap, shaking her head and clamping a hand over her mouth.

Damn.

She dropped her hand. "I'm with Luke."

"So you keep saying." Except I hadn't seen him since the night he'd dropped her off. "Where's he been?"

She maneuvered around the coffee table, putting the piece of furniture between us. "He knows Scarlett is here, and he's giving me some time alone with her."

Wrong move, Rosen. Luke hadn't been here to catch her tears. He hadn't been here when she'd been ready to unload the past. And I had a feeling, if it had been Luke in my seat, Presley wouldn't have told him anyway.

She'd trusted me with that gift. *Me.*

I was winning this goddamn fight.

I stood from the couch and walked to the chair where I'd draped my jacket when I'd come inside. "Luke's a nice guy, but he's not the right guy."

"You don't know that."

"Yeah, I do." The right guy was standing in her living room. "End it."

"No."

"Call it off."

"No." She huffed. "No. No. No."

My voice dropped, smooth and gentle. "End it, Pres. Please."

"N-no," she stuttered, maybe because each time she said no, the corner of my mouth turned up. "You should go."

I shrugged on my jacket. "If you need anything, I'm right next door. No strings. I'll be here."

She nodded, her arms crossed over her chest as she followed me to the door, keeping a safe distance. "Bye."

Forget the door. I spun on her, stepping into her space with one long stride. "Don't say goodbye. I never want to hear it from you again."

"Shaw—"

"Are you in love with him?"

"It's only been a month."

"Give me a month."

She huffed. "You had yours already."

"And I fucked it up. Give me another chance. Please." If we'd reached the begging stage, I'd drop to my knees this second.

"Why?"

Time to lay it all out there. "Because I fell in love with you this summer." I framed her face in my hands as she gasped. "Because you fell in love with me too. And because he'll never kiss you like this."

Then I crushed my mouth to hers, hoping to erase every lick of Luke Rosen with every sweep of my tongue.

CHAPTER TWENTY-TWO

PRESLEY

I closed the door, locked it, then let shame wash over my body.

Shaw had kissed me.

And I'd kissed him back.

I'd kissed a man while dating another.

Shit. I was low. I wasn't this woman. I didn't string men along. Hell, before Jeremiah, there hadn't been any men to string along.

Before Jeremiah, there'd been boys in high school who'd sneak a kiss in an empty hallway. They'd been appealing only because they'd been forbidden. Those boys had been a way to give my father a rebellious *fuck you*.

When I'd moved to Clifton Forge, I'd been too busy growing up to think of dating. Besides that, no one had asked. The eligible men in town saw me surrounded by Tin Kings and stayed far away.

Then came Jeremiah. Then Shaw.

My hand came to my swollen lips and I wiped them

again. Shaw's taste was still in my mouth, and his scent clung to the air.

I'd let him sweep his tongue against mine and devour my lips until I'd realized exactly what I was doing, how I was betraying Luke. I'd pulled away and shoved him out the door.

What was I doing? This wasn't me.

My stomach churned. Luke Rosen was a good man. He deserved better. He deserved a woman who wasn't kissing other men.

A woman whose heart wasn't torn.

Kissing Shaw hadn't felt wrong, not in the moment. Feeling his lips on mine was like coming home after a long day. It was like finding the sanctuary, the solace I'd been missing for months. The boat of my life stopped rocking. The waters of my soul calmed.

My foolish, reckless heart was his.

There was no Luke and me. Me and Luke.

When I looked into the future, I saw a man with dark blond hair and a smile that millions of women coveted but was only for me.

Poor Luke had never stood a chance. Even if Shaw hadn't returned to Clifton Forge, eventually I would have cut Luke loose. I simply wasn't . . . available.

But Shaw had returned. Things would be entirely different this time around. I couldn't hide him from the people in my life. The world would know that Shaw Valance was sleeping in my bed.

"Ugh." I dropped my forehead to the door.

Was I doing this? Shaw had the power to destroy me. If he left me behind again, I'd be shattered beyond repair.

Or . . .

He'd hold my heart and treat it with tender care.

He'd love me.

But before I could think about Shaw, about taking that risk, I had to end it with Luke.

I pushed away from the door and walked into the living room, grabbing my phone.

"Hey," Luke answered. "I was just thinking about you."

Oh, his voice. Not as smooth as Shaw's but it was still sexy. I sank down to the edge of my chair, my shoulders slumping. "Are you still coming over later?"

"I'd like to see you. But if you need more time with your sister, I understand."

I looked down the hallway to the door that was still closed. "No, I'd like to see you too."

"Yeah?" Luke sounded so hopeful. I bet he was smiling.

This was going to suck. "Yeah."

"Give me an hour."

"Okay." An hour would have to be enough time to figure out what to say.

I hung up and tossed the phone aside, pinching the bridge of my nose.

My emotions were all over the place. I hadn't planned on unloading my childhood on Shaw, but with Scarlett here, the floodgates had opened and the horror I hadn't wanted to relive for years had come rushing out.

I hadn't even hesitated. Confiding in Shaw was so natural. So easy. Why was that? I'd kept my past locked up tight. The only person who'd been able to finagle it out of me had been Draven, and even then, there were things I hadn't told him.

I hadn't told him about the red nail polish incident because Draven would have jumped on his bike, ridden to

Chicago and slit my father's throat. It had been hard enough admitting my father had beaten me. I'd cried. Draven had cussed. And when the lid on his temper had blown, I'd clutched his arm and made him promise not to retaliate.

I'd assumed Scarlett was still there and I hadn't wanted to make things worse. And I hadn't wanted my past mixing with my present. The Presley with long hair and a dutiful smile was dead. The Presley who lived by her own design had been thriving.

I didn't want my parents tainting the beauty I'd made for myself.

Shaw had been as angry as Draven. Shaw's fury had pulsed off him in waves, but much like Draven, he'd locked it down. He'd listened and when I'd broken, he'd held me like I was precious.

If I hadn't already fallen for Shaw, today would have been the tipping point.

He'd told me he loved me. He'd been so sure I loved him too.

Was I in love? Being around Shaw was comforting. It was exhilarating. But there was something else—a feeling I couldn't name.

Those were worries for another time because I had a guest coming over. I stood up and straightened the living room. I lit a candle on the coffee table because I didn't want Luke to walk in and smell Shaw's cologne.

Then I waited. My stomach knotted and I couldn't seem to take a deep breath. My palms were sweating by the time Luke arrived, true to his word, exactly an hour after our phone conversation.

"Hey." He smiled and kissed me on the cheek when I greeted him at the door.

"Hi." I took his jacket and hung it in the small coat closet. "Come on in."

Luke followed me into the living room and looked around. "Nice place."

"Thanks." And thank God that elderly woman had crashed into the gym.

It wouldn't have been right, sleeping with Luke. No matter how many times I'd mentally paired us together, there was a gap.

That gap's name was Shaw Valance.

"Would you like something to drink?" I asked.

"Nah, I'm good." He walked into the living room and took a seat on the love seat. He sat right in the middle, leaving no room for me to sit beside him, then leaned his elbows on his knees. "How is your sister?"

"Fine." I took the chair across from the love seat. "She's sleeping at the moment."

"Anything I can do?"

"No." I gave him a small smile, then mustered my courage to break this off. "So, um—"

He held up a hand. "Presley, it's okay. I know why I'm here."

"You do?"

"Shaw Valance is back."

"How did you know? Did he call you?" Because that was going to piss me off. Shaw had no right to interfere.

Luke shook his head. "There's not a lot that happens here that the chief of police doesn't know about. Especially when a famous actor moves next door to my girlfriend's house."

Girlfriend. He thought of me as his girlfriend.

Oh, hell. This was not getting easier, but I took a deep

breath and gave Luke the only thing I had left—honesty. "We were together when he lived here before. It ended when he left."

"But now he's back," Luke said. "I get it. If I had to choose me over Shaw, I might not choose me either. He's surprisingly difficult to dislike."

Ugh. He was being so nice about this. Couldn't he get mad, call me horrible names and storm out the door? "I'm so sorry, Luke."

He hung his head for a moment, then lifted it to give me a sad smile. "So am I."

Silence settled over the room, aside from the candlewick crackling on the table between us.

Luke stood. "Take care, Presley."

"You too." I followed him to the front door and retrieved his coat.

He shrugged it on, then bent to brush another kiss on my cheek. There were no tingles. There were no sparks or butterflies.

I'd been searching for something with Luke that had never been there.

"Give me a few weeks, then tell Shaw he owes me a beer for stealing my girl."

I nodded. "Okay."

Luke opened the door and walked outside, lifting his hand to wave before he jogged down the steps. I stood in the cold, watching as he got into his truck and reversed into the street. Then I closed the door, turned and gasped.

Scarlett was standing in the hall.

"He's cute."

My hand flew to my racing heart. "You scared me."

"Sorry." She shrugged and walked into the living room,

288

curling up on the couch. Her eyes drooped and she yawned, shoving a lock of her stringy hair from her face. "What day is it?"

"Tuesday," I said, sitting beside her.

"Huh. Guess I was tired."

We stared at each other wordlessly.

Looking at her used to be like looking in the mirror. We'd had the same hair, the same clothes. Did I seem as foreign to her as she did to me? Maybe after a shower, she wouldn't look so much like a ghost.

"Do you want a shower?" I asked.

Scarlett dropped her gaze to her hands. "Sure. Can I borrow some clothes?"

"I'll put some on your bed. There are towels and an extra toothbrush in your bathroom."

"Thanks." Her fingers toyed on her lap, picking at something black, probably mascara, caked beneath a nail. Then her hands stilled, and she looked up. "Did you love him?"

"Luke? No. We only dated for a month."

"No, not Luke." She gave me a flat look. "Jeremiah. Did you love him?"

"Oh." My cheeks flamed.

Why couldn't we have talked about anything else first? Like why she was here. Or how she'd left Chicago. Or what she'd been doing with her life. Why did we have to jump right into the Jeremiah subject?

"Yes," I admitted. "At least, I thought I loved him at the time."

"And now?"

"Maybe I don't know what love is."

"I do." Scarlett shifted her gaze to the burning candle. "Because Jeremiah taught me."

289

And there, in her soft voice, was her broken heart.

I'd betrayed my twin sister. "I'm sorry."

For Jeremiah.

For leaving her.

For the years that had gone.

"Whatever." Scarlett stared at the candle without blinking. Without speaking. She was quiet for so long that I gave up and turned to the candle too.

We'd been so close once. If there was love in my past, it was entwined with memories of Scarlett.

Had I ruined us the night I'd left? Was there any hope I'd get my sister back? Or would she hold Jeremiah against me forever?

"I missed you," I whispered, not brave enough to look away from the candle.

Scarlett stood from the couch and exited the room. But before she disappeared into the bathroom, she paused at the mouth of the hall. "I missed you too."

I held my smile until I heard the shower turn on, then hope bloomed.

This reunion wasn't what I'd planned. A reunion wasn't something I'd *ever* planned.

At eighteen, I'd had illusions of the two of us laughing and singing to the radio as we drove away from Chicago. I'd pictured us living our lives separately, but connected—mine in Montana, hers in California. We'd call each other often. We'd vacation on the beach and spend Christmases together.

None of that had come true.

But maybe it would, a decade later.

I went to my bedroom and took out a pair of sweats and a sweatshirt for Scarlett. I also grabbed a fresh pair of panties and a sports bra. I set them on her bed, glancing around the guest bedroom at the bag she'd brought with her.

It was a black backpack, sagging in a corner like it was mostly empty. Where had she been? Where was she living? She'd arrived in a cab. Had she flown here from somewhere? Or taken a bus? Or hitchhiked?

Now that she was awake, we could talk. I went to the kitchen and made dinner. It wasn't anything fancy, but I was hungry and from the looks of it, Scarlett hadn't eaten much lately. I went for simple grilled cheese sandwiches and tomato soup.

When she emerged from her bedroom, our meal was waiting at my round dining table beside the kitchen.

"What would you like to drink?" I asked.

"Water is fine." She slid into a seat, her hair wet and hanging down her back. My clothes were not fitted, but they were baggier on her than they'd ever been on me.

"You can start without me." I filled up two glasses of water in the kitchen, and when I returned to the table, half her sandwich was gone. I sat down, trying not to stare as she inhaled the rest of her food.

"Thanks for dinner." She gulped from the water glass. "I was starving."

"You slept for two days."

"I was tired." Scarlett yawned and stood. "I'm going to go back to bed."

"Oh." So much for talking. "I have to get back to work tomorrow. Are you staying or . . ."

"If that's okay."

"Yes, of course. Stay as long as you'd like."

She picked up her dishes and took them to the kitchen.

I abandoned my meal to follow. "Do you need more

clothes? Or anything? I can swing by the grocery store on the way home from work. Maybe we could talk tomorrow night."

"Tomorrow."

I smiled. "Get some rest."

"Night."

I waited until her door was closed before returning to my plate, but my appetite was gone.

Was she hiding from me? Or was she really this tired? Was she sick?

I ran a hand through my hair, frustrated that I didn't have answers, but Scarlett had always done things on her own timeline. She'd wait until the candles on our birthday cake were dripping before she'd blow them out. She'd take twice as long to jump in the pool. It was the reason she hadn't left Chicago with me. She hadn't been ready yet.

When she wanted to answer my questions, she would. Until then, I'd be patient.

I did the dishes and cleaned up the kitchen. I washed a load of laundry and set a stack of clothes outside Scarlett's door. It was only seven o'clock by the time my chores were done, and I had no desire to watch TV or read.

The yellow house next door was calling my name.

I padded down the hallway toward my bedroom. Shaw's window was dark but there was a glow from deeper in the house. Donning a warm sweater and a pair of wool socks, I tugged on my boots and slipped into the dark night.

The air was crisp, and my earlobes froze as I crunched across the snow-trodden path Shaw had created between our houses. My foot hit the bottom stair and his door swung open.

Shaw looked to my driveway. "Where's Luke?"

"Gone."

"When I saw his truck, I thought you and he were . . ." His face was washed in relief. "I about came out of my skin."

"Oh, well, we were never together. Not intimately."

He blinked and stepped onto the porch, his bare feet oblivious to the freezing temperature. "Say that again."

"I ended it."

He took another step. "You ended it."

"Yeah." I climbed the steps, making my way toward the warmth of his arms. "You better not break my heart."

He stepped closer, placing his palm between my breasts. It flattened on my sternum and the heat from his touch seeped through my sweater. "It's safe. I swear it."

Safe.

That was the word I'd been looking for earlier.

It wasn't as monumental as love, but for a woman who'd lived so much of her life in fear, *safe* seemed almost as important.

"Kiss me, Shaw."

He framed my face. "Where?"

"Here." I pointed to my lips. *Everywhere.*

"I don't want this to be a secret anymore," he said. "But if you take me, it means you get it all. The cameras. The tabloids. I want you, more than anything I've wanted in my life, but I don't come easily."

I arched an eyebrow and gave him a sly grin. "We'll see about that."

Gripping the hand he still had over my heart, I stepped past him and dragged him into the house.

His sexy chuckle drifted away as he kicked the door closed. Then his hands were all over me, and his mouth was on mine.

I didn't care if Shaw came with fans. I didn't care that

he'd drag me into the spotlight. Because I'd rather be by his side than standing in the shadows alone.

With one fast grab, he swooped me into his arms, holding me against his chest as he walked us into the house. He turned to his bedroom, never once breaking away from my mouth.

My arms banded around his shoulders, pulling him close as I slanted to deepen our kiss. To savor the feel of his lips and the wet heat. We panted and licked and sucked, knowing there'd be no stopping.

We wouldn't come up for air until we were both boneless.

I wouldn't mind if that took days.

Shaw's delicious scent filled my nose as we entered his room. The bed centered beneath the window was big and covered in a charcoal quilt. He spun us around, setting me on the edge as he dropped to his knees.

His hands roamed my legs as I whipped the sweater off my torso. My nipples were pebbled in my bra and my core throbbed as he stayed on his knees, removing my boots and socks.

When my feet were bare, Shaw picked one up and placed a soft, gentle kiss to my ankle.

A shiver ran down my spine. "What was that for?"

"I've never kissed you there before."

"Oh." I blushed furiously through a smile that pinched my cheeks.

Shaw laughed, the vibrations of his rich voice rolling over my skin and prickling the little hairs with electricity.

He stood and unzipped his jeans. He didn't shove them off his hips but let them hang open, clinging to the V of his hip bones and teasing me with what was beneath. With one graceful move, he reached behind his neck and yanked his black cashmere sweater over his head.

My mouth watered at the sight of the bare chest and sinewed arms I'd dreamed about for months. My fingers itched to touch the sprinkling of hair that dusted his chest, to feel the hardness of his body beneath my palms.

"Where else haven't I kissed you?" he asked.

I pointed to the inside of my arm, the hollow point opposite my elbow. "Here."

He bent, bracing himself above me with one arm in the bed, then used his free hand to take my wrist. Shaw's touch was featherlight. He skated those lips up the inside of my forearm, the pressure enough to leave a stream of tingles. When he reached the hollow point, his tongue darted out to drop one wet kiss.

The erotic sensation of his lips, the heat of his body hovering above mine but not touching, sent a pool of desire to my center.

"Where else?"

I pointed to the spot behind my ear. Maybe he'd kissed me there before, but I couldn't remember past this lust-induced fog.

Shaw placed the kiss on the exact spot I'd pointed at. My eyes drifted closed as he dragged the stubble of his cheek across the line of my jaw.

"Here." I touched the underside of my chin.

He dropped a kiss there, then another on my lips.

I reached between us, lifting the hem of my T-shirt. He took it from my hands, lifting it off. The jeans I'd worn rode low enough to show the waistband of my panties. I pointed to the red lace on my hip. "Here."

Shaw dropped a trail of kisses from my chin, over the

cotton of my bra to my hip. Once he'd kissed that spot, he nuzzled kisses across my stomach.

I threaded my fingers through his hair, then I pulled him up my body, sealing my mouth over his as my hands dove into his jeans.

The slow, tortured exploration was over. We flew into a frenzy, stripping one another of our remaining clothes. He moved us deeper into the bed, covering me with his weight as he stretched for the nightstand's drawer.

He was going for a condom.

I froze.

"What?" He stilled. "What's wrong?"

"Were you . . ." *Oh God,* if he'd been with another woman—I was beginning to understand how hard it must have been for him to see me with Luke.

"No." He kissed my lips. "There's been no one."

Relief crashed into me and nearly made me weep. I cupped his jaw. "Good. I might have had to kill you."

He chuckled and kissed me again, then went back to the nightstand, but I stopped him once more.

"I'm on the pill. I got tested after the wedding."

"I'm clean too."

"Then stop making me wait." I lifted up and slammed my mouth to his, diving in with my tongue as my hand reached for his shaft between us.

His hand wrapped over the top of mine as he dragged the tip through my wet folds. Then he took my wrist away at the same time he thrust forward.

I hissed, crying out as he filled and stretched me.

"Fuck." Shaw buried his face in my neck and stilled, giving me a moment to adjust.

"Move," I whispered into his ear.

He obeyed, rocking in and out with long, hard strokes that shook me from head to toe. The feel of him bare inside me was incredible. The stretch, the connection, was raw and profound and breathtaking.

We were beautiful together.

We moved in sync with every touch and kiss. We devoured one another until neither of us could hold back from the edge.

I cried out Shaw's name as I came, blinding sparks overtaking my vision. Shaw moaned against my breast as he sucked a nipple into his mouth, pouring into me as I clenched around him.

"Damn, woman." He breathed against my skin as he collapsed onto his back, pulling me to his side. "I missed you. So damn much."

"I missed you too." I hugged an arm over his stomach and kissed his pec.

"I need to ask you something."

"Okay." I shifted up to look at his face, nervous at the seriousness of his tone.

He grinned and rubbed the crease between my eyebrows away. "Will you go out to dinner with me?"

"Like . . . on a *date?*" I scrunched up my nose, holding back a smile. "What's in it for me?"

"Besides a meal?" Shaw's eyes sparkled. "Me."

"Hmm." My smile stretched wide. "Yes. I'll go on a date with you."

His arms came around me in a flash, flipping us both until he'd pinned me to the bed. "Finally I didn't get a goddamn no."

CHAPTER TWENTY-THREE

PRESLEY

"Feelin' better?" Dash asked as he relaxed into the chair across from my desk.

"I, uh . . . wasn't sick. Sorry."

He raised an eyebrow as he took a sip of his coffee. "You okay?"

"I have something to tell you. Two things, actually."

Dash sat up straight. "Are you in trouble? Is this about the Warriors? You haven't seen Jeremiah around, have you?"

"No, it's nothing like that. I haven't heard from Jeremiah in months."

"Thank fuck," he breathed.

Nothing had ever come of Leo's fight with Jeremiah. And I hadn't bothered mentioning to anyone at the garage that Jeremiah had come to visit. If the Warriors cared Leo had beaten him up, they'd let it go, but Dash was never *not* guarded. He had too much to lose. With Draven gone, he'd stepped in to make sure his family, me included, was safe.

"So what's going on?"

"I called in sick because I knew if I told you the truth, I'd have people on my doorstep. I needed a couple days away because my sister is in town."

"Your twin?"

My eyes narrowed. "How'd you know I had a twin?"

I'd never told Dash about Scarlett. Draven had known about my sister, so maybe he'd passed it along, but my hunch was that Emmett had snooped. I didn't mind, but I wasn't going to miss this chance to razz Dash.

"We, uh . . . damn," he grumbled. "Emmett kind of—"

"Emmett kind of likes to hack into people's lives, and you kind of like to know about everything he finds." I giggled. "It's fine. Next time, just ask me."

"In our defense, it was a long time ago, back when you started working at the garage. And there wasn't much to find. Just your high school transcripts and next of kin. You were boring."

If he only knew how wrong that statement was. "Anyway, my sister is here. I haven't seen Scarlett in a long time, so it was a surprise when she showed up at my house on Sunday."

"You two been catching up?"

I shook my head. "Not really. She's pretty much been sleeping since she got here."

"Since Sunday? It's Wednesday, Pres."

"There's something wrong." I cupped my coffee mug, letting its warmth seep into my palms. "She's really skinny. There's the sleeping. I have my theories about what's going on, but until she tells me, I won't know for sure."

I suspected that my father had been abusing her for years and she'd finally found the strength to run away. Or maybe my parents were dead, and she'd been free to leave. But the way Scarlett looked reminded me of my mother on the days when she hadn't tried to hide her pain.

"Want to talk through your theories?" Dash asked.

"That's okay. But thank you. It's complicated and messy."

"I'm always here to listen."

"I know." I smiled. "And I appreciate it."

One day, I'd tell Dash about my childhood. When he undoubtedly got angry, I'd calm him down and convince him to leave my father alone, much like I'd done with Draven. For now, my focus was on Scarlett. And when I needed someone to lean on, I had Shaw.

"What's the second thing?" Dash asked, picking up his mug again.

"I'm seeing someone."

"Luke Rosen." He nodded. "Good guy."

"Yes, he is. But no, I'm not seeing Luke anymore."

"Okay," he drawled. "Then who?"

A vehicle door slammed outside, boots pounded on the sidewalk, and as if on cue, Shaw strode into the office.

I gave him a flat look. We'd agreed this morning when I'd left his house that we'd meet for lunch. It wasn't even ten o'clock yet.

"Morning." Shaw extended a hand to Dash, who shook it from the chair.

"Don't tell me you're making a sequel already."

Shaw chuckled. "No, this time I'm in Montana for personal reasons."

"The guy you're seeing?" Dash asked.

I nodded as Shaw rounded my desk. "You just couldn't stay away."

"From you?" He bent low, chuckling in my ear as he brushed a kiss to my cheek. "Never."

I met Dash's gaze and gave him an apologetic shrug. "He's not nearly as horrible as I thought."

"Baby, you say the sweetest things to me." Shaw grinned and sat on the edge of my desk, staking his claim by my side.

Dash's gaze bounced between the two of us for a moment, then leveled on me. "He's good to you?"

"Yes." I looked up at Shaw, his golden gaze waiting. "He is."

A wave of relief flashed across Shaw's face, like maybe he'd expected me to still be angry about how we'd ended things the first time. But I'd accepted his apology.

He'd been forgiven.

Dash rose from his chair, standing to his full height, and shot Shaw a warning look. "Don't fucking hurt her."

"You have my word," Shaw promised.

"Does this mean you're going to move to California?" Dash asked me. "Because I'm not okay with that."

"No," I said at the same time Shaw said, "Maybe one day."

"Uh . . . we haven't gotten that far yet." Before we talked about long-term plans, we needed to survive a dinner date.

Dash turned and headed for the shop, but before he left, he jerked his chin at Shaw. "Welcome back."

"Thanks."

I pulled in my lips to hide a smile as Dash disappeared.

"Why do I feel like that was important?" Shaw asked as the door closed.

"Because it was."

Dash had never liked Jeremiah. From the moment they'd met, Dash'd had a bad taste in his mouth. He hadn't shaken

Jeremiah's hand or addressed him the few times he'd come to the office. Instead, Dash had pestered me for years to call off the engagement.

That simple statement, welcoming Shaw to Montana, spoke volumes.

Maybe Shaw's reason for coming here in the first place had been to do a project they despised, but the filming was done and the movie buzz wouldn't last forever.

Once the movie was released, we'd forget about it. In a way, we already had. We lived in our corner of the world, far away from the glamour of Hollywood, and no matter what happened with the film, the memory of Marcus Wagner had already faded.

"That went better than expected," Shaw said. "I didn't want you to have to tell them on your own."

This man. "You came for backup?"

"Yep." He leaned down and brushed a kiss across my lips. "And because I missed you."

"It's been three hours."

"Exactly. That's a long time."

We'd spent the night reacquainting our bodies. I'd slept in Shaw's arms and woken in sated bliss before going home to get ready for work.

Shaw stood and took off his coat. "Was Scarlett awake when you left?"

"No. I peeked in on her, but she was still asleep. It's weird, right? It's like she hasn't slept in weeks."

"There's definitely something going on."

"I think it's about my parents. Do you think, maybe . . ."

"Maybe what?" He sat on the desk again, this time facing me after tossing his coat aside.

"That maybe they're . . . dead?" It was hard to say aloud.

I had no love for my parents, but there was something, deep inside, that would mourn my mother.

Never my father.

"Want me to find out?" Shaw asked.

"Find out how? Google?"

He lifted a shoulder. "That or we can hire a private investigator to dig deeper."

"Nah. If we want to do that, I can just ask Emmett."

"Emmett?" His eyebrows came together. "I thought he was a mechanic."

I giggled. "Emmett's handy with more than just a wrench. I'm sure he's got a background check on you on his laptop along with anything else he could scour from the interwebs."

"Oh, Jesus," he muttered.

"But no, to answer your question. I don't want to know about my parents. Not before I talk to Scarlett."

"Would you like me to be there?"

I put my hand on his thigh. "Thanks, but I think we need to talk alone."

"I'm right next door if you change your mind."

"This is so . . . this sucks." I dropped my gaze, voicing one of my fears. "We used to know everything about one another, but Scarlett seems like a different person now. I feel like I don't know my sister anymore. What if we don't like each other?"

"It happens. Families are complicated. My father used to be my hero, and I called him nearly every day. Now, I haven't talked to him in years."

"You will one day."

"What makes you think so?"

"You love your family, Shaw."

Whenever he talked about his mom or sisters, he'd smile and his eyes would light up. And the day he'd told me about his father, there'd been such painful longing in his voice. He wasn't bitter or mad; he was deeply disappointed. Someday, it would fade and he'd be ready to talk to his father again.

"You're not ready yet, but you will be one day. I've never met your father, but I don't think he's an evil man. He's not like Marcus Wagner. Marcus didn't think he did anything wrong. He felt righteous and justified in his actions. Your father confessed."

Shaw stared at the wall behind me, his gaze focused on nothing.

"I know what it is to have an evil father." I squeezed his leg. "My father doesn't think he's done anything wrong either. He thinks it's his right to rape his wife and beat his children. Would your father ever have treated you or your sisters that way?"

"Never," he said quietly.

"He's not your hero anymore, and that's okay. But he's still your father, and I can tell you still love him."

Shaw gave me a sad smile. "I'm not ready to call him."

"Then wait. There's no rush." I patted his leg once more, then reached for my coffee, sipping it before it went cold.

"Is Montana a deal breaker for you?" he asked.

"This is my home."

A home I'd made for myself with a family who loved me unconditionally. A family who'd shown up on my wedding day when they'd hated the groom, but they'd shown up anyway because I'd asked.

I wanted to live alongside them. I wanted to share our lives, blend them together. I wanted to go to Genevieve's house when she and Isaiah had another baby and watch their kids while they took a nap. I wanted to have Christmas dinner with Dash and Bryce. I wanted to meet Emmett and Leo for a beer at The Betsy on a random Friday night to talk about nothing and tease them relentlessly for being eternal bachelors.

"I want it all," I admitted. "I want you, and I want Montana."

"Okay." Shaw nodded.

"Okay? That's it?"

"Okay," he repeated. "Then we live in Montana."

"What about Los Angeles? What about your career?"

"LA isn't going anywhere, and I don't have to live there to do my job. I'll need to travel at times and to see my family, but as long as I can convince you to come with me, this can be home base."

Wow. My head was spinning, trying to absorb his words. We were talking about our future. A long-term future. Shaw had spelled it out so simply, and now that he'd planted the idea in my brain, I wouldn't be able to imagine—I didn't want to imagine—anything else.

We'd build our life here with my family. Our home base. And we'd fly around the world when necessary.

"I've never been on an airplane," I blurted. Why that was the most important fact to announce was a mystery.

Shaw chuckled. "Then you're in luck, because I happen to own an airplane."

"This was not the conversation I'd planned to have today."

Shaw took the coffee mug from my hands and pulled me from my seat, wrapping me in his arms. "Whether you said Montana or California or Japan or Antarctica, it wouldn't have mattered."

I pressed my ear to his heart, soaking in the steady drum. "And if you had said it had to be California, I would have gone."

"Better stop talking, otherwise I'm going to lock us in the waiting room and make use of one of those couches."

I smiled. "I'm pretty sure Dash and Bryce have claimed the waiting room as theirs."

"Annnnd I'm never sitting in there again." I giggled as he kissed my hair and let me go. "I'll get out of here and let you get to work."

"What are you doing today?"

"I've got some calls to make."

"For?"

He winked. "You'll see."

I escorted him to the door, standing on my toes as he gave me an indecent kiss. "I'm going to try and get out of here early so I can talk to Scarlett. Then I'll come over."

"Okay. Call me if you need anything."

"I will." I kissed him again, squashing my habitual goodbye.

Shaw didn't say goodbye. I doubt I would have noticed with anyone else, but Shaw's had always been significant. Refusing to say that word seemed important to him, so I'd stop saying it too.

He waved as he stepped outside and I shut the door behind him, shuttering at the momentary shot of cold. I cranked the heating fan beneath my desk to high when I returned to my chair, and the day went by in a blur as I made up for missing the beginning of the week. My plan to get off early was thwarted, and it was close to five by the time I had deposits ready to swing by the bank and the mail to drop at the post office.

I hurried through my errands, and when I got home, Shaw's truck was in his driveway. I waved, in case he was near a window to see, then went inside to see Scarlett.

She was in the living room, watching a movie. Her hair was tied up in a messy bun. She wore the sweats I'd brought her last night, her feet bare and curled up under her seat.

Shaw's face flashed across the screen.

A swell of pride puffed up my chest as I sat beside her on the couch. Shaw's voice filled the room as he spoke to his commanding officer on the screen. "This is my favorite movie of his."

Scarlett hit pause. "I've never seen it, but he's not hard on the eyes."

She had no clue. Shaw on the screen was sexy. Shaw in his bedroom, holding me, laughing, was ethereal.

"Where did you disappear to last night?" she asked.

"Oh, uh"—I pointed toward my bedroom's side of the house—"I'm dating the guy next door."

Though dating felt like too casual a word. I mean, he'd told me today he'd relocate his life to Montana.

"The guy who was here last night?" Scarlett asked.

"No. Someone else."

She hummed. "You always did get around."

"Excuse me?" I blinked, certain I'd misunderstood her mutter. "What did you just say?"

Scarlett popped a shoulder. "You always had a couple of guys on the hook."

"In high school, when I was a confused teenager who was scared and desperate for some attention. Yeah, I flirted with any boy who looked my way twice. But I've never slept around. Don't you dare insinuate I'm some sort of whore.

I've been with two men in my life." I held up two fingers. "Two."

"This guy next door and my boyfriend? I guess that means we lost our virginity to the same guy."

I flinched. When had Scarlett developed such a sharp tongue? When had she learned to hate me?

"Why are you being cruel?" I whispered. "Because of Jeremiah? He came here. *He* found *me*. I didn't search him out to steal him from you. It was years after I left. Years after you broke up. If you're here to punish me for Jeremiah, I hate to break it to you, but he humiliated me more than you could ever imagine."

And that embarrassment was the best thing to ever happen to me.

"Whatever," she muttered.

"Why are you here, Scarlett?"

She popped that shoulder again. "I got your texts."

"All of them?"

"Yeah." She met my gaze. "Every single one."

"But you never replied. Why?"

"I didn't have anything to say, after you left." The last three words were so quiet I barely heard them.

"I tried to take you with me."

Her gaze drifted to the floor. "I was too scared to leave."

"I'm sorry. I'm so sorry, Scarlett."

She stayed silent.

"I wish I had shoved you in the car and made you leave. I've thought about that day a lot. About what I should have done. And I'm sorry that I left you behind."

Scarlett pulled her arms around herself, hugging them close. "He went into a rage. He was so angry that you'd left, that I wouldn't tell him where you'd gone, that he nearly beat Mom to death."

I gasped, my hand coming to my mouth. "What did he do to you?"

"He made me watch." She lifted her gaze and met mine. "He tied me to a chair in the living room, and other than that, he didn't lay a hand on me. Not once. Instead, he made me watch as he hit her over and over and over again. Until there was so much blood that even she couldn't clean it out of the carpet the next day."

Tears flooded my eyes and I squeezed them shut, trying to block out the mental image, but I saw it with vivid clarity. I saw exactly what she'd been forced to endure. Except unlike the times I'd been tied to a chair to watch the same horror unfold, Scarlett and I hadn't been side by side. I hadn't been there to hold her hand or help get Mom to her bedroom when it was over.

"I'm sorry."

"I should have left," she murmured. "I should have gone to California with Jeremiah."

I wiped my eyes dry, summoning strength to survive this conversation. To set the ghosts free. "When Jeremiah came out here, he said that you were still at home. You stayed?"

She nodded. "I stayed. I went to Dad's community college. I took the job he got for me as a receptionist at his company. I did exactly what he asked me to do, like always. Jeremiah kept trying to get me to leave, he wouldn't stop pressuring me, until finally he said he couldn't stand by and watch me become Mom."

According to Jeremiah, they'd broken up over a year before he'd come to Montana. Even after that year, he'd been so angry that she hadn't wanted to save herself.

He'd had a front-row seat to the disaster that was our home, but he'd never understood.

Jeremiah had watched me run and never look back. He'd found me years later, after I'd discovered confidence and self-worth. After fear no longer ruled my decisions.

But he'd missed the years when I'd been confused. He'd missed the moments of doubt.

The pain of our youth was intermixed with love. The cruelty was tied to affection.

Mom was Dad's toy, but she'd doted on her daughters. She'd hug us fiercely each morning, telling us how proud she was and how special we were. She'd kiss our cheeks and braid our hair. She hadn't protected us, but she'd loved us as best she could.

Dad's love came in the form of attention, and not all bad. If he'd slap me for a mistake, the next day he'd take me out for ice cream. He used to play board games with Scarlett and me. If Hasbro made it, we'd owned it. My favorite had been Clue, Scarlett's Scrabble. Dad had preferred Monopoly.

Dad hadn't been angry every day. Most, but not every. And on those days, the simple joy of playing games had filled our house. We'd laughed. We'd teased. We'd loved.

I loved my parents.

And I hated my parents.

Those two things were hard, even now, to reconcile.

Scarlett had been afraid to leave because of Dad's rage. But I suspected she'd also been afraid to leave her home and say farewell to Mom.

She'd always been the daughter closest to Mom. Scarlett had been the nurse, the first to run for an ice pack or a wash-cloth to sop up a bloody nose. Scarlett had attended to Mom while I'd cleaned up the physical mess.

That carpet stain Mom hadn't been able to remove? I would have scrubbed and scrubbed until the spot was clean, my resentment burning with each stroke. Meanwhile Scarlett would have brushed Mom's hair and stroked her cheek.

"Why did you leave?" I asked.

"Because Mom told me to go." Scarlett's fingers fiddled on her lap. "I told her you were getting married and she cried because she knew you wouldn't invite her. She told me to come and find you. To smile for her at your wedding. I didn't tell her you were marrying my ex-boyfriend."

"Did she know about Jeremiah?"

"No." Scarlett had hid Jeremiah from our parents when we'd been kids and apparently done the same as an adult.

"How'd you leave?"

"Mom gave me a roll of money that she'd kept hidden away from Dad, and one Sunday morning, I snuck out of our pew at church, saying I had to go to the bathroom. And I never went back."

My heart squeezed. Mom must have known what Scarlett's fate would be if she'd stayed. Either Dad would have forbidden her ever to leave, or he would have found her a man like himself to marry.

"Have you heard from her?"

She shook her head. "No. She doesn't have my number. I offered to give it to her, but she said it would be best if I didn't. Besides, Dad won't care that I left any more than he cared that you did. He's got his favorite punching bag. She might have pushed me out the door, but she won't leave him."

Mom's love for Dad would be her death sentence.

"Wait, you left to come to the wedding." That was months and months ago. "Where have you been since?"

311

"Here and there," Scarlett muttered.

Here and there? That wasn't an answer. "How did you get to Montana?"

"A bus."

"Have you been in Clifton Forge this whole time?"

Scarlett didn't answer.

Was that why Leo had claimed to see my doppelganger at The Betsy? It had to have been her. I'd brushed it off as him being drunk, but maybe he really had seen my twin. If she'd been in town, why hadn't she found me? Where had she been living? How was it possible that no one, other than Leo, had recognized her?

"What's going on? What aren't you telling me?"

She shifted uncomfortably, refusing to meet my eyes.

"Scar—"

The doorbell rang.

Scarlett jumped, shaking the whole couch. "Is someone coming over?"

"It's fine," I assured her. Who or what was she so afraid of? Was she worried Dad would track her down? "Don't worry. It's probably Shaw."

"Shaw?" Her eyes darted between me and the screen, where his face was still frozen. "Shaw who?"

"Shaw Valance." I pointed to the TV. "The man who lives next door."

She blinked and her jaw dropped.

I left her there, gaping, as I hurried to the door and swung it open, not bothering to check the peephole. Shaw was probably here for more *backup*.

"Hey—Jeremiah? What are you doing here?"

I asked the question, but as his gaze tracked past me into the house, searching, I knew the answer.

He was here for Scarlett.

"You need to leave." Until I had answers, he was not coming in this house. I pushed the door closed, but he shoved a foot inside.

Then he lifted the gun I hadn't noticed.

And pressed the barrel to my forehead.

CHAPTER TWENTY-FOUR

SHAW

"Hello, Dad."

"H-hi, Shaw."

The phone line went silent.

Before I'd made this call, I'd decided on what to say to my father, but the sound of his stunned, deep voice—a voice that sounded exactly like my own—had blanked my mind.

"You there?" he asked.

"Yeah." I cleared my throat and sucked some oxygen into my lungs. "How are you?"

"Good. You?"

"Doing good."

"Your sister tells me you're in Montana."

"I am. Looks like I'm going to be moving here."

He hummed. "Never been to Montana."

"Maybe one of these days, you and Mom can come up for a visit."

"I'd like that." There was a smile in his voice. "I'd like that a lot."

"That'd be nice." My shoulders fell from my earlobes.

This phone call had become a massive obstacle in my mind. With so much pressure from my mom and sisters to reach out to Dad, I'd built it up to be something huge.

But it was just a phone call to my father, like the hundreds I'd made before.

We didn't have to talk about the past. We didn't need to hash out why I was still disappointed in him and would be for a while.

It could just be a phone call to say hello.

Hello was often monumental in and of itself.

"How about this spring?" Dad asked.

"I'll go through my calendar and shoot some weekends over that would work for us."

Dad didn't ask who *us* was. Matine had likely filled my parents in about Presley too. "Sounds great."

"Okay. Good to talk to you, Dad."

"You too." His voice cracked. "Thanks for calling."

I hung up the phone and set it aside on the couch, dropping my face into my hands.

Then I breathed.

My heart was racing, and I was sweating. A two-minute phone call had drained my energy faster than the one-hour workout I'd done this morning.

Since I'd left the garage after my visit with Presley, I'd thought a lot about what she'd had to say. I'd thought a lot about what we'd decided.

Presley wanted to live in Montana, so we'd live in Montana.

We'd build our life together in Clifton Forge.

This was home.

I wanted to share it with my family, and to do that, I had to let go of the resentment I held for my father.

Presley was right about him. He wasn't an evil man.
Dad's crime didn't seem all that important in the grand
scheme of life. He'd made a mistake. He'd owned it. He'd
suffered the consequences.

He'd weathered the media storm without a word or
complaint, something he wouldn't have had to do if I hadn't
been famous. He'd never once made an excuse as to why he'd
taken that money.

Dad didn't deserve a life sentence. He wasn't Marcus
Wagner.

There'd been a time when I'd wanted to sit across from
Marcus in prison, but that didn't matter now.

I didn't give a fuck about Marcus Wagner's motives. He
was as dead to me as he was to Presley. I'd made the movie,
I'd uphold my obligations to promote it, and once it was
done, I'd simply be grateful that it had led me to Presley.

I was moving to Montana. Hell, I'd *moved* to Montana.
My assistant would take care of the address changes.

Presley's family was here, but I wanted her to be a part of
mine too. She'd love my sisters—the four of them would
commiserate and tease me relentlessly. My mother would
adore her, and my father would cherish a witty, kind daughter-in-law.

I wouldn't deprive Presley of those relationships, so it
was time to heal the rift.

Once I'd made the decision to call Dad, it was aston-
ishing how quickly the anger had just . . . melted away.

I stood from the couch, lighter than when I'd taken the
seat, and walked to the living room window, glancing
outside. Presley's Jeep was in the driveway. I'd seen her roll
in, giving me a little finger wave before she'd parked.

She'd been home for an hour and night had fallen. My

stomach growled, but I didn't want to eat until I'd heard from her. I was hoping maybe if I showed up with a pizza later, they wouldn't kick me out.

Was an hour enough time for the sisters to talk? My stomach growled again. I didn't want to rush Presley, but I also knew this wasn't going to be an easy discussion. Abandoning the window, I shot her a quick text, then flipped on the TV and found a basketball game.

Fifteen minutes passed on the game clock, and I gave in to my stomach, eating a granola bar and sending another text as I chewed. Ten minutes later, when it went unanswered, I called and got her voicemail.

Dread settled in my gut.

Something was wrong.

I didn't care if Presley and Scarlett wanted to be alone, I was checking on them. I pulled on my shoes and a jacket, then opened the front door just as the screech of tires on pavement filled the air and a streak of white whipped around the corner.

Luke's truck skidded to a stop in front of Presley's house.

Another cruiser flew down the street, parking beside him. No lights flashing. No sirens wailing. Two others stopped at the mouth of the cul-de-sac, forming a blockade.

My feet flew.

I leapt down the stairs and sprinted for Presley's house. Blood rushed in my ears, drowning out the sound of a shout at my back, but my legs kept pumping.

"Shaw, stop!"

I didn't stop, not until a pair of arms wrapped around me and tackled me to the snow.

"Get the fuck off me," I shouted and fought, throwing elbows and writhing to be free.

317

"Calm down," Luke barked. The bastard pinned me with his knee in my spine.

"Get off me!" I roared.

"Just listen," he shouted in my ear, making me wince. "You can't go in that house. Get it together."

"She's in trouble." My gut was screaming that I get inside her house.

"You go in there, the risk that this goes bad skyrockets. We both know that."

The truth sobered me up, chasing away the instinct to fight. "Let me go."

"Not until you're calm."

"I'm fucking calm. Let. Me. Up."

Luke hesitated but finally stood and held out a hand.

I ignored it, jumping up and turning to Presley's house, but my feet didn't move. I stayed rooted, long-forgotten training winning out over panic. "What's going on?"

"We got a 9-1-1 call ten minutes ago. An armed man is holding Presley and her sister."

My stomach dropped. "Who?"

"We don't know."

"Fuck." I spat on the ground. My jaw had taken the brunt of the impact when Luke had tackled me and a tinge of blood spread across the snow.

There were eyes on us as I took in the yard. Five of Luke's officers were standing nearby, their mouths hanging open. None of them looked to be more than thirty years old.

Luke had mentioned over a beer that after Marcus had been removed as chief, there'd been some older officers who hadn't liked Luke being appointed his replacement. He'd been slowly encouraging them to retire early and replacing them with younger officers.

We did not need young tonight. We needed experience.

"Go home," Luke ordered.

"No."

He blew out a frustrated breath. "I don't have fucking time for this. Go home. Stay out of the way."

I crossed my arms over my chest, planting my feet. "No."

"Shaw—"

"Chief." One of the officers caught his attention and pointed down the street.

Three men came jogging down the road, the headlights from the cruisers illuminating them from behind.

"For fuck's sake," Luke muttered. "I don't need this."

Dash, Emmett and Leo marched across Presley's yard, bracketing me as they stood across from Luke.

I didn't know how they'd known something was wrong, and I didn't care. Those three would do anything for Presley and that was all that mattered.

"What are you doing here?" Luke asked through gritted teeth. "All four of you need to disappear. This is not a civilian matter."

"I've had extensive SWAT training," I said. "I've been in more hostage recovery situations than you and your men combined. Let me help."

"No." Luke shook his head. "You're not a cop."

"Don't be an arrogant asshole," Dash said. "This isn't about who's wearing a badge."

"Get off this property, Slater." Luke glowered at Dash. "My men have more important things to do than haul your ass to jail right now. You're civilians. I can't—"

"Please." I held up a hand, my voice dropping to let the fear racing through my heart show. "Please. She's my life. If you ever cared about her at all, let me help. We'll stay out of

319

your way. We'll follow your lead. But use me. Use my experience. Please."

Luke's shoulders fell. "We don't even know what we're dealing with. We need to assess the situation. All I have right now is an eleven-second 9-1-1 call."

"Can I listen to it?" I asked.

Luke's jaw ticked. "Fine. But just you."

"That's bullshit, Rosen," Emmett said. "She's one of ours. You want information? The best way of getting it is to let us help."

Luke's molars grated together, loud enough for us all to hear. He glared, then shot his gaze past us to the house. "This is wasting time we don't have."

"Agreed." I unplanted my legs and walked toward his truck. "Let's start with the call."

Luke grumbled something but his footsteps crunched in the snow as he followed. Dash, Emmett and Leo were on his heels.

"Set up a perimeter around the house but stay back." Luke pointed to his officers as he walked. "No one goes in. No one gets out. All units are headed here. I want no one coming or going in a three-block radius. Understood?"

Heads nodded as the officers sprang into action.

Luke took the lead, passing me to reach his driver's side door first. He picked up his radio and called dispatch, requesting the emergency call be replayed.

9-1-1, what's your emergency?

A female's voice whispered through the radio. *He's got a gun. Help us.*

The operator asked some questions, but none went answered. In the background, there was a muffled noise and a woman's cry, then the unmistakable sound of fist hitting flesh before the line went dead.

My heart plummeted.

Luke shut off the radio. "That's it. That's all Presley said. We traced it here from her phone number."

"That's not Presley," I said. "That's Scarlett."

I knew the sound of Presley's voice and even terrified, it wouldn't be as raspy as Scarlett's.

"Her sister?" Emmett asked. "When did she come here? How did we not know this?"

"She told me today," Dash said.

I waved it off. "It's not important. Who would come after Presley with a gun?"

Dash and Leo shared a look, then Dash lowered his voice. "Jeremiah?"

"Her ex?" Luke asked.

"Fuck." I rubbed my jaw. It was almost always someone close to the victim. "Makes sense."

"Any sign of Warrior trouble?" Dash shot a look at Leo and Emmett.

"I haven't heard anything," Emmett said quietly.

Leo shook his head. "Me neither."

Given the Presley-Scarlett-Jeremiah triangle, it could not be a coincidence that this was happening three days after Scarlett showed up in Clifton Forge.

Unless . . .

Could the *he* inside be their father? Could he have come looking for both his daughters and Scarlett had led him right to Presley's door?

But my gut . . . "My gut says it's the ex." It was almost always a current or former lover in these situations. And in this case, Jeremiah counted double. "Scarlett and Jeremiah were together once. Maybe he got wind that she was here. Maybe he brought a gun because the last time he visited Presley, she slammed the door in his face."

"What?" Dash asked. "He was here? When?"

"This summer, before I left town. Pres didn't let him talk much so I don't know what he wanted. She made it clear not to come back and as far as I know, he hasn't."

"You didn't tell us," Emmett clipped.

"Because the guy showed up, Presley ripped him up one side and down the other, and then he was gone. It was a nonissue. Let's discuss that later." I aimed my stare at Luke. "What are you thinking?"

"We need to make contact," Luke said. "Find out if it's him and what he wants."

"Your men don't have tactical gear. You have no snipers. You can't just waltz up to the door. That's a good way to get yourself shot."

"No shit," he deadpanned.

"Chief?" One of his officers approached. He wasn't wearing a stocking cap and the tips of his ears were red. Hostage situations could take hours to resolve and by that time, he'd have frostbite if he didn't find a hat. "We've got the perimeter set up. Should we evacuate neighbors?"

"No, but one of you needs to go door to door and tell everyone to stay inside. Give me a second." Luke held up his finger, then turned to us. "I need to get my team in place and secure the neighborhood, then we can talk through a plan. Stay away from that house or I'll put you in cuffs."

His parting comment was aimed my way.

As Luke turned to address his officer, I walked away from the cruiser, the guys following. I stopped in the center of my yard, where I could get a clear look at Presley's house.

Every light was off. If it was Jeremiah inside, he'd shut them off and probably had Presley and Scarlett huddled together. There was faint movement by the living room window, like a breeze had picked up the curtain.

That motherfucker was inside, watching.

Luke waved two other officers over, huddling with them in the middle of the street, and pointed to houses around the block.

He was doing his job. He was following protocol. Luke had been in some tight situations before when he'd been a cop in Bozeman, and though I trusted his skills, his team was too green for this.

There was no way I was letting some rookie with a twitchy trigger finger walk inside that house and put Presley in danger.

"Like hell he's keeping me out of that house."

Three pairs of eyes turned my way.

"Us," Dash corrected. "Like hell he's keeping *us* out of that house."

"No." I huffed. "You're mechanics."

"Mechanics with more hours in shit situations than any officer here besides Luke. Mechanics who know how to fire a gun and take a life when it means protecting those we love." There was no shaking in Dash's voice. There was no question that he'd killed before. His eyes were hard and calculating.

If Presley's life was on the line, he'd do what needed to be done, no hesitation.

Given the nervous energy pulsing off Luke's team, I didn't trust them to do the same.

"I don't suppose one of you has a spare gun handy."

Emmett lifted up the hem of his coat, pulled out a Glock

22—the same handgun I'd carried as a cop—and handed it to me.

I checked the magazine—*loaded*—then tucked it into the waistband of my jeans, the weight familiar and comforting. "Luke can call the shots. But if he does anything that I think will put Presley in danger, I'm going inside."

Dash nodded. "We'll be right behind you."

I looked at the house again and my stomach pitched.

I'd seen this situation too many times. This was one we'd trained for often because domestic abuse was appallingly common. Every move, every decision, was a wild card. Most of the time, it ended well. Most of the time, the victim walked away unharmed and the assailant was taken into custody alive.

But I'd seen three hostage situations end badly.

Two of them had ended with the shooter killing his captives before taking his own life. One, the victim had already been dead. Her husband had killed her an hour before the cops had shown up, but the bastard hadn't been paying enough attention to realize she'd bled out from the stab wound in her abdomen.

It was hard to remember the good cases, the successful outcomes, when the woman on the other side of the locked door was mine.

I shoved the fear down deep and took a calming breath to slow my racing heart.

She was my life.

Like hell I wasn't going in to save it.

CHAPTER TWENTY-FIVE

PRESLEY

"Fuck." Jeremiah hovered beside the window overlooking the front yard. "I can't believe you called the fucking cops."

Beside me, huddled against the living room wall, Scarlett licked the cut on her lower lip. "You put a gun to my sister's head."

"I wasn't going to hurt her. I told you at the clubhouse, I just needed some money. Last time, she didn't let me even talk."

Scarlett stiffened.

I blinked. The clubhouse? Scarlett had been at the Warrior clubhouse? When?

"You were together?" I asked. "How long have you been in Montana, Scarlett? What's going on?"

My gaze darted between the two of them as Jeremiah peeked past the curtain again. How long had they been together? Months? Years? Was the reason Jeremiah had never truly committed because Scarlett had been sneaking around with him behind my back? Was this her revenge for me falling for Jeremiah?

"Is this why you didn't show up at the wedding?" I asked him, but he was too busy whispering curses at the cops outside to answer.

Jeremiah didn't need to answer because Scarlett's shame was clear.

I'd moved past the humiliation of the wedding day. I was *glad* he hadn't shown. But knowing Scarlett had been a part of it broke my heart all over again.

"Scarlett?" I stared at her profile, waiting for an answer.

A tear dripped down her cheek. "I just wanted to talk to him. I wanted to know if he'd ever really loved me, or if it was always you."

Ironic that I'd asked myself that same question in reverse. "You're the reason he stood me up."

She closed her eyes, squeezing another tear free. "I'm sorry. I didn't go there with the intention of ruining your wedding, but . . ."

But Scarlett had returned to Jeremiah's life and he'd had the sister he'd always wanted. Relief eased a shred of the heartache that this hadn't been a long, drawn-out affair.

When Jeremiah came to find me in Clifton Forge, I'd asked him twice if he was still hung up on Scarlett. We'd met for dinner a couple of times and talked about Chicago. He'd promised—*sworn on his life*—he wasn't in love with Scarlett anymore. They were ancient history.

He'd assured me that *I* was his reason for visiting Clifton Forge. He'd been curious about how my life had turned out. Maybe at the time, his words had been true. Or maybe Jeremiah had been lying to himself as well as to me.

Jeremiah had come out here for a weekend visit and stayed a week. After two, I'd offered him my guest room so he wouldn't waste any more money at the motel. By the third week, I'd lost my virginity, he'd taken up the left side of my bed, and he'd moved here.

He'd never been close with his parents and had no reason to return to Chicago. After a month, he'd proposed. To everyone at the garage, it had seemed sudden, but they hadn't understood our history. I hadn't bothered explaining because my stubborn streak had flared and *why should I have to explain my decisions?*

Or maybe because I'd known, deep in my heart, that Jeremiah hadn't been mine.

I hadn't wanted to explain Jeremiah's past with Scarlett. If I said it out loud too many times, I'd realize I was in second place.

I'd been a poor substitute.

He'd settled for the other sister after the first wouldn't let him save her.

"Why did you come here?" I asked Scarlett.

"I told you, I wanted—"

"No. Why did you come *here*? To my home?" Why had she dragged this heartbreak and humiliation to my front door when I'd finally moved on?

When I'd found Shaw.

Oh my God, Shaw.

I stared at the windows, where the cotton of my curtains couldn't keep out the occasional flash of headlights. Shaw was outside, and he had to be distraught.

"I wanted to see you," Scarlett said, lowering her voice.

Liar. "You could have seen me months ago."

"I tried, but . . ." She blew out a deep breath. "I wanted to come see you sooner but Jeremiah thought it was too soon. We got in a fight and I left. I hitchhiked here and was getting a feel for the town. Before I worked up the nerve to come here, he tracked me down and begged me to wait. To spare you that pain."

That was when drunk Leo had spotted my look-alike. The dates, the events, flashed through my mind as things began to make sense. That was the reason Jeremiah had called me begging for Scarlett's number. The idiot hadn't gotten it from her when she'd been crashing with him in Ashton, but then she'd left and he'd had no way to find her.

"What's the reason you came here now? After all these months?" Because her desire to see me was clearly bullshit, since she'd spent days hiding in my guest bedroom.

"I did want to see you," she insisted. "And because I had to get out of there. The clubhouse."

"You were with the Warriors all this time?"

She nodded. "Since I left Chicago. I traded one hell for another."

I'd spent my fair share of weekends at the Warrior clubhouse, and though I hadn't enjoyed interacting with the club members, I wouldn't have said staying in Jeremiah's room was *hell*.

Though, he had just come into my home with a gun and hit her across the face.

He had changed.

The Jeremiah I'd known had never laid a hand on me. Of all people, he should have known it was the ultimate betrayal.

"What's going on, Scarlett?" I whispered, keeping my gaze on Jeremiah.

He stayed at the window, raking a hand through his hair and muttering to himself.

"I don't know." Her eyes were full of fear as she stared at him. "Something isn't right. It hasn't been for a while. He's edgy and angry. He's been getting into fights. There's been a few times when he's come to the clubhouse bloody. There was one time this summer it was so bad I almost took him to the hospital, but he refused. So I helped clean him up, but he wouldn't tell me what happened."

Leo. That had to have been the night Leo went after Jeremiah. Had Leo beaten him up more than once? When Jeremiah had come to my house this summer, he'd had markings on his face but that couldn't have been from Leo. There was no way Leo would have risked angering the Warriors a second time and luring danger to Clifton Forge.

I leaned in closer to Scarlett's ear. "Why'd you leave?"

"We got in a fight. He wouldn't tell me what was going on and we argued. He got really mad and it was . . ." She swallowed hard. "It reminded me of Dad, so I left."

"Did he hit you?"

Her chin quivered. "Not until today."

I took her hand, gripping it with both of mine. There were hurts to heal, discussions to have and mistakes to forgive, but right now, we needed each other. We'd survive this horror like we'd survived others.

Together.

"Jeremiah." I swallowed hard, willing my voice to be gentle and soothing. That was how Mom used to talk to Dad when he was on the verge of a rage. She'd speak so tenderly, and there'd been times when her words would wash away the fire. "What's going on?"

He turned away from the window, blinking like he'd

forgotten we were sitting on the floor in the dark. After he'd hit Scarlett, he'd shoved us in this spot and run through the house, shutting off every light. If I'd been thinking clearly, that might have been our window to escape, but Scarlett and I had both been in shock after he'd punched her.

"You can tell them it's a mistake." He stepped away from the window to pace behind the couch. "You can tell them I'm not here to hurt you, and Scarlett made that call on accident. Then you can get me the money."

"What money?"

"I need some money, Pres."

I'd heard that sentence so many times, but never with such desperation. My hold on Scarlett's hand tightened. "Why? What happened?"

"You can get me the money and tell the cops it was a mistake." He repeated the words, convincing himself rather than me that his plan would work. "Tell them Scarlett was drunk or something. Then you'll get me the money."

"What money?" I asked again.

"I need one hundred thousand dollars to make this all go away."

My mouth fell open. "Oh my God. What did you do?"

"I need a hundred thousand dollars!" The gun flailed in the air as he shouted.

Scarlett inched closer.

"Tell me what you did," I said, doing my best to keep my voice from shaking. "What happened?"

"I fucked up." His Adam's apple bobbed as he blinked, focusing on me. Something flashed in his eyes—pain or regret—and for the first time since he'd burst inside, I felt like he was actually seeing us. He realized we were cowered on the floor. His gaze darted to Scarlett's lip. "Fuck. I'm so sorry, babe. I didn't mean it. I swear, it will never happen again."

I'd heard that my entire life. For once, I wanted a man to be honest. *I meant it. And it's gonna happen again.*

"Jeremiah, look at me." My voice was growing bolder as his ends began to fray. "What. Happened?"

"I took some drugs."

"Today?" That explained his behavior.

"No," he snarled. "From the club."

My eyes bulged. "You're doing drugs?"

"Goddamn it, Presley! Will you shut the fuck up and let me talk?"

I flinched and closed my mouth.

"I was on a run for the club this summer. We were taking some H to Washington, and when we got there, there was a mix-up at the drop. I thought I'd emptied out my saddlebags, and the guys who made the switch counted it all and said we were good. But when I got back to Ashton, I found a pouch I'd forgotten. And I kept it."

My stomach dropped. He'd stolen drugs from his own motorcycle club. I'd been around the Tin Kings enough; you didn't betray your brothers.

Jeremiah was a dead man walking.

"I have this friend in Chicago," he said. "A guy I met after high school who was connected with some dealers. He sold it for me. We split the money, and he asked if I could get more."

"So you've been stealing from the Warriors," I whispered.

"It'll all go away if I pay them back."

No, it wouldn't.

"I just need some money," he pleaded, sensing my skepticism. "That's why I came. I figured if I held Scarlett hostage or something, you'd find a way to get me the money. Last time I was here, you were with that movie star. I recognized him. A hundred grand is nothing to a guy like that. Just ask him."

He accentuated his last sentence by pointing the gun to my face.

"Okay," I lied. "I can ask Shaw."

"Good." His shoulders fell and the gun dropped to his side. "Then it'll be okay. See, babe? It'll be okay."

Scarlett stayed quiet, keeping her eyes locked on her knees.

"Do the Warriors know you took the drugs?" Were they on their way here? Had they followed him?

"No." Jeremiah's face paled. "They think it was someone else."

Oh, God. "Who?"

His eyes flicked to Scarlett.

"What?" I shrieked. "You told them it was Scarlett?"

She gasped, then schooled her reaction. Her body froze, and her gaze turned to ice. She shut down like she'd done a million times before.

"They would have killed me on the spot. But she was already gone. If I go back with the money, I can convince them to leave her alone. We'll let it ride for a while and I'll see if I can get out of the club in a few years. This will blow over."

Jeremiah was delusional. Men like Tucker Talbot didn't believe in letting things blow over. Members didn't leave his club—alive. Whether they were compensated or not, someone would pay for the theft.

If we didn't fix this, that person would be Scarlett. I would lose her to him like I'd lost Draven.

"Okay. Let's figure this out. Where is the money?"

"I lost it."

"Gambling." Fuck. I should have known. "You lost it playing poker."

Guilt crossed his face for the briefest moment, then his features hardened. "Make the call, Presley. Get me that fucking money. Or your sister is dead."

I gritted my teeth and pushed up from the floor, dropping Scarlett's hand. "I hate you for this."

The fury slipped out with the words.

He lifted his chin, the obstinate gesture twisting his features. "Make. The. Call."

He looked nothing like the boy who'd helped me escape my own personal hell. He looked nothing like the man I'd wanted to marry.

I swiped my phone off the end table, but before I could bring up Shaw's number, the doorbell rang.

The room stilled.

"Clifton Forge Police," Luke called from beyond the front door. "We got a call. Just want to make sure everything's okay."

With one long stride, Jeremiah crossed the distance between us and gripped my arm, hauling me across the floor. "Tell him we're fine. Tell him it was a mistake."

I fought his grip. When I was a kid, I never would have dreamed of fighting my father, but I wasn't that scared little girl anymore. "Let me go."

He pressed the barrel of the gun to my head, urging me forward. "Do it, Pres. Or I'll hurt Scarlett."

I met his glare. "Who are you?"

He pressed the gun harder. "Get rid of him."

I sucked in a breath, then slowly walked to the door.

Jeremiah trailed close behind, shifting so the barrel of the gun was in my ribs. He nodded toward the knob.

I cracked the door. "Hey, Luke."

"Hi, Pres. Can I come in?"

"Now's not a good time. I know my sister called you guys on accident, but we're fine. Sorry about that. We're just talking."

Luke's eyes darted to the side where Jeremiah stood behind the door.

I gave him a slight nod.

"You sure you're okay?" Luke stared at me like he was trying to communicate something, but I had no clue what he was saying behind his serious gaze. He was wearing a bullet-proof vest and no coat. His arms had to be cold.

"I'm okay. Thanks for checking on me. Good night." I closed the door quietly.

Jeremiah stretched past me to flip the lock.

We stood there, barely breathing, as Luke's footsteps echoed across the porch.

"He won't leave," I whispered, turning to Jeremiah, hoping I could reason with him. "He knows something is wrong. Until he sees for himself that I'm fine, he won't leave. Put the gun down, Jeremiah. Please. Let's sit down and talk. This isn't you."

Jeremiah's hard expression held fast. I was sure he'd hit me next, but then his chin dropped along with the gun. "I fucked up."

When his eyes lifted to mine, he looked so broken. Had he always been this lost? Had I missed this in our time together?

His home life hadn't been horrendous like ours, but it hadn't been good either. His parents had neglected him, and when Scarlett had come along, she'd given him the attention he'd craved. He'd given her his devotion in return.

But it wasn't love.

I knew love. I saw it in Shaw's smile. I felt it in his touch. I heard it in his voice.

The second I got out of this mess, I'd tell the world.

I was in love with Shaw Valance.

"Go." Jeremiah nodded for me to walk down the hall. He followed, not closely, with shuffled footsteps. The urgency from his dramatic entrance was gone. The desperation was waning too.

I reached the mouth of the entryway, ready to turn for the living room, when a hand gripped my elbow and yanked me sideways.

"Ah—" My scream was cut short as Shaw stepped in front of me, shielding me as he leveled a gun at Jeremiah's face.

"Put the gun down," Shaw ordered, his voice steady. "It's over."

Jeremiah looked at the weapon in his hand and his entire frame fell. "They'll kill me."

My eyes darted past Shaw, searching for Scarlett. She wasn't on the floor anymore. Instead, she was standing behind Dash, who had his own weapon trained on Jeremiah.

"Yeah," Dash said. "They will."

Jeremiah's eyes turned up, hazy and unfocused. He scanned the room until he found my sister. "I'm sorry."

"It'll be okay." She sniffled. "We can fix this."

He looked at me, then back to her. "I loved you."

My hands gripped the back of Shaw's sweater as time slowed.

Tears streamed down Scarlett's cheeks.

Dash took one step forward.

Shaw yelled, "Stop."

Jeremiah lifted the gun to his mouth.

And I screamed.

CHAPTER TWENTY-SIX

PRESLEY

"Where's my sister, Luke?" I planted my hands on my hips.

"She's safe."

"That's not an answer."

He steepled his fingers under his chin, leaning deeper into his chair with nothing else to say.

"You're wasting my lunch hour," I muttered. Luke had wasted my lunch hour every day this week.

Through the glass window behind him, snow was falling, dusting the bare tree limbs with another white layer. The riverbanks were frozen, and the water flowed black through an icy channel. There wasn't a breath of wind in the air to disrupt the snowfall. The fat flakes floated down in perfect lines to rest on the ground.

It was peaceful. It didn't seem right that the world was so tranquil when there was so much turmoil stirring inside my chest. "Is she okay?"

"Yes." Luke nodded. "She's safe."

Safe was not the same as okay. There was a big difference between the two words after what we'd seen.

I hadn't seen Scarlett in ten days, not since the night Dash had carried her out of my house, his hand over her eyes as she'd screamed and stretched for Jeremiah's lifeless body. Shaw had pinned me to his side, shielding my eyes as we'd followed closely behind.

The moment the gun went off, chaos erupted.

As we hurried outside, a stream of police officers, Luke at the front, raced in. Somewhere between the questioning and the flashing lights and the gurney carrying a black body bag, Scarlett found her way into Luke's truck. She sat slumped in the passenger seat, her head pressed to the glass of the window, her eyes blank.

Shaw and I stood in the snow, clinging to one another though neither of us was cold. We were numb. He wrapped me in his arms, holding me close. I burrowed into his chest, wanting to disappear inside forever.

Then he was ripped away. Arrested. Dash too. Both of them were hauled away in police cruisers while Emmett and Leo stood as my sentries.

In the midst of my panic, my pleas for answers and Shaw's release, I lost Scarlett.

I looked over to Luke's truck and she was gone.

I screamed her name, over and over, until Luke appeared. With his hands on my shoulders, he promised she was safe. That she was giving her statement. Then he drove me to the police station—it wasn't like I could go home—and settled me in this office, draping a wool blanket over my shoulders. Then he'd sat me in the same chair I was in now, across from the same chair he was in now, and we'd talked about what had happened.

When I was finally free to go, I found Shaw waiting for me in the lobby. Bryce had posted bail to rescue him and Dash from their jail cells.

Shaw took me to his place. Sleep had been fitful at best, but he'd held me close, and when the tears had started the next morning, he'd tightened his embrace and promised it would be okay.

Ten days later, the fog was clearing.

I'd returned to work two days after that awful night. Everyone had protested when I'd walked into the office that morning with Shaw by my side, but I'd needed normal. I'd needed the garage's noise, smell and peace.

The day after that, Shaw and Dash had been charged with obstruction of justice. Both had been fined but thankfully, there'd been no jail time. By some miracle, the arrest had been kept out of the tabloids so far. Shaw's manager, agent, assistant and publicist were on high alert. It would happen, we'd deal with the fallout, and life would move on. Though I suspected that when the details emerged, Shaw's image as a hero would only be reinforced.

He'd broken the law to save the life of the woman he loved.

My house had been cleaned. The evidence of Jeremiah's death was gone but his shadow remained. I'd stepped inside once after the cleaners had gone and immediately stepped out. I wouldn't go into that house again. Shaw had spent two days hauling my belongings into his home while I'd been at work.

As he'd promised, we would be okay.

I just needed to find my sister.

"Will you have her call me?" I asked Luke. "Wherever she is?"

"No." He sighed. "She's in protective custody. That means no outside contact. You keep asking but my answer isn't going to change. She's safe. She's where she needs to be. Leave it at that and know that I have her and your best interests at heart."

"Fine." I stood, knowing I'd get no more information. I picked up my purse and turned for the door.

"Pres?" Luke stopped me. "How are you holding up?"

"I'll survive."

"Anything I can do?"

"Besides tell me where my sister is? No. Just take care of her."

"I will," he promised. "And Shaw? Is he taking care of you?"

"Yeah." I gave him a sad smile. "He is."

"How's he doing?"

"He feels guilty. At the moment, he's burying that by fretting over me."

Yesterday, I'd woken up alone. Shaw had been in the living room, sitting on the couch in total darkness, staring at a wall. It had taken some time to coax out the truth, but he'd eventually confessed.

He felt responsible for Jeremiah's suicide.

Luke had listened to Shaw's advice about how best to get Scarlett and me out safely from that house. They'd all agreed that their first step had to be gathering intel. They'd suspected Jeremiah was inside but hadn't been sure. Someone had to approach.

Luke had insisted on taking the risk and ringing the doorbell himself. Meanwhile, one of his officers would attempt to survey the situation from my deck in the backyard.

Shaw and Dash had assured Luke they'd stand down,

stay away and watch. Instead, Shaw had snuck through my bedroom window while Dash had snuck through Scarlett's. The officer at the deck hadn't been able to pick the lock on my sliding glass door.

While Luke had been debriefing his officers on the plan and pulling on a bulletproof vest, Shaw and Dash had crept inside, lurking in the dark, listening as Jeremiah had confessed to stealing from his club.

Maybe if they'd waited, maybe if they'd stayed outside, we would have been able to get Jeremiah out and into police custody.

Or maybe he would have killed us all.

We'd never know.

The guilt of Jeremiah's death weighed on Shaw.

It wasn't in his nature to disobey orders, and because of it, a man had taken his life.

"I get why he did it," Luke said. "If I'd been in his shoes, I wouldn't have stayed out of that house either."

"He thought once he had me and Scarlett safe, it would be over."

Luke shook his head. "I don't think it would have ended any other way."

"Me neither," I whispered.

During the sleepless nights of the past ten days, I'd thought a lot about what had led to the blast of Jeremiah's gun. He'd been so desperate, so manic. He'd known what fate awaited him, and rather than leave his death to the Warriors, he'd taken it upon himself.

We'd lost Jeremiah long before he'd burst into my home.

"Bye, Luke."

He nodded once. "Take care, Presley."

"I'll be back on Monday."

"I assumed you would." He chuckled as I walked out the door.

Until I knew where Scarlett was, I'd hound Luke for answers. He wouldn't be at the station this weekend so I couldn't swing by to pepper him with questions, but I'd be texting often. There were advantages to having the chief of police's personal cell phone number.

I made my way through the bullpen to the exit. Luke had stopped escorting me out yesterday—I knew where I was going. The short dash from the station to my Jeep chased away any warmth I'd found inside. I brushed the heavy snowflakes from my jeans and hair, then cranked the heat as I drove to the garage.

When I arrived, Shaw was in the chair across from my desk, waiting.

"I brought you soup." He stood and kissed my cheek as I shrugged off my coat and dumped it beside my desk.

"Thank you." I warmed my hands on the bowl before taking off the lid and stirring it with my spoon.

"What did Luke say?" he asked.

"Nothing," I muttered. "He won't tell me where she's at."

"Let's just hope he hasn't called in the DEA."

None of us knew what Scarlett had seen in her time at the Arrowhead Warrior clubhouse. Worst-case scenario: federal investigators got involved, hoping to use Scarlett as a tool against the Warriors to take down the gang. She'd be a pawn.

She'd become more of a target than she already was.

I was holding out faith that my sister was smart enough to keep her mouth shut. If Luke had no reason to use her as an informant, eventually he'd let her go.

Especially if we could get some assurances that the Warriors no longer thought she was a thief.

Dash had been forced to make another call to Tucker Talbot and explain that Scarlett had not stolen drugs from the Warriors. Tucker had listened but made no assurances he believed Dash.

Too much money had been stolen.

Which meant we were at a standstill. Either the DEA would show up in Clifton Forge or the Warriors would start hunting for my sister.

"I hate this." I sighed. "I hate that she's missing."

"I know, baby, but it's better this way." Shaw gave me a sad smile. "Until things settle down, it's safer for both of you if she's gone."

"Yeah," I mumbled into my soup.

"I called my dad this morning."

The spoon fell from my hand, splattering tomato basil on my desk. "You did?"

He nodded. "I actually talked to him once earlier. Just didn't get a chance to tell you. But I called him today too. I needed to talk it through."

"What did he say?"

"He thinks I made the right call. Dad said it probably would have ended that way, no matter what happened."

"Luke said the same." I stretched my hand across the desk.

His large grip enveloped mine. "You talking about me?"

"You're my favorite topic." I squeezed his fingers. "I know you feel guilty, but this is not your fault. Jeremiah made his choice."

Shaw hummed, rubbed his thumb over my knuckles,

then let me go. It would take time, but I had faith he'd eventually come to terms with his guilt.

The door to the shop opened and Emmett stepped inside. Isaiah was right behind him.

"Hey, guys." Emmett came over and shook Shaw's hand.

Isaiah clapped Shaw on the shoulder before sitting down.

If there'd been any worry that Shaw wouldn't fit right in here, those fears were long forgotten. A hostage situation had a way of proving loyalty and sincerity.

"What are you doing today?" Emmett asked Shaw as he took his lunch out of the fridge.

"Not much. I had some work to do this morning but it's pretty well wrapped. Why?"

"Leo is finishing up with some pinstripes on a hood in the booth, then he's convinced me to leave early for a beer at The Betsy. Want to come?"

"I can't." He grinned at me. "I have a date tonight."

"A date?" I raised an eyebrow. Since when did we have a date? "Who's the lucky woman?"

"I'm picking you up at four. Can you leave early? We need to make a stop before dinner."

"I'll cover the office until closing," Isaiah offered.

"Thank you." I smiled and ate a spoonful of soup, listening to the guys spend their lunch break telling Shaw about the car they were working on. When they'd nearly convinced him to buy it for my next birthday, they'd returned to the shop to finish up for the day, leaving the two of us alone once more.

"Did you talk to your landlord today?" Shaw asked.

"Yes. I feel so bad for her. How's she going to rent out

the house where a man held two women hostage, then committed suicide?"

"Want me to buy it from her and bulldoze it to the ground?"

"Yes, please." I was joking. Sort of.

I'd loved that house. It had been the springboard for my life in Clifton Forge. It had been my sanctuary. Seeing it now, dark and haunted, was destroying the beautiful memories.

"Done." Shaw nodded. "Consider it gone."

"I was joking."

"I'm not. If flattening that house makes your life easier, then that's what we'll do."

"How about instead, we cover the mortgage until my landlord can rent it out? Then I won't feel guilty about leaving."

"Okay. But if you change your mind . . ." He crashed his fists together, making the sound of an explosion.

"Deal." I giggled.

"There's something else I wanted to run past you."

I narrowed my eyes. "Why do I get the feeling I won't like this?"

"Keep an open mind." He winked. "I have a movie premiere in two weeks. Will you come with me?"

"This movie? Our movie?" I gulped. It wasn't really my movie, but he got the point.

"No." He shook his head. "That won't be out for another year or so."

Good. I'd need time to think about that one. Maybe in a year, I'd be more willing to see the film. Even then, I wouldn't go to support the movie. I'd only go to stand beside

Shaw, to show him I was proud of his accomplishment and that he'd taken a risk beyond his typical role.

"What movie?" I asked.

"It's an action film I shot about a year ago."

"I like action films." I tapped my chin. "Define movie premiere."

"Red carpet. Tuxedo. Gown."

I groaned. "I'm going to have to smile a lot, aren't I?"

Shaw laughed and stood, rounding my desk to drop a kiss on my forehead. "But it's such a beautiful smile."

My heart fluttered. "Always the sweet talker."

"I'm taking that as a yes and leaving before you change your mind." Shaw gathered up the trash from our lunch and dumped it in the trash can, then put on his coat. "Four o'clock."

"I'll be ready." I stood and escorted him to the door, waiting in the threshold as he brushed off the snowflakes from his truck's windshield.

I was going to a Hollywood movie premiere. I was in love with a bona fide movie star.

Shaw Valance.

Shaw *Valance*

Shaw Valance.

There were only so many ways to interpret two words. Only so many ways to alter their meaning with inflection.

But no matter how many times I said his name in my head, Shaw Valance would always be *mine*.

Shaw Valance was the man who'd brought me soup at lunch because he knew how cold I got in the office. He was the man who knew how much I loved my job and would support me working here for as long as it made me happy, no matter how many dollars he could charge on his credit card.

He was the man who'd opened my heart. Who'd become my other half.

Shaw tossed his snow brush into the backseat. "Go inside before you freeze."

"Okay." I smiled but didn't move. "Shaw?"

"Yeah, baby?"

"I love you." The words drifted through the snow, causing a wide smile to spread across his face.

"See you at four." He winked, then got into his truck and disappeared.

My feet floated to my desk. My fingers were lighter than they'd been in days as they flew across the keyboard, wrapping things up for the week.

Shaw loved me, but he'd never said *I love you*—three words, in that order.

He was always the one to make the move first. He'd ask, I'd answer. He gave me that control. There was something freeing about making the statement first—putting myself out there so he knew it wasn't always about me responding to him.

I was nearly done with work for the day, anxious for Shaw to pick me up, when my phone dinged. I opened it to a text from Bryce.

At the grocery store.

That was the caption to a picture of Luke Rosen carrying a woman in a fireman's hold out the front doors.

Except it wasn't just a woman.

It was Scarlett.

Was that his idea of protective custody? Of being safe? Clearly, he'd underestimated Scarlett.

"You better know what you're doing, Rosen," I muttered to the screen.

347

Then I texted him the same, getting a reply ten minutes later.

She's safe.

She'd better be.

———

"WHERE ARE WE?" My boots crunched as I followed Shaw into a field.

The snow had stopped falling an hour ago and the sun was about to set. The air was frigid and the breeze bit through my red parka.

Shaw had mentioned taking a long vacation to California to meet his family and with the weather like it was, that sounded better every second.

"Close your eyes." Shaw took my hand.

"Okay." I obeyed as he stepped behind me and wrapped his arms around my chest.

The chill from the wind was gone, chased away as he shrouded me with his tall frame.

"Straight ahead of you will be the barn."

"The bar—"

"Don't open your eyes."

I frowned, closing them again. "Closed."

"You can pick the color, but I vote for red."

"A red barn." My heart skipped. "Okay."

Maybe he was planning on building Clifton Forge's first petting zoo, but my mind jumped to a much better use for this property, hoping the land ten miles out of town, nestled beside the river and surrounded by trees, was for something more personal.

He spun us to the right ninety degrees, our feet shuffling as we swayed. "This will be the guest house."

A smile cracked my face. "What kind of guests?"

"My parents. My sisters. Your sister."

"I like those guests."

"And this"—he spun us again, this time only forty-five degrees—"this is where we'll have our house."

"What kind of house?" I asked.

"A happy one."

Shaw always had the right answer.

My entire life, all I'd wanted was a happy home.

His arms disappeared but I kept my eyes closed, ignoring the emotion overload prickling my throat. As his boots moved on the snow, I listened, following as he moved in front of me.

"Presley Marks. I love you."

"I know," I whispered.

"Good. Now look at me."

My eyes popped open, dropping to where Shaw knelt before me. In his hand was a black box, the diamond ring inside catching the last glimmer of the setting sun.

"Will you marry me?"

I giggled. "No."

He threw his head back, laughing to the winter sky before shooting to his feet and wrapping me in his arms. "I knew you'd say that."

"Haven't you figured it out?" I whispered against his lips. "Sometimes when I say no to you, it really means yes."

EPILOGUE
SHAW

Seven and a half years later . . .

"Huddle up." I braced my hands on my knees as thirteen six-year-old boys circled around me.

Across the huddle, Isaiah slid in beside his son, Asher. Like the other boys', Asher's eyes were on the grass. The whole huddle had slumped shoulders and pouting mouths.

"It's okay," I assured them. "We have time for one more play."

The other team had just scored a touchdown to take the lead as the ref had given us the one-minute warning.

We were in the first- and second-grade boys' flag football championship game. These kids wanted to win so badly, but the other team was bigger and faster. Hell, it was a miracle we'd kept the game close because at the beginning, when they'd scored back-to-back touchdowns, I'd been sure we'd get crushed.

But we'd clawed our way to a tie.

"Here's what we're going to do. Asher." I pointed to him.

He was lean like Isaiah and damn fast. "You're gonna take the snap. Fake to the left, then hand it off to Nico. Got it?"

"Got it," Asher said, then looked up to his dad, who gave him a sure nod.

"You boys on the line, block." I pounded a fist into my palm. "Hard. Don't let those bigger kids get through."

Cheaters, more like. I'd been eyeing the defensive line on the other team. There were a couple kids who stood head and shoulders over our kids. More like third or fourth graders. And our team was predominately first graders.

"Nico." I turned to my son, who was standing at my side. His face was set and serious, the same look that Presley gave me whenever she was determined. "You'll have the ball. You're going to have to run all the way to the end zone. Do. Not. Stop. If you see a kid going for your flag, stick your hand out and block. Be aggressive."

"But Dad, Mom said not to do that anymore after the last game when I gave that kid a bloody—"

"Forget what your mother said. She's not the coach. I am. And we can win this game." I put my hand into the huddle. "Panthers on three. One. Two—"

"Panthers!" the boys yelled.

A few kids ran to the sidelines while the rest followed me and Isaiah to the line of scrimmage. Isaiah shifted the linemen into the right place while I did the same with those in the backfield. Once everyone was set on both teams, I nodded to the ref, whose whistle was pinched between his teeth.

Isaiah joined me downfield, watching as the boys waited for the play.

"Shit, I hope we win," I muttered.

351

He nodded. "I'm so fucking nervous right now."

Neither of us had expected to end up as coaches for our sons' football team, but when the youth association had asked for volunteers, it had made sense to step up. We both would have been here anyway watching practice, since Nico and Asher were the same age.

Officially, I was the head coach and Isaiah my assistant. But that was to save him from getting bombarded with parent texts, something he refused to handle and I didn't mind.

We'd been playing games every Saturday morning for the past six weeks against teams from nearby towns. One weekend, we'd played in the pouring rain. The next, there'd been an inch of snow on the ground.

But we'd lucked out for the championship. The October sun was shining, there wasn't a cloud in the blue sky, and the spectators along the sidelines only needed a coat to stay warm.

That hadn't stopped Presley from bundling up Noah like he was going skiing in Aspen. Our four-year-old son had shucked his coat five minutes into the game and was currently racing around in the open space beside the field, chasing Genevieve and Isaiah's seven-year-old daughter, Amelia.

Noah was obsessed with Amelia. She was the big sister he didn't have but desperately wanted. Lucky for him, we shared life with our friends. We went camping each summer with the Reynolds crew. We had Thanksgiving with the Slaters.

When our baby girl, Natasha, had been born in August, one month early, we hadn't had to worry about what to do with the boys. Our family had been there to watch them while we went to the hospital, staying an extra four days longer than we'd planned.

And they were all here to watch Nico and Asher's football game.

Bryce and Genevieve stood on Presley's right. Dash stood on the left with his arms crossed. Xander and Zeke stood beside him in the row, their postures mimicking their father's as they focused on the play. The boys had streaked black face paint under their eyes this morning to show their support.

Not all that long ago, we'd been on the sidelines watching their flag football games.

The whistle blew and the kids scattered, boys pushing boys as Asher caught the snap.

"Fake," Isaiah said, watching as his son did just that.

Then Asher handed it off and Nico had the ball.

I bit my lip, taking one step forward as he ran wide, skirting the line to the right. "Run, buddy."

Nico's legs pumped. He had the ball cradled under his right arm so that as a defender came up on his left, he could give him the strong arm.

The other kid tripped, falling into the grass as Nico kept running.

He broke free.

Asher was fast.

But Nico was faster.

"Go," I chanted. "Go. Go."

"Go!" Presley's shout carried through the air. "Run, Nico!"

She was a tiny thing, but damn when she wanted to cheer for her kids, you'd need a megaphone to drown her out.

"Run!" she screamed, covering Natasha's ears in the baby sling strapped across her chest.

"He's gonna make it." Isaiah's hand shot out, grabbing my arm.

"He's gonna make it." I grabbed his arm too.

Time was up but the play was still good and Nico's blond hair streaked down the field, past the orange pylon.

"Touchdown," the ref yelled, blowing his whistle.

"Yes!" I fist-pumped, then clapped loud and fast. I grinned at Isaiah as we jogged down the field to meet our team.

Parents cheered as the kids screamed, all of them jumping up and down around Nico.

We regrouped the kids, getting them into a line to shake hands with the other team. We sent the boys to the refs to say their thank-yous. Then Isaiah and I talked to parents—most of whom wanted to make sure we'd be back to coach next year's team. Finally, the crowd dispersed, and Nico and I joined Presley.

"Good game, bud." She bent to kiss his cheek.

"Thanks, Mom. Can I go play with Noah?"

"For a couple of minutes."

Natasha was zonked in her sling. The coat Presley had put on her made her look more like a caterpillar than a baby.

"How's she doing?" I bent and kissed the baby's beanie-covered head, then dropped a kiss on Presley's mouth.

"We're good." She smiled at our daughter, then looked up at me. "Good game, Coach."

I beamed with pride. "Thanks."

I'd won an Oscar for my performance in *Dark Paradise*, Cameron had been nominated for best director, and the film had been nominated for picture of the year. That movie had catapulted Valance Pictures to the next level, giving us a name to build upon. Investors had come in droves and our staff had doubled in less than a year. It had all come with growing pains, but after the past five years, it had become a huge source of pride.

Watching my son's success was far more satisfying than any I'd earned on my own. It wasn't on the same level as the day I'd married Presley or the days we'd welcomed our kids into the world, but today was a damn good day.

"This is better than any football game I've ever played myself," I told her, picking up the diaper bag.

"This is better than any football game you've made me watch on Sundays."

"Very true." I chuckled as we started toward the car.

Dash waved as he climbed into his truck, his crew already loaded. Isaiah kissed Genevieve before he closed the door to her car. She'd drive herself and the kids home while he'd ride behind on his bike.

"Let's go, boys," I called to Nico and Noah as we walked.

Nico picked up his brother's coat, carrying it for him as they ran to catch up.

We buckled the kids into their seats and got in, driving across town to our home, the one we'd built on the property where I'd proposed to Presley.

A month after I'd proposed, Presley and I had gotten married in Las Vegas.

She hadn't wanted to plan a wedding again, so we'd flown to Nevada one weekend, just the two of us, and gotten married. Then we'd gone to California and spent two weeks with my family.

As I'd expected, they'd all fallen in love with my wife.

We'd returned home and lived in my yellow house for nine months while our place in the country was being built. There were times when I missed that little place because it was where our life had started. Every once in a while, when I was in the neighborhood, I'd drive by. But as far as I knew, the day we left Quaker's Court was the last time Presley had been on that cul-de-sac.

There were too many ghosts for her on that street.

For a while, Jeremiah's death had nearly ripped Presley and her sister apart, but they'd hung tight and fought for each other.

Scarlett would probably be over later today because her Saturday afternoons were normally spent in our living room, where she and Presley would drink wine and talk.

Mostly their conversations were light. Sometimes, they delved into the past and their parents.

After I'd learned about their father's abuse, I'd wanted to ruin the man. It wouldn't have taken much to get him black-listed in his community and shamed for his actions. I'd hoped for it, planned it even, but in the end, I'd talked myself out of it. Hurting him would only hurt Presley's mother and that woman was already living in her own personal hell.

Presley's parents still lived in Chicago and as long as they stayed away from my family, I was content to leave the subject untouched.

There were certain things we didn't talk about these days. Like her childhood. Like what had happened to Scarlett after Jeremiah's death.

And the Warriors because, well . . .

That was a different movie.

"So I got an interesting email today," Presley said.

"From who?"

"Ginny."

I'd be having a call with Ginny on Monday about boundaries. "Why would my agent be emailing you?"

"She said you shot her down and she's desperate, so she's asking me to ask you to reconsider."

"I'm not changing my mind."

Cameron had approached Ginny a few months ago, asking if I'd be interested in doing another movie similar to *Dark Paradise*. He'd come across a script that had spoken to him and he thought I'd be perfect for the part.

I'd given Ginny a flat no. She had other clients to represent these days, but she came to me once or twice a year, hoping I'd changed my mind about *retirement*.

Dark Paradise was the last film I'd done as an actor, though I'd been part of many since—behind the scenes. I preferred a more active role in Valance Pictures to acting. It worked better with the eight-to-five lifestyle we wanted in Clifton Forge. And I sure as fuck didn't miss the goddamn paparazzi.

"Are you sure?" Presley asked. "We could make it work. I can bring Natasha to the garage with me during the day. Noah can go to preschool and Nico has school. We'd be fine for a few months."

I reached across the console to take her hand. "I'm not going anywhere."

I had no desire to spend weeks on location or leave home for a press tour. Presley had survived two movie premieres, but the flashing lights and the screaming fans weren't for her.

They weren't for me these days either.

My legacy wasn't fame or fortune.

It was in this car, the smiles on my children's faces and the happiness in my wife's heart.

This was my legacy.

I intended to nurture it by Presley's side for the rest of my life.

BONUS SCENE
SHAW

"I knew it," Presley whispered as a gorgeous smile stretched across her face.

People in the seats around ours stood. Applause drowned out the orchestra's music. And I was stuck in my damn chair, replaying the name that Matthew McConnell, last year's Oscar winner for Best Male Performance in a Lead Role, had just read from the card in his hand.

Shaw Valance.

He'd said Shaw Valance, right?

Presley stood, tugging on my arm as she got to her feet, dragging me with her. Then she laughed and framed my face with her hands. "I'm so proud of you."

"I won?"

"You won." Her blue eyes flooded. "Oh my God, you won!"

"I won."

She nodded and stood on her toes, pressing her lips to mine. Then she pulled away to give me a gentle shove into the aisle, where an usher was waving me up the stairs to the stage.

The auditorium was packed. My face flashed on the enormous screen, giving the spectators seated in the balcony a closer look at what was happening onstage. Then, before I'd realized I was on camera and center stage, I was shaking Matthew's hand.

"Congrats, Shaw."

"Thanks." I nodded as he handed me a golden statue.

The Academy Award.

The Oscar.

In my goddamn hand.

Matthew laughed and slapped me on the back, giving me and my statue a gentle shove toward the microphone.

An acceptance speech. I had to give a speech. *Fuck.*

The applause in the room dulled and disappeared as people resumed their seats. Beyond the stage lights, I couldn't make out many faces.

That was okay. There was only one I needed to see, and I found her just fine.

"Wow." I cleared my throat and squared my shoulders. I'd practiced this. I hadn't really expected to win, but I'd practiced, because Pres had insisted.

"My wife made me practice a speech. A speech that I've completely forgotten. Which is lucky for you because that means this should be short."

The audience laughed.

"I'd like to thank the Academy for this award. I'm honored." And surprised.

When we'd wrapped *Dark Paradise*, there'd been chatter. But as the movie had gone through postproduction, I'd had other priorities. Namely, building my life in Montana

360

with Presley. Living thousands of miles away made it easy to forget the buzz that came this time of year. It made it easy to miss any Hollywood hype or speculation about who'd win.

Hell, I'd been honored at the *nomination*, especially considering the men who'd been included in my category. When the list had come out, I'd been certain that Dean Alara would win for his performance in *Hector*.

Except here I was, on stage. The winner.

"Cameron Haggen, I'll forever be grateful that you chose me for this part. It was truly an incredible experience working with you, and I'm proud to call you a friend."

I found him in the crowd, second row with all of the other nominees for Best Director.

Cam grinned and did a fist pump.

"Ginny, Juno and Laurelin. Thanks for keeping the wheels on the bus. To my parents, thank you for believing in me. To my sisters, thank you for tormenting me relentlessly and keeping me humble."

That earned another rumble of laughter.

There were people I was forgetting. Cast and crew members who'd done so much. But as I felt the clock tick down, there was really only one way to end this speech.

"Pres." A lump formed in my throat as I locked my eyes with hers.

My God, she was beautiful.

Her hair was styled away from her face tonight. The blond strands caught the glow from the muted chandeliers. Her dress was a strapless number, velvet and the color of wine. An artist had come to the hotel earlier and done her makeup. Smoky eyes. Red lips.

Fancy Presley. That's what she'd called herself.

To me, she was everything.

"I love this movie. I'll always love this movie. Because it brought me to Clifton Forge. It brought me to you. Thank you. Thank you for taking that first motorcycle ride with me. Thank you for being my neighbor. Thank you for the baby carrots."

She laughed and dabbed at the corner of her eye.

"Thank you." That lump in my throat threatened and I swallowed hard. "I love you, baby."

A tear fell down her cheek as she smiled. Then she blew me a kiss and mouthed, "I love you."

And that, right there, was why I'd always be a winner. Not because of a golden statue or an auditorium filled with people cheering or the orchestra playing as I walked off the stage.

My wife was on her feet, clapping with the crowd.

This Oscar was nice. It would be cool to add to the fireplace mantel.

But I'd already won the day I'd walked into the Clifton Forge Garage and met the love of my life.

ACKNOWLEDGMENTS

Thank you for reading *Stone Princess*! I hope you loved Presley and Shaw's story. My readers are truly awesome and your support means the world!

Thank you to the amazing women who helped make this book happen: Elizabeth, Marion, Julie, Karen, Judy and Hang.

Special thanks to my family and friends for their endless encouragement. I am so blessed to have such an incredible support system.

ACKNOWLEDGMENTS

ABOUT THE AUTHOR

Devney Perry is a *Wall Street Journal, USA Today* and #1 *Amazon* bestselling author of over forty romance novels. After working in the technology industry for a decade, she abandoned conference calls and project schedules to pursue her passion for writing. She was born and raised in Montana and now lives in Washington with her husband and two sons.

Don't miss out on the latest book news.
Subscribe to her newsletter!
www.devneyperry.com

Made in United States
Troutdale, OR
01/10/2024

16864962R00228